SURVIVING THE WALL

BOOK 3 OUTLASTING SERIES

LK MAGILL

FIRST HALE PRESS

Surviving the Wall/ LK Magill – 1st ed.

Ebook ISBN 978-1-7336155-8-7

Paperback ISBN 978-1-7336155-9-4

Hardcover ISBN 978-1-950928-07-1

DEDICATION_

To Sara Mae and Jenna, for sticking with me to the bitter end.

ACKNOWLEDGMENTS_

Firstly to God, the master writer of billions and billions of stories.

And to the other usual suspects who provide me with encouragement, support and love in all of its many forms: Mom, Dad, Kathy, Cindy.

PROLOGUE_

THIS IS BOOK 3 IN A RAPID READER SERIES AND IS MEANT TO be read in order.

If you haven't already, please make sure to start with, OUTLASTING AFTER (Book 1) first.

Otherwise, enjoy!

CHAPTER ONE_
HANNAH

"LENA, GET IN THE CELLAR," HANNAH HISSED. HER EYES darted to the corner of the storage room where an old hunting rifle was leaning against the wall. The gunshots from outside were growing closer now. With each fresh burst, Hannah's heart pinched tighter inside her body. It was going to explode, she was sure of it. Making a dash for the gun, she managed to grab it with shaking hands. When she whirled back around, Hannah watched as a debilitating sort of terror transformed Lena's face. She was frozen, eyes wide, mouth parted in horror.

"Now, Lena," Hannah growled, her own chest expanding suddenly with hysteria.

In the background, everything fell silent. The sounds from outside ceased, leaving Hannah alone with only the painful thumping of her pulse.

Someone's coming.

Someone's coming.

Lurching forward, Hannah wrapped her free hand

3

around Lena's arm and dragged her over to the cellar door. It was a simple square of plywood that lay flush with the floor. Its flimsy silver hinges were screwed to a wooden frame. There was no lock, no way to prevent someone from opening it.

Though she knew there was no way out and nowhere good to hide, it was their only option. Hannah had been down the ladder into the cellar countless times to fetch food, so she was familiar with the small space.

Laying the rifle to the side, Hannah lifted the door with one hand and shoved Lena into the dark hole. The other woman cried out before Hannah heard her body hit the bottom. In the distance, a new barrage of gunfire exploded.

Snaking out a desperate hand, Hannah grabbed for her weapon and stumbled down the ladder. The plywood slammed shut above her, dropping the space into pitch blackness. Falling to her knees, Hannah began crawling like a dog, dragging the gun along beside her in the cold dirt. She reached Lena's body quickly, gripping first her small boots, then feeling along the other woman's legs.

"Come on," Hannah whispered, urging her friend to scoot further and further until they were both huddled against one of the storage bins.

For the longest time it seemed... they sat perfectly still. With her knees pulled up to her chest, Hannah bit at her lip until the taste of blood filled her mouth. Beside her, Lena's body shook violently. The sounds of her muffled whimpering crept out into the dark. It was the same sound Hannah had heard so many months ago, wandering through a darkened forest.

That female sort of crying, it was so familiar. It had been Lena lying at the bottom of that metal cage in the bad place. Now here she was again, trapped in the back of a cold dark cellar, waiting for what was on the outside to come in and get her.

"I can't," Lena's voice cracked, her words breaking. "I can't go back. I can't. Please... shoot me."

"No." Hannah's fingers tightened on the gun.

"You shoot me!" Lena's voice raised as her hands shot out to wrap blindly around Hannah's shoulders. "You do it! You shoot me!"

"Stop it!" Hannah screamed the words, but then held her breath.

Above them, the door swung open heavily, hitting the side of the building with a deafening force. Footsteps. Careful, almost imperceptible footsteps entered the space. Lena's hands disappeared from Hannah's shoulders. The room went completely still.

Sucking in a quick breath, Hannah strained to hear what was overhead. The footsteps came closer, then were joined by another set. Blood hummed in Hannah's ears, her heart racing in time with a fresh release of adrenaline. The sudden flush made her feel instantly sick before a line of sweat burst on her forehead.

Giving her head a purposeful shake, Hannah squeezed her eyes shut a moment, willing herself to calm down. *Breathe. In. Come. On. Breathe...*

When the boots stopped at the cellar door, Hannah's eyes popped wide. Easing forward onto one knee, she stopped thinking. The hard ground pushed into her knee causing her body to wobble ever so slightly. Sucking in a breath, she straightened. Then, just like she'd seen Andy do with the wolf, she cradled the weapon against her shoulder and pointed it at the place where the opening should be. It was still so dark, she couldn't actually see anything.

Please be Chan. The words were desperate in her mind. *Please... just be Chan.*

As the plywood lifted up, a faint shaft of light filtered down. Like a ray of sunshine through a sky of clouds, it lit up the ladder and the ground just around it, but not them. There still wasn't any light touching Hannah. She tried to swallow then, but her throat had gone bone dry. With a fingertip looping through the trigger, Hannah felt her whole body go completely numb.

She expected to see a pair of boots descend. She expected a man to jump down, to land on the floor. But instead, a tiny silver canister dropped neatly to the ground where it rolled towards them, spewing a white sort of smoke. Tear gas?

Quickly, Hannah shut her eyes and held her breath. Sliding her hand along the bolt action, she loaded a bullet into the chamber of the rifle and prayed.

Beside her, Lena started hacking. She choked and coughed until Hannah felt her body writhing around on the ground beside her. Then she was retching. Lena was vomiting and letting out these half-strangled cries.

Hannah's lungs began to scream from the lack of air. Her pulse spiked and her throat clenched and her body begged her to inhale. Just as she thought she might pass out, she heard him. She heard a heavy male body drop to the floor.

Why he came then, with the thick of the fog still heavy in the air, she didn't know. Maybe it was the sound of Lena struggling. Maybe he just hadn't heard the cries of a woman in so long, it drove him to reckless action. But whatever the reason, the second Hannah felt his energy join them in the small space, she pulled the trigger.

Sliding the bolt out and along the rifle, she kept her eyes shut and wracked another bullet into the chamber. Then she pulled the trigger again. Then she did it again. Her body was close to convulsing now, it was all she could do not to suck in air through her nose.

She fired until the bullets stopped loading.

She fired until her eyes rolled back in her head and she lost consciousness.

She fired five times, never once taking a breath.

CHAPTER TWO_
COLE

COLE *KNEW* HE WAS RUNNING. HE WAS GOING AS FAST AS HIS body could possibly go, but even so, it didn't seem fast enough. To Cole, he was moving in slow motion. Everything around him was agonizingly slow.

Eyes sweeping the compound, he held his rifle up and took in the vacant deadness that surrounded him. The snow kept right on falling, softer and thicker now than ever before. To his right, the storage building appeared. It was only his training that had him stopping at its door.

Everything inside of him screamed for him to keep moving towards his cabin where he prayed he'd find Hannah. But what if the enemy was hunkered down here? He had to clear everything in the correct order.

Someone had killed Chan. Fuck. *Fuck.*

Just behind him, Cole felt one of his men ease to a stop. Keeping his eyes focused on the door and his hands on his weapon, Cole waited as the other man's arm snaked around him and yanked the door open. In the next second he was inside, rifle swinging to the left while the man at his back entered and faced the right. The space was dark. Empty.

"Clear," Cookie whispered the word.

Together, they moved towards the piece of plywood that served as a cover for the entrance to the cellar. It didn't have a lock, or a chain or a latch. It never needed one.

Hovering above it, Cole stopped breathing. What would he find down there? More bodies? Hannah's body? The sickening twist of his stomach sent bile to bubble at the back of his throat.

Come on, come on, come on.

Cookie came up and crouched low before ripping back the wood with one hand. Below them, the space was near black. With no windows, only the dim moonlight from the main room shone down. In an instant, Cole was jumping the five feet to the floor, not bothering to use the small ladder they had constructed. It was a stupid move, but logic had left him.

Spinning on his heel, he eyed each corner before lunging for the row of bins along the back wall. With Cookie down beside him now, they jabbed the tips of their rifles into the mass of corn cobs, flour and grain.

"Nothing." Cole sucked in a breath and stepped back. It was the first oxygen to hit his lungs in a minute, maybe more.

The ceiling was low so both men had to keep their bodies bent in order to move freely. Cole rotated around and crossed the small space in three steps, making ready to ascend the ladder. She had to be in his cabin. By the grace of God, Hannah had to be safe somehow inside his cabin.

"Wait," Cookie called, causing Cole to look back. "There's blood."

"Shit," Cole spat.

Crouching down, the older man ran his fingers along the hard-packed dirt floor of the cellar. The oval of dried blood had stained the ground where it soaked in. It was an awful lot of blood.

Hands shaking, Cole knelt across from Cookie and let his eyes take in the scene. There was definitely enough blood here to account for one dead body, maybe two. Out of the corner of his eye, he spied a few shell casings.

Reaching for one, Cole held the copper colored cylinder in his hand. It was ice cold and days old, just like everything else here. The more his mind absorbed what was in front of him, the more Cole realized how late they were. Terribly late. Whatever had gone down here had happened long ago. Days... maybe even weeks.

"My cabin," Cole ordered and he didn't wait for Cookie to respond.

Keeping his rifle in both hands, Cole jogged quickly up the few steps of the ladder and into the main storage room. Everything was so still and silent. Silent and dark. The sound of Cookie on his heels was deafening. It only spurred Cole to move faster.

Nosing the tip of his weapon out the door, he hesitated only a second to make sure there was no movement before dashing into the open. Cole crossed the twenty or so yards to his cabin in no time and circled directly around back to his solitary window.

Cookie rushed up beside him then, slamming his shoulder into the wall before coming to a stop. Their twin breaths puffed in the air as Cole peeked through the glass, his heart squeezing tighter each moment. There was no fire inside and no movement.

Exhaling, Cole gave up a terse nod before sliding along the outer walls. He came to a stop when he reached his front door. Same as before, Cookie's hand snaked around him and ripped the thing open. Both of them breached the threshold, one right after the other. The space was small and barren.

Dropping to his belly, Cole aimed his rifle beneath the bed. Nothing.

"Clear," Cookie whispered it once more.

"Fuck." Cole rolled to his side and pushed up off the floor. "Where are they?"

"Stone house?" Cookie let the hope release in his voice. "Maybe they made a stand there?"

Cole nodded and then they were both out the door and chugging up the hillside. The trees were covered with clumps of snow. The substance poured from the sky, dripping from branches and consuming the ground. If there was a trail to be had, it was covered by now. Any tracks, any sign that had been left... it was all gone. The entire story of what had happened here was disappearing with each passing second.

Cole crested the incline without even thinking. All those body aches he'd had before? The tiredness, the hunger and the cold? They were all gone. He was positively soaked in adrenaline. His heart punched its way through his chest, causing the only spike of pain he felt. Somewhere in the background, Cookie chugged right along behind him.

When they reached the clearing, they saw the door of the stone house standing open. It swung lazily on its hinges, the wind having died down. Above them, snow fell straight from the sky.

Despite the thick haze, Cole detected movement through the front window.

Raising one hand, he signaled behind him but kept his weapon focused forward. Boots sinking deep with each step, Cole approached the corner of the building. With his back pressed against the stone face, he waited for Cookie to join him before easing around to peer through the glass. The angle wasn't right, he couldn't see in.

Clenching his teeth, Cole ducked low and moved fast beneath the windowsill until he was standing just beside the creaking door. Shit it was quiet. Why was it so damn quiet?

Blinking hard once, he sucked in a breath and opened his eyes wide. One. Two. Three.

Darting through the door, Cole slid to a sharp stop as he found himself staring down the barrel of another rifle.

"Blue!" Cookie shouted from somewhere behind him, it was the code they used to signal friendly fire. "Blue, blue, for shit's sake!"

Exhaling harshly, both Cole and Ace lowered their weapons. It was just the team. They were all alone.

"Status?" Cole barked, his eyes jumping around the room.

The side windows were all blown out, letting the snow drift in. The white substance was heaped on the wooden floor beneath the sills. And everything else? It was chaos, utter aftermath chaos.

In the center of the room there was a scatter of pots and pans, shards of broken dishes and a tumble of chairs. The long wooden table had been tipped onto its side, then pulled back against the open threshold to the bunk room.

Striding up to it, Cole noted the spray of bullet holes that riddled its surface. Someone had used it as a barricade. With a last glance over his shoulder, Cole noted the look on Ace's face, it was hollow. The other man didn't make eye contact, his brown eyes staring off in the distance instead.

"Status?!" Cole shouted again before he lifted a leg over the table and stepped straight into hell.

There were no windows in this room. When the team had originally designed it, they'd meant it as a safety bunker of sorts. You couldn't burn down stone and with the beds and a cache of weapons and water, they figured the team could wait out a siege if needed. They'd meant to install a thick wooden door in the threshold. They'd meant to make wooden window covers for the living room too... but they hadn't gotten around to it yet.

They hadn't *fucking* gotten around to it.

So instead of a safe room, they'd created a room from which there was no escape. And so here is where Ryder had been trapped, waiting to die.

"They must've hit fast and with numbers," Davey's voice was shaky as he rose to stand over his brother's dead body. *Ryder. Oh, God.*

Cole followed Davey's line of sight. He had no words.

"You can see he started shooting in the living room," Davey continued. "He's probably the one that blew out the windows. From the trail of blood on the floor and the scrape marks, he and Flynn both pulled the table back and ended up in here."

Davey sniffed and swiped a sleeve under his nose. Cole dropped to his knees and ran a hand over Ryder's blank face. He wanted to close those vacant blue eyes, but Ryder was too damn cold. The kid had just made it. He'd just battled death and won... hadn't he?

"He went through every weapon and emptied every cartridge," Davey went on. "From the blood stains in the living room, I'd say he got the better part of at least three of them."

Sucking in a breath, Cole cleared his throat and shoved up to standing. He paced back to the threshold between the two rooms and looked out. Sure enough, off in the far corner there was a series of dried Burgundy-colored circles that spoke of death. Blinking once, he let his eyes follow a set of drag marks. The body, or bodies, had been moved shortly after the fact.

"And Flynn?" Cole asked suddenly. "Why do you think she was with him?"

"She still is."

Davey waited for Cole to glance over his shoulder.

When he caught Cole's eye, he gestured under one of the bunk beds.

"Looks like she shot herself." Davey let his gaze drop back to his brother on the floor. "Probably after they got Ryder."

"Holy shit," Cole exhaled the words.

"Someone tried to move her, though." Davey lowered himself down and crouched next to Ryder's body. Laying trembling hands on his brother's chest, he continued to speak, "Her body's all twisted. Maybe they were just checking for a pulse."

"Anyone else?"

"What?"

"I'm asking if you found anyone else." Cole swallowed hard, hating what a coward he was. He couldn't bare to drop down and look. "Under the beds."

"No." Shaking his head slowly side to side, Davey let himself melt away.

Cole watched numbly as Davey's fingers tightened against his baby brother's chest. He gripped Ryder's bloody shirt in his hands before the tears began to fall. Bending forward, Davey pressed his forehead to his brother's stiff body. His shoulders shuddered and heaved, but the sobs that wracked his lungs were silent.

Backing a step, Cole battled his own mix of unbelief and dread. They hadn't seen anyone in over a year. There hadn't been an errant step on their territory in so long. What had he done wrong? What had he missed? This shouldn't have happened. Cole was better than this. What had he fucking missed?

"Boy-o," Cookie's call was close, the old man had come to stand sentinel. "We've still got three out there."

Hannah. The word hit Cole's brain like a lightening bolt, snapping him back to full awareness. They still hadn't found her, or Lena, or Trey.

"Have the cabins been cleared?" Cole turned his back on Davey's suffering and stepped free of the room.

"No," Ace answered quietly. "The watch tree has the ladder down, but no one is up there. No signs of a struggle or blood on the platform, but there's so much snow on the ground..."

Ace hesitated, letting his unspoken thought permeate the air. The others could be buried like Chan. If Cole hadn't walked directly over the man, it would have taken them days to find him, maybe longer.

"Ace," Cole began. "Go out and hit the fence line then follow it south and check the livestock. Cook and I will clear the cabins."

"Roger." Ace bobbed his head, gripped his weapon and strode out the door.

Mind buzzing, heart pumping, Cole picked up the pace and jogged after him. They had seven cabins left to clear. Part of him prayed he would find Hannah, and the other part dreaded it. It was just too quiet all around, even with the heavy storm and the swirling snow. If there were living people at the compound, they were being too damn quiet.

"Boy-o!" Cookie's voice called from behind him.

Cole didn't stop, he just kept his eyes on a swivel as he pushed into the thick trees.

"Cole!"

17

Cookie's hand shot out to grip Cole's shoulder and spin him around. Shrugging quickly out of his grip, Cole glared at the older man.

"What?!"

"You shouldn't be clearing cabins," Cookie's voice dropped low, but his gaze was steady.

"What?"

"You're head isn't on straight. You're being reckless, charging into the cellar, almost getting shot by Ace."

"Well, you don't give the orders, do you?" Cole backed a step and started to turn but Cookie's voice stopped him short.

"You and I both know if she's in one of those cabins, then she's dead."

"Fuck. You." Cole's words were ragged, he could barely spit them out.

"Do you really want to see her like that? Let me clear them."

"She's not dead."

"Let me do it."

"She's not..." Cole swallowed hard and his whole body started trembling. The adrenaline was wearing off now and the reality all around him was flooding in. Chan, dead. Ryder, dead. Flynn, dead.

Hannah. *Hannah.*

Dropping to his knees in the snow, Cole bowed his head. He'd sworn to protect her. He'd done everything to keep her safe, to keep them all safe. The second Cole's heart burst, he felt it. Or rather, he felt the endless exploding pain that its absence left behind.

THE FIRST TIME SHE CAME TO, ALL HANNAH COULD FEEL WAS the swinging. Back and forth, back and forth, her long strands of hair hung down towards the earth. Eyes fluttering, she sucked in a sharp breath. It was dark out, and icy cold, but the air was clear and fresh. The shock of it had her sputtering.

"She's waking up," a male voice called.

With a groan, Hannah put both hands to her head. That's when she realized she was upside down, being carried over the shoulder of some massive man. Eyes shooting wide, Hannah braced herself against his back in an attempt to see. In the next moment, she was laid out flat in the snow, a heavy hand holding a piece of cloth over her nose and mouth.

Struggling weakly, Hannah stared up into a set of piercing blue eyes. The black helmet covering his head let only a few strands of brown hair escape, but his broad face was half-covered in short stubble. The man pinning her to the ground was not familiar to her and with that dark glint in his eye, he looked downright deadly.

Though her heart pounded hard, the only thing she managed was a pitiful whimper before being swept down into unconsciousness.

THE NEXT TIME HANNAH CAME AROUND, IT WAS TO THE scent of urine and blood and decay. Keeping her eyes closed, she wandered into consciousness with caution this time. Her body rocked a little, but it wasn't with the stride of a person.

A warm continuous rumble filled the space which was punctuated occasionally by a burst of static. *Static*. It's a white noise type sound that comes from a radio. *Radio*. Hannah's head began to throb and her stomach twisted. Before she could stop herself, she shoved up to sitting with vomit bursting from her lips.

"Shit," a man cursed under his breath.

Eyes open now, Hannah held one hand to her mouth and glanced around. She was in the backseat of a... of a... SUV. Beside her, Lena's lifeless form was crumpled against the far window.

Looking over her shoulder, Hannah sucked in a breath and scrambled back. Bodies. So many dead bodies were just stacked up on top of each other. All men. All soldiers with helmets and black clothes and bloody hands.

Instinctively, she searched the door panel at her back until she gripped a smooth handle firmly in her palm. With a glance to the front seat, Hannah locked eyes with the driver. The same blue flash of brutal intensity met her gaze as he slammed a foot on the brake and had them all lurching forward.

In the next moment, Hannah yanked open the door and was tumbling out onto her side. Her body met hard with the snow covered ground, causing her wrist to buckle beneath her and all the air to expel from her lungs. Ignoring the scream of pain from her wrist, Hannah shoved up from the ground and launched herself forward.

They were still in the mountains, with trees flanking a narrow roadway of sorts. It was foggy and dark. She could just make out the forest surrounding her. Hands scrabbling for purchase, she pumped her legs and soon was standing, then running. Her boots sunk in the snow, causing her to lurch and stumble but she pushed forward.

Go.

Go as fast as you can.

Tears streamed from the corners of her eyes as she made for the tree line, the only source of cover. Male shouting could be heard at her back. First one tone and then another. They were gaining.

"Fuck this isn't worth it," a man's voice came out low and breathless, but close, way too close.

The next thing Hannah knew, she was falling. She felt the tug at her ankle and then she was face down in the snow, rolling forward. Her body slid and tumbled to a stop. Groaning, she clutched at her throbbing wrist and gasped for breath.

Then the man was on top of her again, straddling her

body, laying his forearm across her shoulders. He stared into her, through her, as he panted. She felt him reaching into his jacket, searching for something, but his angry eyes didn't leave her face.

"Stop!" The scream erupted from Hannah's lips as she bucked and struggled beneath him. "Get off me!"

"Not a chance, sweetheart," the last word dripped from his mouth as he brought a small square of cloth out and held it down over her nose.

"She's just scared." Another man was standing over them now. His youthful face was frowning down at them, hazel eyes alight with concern. "She's afraid we're going to rape her like the others."

"Oh yeah?" The man on top of her sniffed. "Well, maybe that's just what we're going to do. Huh? You hear that? Now you've got a reason to be afraid... fucking killing my men."

Hannah blinked slowly, the haze of chemicals infiltrating her nostrils, sweetening the lining of her mouth. Just before her eyes rolled back in her head, she observed the younger man throw up his hands and stomp a few feet away. Then the man on top of her got up and they began to argue.

The image disappeared, then came back sharper. The blue-eyed one was pointing at the SUV, then running a hand back through his brown hair. Then it was black. All black.

CHAPTER FOUR_
LIAM

WAS HE REALLY DOING THIS? LIAM HUFFED A BREATH AND adjusted the heavy pack on his back. The barren road stretched out before him, leaving him feeling nervous and exposed. *What the hell else are you going to do?*

Pausing, Liam dug around for the mason jar in his jacket pocket and the sharp taste of relief it held.

He'd been hiking for about five days now, making his way steadily closer to the territory held by Uriah Linfield. On a fool's mission? Maybe. But the interrogator inside of him pushed Liam beyond reason. Hannah's brother or no, Uriah was the key to a puzzle that begged to be solved.

And it wasn't that Liam missed Hannah. No, damn it, that was absolutely *not* it. He wasn't aiming for her brother in some twisted attempt to feel close to her again. Fuck that. Liam just needed answers, that's all. Yeah.

So what if every time he closed his eyes, he saw her beautiful face. The moonshine helped with that. And anyway he'd done all of this to be free of her, to be free of the weakness she brought out in him.

It wasn't like he was planning on staying with Uriah, not a chance. Liam was just going to check things out, maybe ask a few questions and then split. He was just going to keep right on walking. He was sure the further he got, the less hold she'd have on him.

Yeah, by the time he hit the coast, all would be well. So on he went, veering perpetually southwest.

Twisting the silver lid off the jar, Liam stopped only long enough to suck down another shot or two. The alcohol burned his insides, providing both warmth and the ability not to care. The buzz felt good, or at least it felt pleasantly numb.

He'd traded another few knives with good ole Jensen before departing, *unscathed* he might add. Turns out the short shit just wanted to talk. Now Liam's pack was laden with pig jerky and booze, a fantastic combination if he ever saw one.

Returning the lid to the jar and the jar to his pocket, Liam resumed his steady pace. It was cold down here in the lowlands and flat, incredibly flat. In the distance, he could see mountains rise up all around him but they were pretty far off.

Glancing back over his shoulder, Liam frowned at the dark storm clouds that hovered. The compound must be taking a beating, he thought. Looked like snow was just dumping up there, but down here, there wasn't even a whisper of it on the ground. Not my problem, Liam reminded himself before kicking at a clump of withered brown grass.

That's when he first felt it.

Standing still a moment, he stared at the grass, his brow furrowed in concentration. Then after another beat he dropped to a crouch, pressing his palm to the ground. It had been so long, so incredibly long since he'd heard that specific sort of rumble. For a split second he thought maybe it was an earthquake. But then again, it wasn't the ground that was trembling, instead it was Liam's hand.

Sucking it back to his lap, Liam kept himself low to the ground while he turned his head toward the horizon. Nope, he couldn't see anything, at least not yet, but he could *hear* it coming.

It was the sound of a motor. A real live working, running, guttural engine. His heart nearly jumped into his throat but he fought the flood of panic. A cursory glance around him confirmed what he already knew. There was no cover for him anywhere. Even if he made a run for it, the people in the vehicle would see him long before he would be out of range.

Carefully, he shrugged his arms out of his backpack and placed it in front of him before lying flat on his belly. Between his bedroll and the pack, he could at least hide his head for awhile. He didn't have a helmet. The things had been wired with electronics so Cole'd made them all ditch the stuff years ago.

Keeping his eyes on the horizon, Liam pulled his weapon around and settled it over the sleeping bag. He exhaled a steadying breath, closed his eyes a beat, and then maneuvered into position.

With the butt of the gun pressed into his shoulder, Liam adjusted everything until he was perfectly comfortable. Then as the sound of the engine built and a small cloud of dust rose up in the air, Liam lowered his eye to the scope of his rifle and took a good long look.

The first thing he noticed was the shiny metallic flash of a grille. Holding his breath, Liam steadied the scope and kept the distant vehicle in his sights. The windshield winked at him. It was a small truck, a Jeep or maybe an SUV. Gray. No, maybe a faded blue. There were two occupants in the front seat. He assumed they were male, but beyond that he couldn't tell. For the next short while, he watched them approach.

There was nothing else in this Godforsaken valley except the narrow road and the empty fields so of course the vehicle came straight for him. It was moving at quite a clip, too. That left Liam only a handful of minutes to make a decision.

He could shoot out the tires for certain, but crippling the vehicle wouldn't necessarily cripple its occupants. If he could shoot like Cook, then the driver would be dead already. Boom. One shot. Dead.

But Liam wasn't Cook. Sure he was a good shot, but with the moving target and the windshield and the glare… Liam couldn't be certain he'd get a clean kill. Which meant a messy wounded driver and of course one living passenger to deal with, maybe more.

The closer they got, the more his heart hammered until sweat filled his palms. Damn it, damn it, damn it. He had to choose. He had to choose. Maybe the alcohol hadn't been the greatest idea after all. But then the front of the SUV dipped and it swerved slightly to the left. They saw him.

Coming to a halt, the passenger side door swung open and the man inside ducked down behind it. Liam didn't move. He just kept his rifle steady and watched the tip of a gun peek out from around the door.

"Hey, buddy!" The man shouted.

Liam snorted, but made no reply.

"Looks like we've got ourselves in a bit of a pickle!"

Liam grumbled under his breath before raising his voice to answer, "Yeah."

"Well…" the man's boots shifted beneath the door to the truck. He was trying to get more comfortable. "How're we gonna get out of it?"

"Get back in the vehicle and keep driving!" Liam called.

"And let you shoot us in the back?" The man let out an ironic laugh. "Not gonna work."

"Guess I'll just wait then."

"Guess so."

Liam kept his finger on the trigger and his eyes absorbing every detail that he could. The barrel of the other man's gun glinted in the sun, his dusty black boots shifted on the ground and further back another set scooted behind a tire.

"Where're you headed?" The man called again suddenly.

Liam rolled his eyes. Who was this guy? A hostage

negotiator? These techniques were straight out of the military training guide, but even so, they were effective.

Liam let his shoulders relax and cleared his throat. Amazingly he found he didn't want to die today, and neither did these guys apparently. Finally, he shouted a reply, "Southwest!"

"That's our territory," the man responded.

"And who're you exactly?"

"We're Linfield men."

"Uriah Linfield?"

"You heard of him?"

"Yeah." Liam blew out a slow breath. *You could say that.*

"You lookin' to join up?"

"Maybe."

"You a Nor Sider?"

"I was," Liam admitted, then pulled his rifle to his chest and rolled onto his back. Blinking up at the overcast sky, he wondered at the world he found himself in. Quiet footsteps made their way towards him across the ground.

"Well, don't just lie there." The man stood over him, his handgun shoved into his jacket pocket. "We'll take you the rest of the way in."

Rolling over, Liam pushed up to standing and eyed the man before him, then let his gaze slide to the other fucker now standing at the hood of the SUV. They were average. Average in height, average in weight, and likely somewhere in their late-twenties in age. Both had dark eyes and the driver had dark skin to go with it.

Glancing down, Liam considered the hand held out between them. After a beat, he moved to shake it.

"Name's O'Shea," the man said before letting go. "That's Ricks."

"Byrne. Liam Byrne," Liam answered, always uncomfortable giving his last name.

"Well that's Irish as fuck isn't it?" O'Shea laughed, patting him on the shoulder. "Me, too."

Nodding, Liam shouldered his weapon and ducked quickly to retrieve his things. My father was Irish, he thought, hating every inch of his own skin at the remembrance. Your mother wasn't, a voice inside said, and Liam softened just a bit for her. Why did they haunt him so? Even now?

With a slight shake of his head, Liam kept pace beside O'Shea as they walked towards the SUV. The bottle of moonshine bumped against his thigh and it was all Liam could do not to rip it out and take a drink right there.

"Just throw your stuff on the backseat," O'Shea gestured as he slid into the shotgun seat.

Taking a quick glance in the rear compartment, Liam noted it was loaded with fresh cut wood. Yanking open the rear door handle, he tossed all of his stuff onto the long bench seat and sat down. Well, everything except for his rifle. That he kept lying neatly across his lap.

Wrinkling his nose, Liam took a breath through his mouth. The cab smelled of old puke and piss and the floorboards were sticky. Chuckling at his reaction, O'Shea gave the driver a knowing look. As the engine turned over and the vehicle pulled away, he threw Liam a glance over his shoulder.

"Sorry about the smell. Linfield sent out his security

team a few weeks back on a mission and it went a little sideways. We haven't gotten around to scrubbing it out yet."

"Sure." Liam sniffed and rolled down his window. "No problem."

CHAPTER FIVE_
HANNAH

THE FIRST THING SHE FELT WAS PAIN. HANNAH'S LEFT WRIST throbbed with each pulse of her heart. Groaning, she went to reach for it, wanting to cradle her wrist in her other hand. But she couldn't. Metal handcuffs confined her, binding each wrist before looping through a hand hold on the door.

With a cry, Hannah's eyes opened wide and instinctually she tried to yank away. The cuffs stopped her short, causing pain to race up her left arm. In desperation, she stretched her fingers just far enough to pull at the door handle. It moved, but failed to open the door.

"Not this time, sweetheart," the now familiar voice from the front seat muttered.

Sucking in a breath, Hannah glanced wildly around. It was daytime now, but she was still in the SUV. Lena wept quietly on the other side of the long bench seat, her wrists were also bound with cuffs to the other door. The small space was warm, all the windows were up and the stench of death and sickness was overwhelming.

The two soldiers in the front didn't turn around but Hannah knew they were the same as before. Behind her, dead bodies were still heaped in the back compartment. A shudder ran through her.

For a moment, bile rose up in Hannah's throat and she felt a wave of nausea. Battling back, she closed her eyes and tried to control her breathing. When that failed to work, she leaned forward and threw up on the floor.

"Damn it," the driver cursed under his breath, then flicked his eyes up to the rearview mirror. "Just tell me you're going to puke and I'll roll down the window."

Tears welled at the corners of her eyes and snot dripped from her nose. Giving up a few quick nods, Hannah leaned towards the window as the driver pushed a button to make it roll all the way down. The flow of icy air in her face was instantly soothing, so she shimmied up to her knees and hung her head out and over the side.

Spitting and gasping, she took in oxygen and let out vomit. Maybe she should have shot Lena. Maybe she should have shot her, then turned the rifle right around and ended them both.

"Hey, you okay?" The soldier riding shotgun had turned around to stroke at the small of her back.

At the contact, Hannah lunged forward until her body was hanging halfway out the window. Her handcuffs came tight against her wrists again, causing her to cry out as black asphalt zoomed by beneath her. In the next instant, the SUV swerved to the right and sucked her whole body back into the cab where the cuffs jerked on her wrists once more.

"Fuck!" The driver slammed on the brakes then, as he let loose another string of curses.

Rolling up the window, he turned to glare back at Hannah. The passenger had been forced to brace himself against the dash to avoid going through the windshield.

"Easy!" The younger soldier admonished before shoving himself upright and locking eyes with Hannah. "You alright? Do you need some water?"

"Leave her alone," Lena's voice came out low and pleading.

"We're not going to hurt you," the passenger again.

"What do you call this?!" Hannah gestured to her bound wrists as pain continued to pulse up her arm and down into her fingertips.

"Self-preservation," the driver growled. "We lost five good men back there… one of which *you* shot! We risked our ass saving you from those fucking rapists and this is the thanks we get?"

"Rapists?" Lena's voice filled with anguish before she buried her face in her hands and began moaning.

"Those men…" Hannah choked a little, her eyes fixed on the driver. "From the compound. Are they alive? Did you kill them?"

"What do you care?"

"Because they were good men!" Hannah screamed at him, yanking painfully against the handcuffs as the tears rolled down her face. "Did you kill them all? They were our friends! They weren't hurting us!"

"Where's Flynn?" Lena moaned. "Oh God, where's Flynn?"

Her words melted into short tiny gasps. Hannah felt her heart twist inside her chest. Chan. There was Chan and then Trey, he must have fired those first shots. And what about Flynn? If they only wanted to rescue the women, then why wasn't she here?

Ryder. She'd still been with Ryder. They had to still be alive. The others all must have made it. That's the only thing that made sense. The guys were able to keep Flynn safe. They were all okay.

"There were reports of two women being held by a group of men," the driver said. "The rumor was they were being badly abused."

The vehicle kept rumbling along as Lena melted off the seat and onto her knees on the floorboards. Her hands were clasped together, still fixed to the door. For the longest while the only sound in the cab was an occasional burst of static and the strangled noises coming from the little dark-haired woman.

The two soldiers in the front seat sat still, shoulders rigid, bodies tense. Hannah watched the fingers of the driver curl and squeeze along the steering wheel for a bit before she dropped her head. Suddenly, she couldn't hardly bear the weight of it anymore.

"It's time," the driver spoke quietly as he slowed the vehicle to a stop.

Eyes downcast, Hannah let the passenger crawl into the backseat and shift her body to the floor like Lena. With her hands held at eye level now, Hannah leaned her forehead into them and closed her eyes.

"It's only for the drive in," the passenger murmured, as he covered them both with a series of blankets. "We couldn't risk a riot at the sight of you."

Hannah didn't respond. She merely listened as he climbed into the shotgun seat and the driver stepped on the gas. Beneath the vehicle, the asphalt roadway hummed. Before long they were slowing, then turning, then accelerating.

Hannah braced herself as best she could with her body wedged down like it was but soon her head was swimming. Then her stomach turned and if she'd had anything left in her belly it would've come up. Circumstances being what they were, she dry-heaved instead.

Again, the driver swore before finally bringing the vehicle to a complete stop. The engine switched off. Both front doors gave a pop as they opened and Hannah could feel the SUV jolt slightly when first the driver got out and then the passenger.

"What the hell, Jameson?" A new voice spoke somewhere just behind the vehicle. "You said it was bad, but five dead?"

"They were better armed and more highly trained than we anticipated," the driver's deep voice responded. He must be Jameson, Hannah thought.

"And the women?"

"We rescued two," Jameson again. "There was a third, but we weren't able to get her."

"How are they?"

"Well..."

The voices traveled closer as they spoke. Hannah could hear footsteps shuffling to her side of the SUV and then the slap of a palm on the side window. Suddenly her door was being jerked open and Hannah's bound wrists went right along with it.

Tumbling out of the door, Hannah yelped as pain shot down her injured arm. Her body hung there a split second before her legs began scrambling for better purchase. She had to get the weight off of her wrist... and fast.

"Hannah Mae?" The sound of her name in the new man's voice had Hannah glancing up and into his face.

Stunned brown eyes absorbed her before he fell to his knees by her side, propping up her body with his hands. It was the first set of familiar eyes she could ever remember seeing. Her brother. Uriah. He was here.

Opening her mouth, Hannah tried to say his name aloud, but the word just wouldn't come. Someone she knew. Someone from before. Tears poured down her face as her body flooded with a mixture of sorrow and relief.

"H- How?" Uriah stammered. His hands traveled along her arms until they met with the cuffs. A storm cloud passed over his face, his eyes flashing. "What the *fuck* is she doing in these?"

"Well, Sir-"

"The hell is going on, Jameson?" Uriah growled, twisting his head to yell over his shoulder. "Get the damn keys!"

"She killed Meeks with a rifle and jumped out of the

SUV while it was still moving... Sir." Jameson handed Uriah the keys who snatched at them angrily.

Cursing under his breath, Uriah unlocked the cuffs and then gathered his sister close to him. She could feel his chest heaving as his arms cinched around her shoulders.

"He touch you?" Uriah's words were low and charged with energy.

"Not like that," Hannah whispered the answer because it was true. She may loathe the big soldier who'd knocked her out and captured them both, but she was no liar.

Looking over Uriah's shoulder, Hannah's eyes flicked up to lock on Jameson who appeared just a touch nervous. He was standing straight as an arrow, his broad shoulders squared off with about a dozen other men spread out behind him.

They were in a parking garage with dust covered cars lined up everywhere. It was dimly lit with a few flashlight beams pointed at the ground, the walls, and the SUV.

"I told you to stay," Uriah's voice whispered next to her ear before he pulled back to arm's length and shook her slightly. "I told you to damn well stay! What the hell are you doing out here?"

"I..."

"We had reports." Uriah's eyes fell to her swollen wrist and dirty clothing. "We heard rumors, but-"

"Uri, I-"

"How long have you been out? Who the hell got you out?"

Not waiting for an answer, Uriah pulled her right hand towards him in a panic. His eyes tracked to the place the microchip should have been, and he let out a breath as he ran his thumb over the ugly scar.

"Where's the other one?" He called suddenly over his shoulder. "You said there were two women."

Jameson cleared his throat and took a few steps forward before something in Uriah's face stopped him short. When Uriah returned his gaze to Hannah, she looked pointedly at the trembling bundle still stuck beneath a heap of blankets in the backseat. Her brother's brow furrowed and she could seem him physically working to keep his temper. In his youth, he'd been a bit of a hot head. It was a trait he had to try each moment to control.

"Stay back," Uriah ordered. Carefully he helped Hannah to stand before propping her frame against the wide open rear door. "Did this other woman shoot one of my guys, too?"

"No," Jameson's voice was tight. "Sir, we weren't aware you knew one of them."

"Yeah, well I didn't fucking know that either." Uriah ducked low to crawl into the SUV, muttering all the while. "She was supposed to stay put. Stay Hannah Mae. How fucking impossible is that?"

Hannah let her eyes travel over the group before her. Cradling her left wrist in her right hand, she rubbed absently at her swollen skin. Where was she? What had just happened? One moment she was at the compound, her arms linked with Lena's, Chan smiling, the snow falling. The next she was here, with her brother shouting orders and these men all staring.

Because they were definitely all staring, mouths parted, eyes a bit shell-shocked. Nervously, she let her gaze fall to the floor. Her pants were streaked with dried vomit and stained with a circle of her own urine. When you pass out, over and over, you sort of lose control of your bladder. An embarrassed heat rose to her cheeks.

"Please let this be someone I don't-" Uriah's voice hitched, causing Hannah to glance inside. "Know."

Pulling the last of the blankets off, he revealed Lena. Her back was to him, her raven black hair all a mess over her shoulders. For a moment, she looked as if she were praying. Her hands were clasped in front of her, her head bowed towards the door, her knees folded awkwardly beneath her. It wasn't until she glanced over her shoulder, her vivid blue eyes popping wide, her lips quivering, that Hannah watched her brother completely lose it.

Somehow his bulky body sucked back out of the vehicle and into the parking garage in less than a second. Hannah had to step to the side quickly to avoid being shoved into the door. Uriah didn't even seem to notice.

With a singular purpose he closed the distance between himself and Jameson, slamming both hands against the taller man's chest. In the next moment, Uriah pivoted around and threw Jameson down on the concrete floor. They both landed with a hard thump, breath exhaling, legs and arms a tangle until Uriah wound up on top with his forearm pressed forcefully against the other man's throat.

Everyone, including Hannah, stood there in absolute shock.

"You're going to want to be real honest with me," Uriah

hissed. "The next words you say are going to be the most truthful in your entire life. Got that?"

Jameson clutched at Uriah's forearm with both hands and gurgled a bit. Eventually, he nodded.

"Did you put your hands on that woman in there?"

Jameson tried to shake his head side to side but managed only a single jerk to the right.

"I've just got to ask myself... why? Why would you cuff them?" Uriah was shaking, but his eyes were steady, his voice ever so quiet. "Did you force yourself? Hmm? On that woman in there? Or my sister? Did you?"

Jameson struggled a bit, his hands scraping at Uriah's forearm in an effort to get oxygen. Hannah watched his mouth move but no sound came out. He was mouthing the word no.

"Uri... Uriah!" Hannah stepped forward, raising her voice until her brother glanced over at her. "No. He didn't do anything like that. Let him go."

With a final look down at Jameson, Uriah shoved away and rose to standing. His shoulders were heaving as he ran both hands through his hair. Jameson rolled onto his side and sputtered, rubbing at his throat before spitting on the ground. The other soldiers shifted on their feet, looking between the two men and then at Hannah.

"Turn around," Uriah ordered. "All of you turn your backs now."

After a beat of reluctance, all of the soldiers rotated around, their flashlights lighting the distant walls instead. Thrown into a deeper bit of darkness, Hannah watched her brother extend a hand to the man he had just tackled and choked moments before. Her eyes opened a bit wider when Jameson reached for it and let Uriah help him to his feet.

"Grab a light," Uriah said, and Jameson retrieved one from his pocket.

Together, they came back over to the SUV and Uriah crawled slowly back inside. Jameson stood next to Hannah, the flashlight illuminating the interior of the vehicle. Tilting her head up, her eyes traveled over his chest and the redness at his neck before resting on his face. Jameson eyed her, his blue eyes focused and intent.

What was he thinking? She couldn't quite say, but his gaze was not the same hateful piercing from before. Swallowing uncomfortably, she looked down and away.

"Hey Lena," Uriah's voice was soothing and low. Hannah had to strain to listen as he unlocked Lena's cuffs and gathered her to him. "It's okay. I'm so sorry. I'm so, so sorry. Why didn't you stay, baby? Why the hell didn't you just stay behind that wall where it was safe? I didn't know you were out there. Oh God, I didn't know."

Lena and her brother... that was a thing? Hannah squeezed her eyes shut and willed her mind to travel further than it had before. Try as she might, she just didn't remember her whole story. Even the sections she was getting were cut short and distorted, often times out of order and jumbled.

But when she let herself listen to them, to Lena's unintelligible whimpering and Uriah's steady words, she felt in her heart that yes, they had been a couple. They had loved each other. Love.

The idea pounded in her brain and brought all sorts of

memories to flood her. Cole's steady hands, the whisper of his voice, the feel of him close to her. Then Liam, all intensity with his searching eyes and sweep of short black hair. Were they alive? Any of them? Had they made it back to the compound yet? Would she ever see them again?

Swaying slightly, Hannah's knees buckled and she pitched forward. She would've gone all the way down, but Jameson stepped into the breach and caught her, pulling her in close against him.

"Uriah," he called.

"Shit," her brother answered. "Get them inside, and one of you needs to go find that doctor."

CHAPTER SIX_
COLE

THE CABINS WERE CLEAR. THEY WERE ALL MERCIFULLY, hauntingly clear. Despite Cookie's protests, Cole had still insisted on participating in the sweep. He'd allowed Cookie to take the point position, but there was no way Cole could just wait while Hannah lay somewhere inside, stiff and dead. Thankfully, she wasn't.

But then again, a new sort of agony consumed him. Where was she?

Nothing had been disturbed. Nothing had been taken. It was the strangest sort of thing he'd ever seen. If a group of men had come to rob them, then they'd done an exceptionally bad job of it.

The storage building still had all of its food and supplies. Each cabin was untouched, full of clothing, furniture, firewood. Even the blown out stone house, aside from its desecrated furniture and array of dead bodies, was relatively unscathed. They had burned nothing, removed nothing, added nothing. Save for Hannah, Lena and Trey.

The most important things were gone. Long gone, leaving no trace, no tracks and no clue as to what became of them. Had Trey made it out with the two women? Were they camped down with one of their neighbors below? Or, had they all been taken. Were their bodies lying like Chan, just beneath the surface of the fluffy white snow?

On his feet now, just below the slowly swinging ladder of the watch tree, Cole continued to dig. His gloved hands gripped a shovel as he worked mindlessly at the task before him. He'd already uncovered a ten foot circle around Chan's body and found nothing but an empty rifle.

The next best place to start looking was right here, he figured. Someone should've been on watch duty when the attack began. The ladder was down and there wasn't any blood on the platform. Trey. It had to have been Trey up there and he'd made it at least this far.

"You need to stop," Cookie spoke just behind him.

The snow continued to fall, but in light flurries now. It dusted at Cole's shoulders and back as he worked. He didn't bother to shrug it off.

"You've been going since we arrived," Cookie reasoned, his voice monotone and tired in the pale cast of dawn. "It's time to eat, to rest."

"Rest?" Cole gave the other man a disgusted look before returning to his work.

"The horses and mule have been turned out to pasture and fed," Cookie pressed on. "We brought Chan back up to the stone house but Davey won't let us move Ryder's body. We can't just leave them how they are. Someone has to clean them up and prepare them. I need you."

"*She* needs me." Cole hesitated only a moment in his shoveling.

"If she's alive, then she's not under that pile of snow," Cookie again, his voice softening. "Boy-o, if she's alive, then she's not here."

Shoulders slumping, Cole let Cookie's words filter into his worn out brain and bang around for a bit. His hands clenched and loosened on the handle of the shovel. A numb sort of tingling trickled throughout his body. If she's alive. *If.*

Sucking in a breath, Cole swung the shovel back and then chucked it as far as he could. A terrible cry split the air and it took Cole several seconds to realize the sound was coming from him. Helpless.

So. Fucking. Helpless.

He couldn't do a damn thing for Hannah. Collapsing to his knees, Cole buried his face in his hands. How could this have happened? It was all his fault. He had missed something, some sign. She's not here. She's gone. *They took her.*

It was harder than he imagined to force himself to stop crying. But slowly, Cole collected himself back in, got himself under control.

"I agree with you," he said, moving his hands to stare blankly at the snow. "If she's alive, then Hannah isn't here. How soon can you make me a go pack? How soon can I be ready to leave?"

"Leave?"

"Yeah, tonight? Tomorrow morning?" Cole dusted at his hands and pushed up to standing. *Liam.* Damn it, he could really use his best friend right about now. "I'll only take the one horse. I'm not asking for any of you to come."

"You can't just leave. Where do you think you're going to go?"

"I'll start with a sweep of the mountain, then visit each of the neighbors and travel out from there. Someone had to see something… hear something."

"Boy-o." Cookie took a step towards him, his hand raising tentatively to clutch at Cole's arm. "We've hiked for miles, in a blizzard, with little to no sleep. The horses are on the verge of collapse. Hell, you're on the verge of collapse. There is no fresh trail to follow."

"There's common sense. There's people to ask. It's a good enough place to start." Cole jerked back from Cookie's grasp and stomped towards the discarded shovel.

"You want to talk common sense?" Cookie charged after him. "Whoever did this is armed, trained and if we're lucky, has three of our people with them. How many men do you think it would take to pull that off?"

"I don't know."

"You know."

"Six at the least." Cole stopped short of the shovel and glanced back over his shoulder. "I wouldn't do it with less than eight."

"What happens when you do find them? You'll be one man, low on food, low on sleep, low on ammunition. How will you save them then?"

"I don't know," Cole admitted. "But I've got to try."

"You've got to wait." Cookie came around until he was standing directly in front of Cole, looking him in the eye.

"We all want revenge. We all want a piece of these bastards but we need time to prepare."

"She doesn't have time."

"What good are you to Hannah if you show up just so she can watch you die?"

Cole opened his mouth to answer, then pressed his lips firmly shut. What good was he to Hannah? No good. No good at all.

"Come with me to the stone house. Let's eat and clean up our dead. We've got three good people up there that deserve a proper place. When spring comes, we'll be able to dig graves."

Squeezing his eyes shut, Cole pinched the bridge of his nose with his gloved fingers and exhaled a shaky breath. He didn't know how he was going to manage this. He didn't know how he was going to live with himself.

Beside him, he felt Cookie stoop to retrieve the shovel.

"Make that four people." The older man sighed.

Eyes shooting open, Cole looked down. When the shovel had hit the ground, it cast off several inches of the fresh snow. The side of Trey's face was visible now. His eyes stared off into the distance. Frozen streaks of blood stained his chin and lips. He hadn't made it so far after all.

Dropping to his knees, Cole reached out with his hands and once more he began to dig.

CHAPTER SEVEN_
HANNAH

WHEN HANNAH TRIED TO OPEN HER EYES, THE PARKING garage spun in lazy circles. Immediately, she was forced to close them again. Jameson looped his arms beneath her back and legs before picking her up. Cradling her to his chest, he carried her away.

At first, Hannah made a half-hearted attempt to fight him. Pushing her right palm against his chest, she soon lost strength and her hand fell limply down into her lap. She was dizzy, with little white sparks of light winking behind her closed eyelids.

She was helpless, fighting the urge to pass out. All she could do was listen to the opening of doors and pounding of boots on the ground. All she could feel was the rocking of Jameson's steps and the sharp intake of his breath.

Then new sounds of all kinds assaulted her. There was an electronic beeping, a roar of male voices mixing in the distance, the slamming of heavy doors. They hurt her. Each one entered her brain and brought such a mix of strangeness to her mind that she couldn't hardly compute where she was.

It wasn't until a final door closed that they dropped once more into blessed silence. Again, she tried to open her eyes but encountered such brightness, that she had to seal them shut.

"In there," Uriah spoke. He was closer than Hannah had imagined and it was a comfort to her. "Keep the door open."

Jameson's steps slowed and then she was being lowered down. Beneath her, Hannah felt the soft give of a mattress, the crinkle of fabric, the sigh of pillows. Spreading out her fingers against the blanket, Hannah grasped at the smooth linen. It felt fresh, smelled clean.

Again she tried to open her eyes, but only managed a quick glimpse of Jameson standing over her before the room began to spin. The light all around the room increased the throbbing sensation in her head, so she squeezed her eyes shut once more.

"It's the chloroform," Jameson's voice was matter of fact. "I gave you too much, too often. That and you're probably dehydrated."

Hannah exhaled a breath of frustration through her nostrils, keeping her lips pressed together in a firm line. Sure, she had a few choice words for Mr. Jameson, but at the moment it was all she could do not to dry heave again.

Hands gripping the blanket, she listened to another set of boots enter the room. Beside her, the bed dipped suddenly with the weight of a man. She practically jumped out of her skin when a glass was held up to her mouth.

"Uriah!" Hannah shouted, knocking wildly at the cup, splashing its contents over her and the bed.

"I'm across the hall!" Her brother called. "He's just trying to give you some water, Hannah Mae. I can see you, it's okay."

Sucking in a few short breaths, Hannah pushed up to sitting. Her wrist screamed out in protest. Drawing her legs up in front of her, she leaned forward to hang her head between her knees. Damn it, this vulnerability, the not being able to see her surroundings, it was absolutely unbearable.

Muttering to herself, Hannah slid both her hands tentatively along her forehead before she carefully blinked open her eyes. Her left wrist pulsed with the effort.

"You going to throw up again?" Jameson asked quietly.

"No."

"Because if you are-"

"I said no."

"You need to drink some water, it'll help."

In her tiny tunnel of vision, Hannah noted the cream-colored down comforter beneath her. It was thick with feathers and its large quilt-like squares had perfectly straight stitching. With each breath, the vertigo seemed to slow.

Hands trembling as they clutched at her face, Hannah battled with everything she had to maintain this small victory. No sudden movements, no quick blinking. Though she wanted to lift her head and look around, she knew

51

instinctively that her body wouldn't tolerate it. At least not yet. And her mouth, it was so very dry. Licking at her lips, she simply had no moisture left.

"Ready to drink?" Jameson again, he was the one sitting just beside her.

"Not from you."

"He won't let anyone else close to you. Not yet."

"I just watched my brother choke you," Hannah growled. "Why would he have you in here at all? Aren't you pissed?"

"No." Jameson paused before continuing. "He thought maybe I raped his sister. If I was him, I'd have done the same."

Out of the corner of her eye, Hannah watched Jameson's wide hand push a hovering water glass beneath the arch in her knees. Exhaling slowly, she lifted her head slightly and grabbed at the cup.

In order to bring the thing to her lips, she had to shut her eyes and sit up even more. The liquid tasted cool and sweet as it lined her throat on its way to her stomach. She gulped it down greedily, her body demanding more of what it so desperately needed to survive.

When the glass was empty, she shoved it in Jameson's direction before trying to lean back against the pillows. They were further away than she'd anticipated and her stomach muscles quivered. Swinging her right hand frantically around, she tried to slow her fall. Instead, Jameson was right there to prop her up, sliding a hand beneath her shoulders, easing her down flat.

"Don't touch me." Hannah forced her eyes open in time to see Jameson frown.

"You look just like him," he commented, before withdrawing his hands. "I don't know why I didn't see it before."

"Like who?"

"Your brother... only you're pretty, of course."

Hannah maintained eye contact only long enough to witness Jameson's unapologetic stare. Then her world was tilting once more on its axis and her eyelids lowered involuntarily.

"Let's get some more water and a bowl of soup in here," Jameson ordered before Hannah felt his weight lift free of the bed.

Footsteps paced a few steps away from her, then stilled. In the background, Hannah's ears began to pick up the distant murmur of men talking, doors slamming, dishes rattling. There were more people here than just the four of them. And where was here exactly? She still didn't know. Then the sound of Lena yelling broke through all the rest. Hannah's body tensed and she struggled to sit up.

"It's okay," Jameson again. "They're just arguing about something."

"Who?"

"Uriah and that woman. Who is she?"

"She's just a woman."

"You're not going to give me a name?"

"No."

Angling her head to one side, Hannah strained to listen.

Uriah's voice was low and coaxing where Lena's seemed to only grow in frequency and pitch. In all their time together, Hannah had never heard the other woman so vocal. She'd always been a quiet, reserved little shadow, trailing behind Liam and then when he'd gone... behind Chan. Both of the men's names caused a painful twist in her chest.

"Are there really more of you?" Jameson again. "Behind a wall in the north? Is it true?"

"Did Uriah tell you that?" Hannah tentatively opened her eyes. With a sigh, she began to blink things into focus. "That there are thousands of women safe somewhere?"

"Yes."

Jameson's massive frame stood past the end of her bed, his broad shoulders blocking the threshold of her open door. His face was the picture of stone she had remembered it, a five o'clock shadow graced his chin and cheeks. But in his blue eyes, she saw a look of such uncertain hope that she had to glance away.

"Whatever my brother told you about what's behind the Wall..." Hannah exhaled. "You can believe him. He's no liar."

A careful quiet settled between them then. It was in direct contrast to the raised voices on the other side of the hall.

Hannah tried to listen to what Lena and her brother were saying, but the throbbing in her wrist seemed to have traveled up and settled directly between her ears. With each pulse of her heart, Hannah felt a beat of pain in her head and it interfered with her ability to concentrate.

Letting out a low groan, she reached up to pinch at the bridge of her nose.

Jameson shifted and mumbled something about food and more water. Whatever his exact words were, she never did catch them. It was impossible to hear over the footsteps that charged suddenly in their direction.

"You're a liar!" Lena cried, causing Hannah's eyes to pop wide.

Storming into Hannah's bedroom with Uriah hot on her heels, the little raven-haired girl managed to skirt Jameson's heavy frame without actually touching him. Uriah, however, could accomplish no such feat.

Instead of trying to sneak through the gap, he shoved Jameson roughly aside, causing the other man's shoulder to impact the white wall beside him. If this second instance of unprovoked violence upset Jameson, he gave no indication. In fact, as Hannah's eyes darted quickly between them, she noted his face twist up in a slightly amused expression.

"We weren't able to recover Flynn," Uriah explained.

"Just answer the question!"

"You need to calm down."

"Is she alive or dead?"

"I told you… I don't know."

"But he does," Lena accused.

She threw the words over her shoulder as she scrambled up onto Hannah's bed. The bouncing motion had Hannah's stomach sagging along with the mattress and she sucked in a harsh breath as Lena inadvertently knocked into her injured wrist. The little pixie didn't seem to notice, though, as she planted herself firmly along Hannah's side.

Burying her face in Hannah's neck, she wrapped her slender arms around Hannah's waist.

Tangled up there together, Hannah fought a flood of nausea as Lena's tears began to flow. At the foot of the bed, Uriah threw a glance at Jameson who's face fell to sudden seriousness. Almost reluctantly, he gave up a slight shake of his head. *No.*

The word fell like a lead weight straight from Hannah's brain down into the floor. Flynn was probably dead and the idea seemed to drag just about every other thought along with it. Squeezing her eyes shut against the implications, Hannah began to stroke down Lena's hair with her good hand. Dead, they were all probably dead.

"She's…" the words stuttered in Hannah's mouth. "She's gone, Lena. Flynn is gone."

"No," Lena moaned the word, slowly shaking her head side to side.

"I'm sorry," Uriah's tone was pleading as he stepped closer.

"Get out," Lena whispered into Hannah's neck. She could feel the harsh sadness brush against her skin. "Get. Out."

"Come on, baby."

"Get! Out!" Lena pushed up suddenly to scream at the men. Jerking a pillow from behind her, she threw it at the far wall where it fell pitifully short. "Get out! Get out!"

She didn't stop screaming. No, the little woman who'd held everything in for so very long, suddenly could not stop. At least not until the men disappeared through the door. Then the screams fell to sobs and the sobs to moans.

Hannah slowly exhaled. Blinking rapidly, the flood of sorrow that filled her was cut short by an unmistakeable sound. The flip of the lock.

Despite Lena's crying, the slide of the door's lock was clear as a bell in the room. In fact, the metal sound all but echoed.

CHAPTER EIGHT_
LIAM

IT ONLY TOOK ANOTHER HOUR OF DRIVING BEFORE THE CITY rose up before them. And by city Liam meant the shell of what used to be an actual real *city*. The sun was setting and mostly covered by clouds so the view was limited and dark, but still... it caused Liam's breath to catch in his throat.

Cruising down the paved streets, he let his eyes play over the cement sidewalks, fire hydrants and brick chimneys. These had once been sprawling suburbs but they were all burned to the ground now. Cinderblock walls and chainlink fencing seemed to survive, though. Everything else was a blackened shell of what it once was.

Then came the business district with its massive warehouses and sprawling square parking lots with old street lamps and dead traffic signals. Between the stone facades, metal sheet roofing and fire sprinkler systems, these buildings had fared much better. There was still no electricity, and most of the windows were shattered, but the buildings could be used for shelter.

In fact, Liam's mouth dropped open just a hair when he began to see men roaming the streets. They walked casually, in pairs or even all alone. When the SUV roared past them, the men didn't even flinch.

Liam watched in wonder as they merely raised their hands in casual salute as the vehicle tore by. With the window down and the air streaming in, Liam even heard the ripple of laughter. What is this place? He thought. The sheer size was enough to astound him, not to mention the number of men kept growing.

The further in they traveled, the more men there were. Hundreds, maybe even a thousand. And those were just the ones on the outside, starting fires in barrels, cooking food together, talking. They were easy, relaxed and safe. That was it, they all felt *safe* here.

"You been alone long?" O'Shea asked, causing Liam to glance up to the front seat.

Catching the man's eye in the rearview mirror, Liam merely nodded and looked back out the window.

"A man of few words, huh?" O'Shea grinned. He was an unnaturally happy fucker, Liam decided.

The vehicle took a hard right then, and had Liam's body swaying towards the middle of the seat. Up ahead, a series of towering office buildings loomed on either side of the road. The slick glass and steel looked steady enough, though Liam had to crane his neck to see past the first five stories.

Higher up on the buildings there were spots of damage where fires had started or artillery had landed. Whole sections were blown out. Liam shuddered. They'd stood for years this way but even so he couldn't quite shake the vision of them all falling to the ground.

"Did you radio it in?" O'Shea asked Ricks.

"Yeah, he wants to do the interview himself."

"That so?"

"Yeah."

Liam's shoulders tensed and instinctively he stroked his rifle. That was definitely about him, and the others didn't even bother to hide it. Before Liam had time to regret his decision, the SUV was pulling into an underground parking garage. The dark space swallowed them whole until Ricks flipped on the headlights.

Holding up a hand against the brightness, Liam blinked and blinked. He couldn't remember the last time he'd seen artificial light. The orbs swept the concrete walls of the garage as they wound down, down, down.

At the bottom, they pulled briskly into an open space and parked. Glancing to his right and left, Liam noted there were cars parked all around them. The only difference was that they were covered in thick layers of dust. If any of them worked, or had fuel, then they weren't being put to use.

"Here's our stop," O'Shea announced.

Peachy, Liam thought, but kept his mouth shut and his face calm. When Ricks pulled the key from the ignition, they were thrown once more into sudden blackness.

For one brief moment, Liam braced himself, waiting for an attack. But then a flashlight clicked on and O'Shea was shoving out of the front seat. Exhaling slowly, Liam followed suit, keeping his weapon clutched in both hands.

The garage smelled of mildew and mice, but the floor looked like it'd been swept recently.

Scooting out from between the cars, the three of them headed for the corner stairwell. Upon breaching the door, they climbed up one flight of stairs before O'Shea stopped at an entrance marked, *Service*. Turning to face Liam, his eyes were grim.

"The rifle's going to be a problem," he said.

"It won't," Liam countered.

"You're going to have to earn that trust," O'Shea reasoned. "Hand it over."

Bowing his head, Liam took a last look at his rifle. Did they actually expect him to give it up so easily? Hell, their guns weren't even drawn.

The next move Liam made was fast.

Swinging the butt of his rifle up, he smashed it into O'Shea's face before whirling around and taking out Ricks the same way. As they both lay writhing and twisting on the ground, blood spurting from their shattered noses, Liam stepped a boot onto Ricks' hip and bent to fish for his keys.

"You boys are lucky," Liam muttered. "There was a time I would've shot you instead."

Finding both front pockets empty, Liam kicked Ricks over to his belly and resumed his search. Was he going soft? No, that wasn't it at all. This was just plain smart. He couldn't afford the sound of gunfire down here. He was in the heart of the city after all. Not exactly the place to draw attention.

With a jingle, Liam's eyes lit as his fingers closed

around the SUV's keys. Now all he had to do was drive away. *Drive.* The thought made him slightly giddy.

"That'll do," a deep voice boomed.

Instantly Liam froze, but it wasn't the voice that got to him. It was the accompanying click of about a dozen firearms. Shit. He was fucking surrounded. How had he not heard them? Felt them?

Hands raising slowly in the air, Liam kept a grip on his rifle with one hand and the keys in the other. About three beams of solid light zeroed in on him, casting a long shadow over the concrete wall.

"Lower the rifle slowly to the ground," the voice came again. "And drop the keys."

Bending carefully, Liam did as instructed before straightening back up. O'Shea and Ricks were still rolling around, hands pressed to their faces.

"Turn towards me."

Liam obeyed and was instantly blinded by the flashlights, which was the point of course. Calmly, he closed his eyes. Is this what death by firing squad feels like? You stand defenseless and blind while the men around you take aim?

Heart thundering in his chest, Liam flashed back to all those countless men he himself had killed. They were all afraid in the end. None of them wanted to die. And now Liam knew just a hint of how they felt.

Because in that moment, he realized just how much he did not want to die. But if anyone deserved this, he knew it was definitely him. So, inhaling a deep breath, Liam brought Hannah to his mind and waited.

At least she was safe and at peace with Cole. He'd given

her that much. Maybe that was enough for just the smallest slice of redemption when he met his maker on the other side.

"What's your name soldier?"

"Liam."

"Got a last name?"

"Not anymore." Liam would be damned if his father's fucking name was the last one on his lips before he died.

"It's Byrne," O'Shea groaned from the ground. "Liam Byrne."

"Strike Team Three, Liam Byrne?"

Liam's eyes shot open at the question, but the only thing he let in was searing light. Grimacing, he squeezed them shut once more as perspiration beaded on his forehead. Who the fuck would know that shit? Who the fuck was he talking to here?

"Where's the rest of your team?"

"Dead," Liam barked.

"You're all supposed to be dead."

"We are."

"No," the man's voice was incredulous. "I read the reports myself. Your entire team went out in a drone hit down south. It was the last mission of its kind right before the final fall. Lower your lights. Lower your weapons."

Liam felt the flashlights leave his face but kept his hands in the air. Ever so slowly, he opened his eyes and blinked at the scene around him. There were no less than a dozen blacked out soldiers, all in fatigues, cramming the tiny stairwell. How had he not heard them?

Glancing down at the floor, he noted the steps and

landing were all concrete, so there wouldn't be the echoing of metal, but still.

"We were waiting," the voice spoke again, seeming to read Liam's mind. "It's a sort of test of trust. If you were wondering, you failed."

Liam nodded slowly, then let his eyes assess the adversary before him. He was stocky, with broad shoulders and a big barrel chest, though he was by no means overweight. If anything, despite being maybe 5'11" at the most, the guy gave the appearance of being larger than life.

He wore no helmet, no ball cap to cover his thick crop of golden blonde hair, which was an unusual mix of colors.

In fact, Liam had only ever seen it on one other person quite like that, with the streaks of honey blonde and dusting of a light sandy brown. Then there were his eyes. They were the same color brown as his little sister. Fucking family resemblance.

"Uriah Linfield." Liam exhaled, his jaw twitching. "I've heard so much about you."

CHAPTER NINE_
LIAM

"IS THAT SO?" URIAH TILTED HIS HEAD TO THE SIDE, HIS EYES playing over Liam's face. "Who's been talking about me?"

Though the stairwell was dimly lit by the mix of flashlights, Liam could make out Uriah's face plain as day. So, this guy was a North East Side Soldier... one who had access to strike reports and mission plans. The thoughts zoomed through Liam's head as he continued to hold his hands high above him. Only a Command Officer had that kind of clearance. Was Uriah Linfield a part of Command?

"It's all over the high country," Liam explained. "You're building an army."

"I don't do armies," Uriah corrected. "Armies are all about war."

"What do you call this, then?"

"A beginning."

"The beginning?" Liam actually snorted. "Of what?"

"Why don't you come inside?" Uriah gestured for him to lower his hands. "We can talk more about it."

Easing out a breath, Liam dropped his arms down. The men on all sides began to move. O'Shea and Ricks were helped off the ground, Liam's gun was retrieved along with the SUV's keys.

"Search him," Uriah instructed.

Holding perfectly still, Liam let a smirk play across his face as a soldier patted him down. In the end, the guy produced not one, not two, but three different knives. Liam only let his superior expression slide when the asshole removed the jar of moonshine as well. Shit, he was going to finish that.

"Right this way." Uriah gestured for Liam to move through the now open door of the service entrance.

A massive soldier with choppy brown hair and bright blue eyes glared as Liam passed him. Personal space much? Maybe the guy was used to intimidating people with his sheer size, but he was still an inch or so shorter than Liam, who kept his face carefully blank now. He knew what came next. Hell, he'd been on the other side of this sort of thing for long enough.

Once through the door, Liam found himself being led along a narrow corridor. It had the same ugly concrete walls as the parking garage, complete with a high ceiling and exposed conduit running its length. Eyes popping wide for a split second, he nearly gasped aloud but then caught himself.

He could actually see the ceiling. He could see it because the hall had lights. Like working electricity, that flows into a bulb, that's fixed to the wall... lights. As if that wasn't enough, when they got to the heavy metal door at the end, the man in front passed a keycard over a flat black reader and the damn thing beeped before clicking open.

Feeling slightly dizzy, Liam worked to keep his composure as their group squeezed through the threshold and up another flight of stairs. Electricity. They had power here.

At the landing, yet another electronic reader was used and another thick metal door swung open. That's when the sounds assaulted him.

Walking forward, Liam sucked in a breath and came to a stop. There's no way. It couldn't be real. His heart beat an excited pace in his chest and in the background he heard Uriah chuckle. He knew it was Uriah, he didn't have to look.

In the next moment, Liam closed the distance to the railing and looked down.

They were in an indoor bowling alley. Like a pretty damn big one, all the way down here, underground. Below him, no less than a hundred men were laughing, swearing and well... bowling. Lights flashed on electronic scoreboards and pins tumbled with a familiar echo.

Is that *beer*? Liam squinted at a few frosty looking pitchers set on hightop tables. They're even wearing those dopey red and blue shoes, he realized.

"Pretty sweet find, right?" Uriah came to stand beside him.

"What is this place?" Liam was a little awed, he couldn't help it.

"Some rich bastard who owned the building above us was a bit paranoid," Uriah explained. "He had this place built for the apocalypse, complete with bathrooms, food and generators to run the whole thing. We've even got enough fuel and batteries to last a few dozen decades."

"Of all things, he built a bowling alley?" Liam's mind was shaking off the shock and the questions were flooding him.

"It's a safe, self-contained game. Easy to manage for a large number of people."

"Where's the house? The rich guy's residence?" Liam's eyes flicked to Uriah, who let a knowing smile twitch at one corner of his mouth.

"That space is reserved."

"Reserved," Liam repeated. *Yeah, right.*

"Why don't we sit." Uriah indicated a black rectangular table and two matching chairs.

So, this is where the interrogation begins, Liam thought and bobbed his head in acceptance. Pulling out one metal chair, he let its legs scrape along the concrete floor before taking a seat. His long legs stuck out before him as he crossed them at the ankle and leaned back.

Casually, Liam folded his arms over his chest and smoothed the features of his face. The other men in the room melted against the walls, standing, watching, waiting. When Uriah took the seat opposite him, Liam let his gaze lock on the all too familiar brown eyes.

Game time.

"How did you survive that last mission?" Uriah sat straight in his chair, one forearm resting on the tabletop, the other tucked into his lap.

Liam merely shrugged.

"Did any of the others make it?" Uriah paused, his eyes flicking over Liam's face. "Cole Tanner? Ian Chan?"

"No," Liam lied easily, even dropping his gaze to the floor in mock sadness.

"So you've been living alone all this time?"

"I didn't say that."

"You haven't really said anything."

Again, Liam shrugged.

"If you want to stay here, then you've got to give me something." Uriah's tone was easy, his eyes steady and calm.

"Who said I want to stay here? I'm just passing through."

"Is that right?"

"That's right."

"What was your speciality again? For the Strike Team?" Uriah sat back in his seat a bit now, pretending like this was all just cheap talk. The thing was, it didn't fool Liam, not for one red hot second. If Uriah knew them all by name, then he knew precisely what each of them did.

"So, what part of Command did you work for exactly?" Liam watched Uriah's face carefully, saw the quick pass of intelligence before the other man let out a chuckle.

"You like beer?" Uriah leaned over the table, waving a hand absently at one of his men. "Course you do."

The balcony where they sat fell to silence as a soldier disappeared down a far set of steps. Uriah watched Liam and Liam just watched him right back.

He'd never been privy to Command Officer names during the war, actually none of their unit had. The protocol made sense so many years ago. If you didn't know the name of the man above you, then you couldn't give it up in the event you were captured.

On top of that layer of protection, only Cole had ever met with Command in person. All of their subsequent orders came by code on Chan's scanner and if they had any questions, then Chan could communicate them easily enough. Not that their team ever had any questions. Maybe they should have, come to think of it.

In the background, the sound of the alley lifted to fill the air. The thump of bowling balls landing in the lanes, then rolling, rolling, rolling. The echo of pins being struck, then jumbling all around as men cheered or booed.

Inhaling, Liam could smell the mix of alcohol, sweat and food. Stomach grumbling, he glanced to the side, unfolded his arms and let loose an audible sigh. Everything on the outside of Liam screamed boredom, but inside his mind was whirling on overdrive.

"Ah, here it is now." Uriah smiled and scooted back, making room for the pitcher of golden beer.

Before Liam could blink, a plate overflowing with chili cheese nachos landed just beside the pitcher and his mouth dropped open. Instantly, saliva flowed and he yearned to take a bite. Instead, Liam remained frozen in time.

These damn assholes had tortilla chips and fucking melted nacho cheese... like the kind you got at a ball game. Hell, they probably pumped it right out of a giant plastic tub. Maybe they even popped the whole mess in a microwave... a *microwave*.

The unfairness of it all was suddenly overwhelming.

A solid minute of staring passed before Liam managed to shut his gaping mouth and look up. Uriah had both of his hands folded neatly on the table now and a superior twinkle in his eye. Winner, he seemed to say. In the game of getting each other to drop their guard, Uriah had definitely come out on top.

Shaking his head, Liam sat up straight and pulled his chair closer to the table. Without preamble, he grabbed a handful of chips and shoveled them into his mouth. It was so good. So gloriously good.

While Liam chewed, Uriah poured the beer into two frosty cold glasses. He took his time, tipping the cups to the side so as not to create too much foam. When the first full beer hit the tabletop, Liam picked it up and chugged about half of it down. Letting loose an authentic groan, Liam smacked his lips and continued devouring the nachos.

"How do you know I didn't poison it?" Uriah asked quietly.

At that, Liam's eyes cruised up to lock on Hannah's brother. He let loose a wide grin. If these guys used poison instead of a bullet to end him, then they were dumber than shit.

After swallowing another substantial portion of beer, Liam gestured for a refill. "Guess I better get real drunk, real fast then, huh?"

"You got a death wish?" Uriah sipped his own beer and shoved the pitcher closer to Liam, indicating he should pour for himself this time.

"You don't?"

Instead of answering, Uriah bit at his bottom lip a moment and then took another swig. And there it was, Liam realized, the first hint of weakness. Liam hit home with that last comment, and the only reason he knew so was because he'd seen Hannah do the same damn thing.

Whenever she was nervous, or cornered, or avoiding the truth, she pressed her teeth down into her bottom lip and glanced away. It used to drive Liam absolutely crazy, watching her do it. Now it seemed the tell was a family trait. Not nearly so appealing on the hulking brother, but it gave Liam an edge just the same.

"We have space here for a man like you," Uriah began, easing back in his chair, beer in hand. "A man of your talents would go a long way to help our cause."

"What's your cause?"

"What if I told you there were healthy women still alive on this planet?"

"I'd say you were crazy."

"Well, there are thousands of them. Enough to start over, build things back to how they were... eventually."

"Oh, yeah? So where are they then?"

"There are fourteen holding facilities positioned around the world. Each one of them houses approximately thirty-five thousand women."

Liam choked on his last bite and had to pound a fist into his chest to get the damn thing to swallow down. Yeah, he may have known about Hannah and the refugee center, but he had no clue the magnitude of the operation. This thing was bigger than he ever imagined. This thing was worldwide. But the issue remained, he still didn't really know what "this thing" actually was.

"It's hard to believe, I know." Uriah's demeanor relaxed at Liam's reaction. "The closest one is a little over seven hundred miles from here."

"How do you know all this?"

"Because I lived there for awhile. There are some things I can't tell you, but if you join up with us, then I can guarantee you'll see them for yourself."

"What if I say no?"

Liam watched Uriah carefully, his heart rate increasing. There wasn't any way Liam could say no now. He simply had to know more, simply had to see it through. But before he committed himself, Liam wanted to know what type of man Uriah was. Would he let Liam go? Force him to stay? Kill him outright?

"I'd like you to stay." Uriah's brow furrowed, but not in anger. "We've recently suffered some losses to our highest level security team. We need more men with your expertise, more men with your type of training. But if you don't want to stay, then I won't make you."

Liam just eyed him warily, not saying anything one way or the other.

Looking over his shoulder, Uriah gestured with his hand before returning his gaze to Liam. "Give him back all of his things. The gun, too."

Tipping the pitcher up, Liam drained the last of the beer into his glass as his rifle, bag and bedroll were dropped on the floor beside him. After taking another few gulps, he bent to the side, unzipped his bag and checked the contents. All his knives were there, along with the meager supply of jerky, set of clothes, extra ammo and even the jar of moonshine.

Grunting to himself, Liam picked up his black rifle and checked the chamber. Should he do it? Yeah, he should do it.

Careful to keep the barrel pointed at the ground, Liam wracked a bullet into the chamber and watched every soldier there practically jump out of their skin. The massive blue-eyed fucker from before had his weapon drawn and pressed against the side of Liam's head before the count of two.

But that was expected. It was Uriah's reaction that Liam really wanted, and the man himself hadn't moved a muscle. His jaw hadn't tensed, he hadn't so much as shifted towards the handgun tucked into his waistline.

"I said let him go," Uriah repeated, and his men backed down.

Weapons were lowered, the big guy stepped away, but it didn't do much to alleviate the tension in the room.

Liam swung the gun up and laid it flat on the table. The barrel pointed to his left, away from Uriah and away from himself. Leaning back once more in his chair, he reached for a nacho and chomped down on it noisily. After he finished chewing, Liam dusted his hands off on the legs of his pants and sat forward. They were out of beer. Shit.

"So, what kind of rules do you have around here?" Liam asked, and Uriah actually grinned.

"You're staying then."

Liam shrugged. Picking up his empty beer glass he

waved it side to side, eyebrows raised. Uriah tipped his chin up over his shoulder and called again to one of his men.

"Get us some water," he said, and Liam rolled his eyes.

"First off, everything you see down there is earned." Uriah jerked a thumb behind him where the bowling alley hummed just below the railing. "Beer, speciality food and playtime are all on rotation and you have to work for them."

"What sort of work?"

"Most of the guys here are standard infantry. They either dodged the draft or defected at some point in time. Everyone who lives within the city limits has committed a certain portion of their time to me. Maybe they have to cut firewood and haul it back. Maybe they have to repair buildings, clean streets, take on a border patrol shift, things like that."

"What about food?"

"Last season we had a farm and when it's running, most everyone works their asses off from sun up to sun down. The harvest was decent and we should make it through this winter without issue."

"What about guys that don't work?"

"They leave."

"What about fights?"

"They happen." Uriah sighed. "But our security team functions as a sort of police if needed. If there's a dispute that they can't resolve, they bring it to me."

"And you're the ultimate judge?"

"Someone has to be."

"What's your plan?"

"My plan?"

"Yeah." Liam leaned back, eyeing him. "For getting the women out."

Uriah huffed a breath and narrowed his eyes. "We're not quite there, yet."

"And when you do get there?"

"I told you. You'll see them for yourself." Sitting forward, Uriah placed both hands on his thighs and looked Liam dead in the eye. "Meanwhile, you'll need to focus on doing what's asked of you. Like I said before, we've had some recent gaps left in our security force and a man with your training could really be of use there."

"You want me to work security?"

"It's a good start." Uriah gestured to the big blue-eyed soldier who stepped out of the shadows. "This is Garrett Jameson. He was a South West Soldier but you'll find we don't keep those lines around here. I find there's no use for them."

"A Southie, huh?"

"That'll be Sir Southie to you." Uriah chuckled a bit as Jameson's jaw tensed. "He's the head of security and you'll be working for him. He'll show you around, answer any questions you might have."

With that, Uriah pushed up to standing and offered his hand to shake. Eyeing it a moment, Liam wondered at the mess he'd just stepped into. Hannah's brother, a restored city, electricity, shift work.

This hadn't been part of his plan when leaving the compound. Hell, he hadn't had a plan. The point of leaving was to be free of *her*. To walk away and just keep walking, and maybe drinking, until he couldn't remember why he had to go in the first place. Until he didn't see her everywhere he went, until she stopped fucking haunting him.

But here he was, about to commit to working for Uriah *I'm A Big Deal* Linfield, Hannah's very own brother. Was he out of his damn mind?

After a beat, Liam stood and clasped Uriah's hand.

CHAPTER TEN_
COLE

THE FIRE CRACKLED AND SPIT BEHIND A BLACK WROUGHT iron grate, causing soft tendrils of smoke to lift up towards the chimney. That last log had still been pretty wet from all the snow. Despite the frigid temperature outside, it was relatively warm inside the cabin. The owners here kept everything going pretty well.

There was a man of about sixty, his cousin and a younger guy they called their friend. The three of them had lived at the base of Cole's mountain since the first time he'd set eyes on it. Why were they still breathing? How had they survived the team's original assault on this area?

They left well enough alone, that's why. And it was that very reputation for reclusiveness that was saving them all now.

Curling his fingers around the dented tin cup in his hand, Cole sipped at the hot tea but didn't taste it. Hell, he didn't taste anything anymore. He didn't *feel* anything either, for that matter. The only way he knew he was cold was when his body started to shiver, or when Cookie started in on him. The badgering of the older man was an almost constant background noise at this point.

So, no... nowadays Cole preferred the bitter cold of the outdoors, the endless hiking, the empty darkness of night. Because that's what consumed him. That's what drove him on.

"The only unusual thing we've noticed all season is you hangmen stomping down here in the dead of winter," the eldest man said. His name was Ezra and he did all the talking.

"It was about a month ago maybe." Cookie glanced to Cole who's mouth was pressed together in a firm line. "You didn't notice any sign of men passing through? Maybe a shift in your trap line, or game trails getting used this time of year that don't usually?"

"Nope." Ezra rubbed at his ample mustache and glanced distractedly at Cole.

Typically, Cole was the one to do all the talking. And yes, typically they had about five other men with them, not just two. But nothing about this visit was typical and Cole was doing everything he could not to slit Ezra's throat out of pure frustration. The darkness that Liam had always battled, it was engulfing Cole now. And the thing of it was, he welcomed the intrusion.

"What about a visit from just one man?" Cookie changed his tactic. "Or two? Something that wouldn't draw so much attention."

"Well..." Ezra sighed, shifting his boots along the dusty wooden floorboards. "You say they killed four of yours while you's all away trading?"

"Three," Cookie corrected.

"No, no." Ezra shook his head and once more eyed Cole. "You said four."

"We lost three men." Cookie cleared his throat.

"And one woman," Cole spoke finally, figuring they might as well be out with it. They were getting nowhere else wise. And what did they have to lose, anyway? It's not like there were any women left up there to protect.

"Ah." Ezra's faded-gray eyes grew wide a moment, but it wasn't with the utter shock one would expect. Surprise, yes. Shock, no.

"You know something," Cole announced, and had everyone in the room shifting uncomfortably.

They were outnumbered, but only by one body. Between Cookie and Cole, there would be no question as to the outcome. These men weren't trained soldiers, they weren't fighters. They were just survivors, good ones, but still.

Would Cole have liked Davey and Ace to join them? Yes, but he understood why that wasn't possible. Davey had lost it, like his mind crumpled in on itself after Ryder's death and he refused to leave until he could bury his brother. That was months away yet, and Ace had elected to stay behind with him. Davey needed the help. He needed someone to remind him to eat, someone to feed the livestock and keep a fire going.

So here Cole sat, still clutching the tin cup in one hand, missing Liam for all he was worth. That extra man could make all the difference, especially when that particular man was so good at tracking.

Purposefully, Cole kept his off hand visible and empty. There was no sense reaching for a weapon. It would only trigger a blood bath, and as Liam always said, you can't get words from a dead man.

"There was one fella." Ezra gave his head a slight shake. "More of a boy really, about sixteen or so I'd say."

"He come through here?" Cole raised his eyebrows. "A month ago?"

"No, no." Ezra sighed. "He stopped in several months further back. Said he was from even further north, a place up high in the mountains he had with his grandpa."

"What'd he look like?"

"Young, you know. Skinny like that, with clothes that were too big for him. Had light hair, not sure about the eyes." Ezra turned to his cousin who nodded in agreement. "He stayed a few nights."

"And?"

"Well, his grandpa died finally and he was looking for somewhere to land. We pointed him towards Jensen's city and he seemed to walk off in that direction when he left."

"You're telling me this for a reason." Cole gritted his teeth. "I just know it."

"Point is, he's the only other person that's talked about seeing a woman alive in the past three years." Ezra tilted his head to the side. "You get a feel for people after awhile and I believe this kid was speaking the truth, as isolated as he was with his grandpa and all."

"He was from the northern mountains?" Cole's brain pricked at a certain memory of a certain raid he himself had conducted around that time frame.

"That's right. He said it was awful how this neighbor group of theirs had caught two women and they were being held in a cage and such. The boy talked like he wanted to help, but between the old man and himself they wouldn't have made much of a stand against the others. According to him, anyway."

"Yeah, according to him." Cole paused, thinking. "And that's all?"

"That's all," Ezra confirmed, but then he leaned forward. "But you know how that sort of story goes. One man takes it to another, and then another. It wouldn't take long for it to spread through the territory."

"You sent him off to Jensen's?"

"He wanted to see more people." Ezra shrugged. "That's more people."

Cole nodded his head before setting his cup on the floor and pushing up to standing. When he did, so did all the others. Sticking out his hand to shake, Cole waited as Ezra eyed it a moment.

"You the ones with the cage?" He asked finally, eyes darting up to appraise Cole's reaction.

"No."

"You take those women from the north then?"

"Yeah."

"So there's one still out there? That's why you're really tracking them, right? For the other one."

"There's one still out there," Cole confirmed. *And hopefully two.*

"Well, in that case..." Ezra glanced over his shoulder before turning back around. "There was this car..."

CHAPTER ELEVEN_
HANNAH

HOT SOAPY WATER RAN DOWN HER LEGS, OVER HER ANKLES and swirled around her feet before flowing down the silver drain. It was a thing of beauty. A thing of luxury and largess.

And it wasn't just the imposing granite walls of the shower stall. Nope. Honestly, it wasn't even the bottles of shampoo, conditioner and exfoliating body soap. Hell, it wasn't even the disposable razor.

It was the *hot*, running water. That was the most sinful part of the whole experience. And Hannah got to have it all to herself for a total of five minutes, two times a week.

With a sigh, Hannah rubbed at her face with her hands and let the curved silver shower head pour rain down her chest and belly. Tilting her head to the side, she reached out to swipe the mist off the digital control panel. Three minutes and twenty-six seconds to go, then the water would shut off automatically.

On the other side of the door, she could hear Lena knock.

"Need help with your hair?" Lena called. It seemed Hannah had taken over where Liam and Chan had left off... Lena followed her everywhere.

"Not anymore," Hannah called back.

Glancing down at her left wrist, she stretched her fingers wide before clenching them into a tight fist. It no longer hurt. Turns out her tumble from a moving vehicle had only cost her a mild sprain. After a solid week of splinting it, the swelling was gone and her mobility was back.

Methodically, Hannah worked to scrub shampoo into her hair, then rinse and repeat. By the time the water cut off, she was squeaky clean, her skin a lingering bright pink from the heat.

Stepping out of the stall, she surveyed the brightly lit bathroom. It had an ice-white granite counter to match the shower walls, complete with a porcelain sink positioned beneath a wide silver framed mirror. Steam filled the room, and for a moment, she let her body drip water onto the plush bathroom rug. Its long rectangle of sage green ran the length of the space, partially covering the hand-scraped bamboo flooring.

Reaching up to her right, Hannah selected one of the thick cotton towels and wrapped it around her body. Under the cabinet, she would find a hair dryer, a curling iron and an array of makeup. That's right, actual from the Chanel counter, makeup. There were even a few bottles of nail polish.

When Hannah had first discovered them, she'd wanted to smash them all against the expensive floor. It was only her rush of tears that had prevented her. She couldn't hardly see, she'd cried so hard. Somewhere outside of these walls, Flynn was probably lying dead.

Despite having lived underground with her brother for several weeks, it was an outcome that he and Hannah did not discuss. Lena wasn't speaking to Uriah at all and Hannah couldn't decide what to tell him and what not to. Had Jameson left any of their friends alive? What had become of Chan? Or Ryder and Trey? Jameson wouldn't have left without Flynn if she were still breathing, of that Hannah now felt certain.

"Hannah Mae!" Lena's knock sounded against the door once more. "What's taking you?"

"Nothing!" Hannah called back before flipping the lock on the door and pulling it wide.

"Oh." Lena's hand popped up to her mouth before settling. She was still skittish, but working hard not to be. "Can I sit?"

"Sure." Hannah stepped back as Lena swept in and positioned herself on the closed lid of the toilet seat. *That's right, a real flushing toilet. Talk about spoiled.*

The bathroom itself was attached to a large bedroom that boasted a fully stocked walk-in closet along with a queen-sized bed. It was the same one Hannah had been given initially; one that she later found out was meant for her all along.

You see, the clothes in the closet? They were hers. The shoes on the floor? The hair brush in the drawer? The pictures on the bedside table? All of it belonged to Hannah. Because that rich paranoid prick that built the twelve bedroom, seven bath, underground bunker was none other than her very own father. With the specific encouragement of Uriah, of course.

Only... her dad had been killed before he'd had a chance to hole up here. And by the time Uriah was able to track Hannah down, she'd already been shipped to the Wall. He had no choice but to continue on with his service and wait. Eventually Uri was able to join her, when the war was at an end and the pitiful remains of their fighting force were drawn back in.

At least that's what her brother had told her. For all the talking he did, Hannah still couldn't pull up those specific memories for herself. Not the night that their mom had died so long ago and not the day their father left for the office never to return.

Nibbling at her lower lip, Hannah crouched down to fish the hair dryer out from under the sink. Everything was situated in precisely labeled baskets. Apparently Uriah had a thing for neatness. The entire house was laid out in the same way.

Straightening, Hannah plugged in the dryer and flipped it on. Beside her, Lena gathered her knees to her chest and watched. It was bizarre really, the dichotomy of then vs now.

Often times, Hannah would flash back to the compound. She saw the palms of her hands blistered from hauling buckets of water. She smelled the rich earth by the bank of the stream and felt the icy water flowing over her arms as she washed dirty clothes. She heard the whisper of Cole's words close to her ear at night and the ring of metal as Liam fashioned another knife.

It was hard to think of them… either of them. Her heart would stutter in her chest and her throat would close up on her. Cole and Liam had to be okay. They hadn't been at the compound when Jameson's team hit. She missed both of them, worried about both of them, and hated herself for it. She should only be thinking about Cole. Not Liam. But it was always him, too.

Sucking in a breath, Hannah tried to focus on the task at hand. When her golden hair was completely dry, Lena stood up and began brushing through it. Hannah watched her progress in the mirror. They made a strange picture together, the two of them.

"You're still speaking to him," Lena said, almost like a question, but not.

"And you aren't," Hannah replied. Lena glanced up momentarily, her blue eyes going slightly hard before they flitted away. This inner strength was new.

"You could use a trim," Lena commented, changing topics as she fingered the split ends of Hannah's hair.

"I want to keep it long."

"Why? You're never going to see them again."

"Don't say that." Hannah's lungs pinched in on her.

"It's true. Do you honestly think Uriah will let you leave here?"

"Well…"

"Hannah Mae." Lena's eyebrows drew together. "You still don't remember everything, do you?"

Nibbling at her lip, Hannah wrapped her towel more tightly around her body before letting her gaze drop to the sink. No. The answer was no, she didn't remember everything.

Seeming to sense her discomfort, Lena sighed and gave her a slight pat on the shoulder.

"Well, you may not be up for a cut, but I am."

A little smirk transformed Lena's face as she reached into one of the drawers and pulled out a pair of shining silver scissors. While Hannah looked on, Lena proceeded to rid herself of about six inches of hair. Drawing the silky black locks forward over her shoulders, she cut and cut and cut.

"Will you even out the back?" Lena asked, offering Hannah the scissors.

"I've never cut hair before," Hannah replied.

"Haven't you? How do you know?"

Hannah frowned, but then accepted the offered scissors and ran tentative fingers through Lena's hair. How did she know? She didn't.

By the time Hannah was done cutting, the silky black locks fell in deliberate layers all around the little pixie's face, bringing the final length to somewhere just above her shoulders. Stepping back, Hannah eyed her work with mild surprise. It looked good actually.

"You're pretty," Hannah commented absently.

"So are you," Lena responded. Hannah nodded in acceptance, but before she could turn away, Lena grabbed her arm. "You can't tell him, you know. About Cole or Liam."

"I haven't," Hannah said, knowing the him who must not be named was her brother.

And despite Uriah's persistent questions, something had made Hannah outright lie to him about the compound. She'd told him the men who lived there were named John and Jim and George and there weren't any more of them anywhere.

Lena, for her part, had listened quietly to Hannah's lies, and refused to acknowledge Uriah one way or the other. Her brother's face would turn red and his jaw would clench, but he wouldn't press further.

Was he convinced? Maybe. Well, okay probably not, but what could he do to them? Keep asking, of course.

"No, I mean about the *sleeping* arrangements." Lena eyed her meaningfully.

"Oh, right." Hannah's brow furrowed before she shoved out of the bathroom and headed for her closet. "No, I won't tell my brother about your lover."

Lena trailed behind her, a worried line working along her pouty pink lips. "My lover? Um... don't you mean *your* lovers. Plural."

"What?" Hannah hesitated. Lena knew about that?

Standing in the open doorway, the little pixie's fingers played along the carved wooden trim. "And just for the record, Liam and I never slept together... ever. I mean we slept in the same room, but never like that."

"But-"

"My God, Hannah Mae," Lena cleared her throat. "I couldn't hardly close my eyes around a man, let alone do *that*."

"I'm sorry." Hannah ducked her head. "I should've known that, I just... it's Liam, and he has this way about him."

"Yeah." Lena smiled then. "He made me feel really safe. That's all. And then Chan told me about the sharing thing," Lena continued. "It wasn't until after Liam left or I would've said something to you... you know, *before*."

"It's fine." Hannah's heart picked up the pace. "It was over anyway."

"Really?" Lena let a rueful smile play across her lips. "Because it didn't seem over. For him especially."

"I can't..." Hannah sucked in a breath, the months of wasted time flashing through her mind. "What am I supposed to do now?"

"I'm sorry." Lena stepped closer, lowering her voice. "Really, I'm sorry to bring it up, but you just don't remember what Uriah can be like. He was always extra protective over you. Back when we all lived inside the Wall, things got... heated. There was the thing with Andy, and... just keep your private life to yourself. That's all I'm saying."

"Okay." Hannah swallowed the lump in her throat. *The thing with Andy? What thing?*

With a quick shake of her head, Hannah got dressed in a pair of linen pants and warm sweater. It was cool in the house and although they had forced-air heating, Uriah considered it wasteful to keep the space at anything above sixty-eight degrees.

"Do you smell that?" Lena asked suddenly. "He's trying to bribe us again."

The scent of frying bacon had begun to drift beneath the closed bedroom door, that and the smell of coffee. Glorious black coffee. Hannah's stomach grumbled. Uriah was cooking in their kitchen. A real full-sized kitchen, one with a refrigerator *and* an oven.

"You could talk to him, you know," Hannah commented, then sighed at Lena's skeptical look. She was holding a grudge all her own, one Hannah just couldn't maintain. Not with her big brother, anyway.

In silence, the two women left their shared bedroom and walked quietly down the long hall. Their door was only kept locked when other men were in the house, which was actually a rare occurrence. Aside from certain planned meals, Uriah and the two women were the only ones in residence. Although, Hannah's mild exploration of the other bedrooms led her to believe this arrangement was a new one. At the back of the home, there was even a bunk room that could sleep ten.

As they walked, Lena ran one hand along the wall, letting her fingers glide lightly over painting after painting after painting. There were no windows anywhere so the only way to combat the slightly claustrophobic feeling was to cover the blank space with scenes of the outside world.

Sprawling vineyards, thick foggy forests, glassy blue lakes, tumbling dark oceans. They were beautiful, large and expensive, each and every one. But they were nothing compared to the stars at night over the compound. Or the moon throwing shafts of light through the trees.

The memories Hannah's mind did have left her with a dull ache that refused to leave.

"You're up." Uriah lifted his head as they entered the kitchen.

He was hunched over a stainless steel stove, flipping bacon in a frying pan with a set of tongs. Between pieces, he clicked the tongs together subconsciously, his eyes shifting quickly over Hannah before settling purposefully on the dark-haired woman.

"You cut it," he commented, causing Lena to turn away. "It looks good."

When she made no reply, Uriah's jaw clenched and he returned to the bacon. The tension between them was thick and Hannah couldn't help but pity her brother just a little. Try as he might, he was unable to keep from glancing over as Lena strode by. His eyes tracked her all the way to the other end of the room where she took a seat at a mahogany dining table.

Once settled, she kept her back to him, of course. Ever since learning of Flynn's fate, Lena observed a vow of distinct and punishing silence. Well, silence where Uriah was concerned. Clearing her throat, Hannah filled the void awkwardly.

"It smells good," she said, leaning a hand on the swirling granite counter.

Everything in this place was masculine, made of stone and rich wood. The floors were covered in Persian rugs, the furniture custom, blending style and comfort seamlessly.

"Thank you." Uriah shook his head and worked to give his sister an easy smile. "Eggs and toast are ready. Why don't you help yourself?"

Ducking her head, Hannah twisted her fingers together in front of her before glancing back at Lena. How long would this particular war go on? She wasn't sure. Instinctively she knew it was more than just the death of Flynn and the unknown fate of the others that had Lena so clammed up. All that hurt terribly, yes, but the attack on the compound wasn't as simple as all that.

Uriah's men were under orders to evacuate two unknown women from an abusive environment. They conducted the raid based on that information. It wasn't like before the war, when you could sit and use surveillance and ask a bunch of questions before making a move. Hannah hurt for her friends, but she couldn't help wanting to forgive her brother for issuing the orders. He'd thought it was a rescue mission. They all had.

And deep down, Hannah figured Lena understood that as well. So no, Lena's silent treatment wasn't just about the raid. It was about self-preservation. She didn't want to tell Uriah about her months spent outside the Wall and frankly, Hannah didn't blame her.

Skirting around her brother, Hannah reached up into the kitchen cabinets and pulled down three plates. She left one on the counter for Uriah before filling the other two with a portion of scrambled eggs, salsa and toast. Walking back and forth between the table and the kitchen, Hannah brought out a selection of jam for the bread as well as several mugs of coffee and an orange juice for Lena.

It was a personal favorite that the medical doctor who'd examined them both recommended. The jug of juice had come out of deep storage frozen solid. Once it had defrosted, however, it was just as tasty as anything Hannah could remember having. And she *did* remember orange juice from before, of all things.

"This is delicious," Hannah commented as her brother settled into his chair. He was directly across the table from Lena, as always. No matter what she did to avoid him, Uriah's answer was to come one step closer. Relentless. He was relentless.

"Thank you." Uriah bobbed his head and sipped on his coffee, he liked it strong and black.

For several minutes the three of them ate in relative peace. Forks scraped against dishes, cups tapped against the wooden tabletop, the lid twisted noisily off a jar of boysenberry jam.

"So, how's the game room treating you?" Uriah began, sitting back.

"It's good," Hannah answered, her eyes flicking over to Lena who looked away.

"Maybe you'll indulge me in a game of chess later," Uriah persisted.

"Sure." Hannah cleared her throat. "You're going out again?"

"I have to."

"Well, can't we-"

"No, Hannah Mae. I told you it's not safe."

Lena lifted her chin, rolling her shoulders visibly before folding her arms across her chest. On the other side of the table, Uriah narrowed his eyes. She may not be speaking to him verbally, but Hannah found that her friend managed to get her point across regardless.

"What about the library?" Uriah continued, his voice was controlled and calm. "You love to read."

Hannah's gaze bounced between her brother and Lena. When the dark-haired woman stared pointedly back at her, Hannah lifted her hands in bewilderment.

"You do remember that, don't you?" Uriah's whole body shifted then as his energy settled on his sister.

"Oh," Hannah exclaimed at the realization. *She* was the one who loved to read. Right. Of course. "Yeah, I'll check it out. I mean we will. We will check it out."

"Look, I know you've both been through a lot-"

"Here we go again," Lena muttered under her breath, drawing a warning look from Uriah.

"And it kills me that you won't confide in me. It kills me that you won't let me help you."

"We're fine, really." Hannah tugged at the ends of her hair before glancing worriedly at Lena.

"You're obviously not fine." Uriah laid both palms on the table before leaning forward. "Tell me about the microchip. Tell me how you lost your memory and maybe I'll be able to help you get it back."

"Well, the whole thing is kind of fuzzy."

"Try me."

Sucking in a breath, Hannah glanced at Lena who reluctantly shrugged. Maybe she was mad at Uriah, but her concern for Hannah's health still seemed to outweigh it. Clearing her throat, Hannah brought what she remembered back to mind.

Andy. The knife. Her screams echoing inside the Wall.

A chill ran through her and she looked down at her

scar, running a thumb over the circle soothingly. The thing about the microchip… it hadn't *wanted* to be removed. Of all the sensations to remember, the warm pulsing demands of the tiny beacon were the strongest.

"I don't remember a lot about that day." Hannah felt Lena's hand cover hers beneath the table. "The first thing I recall is walking inside the perimeter wall with him. The cameras were all off, I still don't know how he managed it."

"Him?"

"Andy."

"Andy?" Uriah's cheeks flushed as his eyes danced over to Lena who looked uncomfortable before nodding. "I knew I shouldn't have left that fucker breathing."

"What? Why?"

"Don't worry about it." Uriah waved a hand in the air. "Continue."

"No, I want to know why you hate him."

"He had a thing for you, but the feeling wasn't mutual." Uriah's eyes glinted. "He kept going behind his girlfriend's back-"

"You can't say her name?" Lena whispered.

"Flynn." Uriah inhaled sharply. "He kept going behind Flynn's back, finding ways to be alone with you. Of course you were oblivious, thinking he just wanted to be friends. I had to set him straight."

"Tell her what that means," Lena instructed.

"I beat his ass," Uriah admitted. "But he deserved it. He kept applying to partner with you, said he wanted to marry you. I had to change your breeding phase to make it stop. I figured I'd have you all out within two years, your name would never be called in that time."

"But, how were you able to do that?"

Lena and Uriah exchanged a look. It was maybe the first one they'd shared that wasn't full of anger since the day the women had arrived.

"Uriah is the only surviving Command Officer of the Nor East Soldiers," Lena explained. "He had limited access to the coding system within the Wall."

"So, why didn't he change things for you?" Hannah frowned. "And for Flynn?"

"I tried." Uriah's eyes turned pleading, then hardened. "But when I couldn't manage it, that's when I knew I had to leave. I had to stop all of it. Get you all out."

"But you left us," Hannah admonished.

"I had to."

"You could've taken us with you."

"No, I couldn't. It's not safe out here. Damn it, there was no way I could make it all the way down here with the both of you."

"We're here now."

"Yes, and you've been hurt along the way… am I right?"

Uriah pinned Hannah with his gaze until she was forced to look away. Lena sucked her own hand back to her lap where she clenched and unclenched her fists repeatedly.

Silence. Silence and tension bloomed until the only sounds Hannah could hear were the beat of her heart and the rasp of her own breathing.

"Now, tell me what Andy did," Uriah commanded. "I want every detail."

So, Hannah did just that. At least, she got as far in her telling as she could. When Uriah realized that Andy had taken Hannah alone, without Lena or Flynn, things started to unravel. Soon his line of questioning expanded and as it did, Lena squirmed and wriggled in her chair.

It became impossible for Hannah to answer anything truthfully while respecting Lena's privacy. And Uriah was like a dog with a bone. He had the scent, and he wasn't going to just leave it. Finally, Hannah just stopped talking altogether which is when Uriah showed signs of cracking.

"There was a rumor..." His hands tightened into fists on the table before he withdrew them to his lap. "About a pair of women being held in the mountains north of here."

Lena squeezed her eyes closed, her lips firming together in a deliberate line.

"There were two women specifically, not three... not one." Uriah's words grew matter of fact, as if he were distancing himself from the reality of them. "We got word of it several months ago, but I... I..."

Tilting his head back, Uriah stared at the ceiling for a moment. It was unusually high and painted a pale, pale blue, mimicking the lightest shade of the sky.

"I didn't send anyone right away," the words tore from his throat, like he had tried so hard not to say them.

"Maybe I didn't quite believe it, or maybe I thought it was too great a risk..."

"You sent someone eventually," Hannah interjected, watching the self-hate and horror mix on her brother's face.

"But I waited for months." Uriah's eyes fixed on Lena, who began to tremble, her whole body working to keep a lid on her emotions. "And it was you. It was you and Flynn. And Andy put you there... didn't he?"

Shooting to her feet, Lena sent her carved wooden chair flying backwards where it clattered to the floor. Before she could utter a sound, she turned on her heel and ran from the room. In a split second, Uriah was up and after her.

Twisting in her seat, Hannah watched his back disappear through the doorway, listened to the rush of footsteps pound away down the hall. Then there was the slam of a door.

Left alone at the table, Hannah let her eyes drift from plate to plate. She noted that not one of them had left anything. Every bite of food was gone, leaving only smears of purplish jam and yellow eggs to show there'd been something to eat in the first place.

When Uriah failed to return, Hannah exhaled a breath of relief. Perhaps Lena finally let him in. If he couldn't fix Hannah's broken memory, then maybe he could bring some comfort to Lena instead.

Standing finally, Hannah cleared the dishes and washed them in the sink.

With the kitchen tidy and the others gone, Hannah

wandered through the expansive living room with its wide screen television and leather recliners. Beyond that was a door that led to the game room. Circling back, Hannah fled back through the kitchen and into a rather narrow hall. At the end was the front door.

Stepping up to its imposing metal surface now, Hannah pressed her palms against it only to discover it was rather cold. Her brother left from this very spot and entered the outside world almost every single day. Other men, Jameson and a handful of soldiers, used it too, but only to attend dinner, and only when Uriah invited them.

Hugging herself, Hannah let loose a sigh and then turned to one side. The door to the left was open and she knew from previous visits that it housed the library. Well, really it was an office or study of some sort with floor to ceiling bookcases lining each and every wall. It was a big room, maybe the size of two of her bedrooms put together.

Flicking on the light, Hannah walked inside and absorbed its contents maybe for the first time. When she had come here before, it was only briefly, and she hadn't lingered.

There was one large desk situated in the far corner with a brown leather office chair positioned behind it. To her right, as she entered, were a pair of over-stuffed reading chairs with a small table between them. Stacked on it, were several hardbound books.

Tracing her fingers over the surface, she noted one title, *Atlas Shrugged*. Hmmm, had she read it? Possibly. Her brain sparked a moment before stuttering to a disappointing halt.

Stomping past in frustration, Hannah let her eyes play over the array of comfortable furniture made for sitting, reclining and reading. But then there it was. A baby grand piano, black as night without even a sheen of dust to mar its glossy surface.

Before she could think, Hannah was pulling out the little bench and lifting up the fallboard to reveal the ivory and black keys. Sucking in a breath, she lay her fingers along them, feeling their smooth give. Then, ever so gently, she closed her eyes and her hands began to move.

They danced all on their own, producing a familiar melody she hadn't known was inside of her. As the ripple of music rose into the air, her mind relaxed, and her thoughts flowed. She felt suddenly that as long as the piano kept singing, her brain would remain ordered, that her mind would be complete once more.

As the notes came out one after the other, they flowed along to form a perfect symphony. It was so deliberate and yet so un-coerced that Hannah began remembering things. Real, vivid, actual things.

Painful things.

And beautiful things.

And then... *she remembered everything.*

CHAPTER TWELVE_
LIAM

"GET UP."

Liam felt the tip of a boot press into his arm, nudging him insistently from a deep sleep. Groaning into the warmth of his sleeping bag, he peeked his head out and blinked up at Jameson's serious face. His new boss was already dressed for the day, his heavy jacket zipped up to his chin, his breath coming out in puffs in the cold room.

"We don't have all day," Jameson grumbled before turning away.

Actually we do, Liam thought, before reluctantly crawling out into the frigid air. He slept in a pair of long johns and wool socks, all of which were new. Those items had been issued to him along with a set of black military fatigues when he'd arrived that first day. As nice as it was to have some fresh clothing, the perks of being security for Uriah Linfield seemed to stop there.

Hustling to step into his pants, Liam jumped from one foot to the other on the thin carpeted flooring.

"How long did you say you've been staying here?" Liam asked.

"I didn't."

"Wouldn't it be warmer in the bowling alley after everyone's left?"

"It would."

Frowning to himself, Liam zipped up his heavy jacket, slapped his hands together and stepped up to the wide office window. Below them, the asphalt streets of the city were empty and still. A few parked cars were positioned here and there, but they never moved, were never used. It was as if Uriah wanted the place to maintain a look of abandonment, at least from above.

From his position on the third floor, Liam could look directly across the street to the entrance of the underground parking garage. No one ever went inside that wasn't authorized and escorted. Even so, just to Liam's right there was a small section of glass that could be removed in the window. If a breach was called, then Liam or Jameson, or whoever was sleeping here, could shoot through it easily enough.

The rest of the windows on the floor were all intact though, so without proper ventilation they were unable to have even the smallest of fires. That made the overnights here pretty damn uncomfortable. It had Liam asking himself on more than one occasion why he was staying at all. Hell, with any luck he could have marched his ass right down to a beach in Baja by now.

But after a month of working for Uriah, Liam still hadn't moved on, and he couldn't say exactly why that was.

"Ready?" Jameson again, sounding annoyed this time.

"Yeah." Liam knelt to lace up his boots before picking up his rifle.

There were about fifty security guys total for a city filled with over ten thousand men. The split in numbers made Liam nervous at first until he realized how little policing the population actually required. Mostly the security force patrolled key locations throughout the area and occasionally did speciality jobs for Uriah himself. For the past several weeks, Liam had done a stint at the food storage facility, water treatment plant, and stood lookout for a group hauling firewood.

As far as Liam could tell, none of the buildings had running water or electricity, save for the underground bowling alley. The residents of the city made trips to a warehouse a few blocks away where they could get a portion of wood for burning along with a ration of clean water.

Some engineer was practically living at the treatment plant in order to keep the water fresh. Liam didn't quite understand all that the man did, but he knew whenever he stood guard for him, it seemed like one of the more important assignments.

"Come on, it's late." Jameson didn't bother to look back as he stepped over various still sleeping bodies.

The men had shoved the office furniture aside to create open floor space for their bedrolls. Liam had heard some of them grumbling about the arrangement like it was something new for them. One guy had even gone so far as to mention forced-air heating and beds, but then Jameson had walked over and the talk had quickly died.

Liam had made a mental note to circle back to the story later, but he was having a hard time shaking his new boss. The grim-faced giant seemed to be personally babysitting him, which both amused and annoyed Liam in turns. How long did it take to "earn trust" around here?

Of course, admittedly Liam wasn't very trustworthy. Were his intentions good? Maybe. They weren't outright bad anyway, just more curious than anything else.

Pushing through the office door the two men entered a barren hallway. It had crooked paintings lining the walls. They depicted what was once known as modern art. Meaningless lines, with colorful circles and globs of haphazard paint spread along mostly white canvases.

Glancing at the dust that covered the frames, Liam was reminded of a time when these pictures were the height of fashion. A time when you could stop at one in the midst of your busy day and contemplate what the artist was trying to *say*. Hah. Trying to say.

Before Liam could rip one down and split it over his knee, Jameson was through another doorway and jogging down a flight of metal stairs. Following suit, Liam caught up with him and the two men's footsteps could be heard echoing all around as they descended to the ground floor and shoved out into the fresh morning air.

Where would they be heading today? Food pantry duty? Street patrol on the south side? Seemed the food pantry could use some extra eyes and then maybe Liam could swindle his way into a second helping of breakfast.

Stomach rumbling, his eyes darted up and down the street before analyzing the now familiar high rise profiles. Nothing out of place, he noted. Just in front of him, Jameson did the same before grabbing at a small handheld radio and speaking into it.

He announced their entrance into the underground parking garage and had Liam's eyebrows raising. This was new. His shock registered even higher when Uriah himself answered back an affirmative before the damn thing crackled with static.

"No breakfast?" Liam asked, as they traded the dawning light for the dank shade of the garage.

"It'll be there."

Liam wanted to frown, but instead reached into his pocket and drew out a flashlight. Clicking it on, he swept the collection of parked cars as they headed for the corner stairwell. Unlike that trip in the SUV, they didn't need to travel to the bottom floor before seeking out the service entrance.

Jameson flashed a keycard which beeped them along the narrow hall and into the bowling alley which was quiet as a mouse this early in the morning. The lanes were all dark and empty, but the smell of stale beer and sweat lingered. At the far side of the balcony, wedged in the corner near the railing, was a door Liam hadn't noticed before. Albeit, he hadn't been back to the bowling alley often, not since that first interview.

But still, he usually kept better track of that sort of thing. Maybe it had been the moonshine mixed with beer flooding his brain that day. And damn it, the thought made him miss the access to alcohol. It wasn't that he needed it so much during the day. No, his new surroundings had his brain plenty distracted during that time.

It was the nights. The cold, dark, quiet nights when she visited his thoughts and flooded his dreams. Flooded him. Fuck. He really missed the moonshine then.

Trailing behind Jameson, they soon arrived at a single metal door. It appeared to be stoutly constructed with an extra heavy handle and no peep hole. Reaching into his jacket pocket, Jameson pulled out a set of keys. Unlike the others, this door had no electronic reader. It was the old fashioned kind, the one where you needed the exact right metal key to rotate free the lock.

With interest, Liam shifted to watch Jameson slide a key in the lock and twist. Shoving down on the handle, the door swung outward, forcing both men to step back. That's when he heard it.

The sound poured over him, around him, through him even. It was music.

He hadn't listened to a single note of real music in years.

Jaw dropping, Liam stilled as the haunting chords of a piano drifted out of the doorway and consumed the narrow hall. When Liam looked over at Jameson's face, he actually caught the asshole smiling to himself. *Smiling*.

It was only for a split second though. Holding the door open only wide enough for one body to fit through, Jameson seemed to remember Liam was there and his frown returned.

"Stay here," Jameson instructed. "No one else goes in. Got it?"

"Yeah." Liam's eyes narrowed. "Sure."

Then Jameson was over the threshold and the thick metal door swung shut. Once it sealed, the music stopped and Liam was left with the distant echoes of it teasing his mind. A piano. Someone inside there was actually playing a piano.

The song had been slow and beautiful and sad. How could so much be felt in only a matter of seconds? Liam wasn't sure, but that's the impression he got from it. The sadness most of all. Then again, maybe he was just projecting.

Shit... *projecting*? Now he was starting to sound like Cookie.

Pressing the heel of one hand to his eye, Liam fought an internal groan. He hated to think of them. He hated to go down that road. Because it wasn't like he didn't miss his family, he did. And that's what they all had been to him, hadn't they? A family, Cole especially.

Well, now they're just one short, Liam thought, rolling his shoulders. And it was better this way. It was better for all of them, even Liam. Yeah.

Closing his eyes briefly, he leaned back against the wall and did what he was told. He waited.

AN HOUR LATER, THE BOSS MAN HIMSELF APPEARED WITH Jameson in tow. As the pair stepped into the hall, the melancholy ballad drifted out with them. Liam stood up straighter at the sound but kept his expression blank as Uriah eyed him. When the door slammed shut, Jameson turned to lock it and Uriah tilted his head to one side.

"It's Beethoven," Uriah explained. "Moonlight Sonata."

"Ah." Liam's eyebrows raised. "I can't remember the last time I heard music. Let alone a piano."

"It's just a CD." Uriah strode off down the hall, tossing the words back over his shoulder as he went.

A CD... *right*. Liam adjusted the strap of his rifle and glanced over his shoulder. A CD that both Uriah and Jameson had left playing even though they were leaving. Un-fucking-likely.

There was only one logical conclusion a man could draw from this arrangement. Another person lived behind that door. And that other person could play the piano. They could play it well.

Nothing more was said as the three men weaved and beeped their way back out into the daylight. The streets were relatively busy now with men walking together down the open roads. Some carried empty buckets, no doubt heading for a ration of water. Others had makeshift packs filled with chopped wood strapped to their backs. The rare genius among them pushed a shopping cart.

The sun overhead shone down, casting long shadows off the buildings of downtown. It was a rare day, without a spot of clouds in the bluest sky Liam could recall seeing. Breathing deep, the air felt crisp and new and fresh.

Ahead of him, Uriah and Jameson walked with deter-mined purpose. Though both men were alert and focused, it was obvious they had traveled this way before. Ducking down an alleyway, they headed for an ugly brick building, one with splintered glass front windows and a tattered door left swinging carelessly on its hinges.

Once inside, the front reception area made its original use obvious. This was a jail. A bonafide city jail, complete with rows of plastic chairs fixed to the ground and barred doors blocking them from going further. Glancing over his shoulder, Liam realized why the glass at the front was fractured and not caved in... it was bullet proof.

At his feet, masses of paper covered the floor. Bending to pluck one up, Liam frowned at the printed type. It read:

First Phase Evacuation Order
Women and Children only
Bring Identification and bottled water
No personal items allowed
All electronics will be confiscated on site

The crackle of Jameson's radio had Liam dropping the eight by eleven white sheet and standing. He could see two men waiting behind the barred doors wearing black fatigues. Their faces were vaguely familiar. Both of them were soldiers belonging to the security task force.

"Status?" Uriah asked, as the men opened one of the doors.

"Clear."

"Good." Uriah bobbed his head and entered the space. Jameson and Liam followed. "No one's touched him, right?"

"Yes, Sir."

"When's the last time he ate?"

"Last night, Sir. Just like you said."

"Good. Stay here, no one else comes in without my direct authorization. Got that?"

"Yes, Sir."

Pressing further down the hall, Uriah used a set of large keys to override what appeared to be an electronic locking mechanism. Further into the belly of the jail, the hallway widened.

Liam's eyes absorbed what looked like a wing for administration. There was a check-in area, a nurse station and the spot a new prisoner would stand to have his photograph taken. Involuntarily, his mind flashed to the things Flynn had described. How she had arrived at just such a place, summoned by a text message. How there had been a panic, how Hannah had been hurt.

Giving his head a determined shake, Liam tried to clear it and instead focus his attention on Uriah. Did he know what became of his sister? Did he think she was stowed away behind the Wall? Or did he think she was missing... was he searching for her?

"Here." Uriah stopped at a locked door with a shade drawn down over a small square of glass.

Lifting the edge, he peeked inside before replacing the cover and looking back at Liam.

"When we first spoke, you wouldn't tell me what you did for the Strike Team." Uriah walked a few paces away from the door before stopping and folding his arms across his chest. He kept his voice low, but it wasn't a whisper.

"I didn't have to." Liam squared his shoulders. "You already knew."

Uriah nodded. "Do you know how many men you've questioned?"

Liam shrugged.

"Three hundred and seventy-six," Uriah supplied.

"On record," Liam added, his face a blank slate.

"Right." Uriah smiled then. "Did you know that's more than any other interrogator under our command?"

"No."

"Do you know what percentage of the intel that you recovered checked out? Do you know how much of what you got was true?"

"Not formally."

"But you have a feel for it right? That's what they say. All the good ones know when they hit home. Do you?"

Again, Liam shrugged.

"There's a man in that cell that's got information I need." Uriah's eyes darted over Liam's face.

"Who is he?" Liam asked.

"That's the thing, I don't want to tell you."

Liam just blinked. What the hell kind of shit was this?

"The intel I'm after," Uriah continued. "I have no way of confirming if it's true and I've only got one chance to use it. So whatever he eventually gives you, it has to be right."

"You want me to question a man completely blind." Liam huffed a breath and glanced away.

"If you can get his name, what he did for work, things that I can verify…" Uriah reasoned.

117

"Then whatever else he tells me is probably true, right? That's your logic?"

"Do you have a better idea?"

Liam ran a hand up over the back of his head before answering, "Yeah, you can tell me everything. The more information I have going in, the better."

"I can't do that."

"Then you're tying my hands behind my back." Liam looked past Uriah's shoulder at the cell door. "Has anyone else questioned him?"

"Yes."

"Shit." Liam sucked in a breath, his first show of emotion. "How is he?"

This time it was Uriah's turn to shrug.

Grumbling under his breath, Liam stalked to the door and lifted the flap. Through the thick square of glass he observed a smallish man lying on the floor. He was curled on his side with no mattress, no padding or blankets to speak of. A stainless steel toilet was fixed in the far corner along with a single bowl sink.

After a beat of observing, Liam rapped his knuckles on the glass and watched the man jump. Skittish. He was skittish and scared, with owl-like eyes that sported some bruising and too long grayish hair.

Returning the flap to its position, Liam stepped back and sighed. He should've known Uriah was keeping him around for a specific reason. He should've seen it coming from a mile away. But Liam was admittedly not on his game these days. Not since leaving the compound, and okay maybe not since sometime before then.

And on top of that, Liam hadn't performed a traditional interrogation in so long, like well over three years. All of the *things* he had done post-war were extremely non-traditional... *effective*, but not for a case like this.

"You did it, right? You were the one who questioned him?" Liam gestured to Uriah who nodded. "Then you don't get to be in the room."

"Alright."

"No." Liam stepped up to Uriah and looked down on him. And not just physically either, though he had a good five inches on the boss man. Liam looked down his nose at Uriah. It wasn't a sneer, but it was condescending. If Liam was going to get anywhere with the mystery target, then Uriah had to let go of his power so that Liam could take it. "You don't walk in. You don't make an appearance. He doesn't hear you speak. You don't exist without my say so."

"Fine." Uriah gritted his teeth, and Liam narrowed his eyes.

"If you can't follow my rules, then I walk."

"Okay." Uriah put up one hand, his face relaxing. "I get it. You're running the show. He belongs to you."

Liam eyed Uriah a moment longer before pointing to Jameson. "Tell *him* that."

"Interrogator Byrne is running the show," Uriah spoke easily enough. "If he and I disagree, you defer to him. But only on the inside of that room."

Jameson ducked his head and shifted on his feet. Liam watched as the other man's fingers itched uncomfortably at his side. Even after witnessing the exchange, this set up was going to be hardest on Jameson. He would no doubt still defer to Uriah… as he had been doing already for months.

"Good." Liam stepped back and clapped his hands together abruptly. "Jameson, you'll need to escort our boss back outside and send him on his way. Also, I'm going to need two giant cups of coffee and some breakfast. Maybe an egg sandwich or even a burrito?"

Jameson's mouth dropped just a fraction before his eyes darted to Uriah. Ah, still seeking approval, Liam thought, point made.

For his part, their boss simply smiled. It was genuine, with a glitter of laughter drifting up to his eyes. Uriah could appreciate the subtlety that was playing out and he wagged a finger knowingly.

"Don't think I'm not recording everything that goes on in here," Uriah said finally.

"Are you?" Liam glanced at the corners of the room, eyebrows raised in mock surprise.

"It's closed circuit, but still, I'll be watching the whole time."

"Good, you can write down whenever I get an answer correct," Liam mocked.

Rolling his eyes, Uriah handed over a single key before turning on his heel and leaving the room. Jameson was soon to follow.

"I wasn't kidding about the food!" Liam called after them, then muttered under his breath. "Assholes."

Fingering the large copper-colored key, Liam strolled to the cell and unlocked it. Pulling the thick metal door wide, he observed the little man scramble and backpedal until he was wedged pointlessly in the far corner.

Great, there was nothing like working with an already fucked up canvas. And just like with painting, you had to clear away all the mess before you could start over.

Keeping his features calm and smooth, Liam walked casually into the room, making sure to leave the door open behind him. The key, however, he shoved deep into the pocket of his pants.

"Hello." Liam took a seat on the edge of an empty steel cot and glanced around absently.

The other man only whimpered, running a dirty hand beneath his nose.

"My name is Liam and I'm here to save you from this place."

"You... you are?"

"I am." Liam nodded, letting his eyes settle deeply on the other man. "What's your name?"

"I- I'm Dr. Gene Bartholomew and there must be some mistake. You see... I don't belong here."

"START OVER." URIAH LAID HIS PALM AGAINST THE EDGE OF the piano and stared down at her.

"I already told you everything."

"I want to hear it again."

Sucking in a breath, Hannah nibbled at her bottom lip and let her eyes fall to where her hands stretched across the piano's ivory keys. They had been over this, time and again. Why was her brother being so persistent about it?

Hannah didn't like the memory. She didn't like to think of Dr. B bent over his desk, blood spilling across the keyboard, gun glinting on the floor. Squeezing her eyes shut, she let her hands dance out another melody until Uriah cleared his throat and moved forward to shut the lid.

Hannah's brow furrowed but she sucked her hands demurely back into her lap and let him silence her music. She didn't need the instrument to remember anymore, but it made her feel better about it. The truth was, Hannah had gone so long without an intact memory, that she quite preferred it to how she was now. She missed the simplicity of it. The lack of insecurity and remorse.

"When did you get the text?"

"From the source?"

"Yes."

"You had been gone for three months-"

"I thought you said four."

"Okay four."

"No, not okay." Uriah let out a frustrated breath and paced away. "Hannah Mae, I want the truth. I don't want you to just agree with me."

"I'm trying."

"Try harder."

Fisting her hands in her lap, Hannah watched her knuckles turn white before exhaling. They had been at this for a week straight it seemed. Each evening, Uriah would return from wherever it was he spent his days and the first thing he would do was seek her out.

In the beginning, Lena had watched them talk, but then somewhere around day two, Uriah had banished her from the room. She had been interrupting, defending Hannah, telling him to back off. Uriah was a patient man when it came to Lena. He used a light touch, was careful where he stood, what tone of voice he used. But beneath it all, he had a temper.

Hannah always viewed him like a bottle filled with carbonation. It just built and built and built. In the end, if he didn't get his way, then he blew. And he wasn't violent or anything, at least not towards women, but he was heated and controlling.

He was an alpha, plain and simple. Their parents had raised him that way, sure, but he was prone to it. To the power, to the submission of others. From an early age Uriah became an expert at getting his way.

So that meant Lena was forbidden from participating while Uriah and Hannah had their little talks. It saved him from saying something stupid. It saved him from ruining the progress he'd made with Lena thus far.

"When did you get the text?" He asked again.

"In the afternoon, I can't remember the exact time."

"Okay." Uriah nodded, his tone relaxing. "What did it say?"

"To report to the source office."

"Then what?"

"Then I went." Hannah stood suddenly, her stomach dipping with the story. "We've been over this. You know it better than I do now."

"I just need to hear it again."

Uriah was trying to be patient, but his tone belied how close he was to the edge. His jaw was doing that clenching thing it always did and Hannah could practically hear his teeth grinding. She loved her brother, really she did, and he had always been nothing but protective of her, but sometimes she wondered if he thought she was truly stupid. He was just like their father. She could see right through him. After all, she knew him better than anyone.

"No." Hannah shook her head and looked up into his

serious face. "You don't need to hear everything all over again. You're searching for something."

"Han-"

"What are you looking for? Just ask me!"

"He was dead. You're sure he was dead?"

"Dr. B?"

Uriah nodded quickly, his eyes scanning hers. "You're sure it was him?"

"Of course, I'm..." Hannah hesitated, her mind whirling back there once more. "It was dark. The lights were off in the room at first and then they popped on when I asked for them out loud."

"That's when you saw him."

"I saw the gun on the ground, the blood everywhere. He was slumped forward and... and..."

"Did you see his face?"

"He had the same hair color and the same clothes, it was him."

"But did you see his face, Hannah Mae? His face?"

Squeezing her eyes shut against the picture of death, Hannah fought with the impression she had held onto for so long. It was him, wasn't it? It had to be. Who else could it have been? But then here was her brother, asking the one question she hadn't bothered to ask herself. And the answer was sickening and frightening and she couldn't quite name the implications.

"No," she admitted finally, the whisper of words catching like mothballs in her throat. "He shot himself in the head. There wasn't any face left."

"But then you got a text, right? From him," Uriah prompted.

"I got a message from the source," Hannah acknowledged. "And it clearly wasn't him."

"What did it say?"

"It said that I would continue to get my directions, that everyone would continue to get their directions. It said that I wouldn't tell anyone about what happened to Dr. B. It said nothing would change."

"You say *it*… who do you think sent the message?"

"You know."

"I want to hear it from you," Uriah lowered his voice, took a step closer.

Leaning a hand against the piano, Hannah tried to steady herself. They had never spoken of this out loud. Although Uriah had suspected the truth for a long time, he had only ever written it once on a piece of scrap paper for Hannah to see.

After she read what he wrote, her heart thumped in her chest as she watched him rip it into a million little pieces and flush it down the toilet in her apartment. That's when their work schedules changed. That's when she started to see her brother less and less. Access to him became nearly impossible for her until that final day when he left.

"It was the computer program," Hannah's voice wavered. "I think Dr. B lost control of it. The artificial intelligence, or whatever it was, became the true source. The only source."

Uriah exhaled slowly, letting every last bit of air out

from his lungs before speaking almost to himself, "I think you're right."

Looking up at him, she watched the regret flash in his eyes before he purposefully wiped it away. He felt responsible no doubt, just the way Hannah did. After all, they had both been at the highest levels of this thing at one time or another.

Maybe, just maybe, if they'd done something different, made different choices, acted earlier, then things wouldn't have ended up the way they did. Uriah more so than herself, but still. She had been right there in the control room. Time and again, next to the beating heart of this... of this thing... of the source.

"I think that's enough for now." Uriah drew one hand down his face before moving to pat her on the arm. "I'm going to check on Lena. We've got a guest for dinner, so just stay in here until I come get you, alright?"

"Another soldier?" Hannah asked, letting her eyes fall back to the piano.

She hated most dinners now. Jameson was always there, which wasn't so bad in itself, but every so often a new soldier was brought along. They weren't rude exactly, but it was uncomfortable the way they stared. For some of them it was as if they were seeing a ghost, for others the sentiment wasn't quite as innocent.

Lena was often excused from the spectacle, but Hannah never was. *They need proof,* her brother had confided once. *I don't like it either, but I've got to give them something.*

"This one is different," Uriah assured her. "He's an... expert at talking to people. I need you to speak with him."

"Does he know?"

"About you and Lena?"

"Yeah."

"No." Uriah sighed, but his brain was already somewhere else. "Not yet."

Nodding her head in acceptance, Hannah shifted to lean against the piano as she watched her brother go. When he left the room, he swung the door shut but didn't lock it.

Shoving up to standing, Hannah exhaled in boredom and ran her fingertips along the bookshelves absently. They were beautiful, made of rich dark wood and filled with the straight spines of hardbound books. Over the past months she had bounced from section to section, reading a bit of fantasy, then literature, then science fiction, then satire.

Where should she land next? Politics? Hah, there wasn't much need for that anymore, now was there?

Drifting from wall to wall, she pulled a book out here and there, only to shove them back in after flipping through the first few pages. She was tired of being stuck inside. Tired of not feeling the wind on her cheeks or having the sun in her eyes. Sure, there was a tanning bed in one of the back rooms so they could get a dose of Vitamin D, but it wasn't the same. Closing her eyes, she tilted her face up and tried to remember what it felt like to be outside.

When nothing came to mind, her eyes popped wide and her hands fisted on her hips. There was the piano, of course. It was the only way she actually felt peace anymore.

Playing it transported her far away. With her eyes shut, she would listen to the music, letting it fill her soul until she floated off the ground and through the ceiling and into the sky. Better do it now, she thought, before our distinguished guest arrives.

Taking a seat on the bench, she smoothed at her designer jeans and rolled up the sleeves of her cashmere blouse. Then, with a straight back and relaxed arms, she began to play.

Single notes transformed into chords that built sentences that traveled into the air. To her, the music was a story that she was telling. It came out of her slowly at first and brought everything along with it. The beauty and the pain and the hope and the anguish. She was playing Chopin today, and she loved what his music said about life… about people living life.

Smiling to herself, she recalled Uriah's request that she play something more upbeat. *Something happy for once Hannah Mae, it's like a fucking funeral around here.* She had laughed at him then.

Her brother controlled everything about their existence in this house, from what food was available to what company he brought over for meals. The one thing he did not control was what Hannah played.

Maybe he could stop her altogether, but she'd be damned if she pumped out anything to please him. Not now anyway. Not while she was trapped here, like a bird in a cage. At least she could flap her wings a bit, even if she could hardly remember what it felt like to fly.

Fifteen minutes or so had passed when she heard the

door open. Maybe it wasn't even that long, she had only played three songs. Brow furrowing, she kept her eyes shut and continued into her fourth melody, half expecting Uriah to complain about the tempo.

When he said nothing, her mind jumped to the next conclusion. It was Jameson then, he was the only other man who had a key to the house and he often sat in the library and listened to her play. Lena was in the bathroom taking a shower, so it wasn't her. Nope, it had to be Jameson.

Internally, she wanted to roll her eyes. As far as men went he was polite enough. He kept his hands to himself and didn't stare, at least not often. Uriah found him to be trustworthy, and thus far he had proved himself so. But just because her brother liked to have him around, didn't mean Hannah did.

"You're lurking, Jameson," Hannah spoke the words over the sounds of her playing.

She wouldn't stop for him, and she knew he wouldn't want her to anyway. He liked her sad songs, had defended them to Uriah on more than one occasion. When he didn't respond, she listened for his footsteps to come forward or retreat.

Continuing to play, Hannah slowly opened her eyes.

In the next instant, she slammed her hands down against the keys in utter shock. The sound of the thundering chord echoed in the silent room as her eyes locked on the one thing she never, ever expected to see.

"Liam," Hannah whispered the word to herself, tasted the feel of it on her lips as the man in the doorway stared back. He looked just as shocked, frozen there, the color drained from his face.

"Liam," she said it again, louder.

Still, he didn't move.

Shooting up from the bench seat, Hannah knocked it over in her rush to the door.

Before he could utter a word, she flung her arms around his neck and buried her face in his shirt. He was real. So real and warm and tall, she'd forgotten how tall. The weight of her hanging off of him had him bending forward and into her.

After a split second's hesitation, he was clinging to her, running his shaking hands along her back, down her hair. Turning his face to look at her, Liam's questioning eyes sought hers as his lips brushed against her cheek. The flood of heartache and fear and regret all rushed towards Hannah at once.

What had she been thinking so long ago? Was it really that long? Why had she fought this thing with Liam?

Before she could think further, her mouth sought his and she was kissing him.

Kissing him and pressing her body into him and wrapping her legs around his waist. She felt desperate for his touch, for his affection and after a split second he was kissing her back. His chest expanded as he straightened and cinched her tighter into him.

Then he was staggering a few steps and her back was pressed against the bookshelf and he was groaning into her mouth. The heat she felt was exquisite and all consuming.

This was right. This was so, so right. She should never have stopped this. Nothing could ever stop this.

But then there was the click of a gun cocking. Liam's body went rigid.

Opening her eyes, Hannah stared over his shoulder at Jameson and the handgun he held pressed neatly against the side of Liam's head.

"What. The absolute. Fuck." Jameson spat. "I told you not to open any doors."

CHAPTER FOURTEEN_
LIAM

THE METAL BARREL OF A GUN DIGGING INTO LIAM'S SCALP, caused a sickening lick of terror to shoot to his fingertips. It wasn't the first time he had felt this, but somehow the familiarity didn't erase the fear. One wrong pulse, one quick jerk, and his life was over.

Not only that, but Hannah was right here, so close that maybe she could get hurt, too. Swallowing thickly, he held up his hands and felt her lower herself back to standing. And sure, this looked bad.

Here he was, holding Hannah against the wall, his hands all over her, his mouth all over her. She was tiny in comparison to him. He could swear up and down he hadn't meant to do anything to her. But the problem with that excuse was pretty glaring... it was a complete and utter lie.

He *did* mean to do something to her. He meant to do a whole lot of somethings to her, right here, right now, over and over.

Okay... so this looked awful. Really fucking awful.

"Put down the gun," Hannah's voice pleaded.

"Get back, Hannah Mae," Jameson growled it, pushing the gun further into Liam's skull.

"Do what he says…" Liam began.

"You don't talk," Jameson barked, pressing the barrel in harder. "You don't get to talk."

"Stop!" Hannah began to cry. Laying her head against Liam's chest, she wrapped her arms around his waist and refused to move. "I know him, he wasn't hurting me. Please Jameson, put down the gun."

"What the fuck are you talking about?" Jameson was incredulous. "Get out of here. Go get Uriah. Now!"

With his hands held in the air and his heart jumping in his chest, Liam worked hard to control his breathing. Exhaling slowly through his nostrils, his mind whirled on overdrive, trying to think of a solution. He would step back and away, but that movement might be too much for Jameson.

Squeezing his eyes closed a moment, he felt beads of sweat pop on his brow. It was just his luck to see her again like this, to have her kissing him one moment and his head blown off the next.

"Hannah, go get your brother," Liam hissed.

"Get out of here, Hannah!" Jameson shouted it. At least both men wanted the same thing.

For several long seconds, Hannah refused. Her small hands clenched along the back of Liam's shirt. He felt the gentle scrape of her nails, then the press of her chest into his stomach, and damn it if he didn't still want her. *Come on, come on, get going.*

But moments later, when he got his wish, Liam was surprised at the mix of emptiness and relief that filled him. She was safe, yes. But she was also gone.

Out of the corner of his eye, he watched her dash out the door, her long golden hair flowing down her back. But he didn't have long to look, the second she was out of sight, Jameson shoved him hard up against the bookshelf. Liam grunted as the wooden shelves hit along the length of his body, his breath exhaling in an involuntary puff.

"You piece of shit," Jameson spoke quietly into the back of Liam's neck. "I knew you were a piece of shit."

"I wasn't-"

"What?" Jameson's forearm pressed along Liam's shoulder blades, his considerable weight keeping them both stuck there together. "You weren't what? Huh? You think you're the only one who hasn't seen a woman in years? You don't think the handful of other guys that've come in here don't want to do that, too?"

"Other guys?" Liam twisted his head so he could see Jameson. The barrel of the gun scraped along his skin until it stopped at his temple.

"You're the only one who couldn't control himself," Jameson seethed. "That girl out there... she does *not* belong to you."

At that last sentence, Liam actually smiled. Jameson shoved him again. I used to think that, too, Liam thought, before that last kiss. And then there was the way she flew to him. Maybe he had been wrong all along.

Liam's mind flipped to Cole, the other part of the equation, and then on to the rest of the crew. If Hannah was here, then they should be around, too. Bring on the calvary, he thought, and in the distance raised voices and pounding footsteps hailed the return of someone.

It was hard to make out what was being said, though. The mix of female voices was swirling and confusing. But then Uriah breached the doorway, his face a flush of heat, water dripping from his hair onto his bare shoulders and chest.

At least he stepped into a pair of pants, Liam thought, but then all manner of thinking left him when Lena appeared just behind him, wrapped in a fluffy white towel. Eyes popping wide, Liam's mouth fell open completely. Then there was Hannah, shouting and tugging at Uriah's arm while Lena made a dash for him.

"Liam! Oh my God, Liam!" Lena shrieked it, but was stopped short as Uriah caught her about the waist.

"What in the hell?" Uriah roared, while Lena turned to yell at him, gripping her towel subconsciously to keep herself covered.

"We know-"

"He's not-"

"Stop! For shit's sake, stop talking," Uriah growled. "I can't hear myself think with both of you nagging at once."

Uriah's eyes darted between the two women and then up to Liam. Even Jameson seemed overwhelmed, the gun tip relaxing just a fraction as his heavy forearm stilled. After a moment's silence wherein the women just glared, Hannah huffed a breath and tried to walk forward.

Uriah, however, was much faster than she had judged

him. With one hand wrapping firmly around his sister's wrist, Uriah tightened his other arm around Lena. He had both of them in hand now but kept his eyes focused on Liam.

Bending low to speak in Lena's ear, Uriah's gaze hardened. "You know him? *How?*"

"Well, he..." Lena started to explain, but then Liam watched her hesitate, her face turning to search for Hannah. Uh-oh, he thought, this isn't good. The women are hiding something. Liam almost groaned. *Fuck.*

"He helped us," Hannah offered quickly. "He would never hurt us, just put the gun down."

"That so?" Uriah asked, as his eyes flicked over to Jameson.

"He had your sister up against the wall," Jameson explained.

Double fuck.

"It wasn't like that." Hannah tried to jerk her hand free, but her brother's face only darkened as she supplied, "I was kissing him first."

Triple fuck. Liam actually fought to keep his eyes open. *Here comes the bullet.*

"What about you?" Uriah straightened up and looked at Jameson. "I thought you were supposed to be watching him."

"I left him in the living room," Jameson attempted lamely. "I had to use the bathroom. He was supposed to stay. The library is usually locked."

"Just let him go, Uriah!" Lena began wriggling in his grip, her little hands working to loosen the unforgiving arm. "He's the one that saved me. He got Flynn and I out. Let him go right now!"

"Alright... don't fucking shoot him," Uriah instructed. "But you ladies have to go. I can't do this with both of you in here."

Withdrawing the gun, Jameson uncocked it but continued to hold Liam in place. As the women's protests grew louder, Uriah began dragging them out the library door. He actually had to lift Lena off her feet as Hannah clawed at his other hand.

Despite their best efforts though, the women soon disappeared from view. After a few moments, Uriah slipped back inside and slammed the door. When he inserted a key to lock it, Liam heard little hands slapping angrily against the wooden surface. Their voices were significantly dimmed, though, he couldn't make out what exactly they said.

With a final shove for good measure, Jameson backed off, leaving Liam to slowly lower his hands to his sides. For a moment, he turned his face to the wall and laid his forehead against one wide wooden shelf.

Sucking in oxygen, he tried to clear his system of the sickening dip in adrenaline. How the hell had he gotten here? Today was the first time Uriah had invited him to dinner. It was a rare invitation and Uriah wasn't someone you said no to. Besides, Liam was curious.

There was someone new here that he was supposed to question, but carefully so. The person had something to do with Dr. Bartholomew and the mess of bullshit Liam had been wading through for over a week. Secret labs, government projects, the cause of the war.

But then he had walked through the front door. The piano had been playing, the way it always was when he was forced to wait outside. It was beautiful and haunting and the music had called to him. So when Jameson told him to sit and wait, he hadn't.

Shit, what harm could come from opening one little door? From proving once and for all that there was no stupid CD. That it was a real life piano.

And then there she was. Hannah. And his breathing had stopped. And his brain had turned off. And his heart had sunk to the bottom of his chest.

Giving his head a brisk shake now, Liam stepped back from the wall and turned to face the two other men in the room. They both looked positively deadly at this moment. And over the past several months of working with them, Liam knew for a fact that they were.

Brutal, exacting, harsh, deadly. But fair. That was the one thing that stood out. They were always fair, which is why more men flocked to the city each day.

And for all that was worth, Liam was still pretty damn deadly himself. Of course, now he understood why Jameson had taken all his knives. Hell, he even had to leave his rifle leaning up by the front door.

Rolling his shoulders, Liam let his eyes drop to where Uriah's forearm was streaked with fresh scratches. His little sister had scraped the shit out of him. It probably stung like a bitch, but Uriah didn't rub at it. Instead, he watched Liam.

"Explain," Uriah uttered the word through gritted teeth.

"What have they told you?" Liam asked.

"That's not how this works, and you know it."

Ducking his head, Liam acknowledged that statement. He was on the wrong side of the interrogation this time, better get his shit together.

"I came by Hannah on the road." Liam did his best to give them something true, while keeping most of the details to himself. He didn't know what the women were hiding from Uriah or why. He had to find out, but that meant he had to live long enough to see them again. "She was starving and alone. So, I took her home."

"To the compound."

"Yes." Liam managed to keep his face plain, but his insides twisted at the use of the word. Shit, that meant Uriah had been there? Not good. That couldn't possibly be good.

"Go on." Uriah gestured for Liam to take a seat on one small leather sofa.

After a beat of reluctance, he did so, watching the other man come around to sit opposite him. Jameson remained standing, his face a permanent scowl.

"We lived there for a while together and then she told me about Lena and Flynn."

"During that time-" Uriah's eyes glinted. "You acquainted yourself with my sister? Physically?"

In that moment, Liam wanted to clear his throat. He wanted to tug at his shirt collar and look away. But he couldn't allow himself to do any of that. No tells. No guilt. Nothing could pass across his face or consume his gestures.

The most important thing about this interview was that Liam not outright lie. He had to build back some sort of trust with Uriah. But at the same time, admitting you've slept with someone's sister isn't exactly the smartest thing either.

Especially when that someone has a gun and a temper. Which clearly, Uriah had both. So instead of doing anything, Liam did the next best thing... he did nothing. Said nothing.

"When you walked in-" Uriah's questioning shifted to Jameson. "What did you see?"

"Like I said, he had her against the wall." Jameson's face was dark with the memory, his words clipped. "He was kissing her... touching her."

Uriah shifted then like a hulking lion, his shoulders bunching with tension. "Did it look consensual to you?"

Liam's eyes darted up to watch Jameson's face as he battled with the question. Come on, this was subjective as fuck. Sometimes your eyes see what they want to see. And clearly Jameson hadn't wanted to see any man, especially Liam, with Hannah.

"I guess so," Jameson admitted finally, his eyes fixing on some spot just over Liam's head.

"What about Lena?" Uriah focused on Liam now, biting down on his lower lip so hard that it had to hurt. Here comes the weakness, Liam realized. This man was as tight as a drum talking about Lena. Even more so than with his own sister. "Did you *acquaint* yourself with her, too?"

"No." Liam shook his head. "Never."

"And Flynn? What about her?"

"No."

"Just Hannah, then?"

Liam pressed his lips together in a firm line before making a final decision.

"Only Hannah," he admitted. "It's always only been Hannah."

THE QUESTIONING WENT ON THAT WAY FOR HOURS. LITTLE hands slapped occasionally against the door, women's voices called through it, unintelligible, infrequent. Uriah circled back, moved forward in time, then retreated. He demanded details of the raid on Lena's prison, the names of the men Liam had been living with, touched on the issues with Hannah's memory.

As in the past, Liam did his best to dodge him. They both knew what he was doing, but Uriah stopped short of threats and violence. If this was a boxing match, then it was just the first round. They were feeling each other out, so to speak. And for his part, Liam refused to give Uriah any names, numbers or specific locations.

He admitted only to the fact there had been more men with him at one time, which made his pulse jump and his chest tighten. If Uriah wanted this information, it meant only one thing. He didn't have Cole. He didn't have any of them, just the girls. How could such a thing be accomplished?

Shit, Liam could only think of one way. *Where are you Cole, buddy? Tell me you're still fucking breathing.*

By the time Uriah had exhausted himself, Liam's nerves were fried. He didn't let it show, of course, and only shrugged at the other men's departure.

"I'll bring you a bucket to piss in," was all Uriah gave in parting.

A few minutes later, said bucket was slipped inside the door before it was locked shut once more. The damn thing could be bolted from inside or out and needed a key to do both. Damn, but whoever designed this underground fortress had done so with many, many ideas in mind.

Exhaling slowly, Liam leaned forward and put his face in his hands. Holy shit. Holy shit. It was the only phrase playing in his mind. Hannah, Lena, Cole, the others. The implications scared him too bad to truly contemplate.

Not only that but all the crap that Dr. Bartholomew had been spewing was getting to him, too. The source. Artificial Intelligence. A cure for human disease gone terribly, terribly wrong. The war. Losing any semblance of control. What really lived behind the Wall. Fourteen fucking walls to be exact.

Shoving up to standing, Liam paced back and forth, burning through the sudden flood of emotion. It was too much. This was all too much to take in. Lifting his head, he spied an imposing desk in one corner.

Within three seconds he was behind it, opening drawers, shoving his hands inside, searching for hidden compartments, papers, anything. Hissing out in frustration, he rocked back on his heels as he drew out a few blank leather bound journals and a collection of blue ballpoint pens. He should've known Uriah would never leave him with anything remotely of value. Still, he pocketed a pen, just in case.

Hours passed. Maybe less, maybe more.

The overhead lights in the room grew increasingly dim until they faded out altogether. Flipping on a table side lamp, Liam was unable to stop himself from marveling at the bulb's light. Eventually though, he gave in to his aching body and curled up on the longest couch he could find.

With his boots strapped to his feet and his hand stroking the pocket where his largest knife should've been, Liam brought Hannah to his mind. She was here and she wanted him again. It was the last thought he had before he slipped into reluctant sleep.

CHAPTER FIFTEEN_
LIAM

AN OLD FASHIONED KEY SLID INTO THE LOCK. THE SOUND OF its metal grating, though quiet, shook him awake. Eyes popping open, Liam kept his body completely still as he watched the far door to the library swing wide. His heart beat heavily in his chest, sending blood to pound in his ears.

It could be morning. There was no way to tell time in here but for some reason Liam knew that it wasn't. No. It was late at night. His internal clock groaned with the feeling.

So maybe Uriah subdued the girls, got them all calm and shipped them off to bed. Now he was ready for round two. If Liam was in his position, this is the exact time he'd begin another line of questioning, or worse.

Muscles tingling at the idea, Liam forced himself to swallow and slow his breathing. It was a good thing too, because what he actually saw cross the threshold had him sputtering.

Hannah.

Damn. Fucking. It.

She slipped into the room, her back to him, her hair all a tumble of soft silk flowing over her shoulders. Her legs were bare, just like that first time he'd seen her, but now she was healthy and glowing and clean. Biting back a small groan, Liam tried to wrench his eyes away, but simply could not. Whatever nightshirt thing she had on wasn't covering nearly enough for his weakened state.

Shifting uncomfortably, Liam shoved up to sitting and bent forward, his forearms pressed against his thighs. Before he could blink, she shut the door carefully and re-locked it. The sound had his gut twisting as his mind began to function again. What the hell was she thinking? Her brother owned this entire city and everyone in it. No one defied an order. No one.

It wasn't that he thought Uriah would hurt her, but if he caught Hannah in here without his permission... Well, shit wouldn't be going so well for Liam, that's for sure.

Hannah crossed the room to him quickly. Her bare feet didn't make a sound on the hardwood floor. Liam's eyes betrayed him, darting over her face, falling to her pretty pink lips and lingering over her breasts. He could just see the outline of her nipples through the thin cotton shirt and it had his mouth going completely dry.

Get it together. Get it together. That kiss from earlier, it was just a spur of the moment thing. She regretted you before, maybe she's going to regret you now.

"What are you doing," Liam hissed, but Hannah held a slender finger up to her mouth to shush him.

As she neared, he sat up straighter, letting a frown take over his face as he tilted his head up. He couldn't let her stay in here. Whatever her brother had planned for him, he could handle it. But Hannah shouldn't be around. She should just go back out the way she came. She needed to stay on Uriah's good side. She needed-

"Hannah." Liam's eyes popped wide when instead of stopping in front of him, she kept right on coming. In fact, she had him scrambling backwards until he came up against the cushions of the sofa. "Your brother-"

"Don't worry," Hannah whispered, lowering herself onto his lap. "Lena's taking care of that."

"But-" Liam's breath hitched in his throat as her hands slid along his cheeks.

Those eyes. Those doe brown eyes were staring into him, then cruising down to his mouth. Damn it, she was the most beautiful woman he had ever seen. And she lit every nerve in his body on absolute fire.

Did he want her? Oh hell yes he did. His pants were beyond tight and he knew she could feel him through those tiny little panties she was probably wearing. Operative word there being probably. Because maybe she wasn't wearing any underwear at all. He could find out right now. He could-

Then she was kissing him. Her arms wrapped around the back of his neck as she pulled him up and into her body. He felt the brush of her tongue on his lips then the shift of her hips grinding down against him and he was gone. A groan escaped him. Long and low as his mouth took possession of her. Mine, he thought, this is mine.

His hands shot up to twine in her hair, to feel the silky length of it before he tugged her head back to expose her neck. As his lips teased beneath her chin and down to her collar bone, he was rewarded with one of her quiet little gasps. It had his blood racing and his heart pounding in his chest.

He loved how she sounded. He couldn't get enough of those panting cries she used to make when she was under him. They haunted his dreams long after she'd turned him away.

Shit.

And this was exactly why he had to leave in the first place. He remembered now. She consumed him. Hannah had him. All of him. And then she just threw him away.

"I can't." Liam broke off the kiss, swiping a hand quickly down his face.

"What?"

"I can't do this." He glanced up at the ceiling momentarily, then back into her eyes. "I can't play this game with you."

"Lee, what-"

"Because you were never a regret for me. And I can't be one for you. Not again."

"I'm sorry, I-"

Liam tried to get up but Hannah wouldn't budge.

Spreading her palms over his shoulders, she kept him in place, her eyes frantically seeking his. He couldn't very well shove her aside, so his frustration grew. Didn't she get it? Every second he touched her was a second he was losing the battle. Did she realize how hard it was, literally hard it was, to stop? He didn't *want* to stop. He had to stop. She had to let him-

"I'm in love with you." Hannah reached out to grasp his chin, angling his face towards her. "There was never a time that I didn't love you. I'm sorry I lied about it. I thought you were supposed to see a liar from a mile away."

Liam sputtered at that. His mouth dropped in shock, his hands, too. She had lied? She'd pushed him away on purpose. And he *let* her.

Well, damn. He couldn't see anything clearly when it came to her. She had him totally blind. Totally and completely kryptonite blind. And the thing of it was... he absolutely did not fucking care.

"Say it again." His eyes sought hers, looking for the truth.

"I'm sor-"

"The other part," he cut her off, then watched her slowly smile.

"I love you."

As his lips took hers, he felt her respond. His heart expanded. Then she pulled back.

"I love you," she said it again, and this time she watched *him* smile.

"I love you, too," he whispered it. "Don't ever fucking do that to me again."

"I won't." Hannah shook her head.

"Because if you let me have you now..." Liam held his breath a moment before continuing. "Then I'm going to need you for the rest of my life."

"Okay."

"Promise me," he demanded, his heart hammering sickeningly inside his chest. If she let him inside her again, but then turned him away, he would never recover. Never.

"I promise."

Then he kissed her. It was slow, agonizingly slow, and deep. He wanted to taste her. To savor what he had missed, what he had tortured himself over for months. And he had to have more of her. He had to have more right now.

His hands clutched impulsively at her hips, then snuck beneath her shirt to stroke at her chest. She jerked and pushed into his palm as he teased first one nipple, then the other.

His blood surged with the power of it, with what he could do to her. He would have her writhing under him, yet. She would be screaming his name. She would never be able to deny him again.

Lifting her shirt over her head, he let his mouth fall to her shoulder, then slide down to her chest. She arched her back, grinding down against him. He could feel her clutching at his arms before running her fingers up and through his hair. Taking each breast in his mouth, he sucked and licked as his hands ripped apart the tiny lace panties she was wearing.

Thankfully the fabric was flimsy because he didn't want to lose any contact with her. None. And she must feel the same way because she was tugging at his shirt in frustration until he helped her lift it off. Then her skin was rubbing against his skin and her hands were working at the button of his pants and he about lost it.

"You're not ready for me," he spoke into her mouth.

"I am," she whispered back.

He hissed out a breath as she worked his zipper loose and reached in to wrap her hand around him. He'd meant to draw this whole thing out. He wanted to have her under him where he could control the pace, make this last all night. But then Hannah was stroking him and his mind was no longer his own.

Shit. She did this to him. He had forgotten just what it was like. His pants were barely past his hips and she was already lowering herself down on him.

Letting loose a low groan, his eyes flicked up to her face as her breath hitched in her throat. Guess he was wrong about the ready part. She was slick and hot, and he was completely at her mercy.

Reaching out, he wrapped his arms around her body and drew her in tight against him. With each movement she made, he shifted his hips, trying to keep up the pressure where she needed it most. Up and down, she moved against him.

Before long she was whimpering and moaning into his ear. It sent a rush straight down his spine and he squeezed his eyes shut, trying to focus, trying to last. Just a little longer. Just a little-

But it was too much. She was too much. The feeling of her, of having her over him.

Eyes shooting wide, he stared into her face as her climax hit. And then she was looking back down at him, moving with him, around him and the pressure he felt wouldn't hold back any longer. So he gave in to her.

In the end, he was the one gasping for air beneath her.

He was the one calling out her name. And though he emptied himself inside of her, she was the one filling him up. His Hannah. *His.*

CHAPTER SIXTEEN_
COLE

THE FIRE WAS CRACKLING. THE WOOD THEY'D COLLECTED was still damp. Cole could hear the hiss and spit of the branches burning but he wasn't listening to them exactly. He couldn't truly listen to anything anymore. Up above, the clouds were low and heavy. Between them and the fog that flowed through the woods, it was hard to tell where the earth ended and the sky began.

It was otherworldly. But that was fitting, Cole didn't quite connect with his body anymore. And they were so close to Jensen's now, even with as small a fire as they had, it was a risk. Not that Cole cared so much about risk at this point. In fact, he had ceased caring. He only felt sick dread. He only felt burning hate. The combination kept him going, nothing more.

"It's not your fault you know," Cookie's voice was low but pressing.

Hunching his shoulders, Cole tucked his hands further

into his pockets and watched the flames. Not his fault? Huh. The old man knew nothing.

"You sure you want to go through with this?" Cookie again, his voice was gravely, he was unsure.

"Yeah," Cole offered finally, clearing his throat.

"You got a death wish?"

With a shrug, Cole dismissed the question. More like, he had his old death wish back. It was just like before, pulling missions for Command. He was driven towards the edge, wanted to walk along the line. Tip toe over it. Dance on the line's fucking grave.

If he didn't find Hannah alive, then there was nothing left in this world for him. And the suffering he was going through right now? It didn't compare to the hell she and Lena were probably facing.

Fuck. Cole was such a damn screw up. Everything he touched turned to ash. Everyone he swore to protect wound up dead.

Squeezing his eyes shut, the faces flooded him. His parents and sisters, dead on the floor. The four soldiers he'd lost down south. Chan with his eyes frozen open. Ryder's bloody body. Flynn's head blown off. Trey beneath the snow.

Fault? This went way beyond that.

Fighting the bile that rose in his throat, Cole stood abruptly and paced away. Focus, focus. If he didn't dial himself in, then Hannah didn't stand a chance. And he owed her that much at least.

Forcing his eyes open he surveyed their campsite. There was snow still on the ground down here but nothing like on top of the mountain. Nothing like at the compound.

They'd left the horses behind along with Davey and Ace. It was just Cookie and him now. The rescue party of the century. Pressing the heels of his hands over his eyes, Cole groaned. Where was Liam when you needed him? Damn he could use the tall bastard right about now.

"You can't blame yourself," Cookie started in again and Cole lost it.

"I can't?!" Cole whirled around. "This. Is. Because. Of. *Me*."

"No-"

"My unit. My choices." Cole thumped his chest. "Me."

"The team-"

"Is dead. Holding the positions *I* assigned to them." Cole sucked in a breath, shuddered. "I missed something. My head wasn't in the game. It was just like down south. It was-"

"No, damn it!" Cookie stood too, his face pleading now. "Will you just listen to me for one damned second?"

Chest heaving, Cole swallowed his words. They burned down his throat like the tears he absolutely refused to shed. Cookie gulped once. Lifting his faded ball cap, he ran a hand back through his thinning hair before replacing it.

"The four we lost down south were because of me." Cookie cleared his throat before leveling Cole with unblinking eyes. "I failed in my assignment. I wasn't providing them with cover."

"What?" Cole stammered, his heart dropping.

"I was covering you." Cookie spread his hands out,

glancing around pityingly. "I knew something was off between you and Chan. I... I... left my post and I covered you instead. I watched you instead."

Cole blinked, his mind clicking back to that night. The face off between him and Chan in that room. The painfully long minutes where Chan had held a gun pointed at his face but couldn't bring himself to pull the trigger.

"You watched..."

"I saw Chan holding you there," Cookie explained. "I watched through the scope of my rifle. You were standing in the window, third floor up."

"But-"

"I was waiting for a clear shot on Chan. I never got one."

"He was supposed to-"

"I know." Cookie sucked in a breath. "I cornered him after. He told me about the orders. He told me what you wanted him to do."

"What he *should* have done," Cole corrected.

"No." Cookie shook his head. "Don't you see it? You're the only one capable of leading us. You're the only reason we all got as far as we did. You were willing to sacrifice your life to keep us living. No one could've done better. No one."

"You shouldn't have left your position."

"I know that." Cookie bobbed his head. "But I would do it again, if given the choice."

Blowing out a breath, Cole staggered to the fire and crumpled down in front of it. He wasn't sure how he felt about Cookie's admission. Anger at having been defied?

Disappointment that anyone would choose him over his brothers? His soldiers? Just a tiny twinge of relief that in the end, if his orders would've been followed, the four down south would probably have made it?

Cookie paced a bit, then stooped beside his pack. Pretending to fuss with their food stores, the older man lost himself in the silence.

"Are they among your dead?" Cole asked finally. "The faces you see?"

"They are," Cookie admitted. Pausing in his rummaging, he looked over. "You all are though. We're dead men walking, Cole. None of your careful planning and finesse is going to change that. You're just buying us more time."

Blowing out a breath, Cole tilted his head up and studied the fog as it filtered through the trees. Was that it? They were all just living on borrowed time? Every second was for sale and he was simply the best bet to get them more of it? Perhaps.

"I forgive you," Cole said. "For leaving your post. I forgive you."

"I don't need your forgiveness." Cookie rose to standing and shuffled closer.

"What then?"

"*You* do." Cookie crouched down, one hand reaching forward to balance on the ground. "You need to forgive yourself for the things you cannot control. You need to let go of this compulsion to punish yourself. We still have folks out there and they need you. I need you."

"Why?" Cole whispered it.

"Because as much as I don't deserve it, I want more

time. So this little plan you've got cooked up with Jensen? You've got to be sure. We can't go in with you hoping never to make it out."

Swallowing hard, Cole sniffed and glanced away. Damn Cookie and his fucking reasonable bullshit. Cole'd wanted the two of them to march into Jensen's town, demand information and maybe get the opportunity to burn the place down. He wanted to torture and to cut, the way Liam always did. He understood it all so much better now.

But what were the odds of surviving to put that information to use? Not good. Not good at all.

"Alright," Cole conceded. "You can cover me. But if I give the signal, then you waste him, okay?"

"Okay." Cookie, ducked his head before nodding. "I better get a move on if I'm gonna get into position before daybreak."

"Yeah." Cole narrowed his eyes as his head began to clear. "And a few more things…"

THE BUILDING WAS JUST LIKE EVERY MEMORY COLE HAD from before. The big blue accented sign. The painted gray block facade. The classic white letters that read, *Walmart* with the little yellow addition, *Supercenter*.

Despite the fog and the bone deep cold, Cole stood resolutely still in the middle of the abandoned parking lot. All around him, useless vehicles sat parked haphazardly, covered in ice and snow. Overhead, darkened light poles arched into the sky every so often. Would they ever be capable of shedding light again? No, Cole thought, and no busy families would be shoving through the front doors, either.

Glancing up, Cole squinted at the roofline. Cookie was up there somewhere with his rifle, waiting. Even knowing that the older man was around didn't make it easier for Cole to spot him. That was the point of being a sniper, if you were worth a shit no one ever saw you. Not until after the shot was fired. And then, only if you weren't the intended target.

Rubbing his gloved hands together, Cole rotated a tiny circle. It was dawn now, he should have company any second.

Just like clockwork, there was a bit of movement across the street. It was a shadow of movement really, a shift of light where there shouldn't be any, then it was gone. Whoever was out doing rounds was probably scurrying their ass back to Jensen right about now.

Cole jumped up and down a bit in an attempt to warm himself before adjusting the weapon in his hands. In his head, he counted three minutes before the calvary arrived. And arrive they did.

Men materialized all around him. They crept out from the surrounding streets, guns held close, though not pointed directly at him. Glancing over his shoulder, Cole noted a few appear from behind the Walmart itself. But then his focus was back forward, riveted to the voice that called easily to him. The voice that was all cocky command, if not a touch curious.

"Well, well, well." Jensen chuckled a bit. "You hangmen sure are showing up more frequently these days."

Cole forced an easy smile and let the man approach. If this went south, all Cole had to do was raise his hand in the air and the guy was dead. Cookie would smoke him. It was a comforting sort of fact.

"Where is everybody?" Jensen looked pointedly around before coming to a stop a few feet in front of Cole. "No horses? No cart? Where's your people?"

"I've come alone," Cole lied.

"Ah." Jensen bobbed his head, but it was obvious he wasn't convinced. "I take it this isn't about trading then."

Cole shrugged. "Everything's about trading, isn't it?"

"Doesn't seem like you're offering much," Jensen commented, glancing around Cole's body this way and that. "What are you after?"

"Information."

"Ah." Jensen eased back on his heels, seeming to relax. "This is about your boyfriend, then. Isn't it?"

Cole's eyebrows shot to his forehead, he couldn't help it. Boyfriend?

"The tall one." Jensen chuckled. "Or maybe the feeling wasn't mutual. That's why he left in the first place."

"Where is he?" Cole's voice sharpened. He was talking about Liam. There was no way these bastards had got the drop on his best friend, but still, the very idea terrified him. Liam hadn't been himself when he'd left, so maybe...shit. Cole's throat burned. "What'd you do to him?"

"Relax." Jensen held up his hands. "Last we saw he was heading south, making for Linfield territory."

"*Linfield?*" The word pounded between Cole's ears. What the?

"Yeah, Uriah Linfield holds a city about a week's worth of walking in that direction." Jensen pointed south then crossed his arms over his chest. "Now you have your info. What do you have to trade for it?"

CHAPTER SEVENTEEN_
HANNAH

Blinking her eyes open, Hannah inhaled a deep breath and smiled. *Liam.* He was amazing and she still couldn't believe he was here. Standing a foot away from her, stepping into his pants, the man himself glanced at her sheepishly before zipping up.

"Trying to sneak away?" Hannah teased. "You forget, I have the keys."

She was rewarded with Liam's quick smile. Coming to kneel on the floor beside her, he leaned in close and consumed her with one of his kisses. His shirt was still off and his hair was all messed from their night together. Between his chiseled chest and flat stomach, he looked like a sex god. One she could no longer resist.

Immediately her body responded, flooding with heat and desire as she reached for him. But then he was pulling away.

"You're the one that needs to be sneaking out," he said.

When she only giggled, he frowned.

"I'm serious, Hannah. Get out of here before-"

The sound of the doorknob twisting cut him off. It was followed by a hard slap to the thick surface, then a man's voice shouting. Too late, Hannah thought, before nibbling at her bottom lip. *Brother dear is on the war path early.*

Sitting up, Hannah glanced around. She shoved the blanket they'd slept beneath off and found her nightdress crumpled beside her on the sofa. Only after shrugging into it did she notice her shredded underwear on the floor. *Wow, that really happened.*

"Hannah," Liam hissed, tugging his shirt over his head. "Tell me there's another way out of here."

"Not that I know of," she replied, then quickly kicked her wasted panties beneath the couch.

"Shit, shit." Liam paced, grabbing for his socks and boots. "Why didn't we leave last night?"

"I don't know." Hannah ran her fingers through her hair. "I just fell asleep after..."

"Me, too," Liam admitted.

Ducking his head, he let loose a groan before glancing back at the door. A key was twisting in the lock and the doorknob was turning.

"They're called master keys," Uriah spat as he stormed into the room. "What the hell are you doing, Hannah Mae? Don't you realize who this guy is? How badly he could hurt you?"

Cocking a gun, Uriah pointed it smoothly at Liam and motioned for him to step back. Hannah's heart skipped a beat while Liam raised both hands in the air and complied.

"Stop, Uri. This is crazy, I'm not a little girl anymore."

"He's a fucking Nor Side Soldier. One of my own, in fact." Uriah didn't lower the weapon and he didn't look at her. "Do you know what his speciality is? Do you know anything about him?"

"Yes, I-"

"No," Uriah interrupted. "No, you don't. He's the only survivor of a fucking suicide mission. The rest of his team are dead. He's a stone cold fucking killer, Hannah Mae. He has no feelings. We made sure of it."

"That's..." Hannah blanched. Cole's dead? Staggering, her arm searched wildly for the edge of the sofa.

"Do you know where he came from?" Uriah stepped closer as Liam narrowed his eyes. "Do you know what happened to his mother? What he helped his daddy get away with?"

Gradually, the room began to spin. Hannah sat hard on the couch, her heart fracturing and bursting inside of her chest. Cole's dead? It was all she could think of.

Out of the corner of her eye, she saw her brother take one more step towards Liam. Turns out, it was one too many.

It all happened so fast. One second, her brother was holding a gun. The next, Liam had the weapon in his own hand, his arm wrapped tightly around Uriah's neck, the gun pressing hard against her brother's temple.

"No, stop!" Hannah sprang to her feet, but the two men were focused only on one another.

"You think I helped that piece of shit!" Liam gritted his teeth, his forearm flexing against her brother's throat. "I was fucking six years old!"

"You didn't testify," Uriah managed. "You stayed living with him. You had a way out."

"A way out?!" Liam was incredulous, his eyes bright with loathing. "There was no way out. Do you know what would've happened to me if I talked? Fuck. Fucking. You. You're just a spoiled rich boy. You have no idea."

"We read the reports. Even after you were removed from the home. The CPS interviews." Uriah gripped Liam's arm with both hands. "That's what made you so perfect for the job. You don't feel anything. All your foster families, the shrinks you went to-"

"Shut your fucking mouth," Liam growled.

"Hannah Mae," Uriah sputtered. "Run."

"Cole's dead?" Hannah clutched at her throat before screaming. "Liam! Stop!"

His eyes jerked over to her, they were cloudy and dark. It was hard to see her Liam in there. Hard to see him through the tears that spilled from her eyes. Hard to see past the gun at her brother's head.

"See?" Uriah whispered. "You're just like your daddy. You're scaring her."

"Liam," Hannah pleaded. "Stop, please, stop. Let him go. He said Cole's dead. Is Cole dead?"

"I don't know." Liam released his arm, letting Uriah stumble forward a few steps before un-cocking the gun. "You'll have to ask him that."

Despite the angry red mark that slashed across his throat, Uriah managed to stay on his feet. In three strides he was at Hannah's side, hugging her tight to him. Swiftly he pulled the master keys out of his pocket and shoved them into her hand. Then he was whispering in her ear.

"Get Lena and go." Uriah kissed her head. "Take a gun. Lock us in here and wait outside the door."

"Uri."

"Jameson should be here anytime." Uriah pulled back to look at her. "He'll take care of you."

"What? I..." Hannah was at a loss.

Glancing over her brother's shoulder, she was just in time to see Lena enter the room. She'd heard the yelling. The door was wide open. Who wouldn't have heard them?

Dark hair hanging loose, blue eyes filled with concern, Lena let her gaze travel from Liam to Uriah. The two men both absorbed her presence in a similar fashion. Liam's shoulders slumped forward a moment while Uriah's hand shot to his forehead.

They hadn't wanted her to see. They hadn't wanted her to hear. The thing was, they both thought she was too fragile. Hannah watched as Lena crossed the room quickly, though Uriah was already calling for her to leave.

She wasn't listening though. Lena rushed to Uriah's side, reaching her hands up to run over his injured throat before looping them around his neck. Hannah stepped away from them as her brother broke and clung to the little dark-haired woman. He couldn't help himself.

And that was when Liam slipped from the room, the gun tucked neatly into the back of his pants.

"Wait!" Hannah called, but he didn't stop.

She jogged to the threshold, gripping the walls as she leaned out. Looking first right and then left, she saw him already at the front door. He was stooping to pick up his rifle. He was on his way out. Liam was leaving her... again. Inside her chest, her heart wanted to explode.

"What are you doing?" Hannah demanded.

Liam tensed at the sound of her voice, but didn't stop.

"You're running," she accused, unable to keep the hurt from her voice. "Cole's dead and you're running away."

"Fuck, Hannah." Liam turned on her then, his eyes bright. "Didn't you hear a word your brother said? I'm no good for you. And I don't know if Cole's dead. I don't know how you got here, or what the hell is going on."

"I don't care what Uriah said." Hannah reached out for him, but Liam backed a step and it hurt. "I made a promise to you last night. I guess you didn't make the same one to me."

"Don't." Liam rubbed a hand down his face. "Don't use that. You can't use that. I am what he says. I watched my father kill my mother and I did nothing."

"It sounds like you were a little boy."

"I didn't stop him." Liam sucked in a breath. "I didn't testify. I failed her and I'm a danger to you. Please. Just let me go find Cole."

"A danger?" Hannah didn't know if she wanted to laugh or cry. "Is that what you were to Lena? To Flynn? What about all those times with me? Were you a danger then?"

"That's not-"

"If Cole is dead, and you leave me..." Hannah hiccuped and looked away. "I am asking you to stay, Liam."

"I can't."

"Stay with me." Hannah straightened, staring up at his face. "Or do I have to get Lena to come ask you? Is that it?"

"Hannah."

"Because you'd stay for her, right?"

"That's not fair."

"But you would!" Hannah shouted it. "You'd stay for her and not me. Why? Why is that, Liam?!"

"Because Lena's just like her!" Liam sucked in a breath, ran a shaky hand back through his hair. "Do you want to know what my mother was like? What she looked like? How fucking frightened she was all the time? Go look at Lena. She's just like her. Black hair, blue eyes, the only thing she's missing right now are the bruises to match, okay?"

"Lee," Hannah exhaled it.

Closing the distance between them, she wrapped her arms around Liam just as his face crumpled. He bent into her, his head buried in her neck. She could feel the wet tears coming off of him, but he was silent.

"I love you so much," Hannah whispered. "I'm so sorry that happened to you. I'm so sorry you think it's your fault. But it's not your fault, Lee. It was never your fault."

Finally, his arms cinched around her waist. She could feel the moment he broke, the moment he gave in to her. For the longest while, they stood there together. His breath hitched at first as she continued to whisper soothing words in his ear.

This man. It hurt to think what he'd gone through. It hurt to think how other people had used him for it, for the guilt he carried. And Uriah. Hannah wanted to shake him.

She wanted to yell and scream at him for being such an asshole. But that was Uriah. He always got what he wanted, even if he had to manipulate other people to get it.

"We need to talk," Uriah's steady voice came to fill the entryway. *Speak of the devil.*

Looking back over her shoulder, Hannah spied him in the threshold of the library only a few yards down the hall. Lena's arm was looped around his waist. They both had this look about them, like maybe they'd heard some of it.

Liam drew back and away from her, but Hannah gripped his hand before he could protest. She wasn't about to let him walk.

"Where do you suggest we do that?" Hannah asked, turning to face her brother, her chin tilting up.

"How about over breakfast?" Uriah's eyes drifted from her to Liam, then back. "No guns."

"No deal," Liam's voice was short. "We're leaving."

"No, you're not," Uriah corrected, his shoulders tensing. "It's time to come clean. You, me, them. There's a lot to discuss."

"I'm not sitting quietly at a table while you call in the calvary," Liam reasoned. "I'm going now and if Hannah wants to come, then she can."

"No calvary and Hannah's not leaving." Uriah gave his head a shake. "But if you want to go, then there are things you need to know. Things we all need to know."

"We'll stay," Hannah spoke up, squeezing Liam's hand harder as he tried to suck it away from her. "But we all get guns. Me and Lena included."

"Sounds reasonable to me," Lena piped up, and had Uriah's eyebrows lifting. "I want a 9 mil."

"Holy shit," Liam muttered before letting loose a low whistle under his breath.

He'd stay, Hannah thought, at least for now, he'd stay.

THE ROOM WAS BRIGHTLY LIT. DESPITE BEING SEVERAL stories below ground, the high ceilings and white walls left you with an airy impression.

Glancing around, Liam noted several massive oil paintings hanging on the walls. One in particular caught his eye. A violent ocean. Crashing waves, a mix of blues and whites as the sea turned over on itself. Fitting. Very fitting.

"This is stupid," Jameson grumbled, standing just beside the painting in question. He was leaning up against the wall, his foot propped beneath him. His fingers clenched. No doubt they were uncomfortable being empty as his handgun lay feet away from him in the center of the dining room table.

"Yet necessary," Uriah countered.

Easy for him to say though, since his hand was tucked neatly in his lap, wrapped tightly around his weapon. Liam's gaze fell from Jameson down over Uriah and settled on Lena who was sitting just next to the asshole. Beneath the table, she too was holding a gun. The thought made Liam's stomach pinch. Did she even know how to use the damn thing?

Running his thumb over his own weapon, Liam didn't have to look down to know it was ready for use. Safety was off. Bullet in chamber. All Uriah had to do was flinch wrong and Liam would have him covered. But then Uriah would draw too, and Jameson would jump for the table and Lena would... do what? Shoot one of them, or Liam, or maybe Hannah by mistake?

Sliding his eyes to his left, Liam absorbed Hannah's presence just beside him. She was focused. Her left hand was poised on top of the table, her fingers drumming incessantly at its mahogany surface. But her right hand? It held a gun, too.

A line of perspiration beaded on Liam's forehead then. The thought of the women here, in the middle of all this potential death and destruction, it made his insides fucking shake. He couldn't let them get hurt. Not the way his mom had been. Not ever again.

And so he held himself in check. Though he desperately wanted to have a go at Uriah, he would be careful about what he said and the movements he allowed his body to make. Come to think of it, the man across the table was probably dialed in in the exact same way.

Liam flicked his eyes over to Uriah once more. Yeah, the guy was strung tight. So maybe Hannah's demand for a gun had been a good thing. Everyone was being extra careful. No one wanted to draw.

"Someone mentioned breakfast," Liam began, wanting

to break the ice but also to establish the order. He had to control this interrogation. Because that's what it was, a chance to ask questions. And Liam simply burned with those these days.

Of course, he couldn't lead with the most pressing of them. He couldn't tip his hand, couldn't let Uriah know how little Liam understood about what was really going on. How did the women get here? Where the *fuck* was Cole? Was his oldest friend even alive? Were any of his brothers?

The idea of their possible end made Liam positively sweat. But on the outside, he was all cool, all control.

"Jameson," Uriah spoke finally. "Make us something."

"This is bullshit," Jameson spat, but he shoved away from the wall and strode the few steps towards the kitchen.

Even though Uriah's right hand man would be doing the cooking, he could still keep everyone in his line of sight. The room they were in was large, encompassing the kitchen and dining area before spreading beyond to a massive living room. Talk about money, this place was set up for the long haul, Liam thought. Might be a good place to start.

"So you happened to find this place, huh?" Liam tilted his head to one side, watching Uriah's face become impassive.

"No," he admitted, much to Liam's surprise. "My father built it. Well... I used his money anyway."

"Why?"

"For fun."

"Uri," Hannah warned. "You want me to stay, right? Want me to do what you say? It's time to be honest."

Liam watched Uriah's eyes flick over to his sister, then return to Liam. Settling back ever so slightly in his chair, the boss man battled a mob of tension that filled his eyes. Clearing his throat, Uriah exhaled slowly through his nostrils before speaking.

"I just want to get one thing out so we're all clear," he said. "If you take my sister out of here, then you *will* be killing her. You get that right?"

"Uri!"

"No!" Uriah slapped a palm on the table. "I can keep her and Lena comfortable for at least thirty fucking years down here. If you walk out with Hannah, then you'll be the one murdering her. So help me... if that happens I will run you down like a damn dog."

Liam kept his face relaxed, his thoughts safely swirling inside his own head. Everything Uriah was about to confess was predicated on the idea that by doing so, he would get to keep his sister in place. Liam couldn't let him know the truth. He couldn't let Uriah know that he didn't have to say a single word.

Answers or no, Liam would never let Hannah come with him when he left. And he *would* be leaving this place... soon. To find Cole. He had to find Cole.

"Deal," Liam agreed.

Sliding his eyes briefly to the left, he caught Hannah's tentative smile. She thought he was committing to staying, too. She didn't realize what a complete asshole he was. He really didn't deserve to have her. But he would go find the guy who did, and if Cole was still alive, he'd bring him back to her.

"You've been talking to our good doctor right?" Uriah asked.

"That's right," Liam acknowledged, not sure where this was going.

"And what has he told you so far?"

"You already know that," Liam narrowed his eyes. "You've been taping the sessions."

"Doctor?" Hannah's voice shook. "What doctor?"

"Humor me." Uriah shrugged, ignoring his sister.

"He's a geneticist, one of the best in his field," Liam recited. "His focus was inherited disease but he also researched variation in human DNA. He believes he's discovered the cure to AIDS."

"Just AIDS?" Uriah prompted.

"No." Liam frowned. "He believes he's discovered the cure for all disease and illness of every kind."

"Uriah," Hannah hissed. "What doctor?"

"You know what doctor," Uriah supplied, glancing at his sister. "Sort of."

"You've questioned Dr. B?" Hannah turned on Liam, her eyes worried. "Dr. Bartholomew?"

"Yes." Liam frowned before tipping his chin at Uriah. "He has him."

"But- but how?" Hannah stood abruptly. "He's dead!"

Dropping her gun, Hannah began back pedaling, her chair scooting in fits and starts across the carpet. At the sound of the weapon clattering against the table, everyone in the room jumped. Lena's eyes went wide as Uriah swore.

Out of the corner of his eye, Liam saw Jameson drop behind a counter in the kitchen.

"Easy now," Liam coaxed, his heart pumping in his throat. "We're all being easy. Right Jameson?"

When there was no answer, Uriah added his voice to the request, "Right?!"

"Yeah!" Jameson called, as he slowly rose back to standing. "Holy shit, I need a fucking gun. It's just not fair."

"I'm sorry," Hannah said. Her eyes darting from face to face. "I'm sorry. It's just. He's dead. I saw him dead. I saw him."

"I know you did." Uriah nodded, motioning for her to sit back down. "Or a version of him, at least."

"A version of him?" Liam narrowed his eyes. "What the fuck is that supposed to mean?"

"The truth is I don't really know." Uriah shrugged. "I don't know how he could be dead but also be in my jail cell at the same time. I haven't figured it out yet."

"That's easy," Liam said. "He's not the same person."

"Isn't he?" Uriah's eyebrows raised. "You didn't think he had the cure, either. But he did."

"What are you talking about?"

"My father and I were majority investors in Dr. Bartholomew's research." Uriah sighed. "My dad because he thought it could make him more money and me because I thought it was a noble cause. What would the world be like free of sickness?"

"You expect me to believe you gave a shit about curing people?" Liam snorted.

"I don't care what you believe, actually." Uriah shifted

before rolling his eyes. "It doesn't really matter anyway, does it? The cure is upon us and that is that."

"The cure? Oh, you mean what those assholes are doing to all those women inside the Wall? The selective breeding bullshit? The sterilization?"

"I didn't know that would be part of it," Uriah protested. "We funded the project. A lot of companies did. We thought we would be getting something like a flu shot or an implant. We didn't know the damn thing would trigger a world fucking war."

"Is that so?" Liam clenched his teeth. "Then why build this place? If you didn't know, then why have the protection?"

Uriah's shoulders tensed at the question and he grew silent. Liam watched the other man's eyes blur in and out as if he were seeing something, some memory none of them were privy to. Then just as suddenly, his gaze focused and he frowned.

"It was about six months after Dr. Bartholomew's lab took our investment. That's when I figured something was going wrong." Uriah sucked in a breath, wiped a hand down his face. "I flew to their office in New York to review their progress but all I got was a tour of the facility and some bullshit song and dance. When I requested their financial statements, I was escorted out."

Uriah's gaze traveled to his sister. Out of the corner of his eye, Liam watched Hannah give him a little nod before he continued.

"I went to my dad but he was busy. He said I was being paranoid, that I was young, just out of college and new to how this whole thing worked. He said I needed to focus my energy elsewhere. But... I just couldn't shake it, you know? That feeling you get when you know something's wrong?

I had this friend back at MIT. He was a genius with computers so I had him hack the system. When he finally got behind the firewall, he said it was unlike anything he'd ever seen. The damn thing was beyond him, changing and shifting, spitting him out, throwing shit at him, tracking him, destroying his software, his hard drive. It shut the power off to the entire school."

"You said *thing*. What thing?" Liam interrupted.

"At the time we didn't know." Uriah glanced once more at Hannah. "But now I think it was the source, or artificial intelligence, whatever you want to call it. I believe that Dr. Bartholomew's 'cure' was actually invented by the AI or maybe in partnership with it. He was merely doing what the computer told him to, in the steps that it revealed to him at the time. Maybe. Anyway it's just my theory."

"And that caused you to build this bunker?"

"No." Uriah shook his head. "It caused me to go to the FBI but they shut me down. That's when I enlisted. That's when I left for West Point."

Liam's eyes widened a bit before he closed his expression. That would explain Uriah's rank within Command. That would explain the military training and the holier than thou officer complex the other man walked around with. But it still didn't explain the bunker, the planning, the prepping.

As if sensing the track of Liam's thoughts, Uriah continued.

"I had my friend hack the government's satellite feeds, their data bases, everything he possibly could that linked back to that lab and any property they owned or were involved in," Uriah explained. "When I saw the blueprints for the refugee centers and the agreement with the UN, that's when I authorized this build. That's when I started planning for the worst."

CHAPTER NINETEEN_
HANNAH

DIRTY DISHES LITTERED THE TABLE FOR AS FAR AS THE EYE could see. Hannah sucked in a breath and ran a hand back through her mass of golden hair. They'd been at this all day. Liam and her brother, going round and round and round.

Breakfast had come and gone, then lunch. Dinner was just on the horizon, with Jameson still grumbling unhappily in the kitchen. Pinching the bridge of her nose, Hannah shoved back from the table and walked a few steps away. Her whole body hurt. Her muscles ached and her butt was numb from the hard wooden chair.

Leaning back against the wall, she folded her arms across her chest and closed her eyes. Every once in a while, static from Jameson's radio would sound out. Hannah could hear her brother's trusted soldier barking out orders, then fielding requests. Something about a new resident interview and a trust check, whatever that was.

Despite the mountain of information Liam had already

picked through, he had yet to bring up what Hannah so desperately needed. He still hadn't asked about Cole. And for that matter, her brother hadn't brought him up either.

Uriah's words from earlier still echoed inside her mind. The phrase *suicide mission* and *sole survivor* kept slicing at her insides. Hannah's eyes popped open. Could Cole be dead?

"You alright?" Liam glanced over his shoulder at her as Uriah narrowed his eyes.

"I'm fine," Hannah answered. So not fine.

"Let's take a break," Uriah said before turning his attention to Lena who sat slightly slumped by his side.

Arching his back to stretch, Liam kept his eyes glued to Uriah for a few moments more. When Hannah's brother continued to ignore him, Liam rose from the table and tucked his gun in the holster now strapped to his back.

Carefully, he turned to one side and closed the distance between them. Hannah watched his long body move, so alert still, even after everything they'd discussed. He wasn't taking any chances. He still didn't trust Uriah.

"Hey," Liam's voice was low as he wrapped his arms around her body, drawing her up against him. "Maybe you should go lie down."

"When are you going to ask about Cole?" Hannah whispered. "Weren't you supposed to be with him? With everyone?"

"Shhhh," Liam soothed, running a hand down her back. "I left them after our trade deal. They turned for home and I came here. I don't know what happened after that. It would help if you told me how you got here, Hannah. How did you and Lena get to Uriah?"

Hannah's breath hitched in her throat as she tightened her grip on Liam's shirt. The raid was something she absolutely did not want to think about. But Liam wouldn't ask unless he needed the information; so, steeling herself, Hannah told him what she knew.

All the while, Liam stroked quietly at her back and said nothing. He let Hannah whisper and hiccup into his chest as she stumbled her way through the past few months of her life. When she was done, he pressed his lips to the top of her head before glancing around.

"So, Jameson's team hit the compound before Cole and the others returned?"

"Yes." Hannah nodded.

"And you think everyone there is dead."

"Uriah would never confirm it, but they admitted they couldn't recover Flynn." Hannah pulled back, tilting her head up to watch Liam's face. "Jameson wouldn't have left without her, not if she was still alive, not if any of them were still alive. I know that now."

"Okay." Liam's jaw clenched as he looked over his shoulder at Uriah. "Alright."

Hannah's chest heaved once before she got herself under control. Her mind was whirling a million miles an hour now, running through the implications. And she knew what Liam was thinking, too. About how her brother was responsible for all those deaths. The deaths of Liam's men, of his friends. *Their* friends. She'd loved them, too.

"Please-" Hannah exhaled in a rush. "It was just a rescue

mission to him. It was the same thing we did for Lena and Flynn."

Liam gave a grunt and looked as if he might pull away. Hannah curled her fingers tighter in his shirt, keeping him close, willing him to look down at her.

"They didn't know we were okay," Hannah reasoned. "They thought we were being hurt. Please, Lee. Can't you see that?"

"It wouldn't have taken a lot of watching to verify." Liam gritted his teeth, his whole body tense.

"You know how hard it is to see into the compound," Hannah reminded him. "Once you're close enough to look inside, whoever's on watch would know."

Exhaling through his nostrils, Liam made a non-committal sound. Behind him, Lena was clearing dishes while Uriah spoke to Jameson. Everything was so normal down here, just like before the war. It was easy to forget the chaos and disarray back on the surface. Easy to forget about the split second decisions you had to make. The choice between life and death was a fast one and you didn't get a second chance.

"He's my brother, Lee." Hannah's heart kicked painfully. "He can be a real jerk, but he's always taken care of me. My father… he wasn't really around a lot. But Uri was. I remember now, every piano recital, every ballet perfor-mance, every school function."

"I see." Liam sighed before reaching up to run his fingers through her hair. "You don't want him hurt, is that it?"

"Yes." Hannah nodded. "Or you either."

For a moment, Liam's eyes grew distant. It was as if he was looking at something far away, though his hand kept stroking through her hair and his breathing remained even. Hannah held her breath, her eyes dancing across his face. Then all at once he seemed to come back to himself.

His eyes dropped to hers and held. His fingers stilled, then drifted to trace over her lips. Leaning down, he pressed his mouth to hers. The kiss was soft and sweet, making Hannah forget herself and the room around them. Maybe it was the same for Liam. Maybe she made him forget himself, too.

"I thought we were all clear on the rules around here," Uriah's voice sounded out, causing Liam to break away.

"Oh yeah?" Liam rubbed his thumb across Hannah's chin once before turning to face him. "And what's that?"

"You and my sister." Uriah squared his shoulders and rose up from the table. "It's not going to happen."

"Uriah," Lena hissed, tugging at his arm.

"You took advantage while she was out there," Uriah accused, his eyes flashing. "She didn't remember anything, she was vulnerable and you used that. You manipulated her."

"That's not how it was," Hannah cut in, her eyes darting between them.

"You're not good for her," Uriah continued, leaning forward over the table. "We both know that. You and I both know that's true."

"Stop it, Uriah," Lena interjected, her voice strengthening. "Just stop!"

Jameson paused in his cooking in the kitchen, steam

rising in swirls above a boiling pot of water. Hannah's eyebrows raised and her mouth dropped a fraction. The little dark-haired woman had her brother's full attention now, and everyone else's for that matter.

"You need to apologize," Lena continued, tilting her chin up just a touch. "To Liam. You need to apologize to him for what you just said. And for what you said earlier."

"Wha-" Uriah started a sentence but it dried on his tongue.

Tearing his gaze from Liam, he let it land squarely on the demanding woman at his side. Seconds ticked by as he simply stared, his expression shifting from shock to disbelief. No one spoke to him like that. Not here in the city he ruled, nor back in their life before the war. Hannah remembered clearly now. Not even their father held him that accountable, though he wasn't around all that much, considering.

"You keep telling me that I'm safe here," Lena began. "That you'll protect me. That you... that you love me."

Uriah's brow furrowed, his mouth opening as if he were going to speak, but then Lena gave a shake of her head and pressed on.

"That man across the table from you." Lena gestured, her eyes following to lock on Liam. "He saved me. *He* got me out. You said you feel guilty about not sending the security team earlier, about waiting too long. If that's true then you owe Liam. He stayed with me when I needed him. Even when it cost him time with Hannah, he stayed with me... only because I asked."

"Lena." Liam sighed.

"No." Her voice wavered for only a moment, then held. "I won't hear another word spoken against you. Not ever." Turning to Uriah once more, she repeated her demand. "Apologize."

The air was thick. All activity from the kitchen had long since ceased. The only thing Hannah could hear was the thump of her own heart and the breathing of Liam just beside her.

"Jameson," Uriah spoke finally, his voice tight. "Give us a minute."

"I've got some business up top." Jameson ducked his head before making a quick exit.

The sound of his footsteps could be heard leaving the kitchen. Hannah didn't turn to look, but she listened as he walked off down the hallway. Then the heavy front door was swinging open for a second before clicking shut.

Uriah let his eyes fall to the tabletop a moment, his fingers balling into fists before spreading out flat. Hannah could imagine what he must be thinking. This was a sort of betrayal on Lena's part, at least that's how Hannah was sure her brother would perceive it. She'd chosen Liam. She'd called Uriah out in front of everyone.

But then Uriah glanced to the little dark-haired woman and straightened his shoulders. Shifting around to face Liam, he spoke.

"Forgive me," the words were clear and surprising.

Liam nodded his head, but said nothing.

Clearing his throat, Uriah pushed back from the table and stalked from the room. Without another word, Hannah's brother followed Jameson's path out of the house. She could hear the front door open once more before it slammed shut.

Lena exhaled and pressed shaking fingers to her closed eyes. Hannah glanced sideways at Liam whose expression was one of concern.

"I want to get you both out of here," he confided quietly. "But I can't figure out a safe way to do it. Not yet."

"No." Lena raised her head and smiled sadly. "He told me what he said about your mom. About you not testifying. He knows it was wrong Liam. We all know."

"But-"

"You were a very little boy with no power for so long," Lena continued, her eyes bright. "I heard you say I remind you of her... of your mother."

Liam swallowed, his face going tight a moment before he nodded. "You do."

"Well then let me tell you how very proud I am of the man that you've become." Lena smiled then, her lips trembling just a touch. "You aren't your father, you're nothing like him. And Uriah isn't your father either. I can handle myself now, Liam. Okay? He won't hurt me and he won't hurt his sister. Not in that way. I'm a big girl and I'm choosing to stay with him. Do you get that? I don't want to leave Uriah."

"Okay." Liam exhaled a long breath. "And Hannah, you'll stay too. Right?"

"What?" Hannah grabbed onto his arm, then let her hand slide down to circle his wrist. "I'm going with you. Wherever you go. We agreed."

"No." Liam shook his head and stepped back from her.

"I have to look for Cole. I can't have you with me when I do. It's too much."

"But-"

"Han." Liam reached for her face, traced his fingers down it. "He always called you that, *Han*. I never liked it before now."

"What's changed?"

"Him." Liam shrugged before letting his hand fall and his eyes shift towards the hallway. "I… I guess I just miss him. I've got to find him, to make sure he's okay."

"I want to go with you."

"You can't," Liam stated flatly.

He looked at Lena once more, then back to Hannah before he started through the kitchen. Hannah was on his heels the whole way. Begging, pleading, insisting. Lena let them go, her eyes all full of apology and regret.

Through the kitchen and down the hall and back into the library they traveled. Liam ignored Hannah's protests as she pitched them at him, shifting quickly between demands and hysterics. Nothing fazed him though.

He gathered his jacket, his knives, his rifle by the door. Pausing, Liam gripped her chin in his hand and pressed a final kiss to her lips. Without a word, he was gone. Open. Shut. Just like that.

Leaning her forehead against the front door, Hannah let the tears continue to flow down her face. She could rush out, rush after him. But then where would she be? In the middle of a city full of soldiers and men who were training to be soldiers. Even she knew it wasn't a good option.

"Lock it," Liam spoke quietly through the closed door.

He was waiting there.

It was that final act that had her breaking, giving in to the ache and stabbing reality that he may never come back. That she might be left waiting there, wondering with each open door whether it would be him, or Cole. That she might be waiting forever for an end that would never come. That she could do nothing about it.

Finally reaching for the lock, Hannah flipped the bolt into place before her body slipped slowly to the ground.

CHAPTER TWENTY_
COLE

Tilting his head up, Cole surveyed the surface of the shining blue-black building before him. It was pristine in places, and completely blown to hell in others. There wasn't any snow down here in the city, though it was still plenty cold.

Shoving one hand further into the pocket of his jacket, Cole wondered how the damn thing had withstood so many blasts. Then again, the sky scrapers all around them seemed equally damaged. And yet here they all stood. All steel and glass and concrete. All manmade monstrosities that would linger for God knew how long.

Shifting his eyes to the right, he absorbed the nervous impatience of at least half a dozen other men. They were all like him. Dirty, disheveled, hungry looking. Some had guns, all had knives. They'd come into the city around the same time, or at least that's what Uriah Linfield's security force thought.

The truth was, Cole and Cookie had been here for quite

a bit longer. Slinking and sneaking and blending in. And it was a good thing, too. Because now the two of them knew what came next. They knew about the "trust check" and the entrance interview that each new man had to go through in order to stay.

They knew that some big bastard called Jameson would come out and talk to them. They knew most men would be allowed to stay, and a handful of others asked to leave. Well... really they were made to leave and then buried in a field if they ever came back.

It was an efficient system at least, Cole had to give them that much. How else could you manage so many men in one place? And there were thousands upon thousands here. It was incredible, and slightly sickening.

Around him now, the security guards began murmuring and shuffling their feet. Lowering his eyes, Cole saw what made them squirm. Here came the head of security now, out from the depths of a parking garage that lay just across the narrow street.

Jameson was tall, with broad shoulders and a calm demeanor. Cole and Cookie had watched him before, tracked him even. They hadn't yet caught a glimpse of Uriah, though, Hannah's brother. Word was he'd been spending a lot of time underground lately, or in a nearby jail.

That was the next item on Cole's list, find the jail, surveil it. But not today. Today he had to be accepted into Linfield society.

The other guards, all dressed in their clean black fatigues, straightened up before forcing the mass of new men against the flat of the building. With his back pressed against the cold glass of some abandoned office, Cole chanced a quick look up and over.

Cookie was hidden up there somewhere, rifle poised and ready. All it would take was Cole's signal. A hand up to his head or even in the air, then there would be bodies dropping like flies. It wouldn't matter if Cole was armed or not.

And that extra layer of protection had his pulse easing up a bit if not quieting down altogether. Because the next step here involved him handing over his own rifle, calmly. Cole hoped he wouldn't need to start a blood bath. He hoped he would pass into favor and be able to scope the city in more detail, for longer. He hoped to track down Liam. He hoped Liam wasn't buried in a field just southwest of here.

And then of course there were Hannah and Lena. Finding them and the infamous car that took them. If Cole could locate Liam, then he'd have the best tracker around to help. It was a lot of ifs... but also a lot of hope. Cole hadn't had so much of either in months.

"Morning gentlemen." Jameson came to a stop before them, his blue eyes darting across the array of new faces.

"Morning," most of them murmured back. The tension was clear. There was so much riding on this exchange for all of them.

"As most of you know, you have entered the territory held by Uriah Linfield. This includes the city you're standing in and extends to the Great Salt Lake to the west and the mountains to the east. The suburbs situated to the north and south of here will serve as the markers for those particular borders. If you are asked to leave, you will move past those boundaries and not return. Is that clear?"

"Clear," a few muttered, ducking their heads. Cole nodded, too.

"We enjoy order around here and a fair amount of quiet," Jameson went on, letting his gaze slide over the men slowly as he spoke. "There's no killing, no stealing and no hoarding. You can't claim an entire building for yourself. Take only what you need. Like back when your mommy was trying to teach you to play nice…you've got to *share*."

This last comment got a bit of a chuckle from the group. Cole forced a smile.

"We've got food stores, fresh water and a daily ration of firewood. To get these things you'll be expected to work. During the growing season, that means long hours. If you can't handle it, then walk away now."

Jameson paused. No one moved.

"If you're going to live here, then you have to commit some time out of your busy schedules to train as a soldier. You'll belong to Uriah Linfield and will follow the commands of his officers. When we say wake up, you wake up. When we say march, you march. When we say fight, you fight. Questions?"

"How often is that?" One man asked.

"How often is what?" Jameson narrowed his eyes, took a step closer.

"The marching and the fighting."

"We haven't done any yet," Jameson qualified. "But someday we will. Anything else?"

"What if we break the rules?" A younger man asked, his eyes shifting.

"Then we shoot you," Jameson's answer was quick, nonplussed, causing the others to chuckle nervously.

"What about the women?" The first man spoke out again, causing Cole and every other man to turn and look at him.

"What women?" Jameson countered, then gave a rare smile. "Yes, the rumors are true. There are healthy women still alive, thousands of them and eventually we will work to set them free. That's what this is all about."

Gesturing around him, Jameson let the others murmur and exclaim and whisper to one another as his words sunk in. Women. The Wall. Everything Cole had heard over the past half a year was true. And Hannah's brother, the one she absolutely refused to talk about, he was up to his eyeballs in army building. Well.

Cole sucked in a breath, maybe big brother would like to know where his baby sister had gotten off to. Maybe he'd move his fucking army to hell and back to find her. Might be worth a shot, Cole figured as Jameson stopped in front of him.

"I'm going to need you to turn over your weapons," he said and held out both hands.

For just a moment, Cole hesitated. It was a hair breadth, not even a full second, but it was there just the same. This was something you never, ever did, not willingly. You didn't give up your firepower, not to any man. But this was quiet, covert work, an undercover job of sorts. He was doing this to get Hannah back, and to do that, Cole would give up anything.

Quick as you please, he shrugged his trusty black weapon off his shoulder and handed it over, followed by a single knife. Jameson grabbed at the strap of the gun and the blade, then handed them both to the guard just beside him. Looking Cole up and down, Jameson kept his hands extended.

Cole cleared his throat, then emptied his pockets, lifted his jacket and shirt, turned a small circle. Hell, he even unlaced and stepped out of his boots. When Jameson appeared satisfied, he moved down the line.

As the man next to him gave up a series of small knives, Cole stepped back into his boots. Crouching low, he began to work the laces up and secure them in place. Just when he'd finished, Cole felt a ripple pass through the others. Glancing up, he saw Jameson turn his head to look and so Cole followed his line of sight.

Striding out from the parking garage, like a blast from the past, was a man Cole knew. His face was just the same, set in a grim line beneath a short crop of golden hair. If he'd have been closer, Cole knew the man's eyes would be brown, he knew his fine white teeth would be straight and perfect as his clothing would be perfect, as his words would be careful and calculated.

Because the man that drew near to them, the one that caused the Linfield guards to stand at attention, was Cole's own personal nightmare. Command Officer Twelve. Because they never used names. Because it wasn't safe for the leaders of the Nor East Side Soldiers to be identifiable, accountable.

No, no need to be responsible for your orders, your actions. But in the end, all of that smoke and mirror bullshit didn't prevent Cole from knowing the truth. *He* didn't need a name to recognize the man who'd ordered that suicide mission. Cole didn't need a name to remember the man who'd ordered Chan to kill him.

Nope. Cole only needed a face. And unlike his poor Hannah, Cole's memories were still clear as day. And a face is what he had.

Slowly, Cole rose to his feet and stood stock still. His hands itched and quivered for his weapon. If he slid his eyes just to his right, he knew he'd see his rifle dangling from the back of some guard standing not three yards away. Too far. Much too fucking far.

As Command Officer Twelve approached, the others all stared at him, too. They all knew him, or if they didn't, he drew enough attention to make them realize they should. Cole couldn't take his eyes off the fucker. He just couldn't.

And he felt the instant his old superior connected the dots. It was in his eyes, the flash of knowledge, the glance to the his left, the motion to Jameson, the frown.

"You have the names of these men?" Command Officer Twelve asked, coming to a stop in front of Cole.

"Not yet," Jameson answered, shifting his attention back around.

Inhaling, Cole studied the face of the man he'd trusted for years. The one who he met with over and over, to get his missions, to offer his reports, to strategize. Try as he might, he almost still couldn't believe it. But there the orders had been, clear as day on Chan's scanner.

And then again in that South West Soldier building down south. Every computer, every monitor had been splashed with their fucking code. How long had Officer Twelve been working for the other side? Did he have a side? How long had he plotted to exterminate Cole and the others? His team? Fuck. This. Fucking. Prick.

"How'd you do it?" Officer Twelve lowered his voice, spoke just to Cole, like he had so long ago.

"You mean survive your suicide mission?" Cole asked, biting back every bit of energy that surged and roared and demanded he gut this fucker right here, right now. "Or would you rather know how I survived your extermination order?"

"I didn't give that order."

"The fuck you didn't." Cole stepped closer. The toes of his boots bumped Officer Twelve's. He could breathe the guy's exhaled air, they were that close.

And in the background, everyone was all static. Cole knew Jameson was saying something, that the others were circling, that guns were drawn and aimed at him. He just didn't care. All he had in this moment, he had for this man, for the betrayal of it all. For the four down south. For Chan and his guilt, and Cookie and his guilt, hell even for himself and his unnecessary fucking guilt.

"*You* are the double agent," Cole whispered. "It was you all along." *And now it's time for you to die.*

Cole couldn't hear what Officer Twelve was saying anymore, the blood pounding in his head was so loud.

Flexing his fingers, he began to raise his arm. It was slow at first. At least it felt slow to him. For he knew that when his hand reached his head, or anywhere near it, Cookie would take that shot and waste this asshole.

After that, Cole would get a bullet to the head too, no doubt. Maybe it would come from Jameson, or one of the other guards.

So this was it. A mutual death. One much deserved.

Cole didn't let himself brood or think too much about it. He just knew if this was the last thing he did, then he'd fulfill a glorious purpose in the end.

And Hannah? God. Cookie would push on, surely. He'd find Liam, they'd get her back, or whatever was left of her.

Cole figured that he'd see her on the flip side. Well... if God let men like him go to where good people like Hannah ended up, then he'd see her. It was more likely that the Almighty would let his Han give him an occasional visit in hell. Yeah, that was much more likely, Cole reasoned, and smiled.

HE KEPT HIS HAND WRAPPED AROUND THAT DAMN DOOR handle for much too long. With his eyes closed, Liam felt the press of cold metal in his palm as Hannah finally slid home the lock on the door. She'd taken long enough, but now she was safe. Her and Lena. Shit.

Sucking in a breath, Liam opened his eyes and backed away. For a long moment, he surveyed the steel door at the end of the long dark corridor. It was solid. The underground bunker would hold, just like Uriah said, no matter what. And wasn't that the kicker of it? Hannah's brother was right. Despite the apology and all that crap, he could keep the women safe, comfortable, alive when no one else really could.

And that's what Liam would tell Cole, when he finally found his old friend. Because he *would* find him, eventually. The guy had to be out of his mind right now, Liam thought. He couldn't imagine returning to the compound to find everyone dead and the girls gone. Hell... Cole was definitely in absolute hell right now and Liam had to dig him out of it.

Turning on his heel, he hesitated only a moment longer as the subdued sounds of a piano began to play. It was another sad song. So damn sad. He could almost see Hannah sitting there, her hands floating over the keys. When he'd first walked in, she'd been so beautiful like that, she hadn't seemed real. Maybe the past twenty-four hours was just a dream, he thought.

With a shake of his head, Liam strode away. His boots echoed off the concrete floors as he made his way through a series of doors. The final one opened onto the terrace above the bowling alley. Men were inside, enjoying the fruits of their labor. The smell of beer and sweat and nachos wafted in the air, like it always did. Liam ignored it and pressed on.

Out in the parking garage, the fading light in the distance beckoned him. It was late in the day, almost dusk in fact, though the sun still shined. Liam wasn't exactly sure of the protocol, but he figured he should give Uriah a heads up that he was leaving.

Despite everything that had gone down, Liam knew Hannah's brother would not want him to go. He might not approve of Liam with his sister, but the interrogation job he'd been doing wasn't quite complete. Uriah wanted more.

But Liam simply couldn't wait any longer. Maybe he'd tell Jameson he was going out, then he could dodge the typical flood of questions that would flow from the boss man. He didn't want to say he was going after Cole. He didn't want to give the guy any more information than he had to. That was rule one of interrogator school.

Get more than you give. Don't give.

Liam almost smiled. Then he reached street level.

What he saw before him had the smirk falling right off his face.

"Cole!" Liam shouted it, then broke into a run. "Stop! Cole! Don't fucking do it!"

Guns that were aimed at Cole's head soon swiveled toward Liam, then back. Jameson was yelling, the security crew was tense as fuck. Liam recognized all of them, so that was good. To them, he belonged, he could be trusted. They maybe wouldn't shoot him, or at least they'd hesitate.

"Cole!" Liam screamed again, but his friend didn't seem to hear him. That arm just kept creeping up his side, poised to give a signal. *The* signal of death.

Uriah was toe to toe with him. They were practically kissing at this point, from what Liam could tell. And then Hannah's brother was glancing over at him, then down at Cole's arm and Liam knew he recognized what was about to happen. That's when all hell broke loose.

Uriah tackled Cole, wrapping his heavy arms around Cole's body, keeping that signal hand down. They hit the ground with a thud and then the shot rang out.

One. Loud. Boom.

The echo down the narrow street with its high rise buildings made the single bullet seem like a dozen. And then there really were a dozen as Uriah's security force opened fire.

Liam dropped to the ground, covered his head. The

unlucky fuckers crouching next to the building were riddled with bullets. Some managed to run, some didn't. Blood splattered and poured and Jameson was shouting.

Laying his face to one side, Liam peered up and saw Uriah and Cole. They were struggling, wrestling, rolling over one another. Jameson was standing above them, pointing his weapon this way and that, he couldn't get a clear shot. Liam couldn't let him.

Leaping to his feet, Liam raced over, motioning at the others with his hands, then up to where he figured Cookie was poised to drop Jameson.

"Stand down!" He ordered it, his chest heaving on each word. He could only hope that Cookie recognized him. "Sniper fire! Sniper fire! Get down now!"

This got Jameson's attention. He flattened himself to the pavement as did the others and began to belly crawl for cover, though there wasn't much around. In the middle of it all, Uriah and Cole grunted and swore at each other.

Coming to stand over them, Liam took a quick inventory before diving in for the gun they were battling over.

"Fuck!" Liam threw his weight down on them, added his hands to the mix. "Cole, fucking stop. It's me. Uriah. Shit. Let. Me. Fucking. Have it!"

With a final tug, Liam jerked the gun free and fell back. Unfortunately that didn't stop the battle before him. Uriah flipped over, Cole was on top, then the reverse. They kept at it, throwing punches now that the gun wasn't an option.

Liam glanced at the glinting windows of the surrounding buildings and stood up. Waving his hands he turned slowly, trying to let Cookie get a good look at his face. He motioned again for a stand down, not sure if it would fly, then stomped back over to the fight on the ground.

"Jameson," Liam called. "We've got to separate them."

"And get dropped?" Jameson hissed, his eyes shooting to the very same buildings high above them.

"As long as you don't try to kill Cole," Liam reasoned. "You should be alright."

"Should be?" Jameson was incredulous.

"Save your boss!" Liam taunted, trying to get a reaction.

"He's your boss too, asshole!" Jameson countered, but then made a low dash forward.

Darting over, Jameson wrapped his arms around Uriah while Liam made a grab for Cole. With the two of them heaving, they managed to separate the pair. Jameson just kept dragging Uriah towards the parking structure, while Liam pressed Cole up against the nearest building.

Chest heaving, face flushed, Cole panted, his fierce eyes still tracking his prey as it was led away from him. For a moment, Liam panted along with him. There was blood covering his friend's clothes, the front of Cole's shirt, his hands, his face, his hair. Someone was hit. One of them, or maybe both, Liam thought.

"Lee?" Cole's voice came out shaky all of a sudden, and Liam met his eyes.

"Cole, damn it," he exhaled the words before crushing his buddy against him. "You come all this way to die in front of me?"

"Hannah," Cole choked on the word.

"I know." Liam held him tighter. "He has her. Her brother has her, she's safe."

"Wha-" Cole's knees buckled as he worked to shove Liam back.

"That guy you just tried to smoke is Uriah Linfield." Liam eased back, ran a hand through his hair. "He's Hannah's brother and he's got her stashed in a bunker over there."

Jerking his thumb behind him, Liam watched the shock drain the color from Cole's face. His friend's eyes danced to the entrance of the parking garage, then back to Liam.

"That guy is Command Officer Twelve. He ordered the suicide mission. He ordered my assassination."

"What?" Liam's eyes narrowed before he glanced over his shoulder.

Just under the protection of the garage, Jameson was pressing his hands to Uriah's shoulders, holding him down. The others were zipping across the street now. A few radios crackled and snapped. One announced the need for a medic. Uriah Linfield had been shot.

"I hope he bleeds out," Cole muttered.

"No, you don't." Liam's eyes snapped back to Cole. "She'll never forgive you if you kill her brother. Trust me, I've wanted to."

"You've seen her?" Cole's eyes grew big before he cleared his throat and ducked his head. "I thought. I thought she was dead. Or..."

"His team got her and Lena." Liam grabbed Cole's shoulder, shook it a little. "They've been fine this whole time."

"I'm not fucking crying." Cole sniffed, pressed his hands to his face. "If that's what you're thinking, I'm not."

"I know."

"Gentlemen," a man's voice announced. Liam felt the harsh tip of a barrel press into the back of his skull, then another cross his line of vision and center on Cole. "Looks like you'll both be coming with us."

"Alright," Liam responded quickly, there were three soldiers flanking them. At least that's how many he could see.

Raising both his hands in the air, Liam hoped Cole would get the hint. Now wasn't the time to blast their way out of here. Cole had no gun, Cookie had undoubtedly ditched his post by now and Liam's array of weapons were currently being lifted from his body.

After a moment's hesitation wherein Cole's blue eyes flashed, he too raised his hands and placed them on top of his head.

"Have to say that took me by surprise," the man admitted. Liam recognized the voice as belonging to a guy named Roger. They'd worked together over the past months on Linfield security detail. "Didn't figure you for a turncoat, Liam."

"I'm not," Liam countered, but let the guy cuff him. "This is all a misunderstanding."

"Is it?" Roger again.

Keeping one hand looped tightly around Liam's elbow, he motioned for another guy to move forward and hand-cuff Cole. Liam held his breath, willing his friend to simply comply. The way Cole's eyes snapped and his muscles tensed, Liam knew it was the last thing he wanted to do.

Letting anyone detain you wasn't wise. Hell, it went against everything they'd done in the past five years. But this time they didn't have a choice. Hannah was just across the street. There was only one way to see her again, and it involved staying alive.

"Yeah," Cole said finally, turning his back to the soldier and offering his wrists quietly. "A misunderstanding."

Liam exhaled and as they were led away he allowed himself to hope.

He hoped like hell they were going to be detained until Uriah or Jameson could question them. He hoped like hell Uriah survived. He hoped like hell they weren't being led out to that field just outside the city.... the one where problem men went and became problems no more.

SHE WAS ONLY ABLE TO PLAY THE FIRST FEW CHORDS OF THE song, after that Hannah found she couldn't go on. Folding her arms down over the smooth ivory and black keys, she slumped forward. The piano pressed against her forehead, dug into the soft flesh of her arms and let out a last echo from the depressed keys.

Several sheets of music broke loose and fluttered to the ground below her feet. She could see them land in disarray and couldn't help feeling similar.

All the parts of her life were out of order. Like the pages, they were overlapping, off center, out of place. She couldn't recall the last time she felt in control. She couldn't recall the last time she felt things were okay. Maybe back at the compound in that rare slice of time when she, Cole and Liam all knew their place, had all agreed to their respective roles. How long ago was that? Seemed like too long all of a sudden.

"He'll come back," Lena's voice crept into the space,

causing Hannah to raise her head. "He just needs time to process, I think. He just doesn't know how to handle it."

"It?" Hannah frowned, brushing the hair from her eyes.

"Being happy," Lena supplied. "Feeling love. He doesn't know how to deal with it."

Nodding, Hannah blew out a breath and let her gaze travel haphazardly over the library. So many neat, perfectly bound books, the space was beautiful. If only she could keep herself feeling the way this room looked. Maybe then she'd know better how to act, how to take back her own life.

Giving her head a slight shake, Hannah looked back to Lena. Her eyes were all red-rimmed. Her life wasn't exactly going as planned either.

"And what about you?" Hannah asked her. "Are you and my brother..."

"We'll be fine." Lena offered a tentative smile. "He kept telling me to stand up for myself... I guess that's not what he had in mind."

Hannah huffed a short laugh before pressing her fingers over her eyes. "No, I don't think it was. But I'm proud of you. I guess I wish I would've done it, but I just can't seem to do anything like that against Uri."

"I know, it's so hard." Lena crept forward, leaning a hand on the piano's shiny black surface. "He's been more of a dad to you than a brother. That's why he's so overprotective. He still sees you as a little girl."

"I still feel like one," Hannah acknowledged. "Whenever I'm around him."

"I'll talk to him about it," Lena offered.

"No." Hannah's brow furrowed. "Back when I couldn't remember, it was like I was a different person. I really liked being *her*."

"Yeah." Lena smiled. "That Hannah was pretty badass."

"Yeah she was." Hannah smiled back. "So I'll talk to Uri myself. I know he'll love me no matter what but I just don't want to disappoint him."

"You won't."

"Ugh, he's got me so twisted up." Hannah nibbled on her lip. "I guess he'd of made a really great dad."

"You think so?" Lena's eyes lit a moment before darting away.

"Lena." Hannah frowned, watching as her brother's woman squirmed. "That look. Why do you look like that all of a sudden?"

"Like what?" Lena cleared her throat, drummed nervous fingers on the piano.

"When I mentioned Uri being a good dad." Hannah narrowed her eyes. "You looked guilty. Wait... you aren't..."

"No," Lena rushed, putting out her hands in defense. "I mean, I'm not sure really. It's too soon."

"But... what? How is that possible? We all have IUDs."

"I removed it."

"You..." Hannah's mouth dropped. "Does Uri know?"

"No." Lena shook her head. "I didn't tell him... but he never asked. He never said anything one way or the other."

"Why would you..." Hannah gestured around them. "Take that kind of a risk?"

"It's so safe here." Lena stepped forward, pleading. "There's food and heat and water. No one gets in here."

"But-"

"I know it's hard to understand," Lena interrupted. "But I- I- I wanted to die for so long. When I was... you know. And then after, I was always so scared and lost in the... in the evil. And then one day I woke up here and I realized this was the only chance maybe I'd ever get. I want to only focus on love. I want to only feel love now, to feel *life* now."

Hannah pursed her lips as Lena's hand drifted down, stroking at her flat belly. It was true, Hannah didn't understand. The idea of getting pregnant and bringing another life into this world as it was now, seemed beyond frightening to her. But then Lena had endured so much worse than Hannah ever had. Who wouldn't want to focus on a new beginning? Who wouldn't want to forget their past?

Taking a few steps forward, Hannah embraced her friend. If anyone deserved a memory swipe, it was Lena. They swayed there a moment, Lena clinging and hiccuping on Hannah's shoulder; surrounded by luxury and safety and everything that had marked their whole lives before. Maybe this was going to be okay. Well, it was going to be what it was anyway.

"Promise me you won't say anything," Lena whispered.

"I promise," Hannah murmured, telling herself there wasn't anything really to keep secret... yet.

Behind them, the front door banged open. Lena cringed and Hannah glanced over her shoulder. A flood of boots entered the space, accompanied by the shouts of men, many men. With a frown, Hannah jogged to the threshold of the library and stared out into the hall.

Half a dozen soldiers were squeezed into the tight space with Jameson behind them, shouting orders. They were carrying something between them, something… big. Beside her, Lena sucked in a breath and clutched at Hannah's arm.

"It's nothing," Uriah gasped, writhing on a stretcher suspended amongst his men. "Put… me down."

"No," Jameson's answer was clipped as he turned his attention to the soldiers. "Take him to the back bedroom, third door on your left."

The herd of noise proceeded past the entrance to the library as Uriah continued to protest. Hannah's gut dropped as she watched him twist against the straps that held him to the board. There was so much blood. He was covered in bright red blood.

"Get back in there." Jameson turned to the two women, a radio held in one hand. "I'm locking you in."

"Uriah!" Lena called suddenly. "No. What? What happened? Uriah!"

Breaking forward, she made as if to follow him down the hall. Jameson blocked her easily. In his hand, the radio burst with crackling voices. It said something about having two men in custody and a doctor five minutes out.

Hannah's throat felt so tight and clogged all of a sudden. What happened out there? What happened to Uri? Where was Liam? Craning her neck, she tried to see past Jameson's hulking figure.

"You too, Hannah Mae." Jameson pressed them further into the room. "Stay in there."

"What happened?" Lena demanded again.

Hannah couldn't find the words to speak but her eyes darted up to Jameson's face. He looked drained. Static burst again on the radio and Jameson held it to his mouth, all the while keeping his eyes locked with Hannah's.

"Take them both to the jail," he instructed. "Do nothing until I get there."

"What happened?" Hannah whispered it this time.

"Uriah's been shot," Jameson answered. "Your boyfriend was in on it, not sure how yet."

"No." Hannah shook her head. "No, Liam wouldn't do that. You're wrong! You've got it wrong!"

Pushing at his chest, Hannah fought a flood of fear. Jameson didn't hardly move. Clasping a hand over hers, Jameson held on tight, willing her to believe him. But it just couldn't be true. Could it?

Then Lena was ducking around them. Skirting quickly around Jameson's big body, she headed out the library door at a dead run.

"Lena!" Jameson called, dropping Hannah's hand. "Shit."

Spinning on his heel, the big soldier turned and tore off after the little dark-haired woman. Hannah was soon to follow. Her brother. He'd been shot. Would Liam shoot him?

No, he wouldn't do it. He wouldn't.

Running down the hall, Hannah's breath hitched and burned in her lungs. Jameson was pounding away in front of her, the sound of him cursing came to buzz in her ears.

Suddenly his big body slid to a stop in front of her, his arms catching Lena by the waist just before she breached Uriah's bedroom door.

Hannah skidded to a stop behind them. Lena started shrieking.

Inside the bedroom, Uriah about lost his shit. The sound of her calling for him was too much. He was swearing and yelling and several soldiers were backing out of his bedroom, their heads on a swivel between their bleeding boss and the appearance of not one but two women. Hannah recognized one soldier from a prior dinner but not the others. They stood stock still, shock etched clearly into the lines of their faces.

Jameson's radio crackled again, but he wasn't able to answer it.

After a moment's hesitation, he released Lena. She brushed past the other men and into the room, the simple dress she wore fluttered out behind her body. Her hair was loose, like a tangle of soft silk. One soldier reached out as she went by, touching the black strands as they slipped quickly through his fingers.

"You three," Jameson barked at the men, his face turning to stone. "Up against the wall. And you, go open the front door for the doctor, then post up outside."

Reaching beside him, Jameson grasped at Hannah blindly before shoving her further behind his body. She ducked her head and complied.

"I told you he was telling the truth," Jameson informed the soldiers. "There are living women out there, many more than this. Now you know. But you keep your hands to yourselves when you're in here and you keep your mouths shut when you leave. Got it?"

"Yes, Sir," they muttered it together, their eyes still staring.

"Hannah Mae," Jameson spoke her name, but he didn't turn to find her.

Holding out his hand, he simply waited, keeping his gaze focused on the soldiers. Without a second thought, she placed her hand in his. He held on tight and in three steps he had them both inside the bedroom.

The backboard had been placed on the king sized bed in the center of the room. Uriah was still strapped to it, but he had calmed considerably. Lena was sitting beside him, her head bent, one hand gripping his arm, the other held against his cheek.

Her brother murmured quietly to his woman.

Reassuring words poured from his mouth even as Hannah's eyes traveled over his blood soaked clothes and the strained features of his face. She staggered a bit, leaning into Jameson who pulled her in tighter.

"Get two chairs in here," Jameson barked at the last remaining soldier who then scurried out.

Lifting the radio to his mouth once more, Jameson began issuing orders, calling for the doctor, demanding an update on the jail. Hannah squeezed her eyes shut. She didn't want her brother to die and she didn't want Liam to be the one responsible.

In the distance, there was shuffling, doors opening, closing, boots stomping. Then the doctor breached the bedroom and the requested chairs followed him. Jameson grabbed one, shoved it in the corner of the room and sat Hannah in it. Crouching in front of her, he tipped her chin to him. His face was grim.

"You will not leave my side, do you understand?"

Hannah's eyes left his face, searching for the doctor. Her brother was cursing now. Lena was shushing him.

"He'll live." Jameson drew her attention back to him. "But if you get hurt while he's like this, then I won't. Got it?"

"Yeah," Hannah stumbled on the word, ducking her head. "I got it."

"Promise me," Jameson demanded.

The words resonated inside her head, dinging around and making her heart ache. It was the second promise she'd had to make in the past five minutes. She much preferred the loveliness of the first one.

"I promise," she said.

CHAPTER TWENTY-THREE_
COLE

THE METAL BARS OF THE CELL WERE COLD. COLE SLID HIS hands down one, then squeezed. This was a city jail so it was pretty small. Nothing like a county facility or even a state prison. It had been constructed for your run of the mill processing stuff. Drunks, assaults. Local crimes that would have a criminal passing through, not staying long term.

Stepping back, he surveyed the gray concrete floor with its many splintered fractures and cracks working this way and that. Off to one side, two metal bed frames were attached to the wall. In the back, there was a stainless steel sink and toilet. They no longer worked.

Above his head, the solitary light fixture in the ceiling was dark. This place didn't have electricity, and it didn't have heat either. Slapping his hands around his body, Cole jumped up and down, watched his breath puff out before him.

"You're wasting your energy," Liam's voice spoke from the cell next door.

"I've got some to spare," Cole countered, but stopped his jumping to shake out his arms and legs.

"That's the adrenaline."

"I forgot what a pleasure you are to be around," Cole countered, but found himself smiling.

Smiling. He hadn't had a reason to feel halfway close to this good in so long. Hannah was alive. Lena was alive. Liam was alive. Shit, despite their surroundings, today was a great fucking day. And Cookie was still out there, lurking.

"I missed you, too," Liam's voice dropped low. Cole could almost imagine his friend leaning his head back against the wall, closing his eyes.

"You should never have left." Cole stood still, remembering.

"I know it," Liam agreed. "But she didn't want me anymore... I thought."

Cole nodded, dropping his head. His chest tightened, he couldn't help it. Did that mean...? He couldn't finish the thought in his own mind. All he'd wanted since he saw Chan's face frozen in the snow was to find Hannah safe. Now she was. He hadn't let himself go beyond that. Hadn't cared.

"So, you two..." Cole trailed off, cleared his throat.

Liam, as usual let the silence drag on. Cole listened to his oldest friend shifting around in his cell, envisioned him pacing, trying like hell to get comfortable. But there was no comfort to be found in here. Not physically from the imprisonment, nor mentally.

In Cole's mind, this talk between them was long overdue. Might as well have it now, before the next thing came for them, whatever that thing might be.

"This is awkward as hell," Liam said finally.

"Yeah, well we're in love with the same woman." Cole swallowed. There, he'd said it.

"I think..." Liam sucked in a breath, blew it out slowly. "I think she can't choose. I think she doesn't want to choose."

Cole bobbed his head, jumped up and down again a few times. He felt relief. Relief at the idea Hannah still wanted him. That was all he could think of, all he was worried about. Although he *should* be concerned about her brother. He should be freaked out about being locked up, about Uriah asshole Linfield actually being his Command Officer.

But again, it was Han that dominated him, consumed his thoughts, dictated his actions. He had to get to her, convince her never to leave him. And Liam? Well, he didn't want to lose his best friend again either. He needed to get both of them to stay with him, needed to get all of them back to the compound, make it safe again, like before.

"Will you make her choose?" Cole asked. Walking to the bars, he looped his hands around the cold metal rungs once more.

"Will you?" Liam countered.

Silence. The two of them waited there.

Darkness was quickly falling outside. The cells they

were in didn't have windows, but across the way, there were a few thick glass windows high up in the wall. They weren't the kind that opened. Through them, you could see the side of another building, but just barely now.

"What about…" Liam trailed off, sucked in a breath. "What about the deal we had before. You know, the one she came up with."

"The sharing thing?" Cole frowned. They hadn't ever really let that work had they?

"Yeah, but… like more permanent maybe," Liam mumbled the last words.

Cole smiled. "You proposing to me, Lee?"

"You're an asshole, you know that?" Liam bit out the words, but then groaned. "But we *are* in Utah. What was that word they used? You know, with all the wives and stuff."

"Polygamy," Cole supplied. "But it wasn't for multiple guys."

"Well," Liam countered. "Kind of a chick shortage if you haven't noticed."

"Yeah." Cole furrowed his brow. "Yeah, I noticed."

"So they made it work."

"Because they thought God wanted them to do it like that," Cole reasoned.

"Does it matter why you do it?"

"I guess not."

"So… could you?" Liam pressed.

"Could you?" Cole countered. Did he want this? Was he okay with this?

"It'd be hard." Liam sighed, shifted around again. Cole

could hear the sound of his jacket rustling, then settling.

"What isn't hard these days?" Cole asked finally. Wait, now he was the one convincing Lee?

"Yeah," Liam agreed. "No harder than walking out of here alive."

"Good point." Cole frowned, then glanced around him.

The adrenaline was wearing off and reality was sinking in. He'd gotten Uriah Linfield shot, in the middle of a city owned by same. And now he and Liam were here locked in an old jail. No guns. No knives. No heat. No water. Huh. Suddenly the Hannah arrangement seemed like a piece of cake.

"I guess," Cole began, squeezing the bars hard once before letting go. "I guess it depends on what Han wants. I could do it for her, if she wants to... then I could."

"Yeah, whatever she wants then."

Cole pursed his lips. He thought back to the past month. The agony of not knowing. He remembered what it felt like to leave Liam in that city. To just walk away from his brother, then come home to find the rest of them dead. It was unbearable. Hannah and Lena had been gone and Cole was so alone in it all, without Liam to help. He hadn't known if maybe Liam was dead somewhere, too.

"But, I would want you to stay close either way," Cole added. "I don't want to lose track of you again. You're my family, Lee. I can't do it again."

Stillness.

Utter quiet.

All Cole could hear was the pump of his own heart, the rush of breath in and out of his lungs. The burning around his eyes, he dismissed as him being too tired. They weren't tears wanting to come through. No way.

"I guess we're in it then," Liam said finally.

"Yeah," Cole cleared his throat, looked up at the ceiling. "I guess we are."

TREMBLING BONE DEEP COLD. HOW COULD ANYONE SLEEP with their body vibrating constantly, trying to keep warm? Cole didn't know how it was possible, but it was. He'd closed his eyes, slumped down against the wall and sleep simply took hold of him.

Hours later, in the pitch of night, a sound woke him. At first, he wasn't sure if he'd dreamt it. A single shot, the thump of a body. But then his eyes were wide and his senses were on fire. He inhaled through his nose, the tang of too much metal greeted him.

"Hear that?" Liam hissed.

"Yeah," Cole answered.

Thank God, for a minute there he'd thought the worst. For a few precious seconds, he thought someone had come for Liam, killing him in the night without so much as a protest. But his buddy was still here and alive, that was good.

The sound of careful footsteps floated towards them. Cole held his breath, worked to calm himself down. Boots were placed as quietly as possible in the dark. Then there was a beam of light. Cole squinted and held up his hand as a flashlight passed over his cell.

"Boy-o," Cookie exhaled. "What sort of trouble you got us into, huh?"

"Cook, shit." Liam gasped in the cell next to him. "How the fuck did you get in here? Tell me you didn't waste the guys guarding this place."

"No," Cookie assured him, then grinned. "Just the one. The other two took off running when his body dropped between them."

Groaning, Liam lurched and shuffled in the cell next door. Cole smirked, rising to his feet. His bones cried out in protest, aching from the cold, but Cole ignored the feeling. Time to get out of here, he thought. His eyes traveled over Cookie's body, to both his hands and pockets.

"Where are the keys?" Cole asked, squinting.

"About that." Cookie sighed. "I figured they'd be at the front desk or even on the guy I dropped. No such luck. Any idea where they'd be?"

"Holy. Shit." Liam cursed. "You already shot Hannah's brother, and now you've killed another one of his men. We're so screwed."

"Hey." Cookie frowned. "Nice to see you too, you ungrateful bastard. And I didn't know it was Hannah's brother, only heard about it after. Plus, he's lucky you came out and ruined my shot. He'd be dancing with the devil right now if not."

"Well, Cookie..." Cole ran a hand down his face. "You don't happen to have a few sticks of dynamite on you, do you?"

"Nope."

"Great. That's just great."

HANNAH'S HEAD SHIFTED ON THE PILLOW. HER NECK WAS stiff and her back was sore from the few hours of sleep she'd gotten on the floor. Groaning, she rolled onto her back and rubbed at her eyes. Lena was asleep on the bed beside Uriah and the last time Hannah had checked, Jameson was positioned in a chair by the door.

The room was dimly lit, with a bedside lamp providing a small splash of light. Outside the door, soldiers roamed about the house. They paced the hallway, filled the living room and wandered the kitchen. The place was on lockdown and therefore, so was Hannah.

The good news was, Jameson had been right, Uriah would live. The bullet had grazed his upper arm, taking out a significant chunk of flesh, but not causing mortal injury. After the medical doctor finished cleaning it and applying a few stitches, Uriah was prescribed some pain medication and rest. The former he had staunchly refused, the later he accepted only because of Lena's insistence.

Hannah figured that her brother only laid down in the bed to placate his woman. It was happenstance that he ended up falling asleep, too. That's when Jameson had brought Hannah a few blankets and a pillow. She'd curled up in the corner and listened to the occasional static on his radio until she too had gone lights out.

But now she was awake, and she wasn't entirely sure why. It wasn't morning, her body told her that much. Lifting up on one elbow, Hannah peered over the top of the bed. Jameson was standing still in the doorway, facing out. It was open several inches.

The light from the hall fell into the room, casting a long shadow over the floor. He was talking to someone. Another soldier. Their whispers were heated.

Hannah held her breath, straining to listen.

"Give them to me," Jameson hissed.

Reaching out, he snatched something from the other man. The dark bundle clinked and clicked as Jameson held it tightly and thumbed through whatever it was. Keys maybe? Sounded like it.

"You sure he's dead?" Jameson again, this time with a sigh.

"Yes, Sir," the soldier answered before giving a quick duck of his head.

"Anyone else?"

"No, Sir."

"Alright." Jameson paused. Glancing over his shoulder at the bed, he frowned as he met Hannah's eyes. "Dismissed. Wait in the living room."

"Yes, Sir."

The soldier disappeared and Jameson shut the door. With a twist of his wrist, he locked it before rotating fully. Hannah watched him. His face was drawn, he was tired but steady. Swiping a hand down his face he approached Uriah's side of the bed and looked down.

"Tell me," Uriah's voice came out gravely, he'd been awake, too.

"Your sister's up." Jameson nodded towards Hannah, still crouched on the ground. "I've got a full team inside and another out tracking the shooter. We haven't found him, yet."

"You won't," Uriah commented. "If he is who I think he is, then you won't find him."

"Well-" Jameson exhaled. "Looks like he found us, relatively speaking. The jail's been hit. We lost Martinez there, but the others fled without injury."

"The keys?" Uriah pushed up to sitting and grimaced.

"We've got them," Jameson assured him. "All three sets are here, so our prisoners aren't going anywhere."

"You're certain?" Uriah pressed, glancing quickly at his bandaged arm.

"You should lie down." Jameson frowned. "The doctor-"

"Wasn't necessary," Uriah interrupted. "Like I said before, it was only a graze wound."

"You're bleeding," Jameson commented, and had Uriah cursing softly.

"Bring me a fresh bandage before she wakes up." Uriah bit his lip, his eyes sliding down to the sleeping figure beside him.

Hannah followed his gaze. Lena's breathing was even,

her dark hair splashed across the pillow. She was still out. At least one of them was.

"Hannah Mae," Uriah's voice settled on her as Jameson handed him a new swath of gauze and some tape. "You lied to me about who you'd been living with. I need you to tell me the truth now. What were their names? What did they look like?"

"Liam wouldn't have done this," Hannah pleaded.

Pushing up to her feet, she skirted the edge of the bed until she came to stand alongside Jameson. The big man looked down on her, his eyes frustrated, but said nothing. Hannah refocused on her brother, he'd pushed himself back against the headboard now. His fingers ripped at the soaked bandage, revealing the angry patch of flesh underneath.

"Just tell me," Uriah said calmly, keeping his eyes on her. "I'm not going to hurt your precious boyfriend. He's the only reason the shot landed here." Uriah tapped a finger close to his wound before swiping across his bare chest and stopping at his heart. "Instead of here."

Hannah sucked in a breath and bowed her head. Leaning forward, she braced both hands on the mattress. Had she really come that close to losing Uri? What had happened out there? And where was Liam?

Jameson cleared his throat and Uriah sighed. Hannah lifted her head, brushing quickly at the tears that threatened to fall.

"Can't you answer your brother?" Jameson asked. "Why are you protecting the men trying to kill him?"

"I'm not," Hannah hissed. "I would never-"

"Then tell us," Jameson insisted. "Who did you live with? Who was with Liam at the compound?"

"You don't understand," Hannah protested, looking from one man to the other. "They were good men, *are* good men. They wouldn't do this."

"Then they have nothing to hide," Uriah reasoned, his mouth set in a firm line. "Let me make this easier for you. How about I say a name and then you just nod your head? How about that?"

Hannah sat on the bed beside him and bowed her head. So much for being the Hannah from before. So much for being a badass who could defend the compound and lead a rescue. In here, in front of her brother, her loyalties were truly divided. The truth was, someone had shot Uriah and that someone was still out there, shooting more men. Hannah couldn't refuse him when he needed her.

"Let's start with an easy one," Uriah went on, seeming to take her submission for what it was, an agreement to participate. "I've heard you say his name before, but in all the chaos of the past few days, I haven't had time to talk with you about it. Cole Tanner. Did he live at the compound with you and Liam?"

Swallowing hard, Hannah nodded her head but kept her eyes averted.

"Alright." Uriah paused. "He was the lead of a unit under my command. It was maybe the best unit we had towards the end, but there were twelve guys in it. How many did you live with?"

"Eight," Hannah whispered it, feeling so incredibly guilty all of a sudden.

"Jameson," Uriah refocused his questioning. "How many did you leave at the compound?"

"Three men and one woman," Jameson answered. Hannah knew by *leave* they meant kill. Chan. Trey. Ryder. Flynn. The names pounded around inside her head, hammering at her heart.

"That leaves three more," Uriah confirmed. "Why weren't they all at the compound when our team hit?"

"Because they were going to get supplies." Hannah fisted her hands and pressed them over her eyes. "They took me in when I was starving and fed me, clothed me. Then they saved Lena and Flynn. We needed more food, more clothing, more everything. And Cole and the others went out to get it, okay? They left because of me and Lena. For *us*."

"I get it Hannah Mae," Uriah said softly. "And between you and Lena I can promise you I will keep all of that in mind. But I need this information. I need you to give it to me."

Nodding, Hannah dropped her hands back to her sides and studied the soft beige quilt beneath her.

"Another name then," Uriah continued. "How about Lawrence Smelt? Maybe they called him Larry?"

"No." Hannah's head popped up, her eyes darting between her brother and Jameson as they exchanged a glance. "I've never heard that name."

"He'd of been older than the rest of them by two decades," Uriah continued. "Maybe he had a nickname. Graying hair, real smart, but he wouldn't have talked like it at first."

"Cookie?" Hannah frowned, then nibbled at her lip. He was the only one who fit that description.

"Anyone else there like that?"

"No," Hannah blinked. "No one."

"Then that's him." Uriah looked up to Jameson. "He's the best sniper we had, I mean *the* best. We need him. We could really use him."

"You're kidding," Jameson huffed, then swore. "You want to bring him in... *alive?*"

"Yeah." Uriah smiled. "It's doable. You just need to bring in Byrne and Tanner. The old man won't be able to resist. He won't leave without them."

"Wait," Hannah's voice pitched, causing Lena to stir. "Tanner. You mean Cole? You have him? And Liam? Where are they? Are they hurt?"

Uriah glared at Hannah as Lena rolled over and blinked up at them. She hadn't meant to wake the other woman, but the mention of Cole had its affect. Hannah's heart kicked as her mind began to spin on overdrive. Cole. She hadn't seen him in months. She missed him like crazy. He must be so worried. Was he okay? Was Liam with him?

"Hey," Lena's sleepy voice entered the space. "You should be resting."

"I'm good," Uriah assured her, before gesturing to the fresh bandage. "See? No blood."

"Oh," Lena sighed, then stretched. "That's great, but why are you up? Jameson? Hannah Mae?"

"Just a little business," Uriah intercepted as Hannah went to open her mouth. "Jameson's going to prep the back room for a few new visitors so I've got to take a little tour around, okay?"

"What?" Lena pushed back her hair and rubbed at her eyes.

"You're going to go get Cole?" Hannah asked hurriedly. "And Liam?"

"Cole?" Lena sat up straighter. "He's here?"

"Oh, another one of your heroes?" Uriah's brow furrowed before he flicked his eyes up to Jameson. "We'll make sure to give him a warm welcome. Right?"

"Right," Jameson confirmed. "But that means you two will have to stay here while we go out. I'm going to lock you both in."

"But-"

"Wait-"

"Come on now," Uriah cut the women off with an easy sweep of his hand. Scooting to the side of the bed he barely hid a grunt of pain as he stood up and accepted a shirt from Jameson. "I'll be in the house the whole time but I've got to manage the soldiers here while Jameson steps out. You two just cozy up back in bed, okay?"

"You're not well, you need to-" Lena stopped short as Uriah bent over and silenced her with a kiss.

"Sleep," he instructed as he stepped back. "Both of you."

SLEEP DID NOT COME EASILY. OF COURSE, IT SEEMED everything surrounding Uriah did not come easy these days. Hannah paced in front of the bedroom door for awhile, occasionally pressing her ear against its surface. Men mumbled and strode back and forth, but none lingered close by.

"Come lay down with me," Lena called from the bed. "You're making me nervous and there's nothing you can do."

"It's Cole." Hannah turned, running her hands through her hair. "He's out there somewhere, and Cookie. Maybe Ace and Davey too, I don't know."

"Come on," Lena insisted. "I'm cold."

Huffing a breath, Hannah gave a last look to the door before crossing to the bed. Lena couldn't possibly be that cold, she thought. There were several heavy blankets and the house itself didn't fall below sixty-five degrees at night. Lifting the sheet, Hannah watched Lena scoot over to Uriah's side before sliding in beside her friend. Huddled together, they breathed in the quiet for a few moments.

"I told him their names," Hannah admitted finally. "I gave up Cole and Cookie."

"Hey," Lena shushed her. "It's okay."

"But what if... you know... they get hurt."

"Giving your brother a name isn't going to make a difference," Lena reasoned. "You're only making yourself upset. Let's talk about something else. Something happy."

"Something happy?" Hannah frowned, trying not to outright sneer.

"It's how I've been dealing with..." Lena trailed off. "It's what I do now, okay? When I start to have the flashbacks, then I just redirect. I just replace them with another thought."

"Is it working?" Hannah closed her eyes, felt Lena's fingers twine with her own. She could only imagine what Lena's mind was flashing back to. Months and months of horror.

"It helps." Lena sighed. "Uriah suggested it, sort of like a thought replacement therapy. It's easier now than in the beginning."

"God Lena, I'm so sorry."

"Something happy," Lena insisted, giving her hand a tight squeeze.

"Okay, okay." Hannah scrunched up her face, studied the ceiling. "This bed is soft."

"Yes, it is."

"And it's my turn to shower in the morning."

"Oh, I'm jealous of that."

"Your turn," Hannah said.

"Uriah isn't dying," Lena began. "And maybe I'll get to have a baby."

"Yeah." Hannah nibbled at her lip. "Those two are way better than mine."

They both smiled. The tightness in Hannah's chest eased.

"More happy," Lena insisted.

"More happy," Hannah echoed, closing her eyes. "When will you know? About the baby."

"I'm not sure, another week? Maybe more?"

"Will you tell him?"

"Of course." Lena paused before adding. "Eventually."

"Lena," Hannah warned.

"More happy."

"More happy, right." Hannah sighed. "Names. Baby names. What are you thinking?"

"Well, I was thinking Flynn for a girl and maybe Ian for a boy."

"Ian." Hannah's heart saddened. "That was Chan's first name?"

"Yeah."

"Those are the best names ever."

"They are."

"YOU'VE GOT TO GET OUT OF HERE, COOK," LIAM demanded. The old man was out of his mind. "The guards that got away will be heading back soon, and not alone."

"I'm not leavin' ya," Cookie countered. "I'll just post up outside and drop em' one by one."

"Better to wait until they bring us out first," Cole cut in. "Unless you're sure they've got the keys."

"No." Liam shook his head. "No. No. No. You two aren't hearing me. You've got to stop killing Linfield men."

The flashlight beam swung up from the ground and caught Liam dead in the face. Holding up a hand, Liam blinked against the immediate blindness and backed a step further from the bars of his cell.

"If I didn't know better," Cookie commented. "I'd say you've been converted Liam."

"I'll be loyal to Cole till the day I die," Liam spat, as Cook lowered the beam back down. "But I've been here a lot longer than either of you. There's more men here than you could kill in a lifetime, and Uriah's not going to give you another shot at him."

Grumbling, Cookie rubbed at his scruff of gray beard and looked towards Cole's cell. Just next door, Liam could practically hear the wheels turning inside his friend's head. They were up shit creek, never had a paddle, let alone a good boat. The city was huge and their apparent suicide mission had been blown all to hell, thanks to Liam.

"What do you suggest?" Cole asked finally. Liam exhaled.

"Cookie posts up outside, but only to monitor." Stepping up to the bars once more, Liam gripped the rungs in his hands. "You do not shoot anyone else. You just watch, got it? If it looks like they're going to kill Cole or me, then yeah, drop 'em. But you've got to be absolutely sure."

Cookie's eyes danced over to the cell next door a moment before traveling back to Liam. When the older man ducked his head, Liam knew Cole had given the okay.

"If I've learned anything, it's that Uriah has his hand in everything," Liam continued. Time was ticking, he had to keep this brief. "He's going to want to talk to Cole. He's going to want to talk to me. Not sure if he'll do it here, most likely not."

"Meaning they'll bring us to him?" Cole suggested.

"One way or another we'll be meeting up with him," Liam confirmed. "If we stop killing all his men, then I think we may just be able to talk ourselves out of this one."

"Since when have you preferred talking to cutting?" Cookie snorted.

"Since the man in charge has Hannah and Lena," Liam snapped. "That's when."

"Shit," Cookie swore, his face going slack from the shock of it. "They're here?"

"Yeah." Liam nodded. "He's had them the whole time. Now get the fuck out of here and don't show yourself until me or Cole comes to find you."

"If you don't see us for a month or more," Cole added. "Then bug out back to the compound, okay?"

"Don't know if I could do that last part," Cookie admitted. "But the first part I'll commit to."

Stepping forward, the older man shook Cole's hand, then reached for Liam through the bars. His hands were warm as they clasped Liam's flesh. Wherever he'd spent the first part of the night, it had a fire. Must be nice.

Fading back, Cookie disappeared out the way he'd come in. Quiet as you please, just the faint press of boots trailed off in the darkness. Not even a door could be heard closing. After a minute though, Liam felt for certain he was gone.

"You'll be loyal to me till the day you die, huh?" Cole asked, a hint of laughter in his voice.

"You doubt it?" Liam snapped, then ran a hand down his face.

"No," Cole's voice sobered up. "But if you had a choice... between me and her?"

"If you want me to walk away," Liam sucked in a ragged breath before continuing. "Then I will, Cole. Just say it and I'll do it."

"No," Cole was quick to answer. "That's not what I want."

"Okay. Alright." Groaning, Liam paced away, running one hand along the concrete wall of his narrow cell.

All that stuff he'd said? About talking their way out and not killing more men? He wasn't sure where it had all come from, or why he suddenly found this new person so hopeful inside of him.

Maybe it was that last time with Hannah; the way she hadn't wanted him to go. She left him wanting. Not that she hadn't always left him wanting, because she had. It was just that this time he knew he had to choose life.

His own life, Cole's life, Uriah's life. Hannah simply required it of him. So he would rise to the occasion. Do everything in his power to live, to help them all live.

"You know how you were talking before?" Cole's voice broke through the silence, a lilt of teasing in his tone. "About us being polygamists?"

"Cole," Liam warned, gritting his teeth. This was so not the time for shit talking.

"Well I accept," Cole's voice held a smile, Liam could practically see it.

"You're an asshole."

"No, seriously though," Cole continued, his voice dropping low. "I could do it. You've always been like a blood brother to me and I have this… this love for you. Not like that. I mean I don't love you like *that*. But… you know what I mean?"

This time Liam was the one smiling. He'd let Cole dangle and ramble and try to talk his way out of that one.

"You gonna help me out here?" Cole asked, exasperated.

"No," Liam answered. "No, I'm not."

SOMETIME JUST BEFORE DAWN, THE SOLDIERS CAME FOR them. Through the windows high up on the far wall, Liam could see a gray sort of tinge lifting the dark. Rolling his shoulders, he tipped his head first to the left and then to the right. His neck was stiff, his muscles all bound up from a night of restlessness in the frigid cell.

In the distance, a door slammed. The stomping of boots, so many boots, followed. The noises grew louder and louder as they approached. There was no way Cole wasn't awake. No way he wasn't tense with anticipation. The rush of adrenaline alone worked to heat Liam's blood, loosen his body, prepare it for what came next.

There were more men than he had expected, sweeping through the space, checking cells, pushing further into the jail. They would inspect each and every inch of the place before finally settling. Of course, it was Jameson's familiar face that Liam waited to see.

And that big fucker kept him waiting until the last boot stilled and the whole place flooded with quiet. Then he entered. Liam heard him stomp, stomp, stomping. The sound echoed and rolled as he drew closer.

Pressing his face up to the bars of the cell, Liam tracked Jameson's grand entrance. And boy was it grand. All of the soldiers were in blacked out fatigues, but Jameson completed the effect with a helmet, vest and AK slung over his shoulder.

Stepping back, Liam watched Jameson settle before him. Those massive arms crossed over his chest, his intense blue eyes narrowed, face grim. The only comforting thing about it was that Liam didn't have to look up. Jameson was still shorter than him, if only by an inch or so.

"Byrne," Jameson began.

"You know I don't answer to that," Liam countered. He'd long since decided to drop his father's name. He didn't need it. It wasn't him.

"Where's your other friend?" Jameson kept his eyes steady on Liam. "Or should I say, friends?"

"What friends?" Liam asked, causing Jameson's gaze to dart to the cell next to him, then back.

"Well, I believe that's Cole Tanner, your unit leader and life long buddy." Jameson smirked. "And of course Lawrence Smelt is sliding around here somewhere. Or maybe you'd remember him better if I called him Cookie."

Liam narrowed his eyes. Cookie. Where'd Jameson get that name from? It wasn't like they'd called him that during training and nicknames weren't sent back to Command on any reports. No. Jameson had been talking to someone. Hannah. The word jumped into Liam's brain as his gut pinched.

Seemed Cole'd been going through the same process as he shifted nosily in the cell next door.

"You questioned Hannah?" Cole accused, his voice rasping. "What the fuck did you do? I swear-"

"Relax." Jameson rolled his eyes. "I don't hurt women. Not that I had to, she came out with the information easily enough."

Liam swallowed the words he was about to say and could only pray Cole would do the same. After a string of mumbled curses, the jail fell once more to silence. Jameson tilted his head to the side, analyzing first Cole's over-reaction and then Liam's non-reaction.

Huffing a breath through his nostrils, Jameson rocked forward on his toes a beat before motioning behind him. A soldier stepped forward and presented him with two sets of black fatigues.

"We have a clothing change here for you boys," Jameson announced before shoving the material through the bars of the cell.

Liam frowned at his old uniform, ran his fingers over the material.

"You'll be cuffed along with half the guys in here, and with a helmet, you should blend right in. When we walk out of here together, your sniper buddy won't be able to tell you two apart from us. Should keep him from doing too much damage, right?"

Looking back into Jameson's face, Liam frowned. It wouldn't stop a good sniper from picking off the men who weren't cuffed. It was a risk, but one they were apparently willing to take.

"Time to strip down," Jameson instructed. "Uriah Linfield has a lot he wants to discuss."

CHAPTER TWENTY-SIX_
HANNAH

HER BROTHER DIDN'T LET THEM OUT FOR THE NEXT TWO days. Even though Hannah raged and Lena whined, Uriah refused to make an appearance. There was an attached bathroom with plenty of good water to drink from the sink and of course the shower and toilet worked just fine.

Jameson came three times a day to deliver meals and occasionally a fresh set of clothes. When he arrived, Hannah would cling to his arm, her eyes locked on his, trying to convince him. She wanted out. She needed to get out of the stifling bedroom with its mind numbing same-ness. But Uriah's second in command remained unmoved. Apparently, he agreed with the forced seclusion.

Patting at her hand, Jameson would promise her it was temporary before peeling her off and sliding back out the way he'd come. Boredom threaded itself with anxiety. Despite the women's inactivity, so much seemed to be taking place on the other side of that locked door.

Pressing her ear up to it, Hannah would listen for men

passing along the hall. Doors would open, muted words were spoken from further down.

On the bed, Lena would press her face into her hands and sigh. She'd sit for hours, propped up against the headboard, staring at the television screen fixed to the wall. It played movies, so many old time movies. But Hannah hated them. Refused them on principle.

"Wasn't it your turn to shower?" Lena's voice broke Hannah's constant vigil.

"Are you trying to tell me something?" Hannah asked, her chin balanced on her drawn up knees as she sat by the door.

"It'd break the monotony," Lena suggested, stretching. "And if you don't take the water ration, then I'm going to."

"Alright." Hannah blew out a breath and shoved up to standing. "I suppose you want me to get dressed like a proper person, too?"

"That'd be nice," Lena ducked her head. "And when Jameson brings lunch, maybe we can convince him to give us a walk around."

"Oh?" Hannah's eyebrows lifted. "You have something in mind?"

"I do."

An hour later the women were set up in the bathroom when they heard Jameson enter the room. He knocked first, he always did, and then there was the twist of the lock and the gentle shove of the door across the thick carpet.

Hannah looked at Lena and couldn't hardly suppress her smile. This just might work.

Lena gave her a small wink before burying her face in her hands. Then the rocking started, back and forth, back and forth. It was good, Hannah had to admit, real convincing.

"Hannah Mae!" Jameson's voice called. "Lena!"

The women didn't answer. In the ensuing silence, Hannah listened to Jameson shut the door before putting the food tray down with a clink.

"Girls!" He called again as his footsteps moved about the space.

"In here!" Hannah called back, making sure to put just a bit of strain in her voice.

"Hannah, what?" Jameson stopped short as he breached the bathroom door.

"I don't know." Hannah tossed him a worried look over her shoulder. "She's been like this all morning. I can't snap her out of it."

"Hey Lena," Jameson's voice came out soothing, like he was speaking to a frightened child. "You okay? You feeling sick?"

Lena didn't answer and she didn't stop her rocking. Keeping her hands over her face, the little dark-haired woman breathed heavily but otherwise didn't make a sound. Hannah ran a hand down Lena's arm and looked between her friend and Jameson.

"I think it's being locked in," Hannah explained, all innocence and concern. "It reminds her... you know... of the cage. It's too much."

"Shit." Jameson ran a hand over the back of his neck. "I didn't think about that. Damn it."

Crouching down, the big man braced one hand on the floor. For a moment, his eyes traveled over Lena's form, then to Hannah and back. Sucking in a breath, he shook his head and cleared his throat.

"Hey Lena," Jameson began again. "Let's get you both out of this room for awhile okay? You want to take a walk around? We can go to the library, maybe listen to Hannah play?"

The rocking slowed. Reaching forward with both hands, Hannah braced herself against Lena's arms and forced her to a gentle stop.

"You hear that Lena?" Hannah worked hard to keep the victory out of her tone. "We're going to go for a little walk. That sound good?"

Keeping her face covered, Lena nodded, slowly.

"Yeah," Hannah continued, her face turning back to Jameson. "Let me just clean her up a bit, okay?"

"Okay." Jameson nodded, his face flooding with relief.

In that moment, Hannah felt maybe just a tiny twinge of guilt. But then she remembered the past few days of forced isolation, and it disappeared. Jameson stepped out of the bathroom and closed the door. Lena's hands dropped and she couldn't hide the smirk that covered her face.

"You're a genius," Hannah whispered. "A brilliant little manipulator fairy."

"Sometimes you've got to fight fire with fire," Lena whispered back, then rose to her feet.

By the time they were all set to go, Uriah had appeared in the hallway. Apparently, Jameson had contacted him about Lena's little display because he was all tentative and twisted up. Hannah couldn't help staring as her brother stepped to Lena, ran his hands through her hair and whispered to her. She nodded and mumbled some response that had him looking like a guilty bastard.

Well, Hannah thought, serves him right anyway. Then down the hall they went with Uriah in front holding onto Lena's hand. Hannah followed just behind them with Jameson beside her. There was no noise in the house, which was eery because Hannah knew a ton of soldiers had been staying here. Just that morning she'd heard their voices and boots stomping all over the place.

When they reached the opening to the kitchen, Hannah tried to get a look through the threshold but Jameson's heavy frame blocked her. Squinting up at him, she noted his brow furrow and his eyes darting all around. He was checking things out, like all of sudden the space here wasn't safe.

It reminded Hannah of being on the surface, a lifetime ago. Of Andy when he used to hunt, or Cole and the team when they were outside the compound.

"What's going on?" Hannah hissed at him.

"Just keep moving," Jameson said, taking her upper arm in his grasp.

She allowed him to shuffle her along another few steps. They were heading for the library at the end of the hall.

That's where he had suggested they go, that's where they'd agreed to go, but suddenly it wasn't where Hannah needed to go.

Enough with this, she thought. Uriah and Jameson were hiding things from her. They'd said they had Cole. They'd said they had Liam. Well, where the hell were they? Wrenching her arm from Jameson's grasp, Hannah turned on her heel and made a run for it.

In the background, she heard Jameson curse, heard her brother shout her name. She didn't have much time. Maybe she had a head start on Jameson, but he'd catch her quick enough. She just had to make it to the doorway of the kitchen. Had to see what was beyond.

"Cole!" Hannah called his name. "Liam!"

The scuffling behind her became deafening, her ears pounded and her heart raced. Lunging forward, Hannah grabbed at the frame of the door and hauled herself into it just as Jameson caught up to her.

And there they all were, through the kitchen, out where the orderly space opened into a massive great room. Cole, Liam and Cookie. All sitting neatly at the long mahogany table, their hands bound in front of them, half a dozen soldiers lined up behind them.

All eyes were trained on her and time slowed.

Jameson wrapped her in his arms, hauled her up off the ground. Hannah's nails scratched at the white painted wood of the doorframe.

"Cole!" She called again, causing him to lurch to his feet.

"Han!" Cole shouted it as the soldiers behind him grabbed for him.

"Stop!" Hannah struggled in Jameson's grasp. "Stop it!"

Just before he hauled her away, Hannah watched Liam push up and position his tall frame between the soldiers and Cole. Guns came up. The soldiers took aim.

Squeezing her eyes shut, Hannah screamed again, then the scene was gone. Jameson was carting her away. Lena was crying. Uriah was shouting.

And she waited for the shots.

And she waited.

And she waited.

COLE GRITTED HIS TEETH. THERE WASN'T MUCH ELSE YOU could do with the barrel of a rifle pressed against the back of your head, and the heads of your friends. The plastic zip-ties bit into his wrists as he braced himself against the tabletop.

His eyes were wide open though, seared open at the sight of her. He kept his gaze focused on the far door, just in case Han showed back up. Just in case that Jameson fucker lost his grip.

"What more do you want?" Liam was asking, not quite able to keep the plea from his voice. "We brought in Cookie, nice and easy. We're all here now, like you wanted."

It was clear the sight of her had spooked Liam, too. Hell, they were all on edge now. The grumblings from the line of soldiers behind them told Cole that much. They didn't get to see her either, at least not as much as they'd like. It sickened him, everything suddenly sickened him.

"I want your loyalty," Uriah was saying. "I want your commitment to our cause."

"We're committed," Liam responded quickly. "We all want the same thing."

"No, I'm pretty sure your buddy here wants me dead," Uriah countered, leaning back in his chair.

Liam's eyes flicked sideways at Cole but God help him, Cole was unable to hide the desire. Killing Command Officer Twelve sounded pretty damn good right about now. Said Officer, also known as Uriah Linfield, shifted in his position across the table. They'd been at this for days now. *Days*. They were getting nowhere fast.

"You want me dead, too," Cole spoke finally.

"I didn't issue that order."

"Well…" Cole cleared his throat, shifted his eyes up to indicate the bastard standing at his back. "Seems like you do now."

Rolling his eyes, Uriah huffed a breath before motioning for his soldiers to stand down. Cole felt the tip of the rifle recede from his head, then listened as the men backed a few steps towards the wall. When the shuffling and sighing and general positioning ended, he took the chance to ease the tension from his own neck. Stretching this way and that, he exhaled slowly before leaning back in his chair.

"It's not good for them to be locked up like this," Liam said quietly. Everyone knew who he was talking about. "And I know you don't like your sister handled that way."

"You don't talk about her." Uriah pointed a warning finger at Liam. "I'm keeping them safe."

"From us?" Liam countered. "We had both of them for months and-"

"Don't-" Uriah warned. "Remind me."

"We'd never hurt them," Liam continued. "There's no reason they can't move around while you do this... whatever this is. Unless it's your own men you don't trust."

The soldiers behind them grumbled and Cole smirked. Liam was on a roll lately. It was like he had some special pass none of the rest of them had. He was constantly pushing buttons that Uriah raged at, but took.

Every time Liam did it, Cole waited for his friend to get the shit kicked out of him, but then the beatings never came. It was the strangest thing. For his part, Cole had a black eye, sore as shit ribs and maybe a broken finger.

Cookie hadn't said anything, a highly difficult feat for the old man, and therefore was squeaky clean. And this was despite the fact he'd actually shot Linfield himself. Go figure.

"I'm maybe six months out on making a tactical assault on the Wall," Uriah said. "The longer we wait, the more advanced their defenses will be. We could use a team like yours in the strike. A sniper as good as Smelt would be pivotal in making that initial breach."

"So we'll do it," Liam agreed, his eyes shifting to Cole who was non-committal.

"It's another suicide mission," Cole supplied. "I'm just waiting for the knife in my back."

"Again, I did not issue that order."

"Oh, that's right. A *computer* did it." Cole smiled broadly, nodded his head. Uriah's bullshit excuses meant nothing to him. "You didn't see it go by and put your little stamp of approval on the damn thing."

"I do not *have* to explain myself to you." Uriah squeezed one hand into a fist. "But it *is* the truth. At that time we weren't aware of the source's involvement and how exactly it controlled everything. I was given the order from above me and handed it down because I was told the information had been vetted. So yeah, I stamped the fucking thing."

"So, who gives the orders now?" Cole asked.

"I. Do." Uriah's hand went flat against the table.

"Not the source?" Cole mocked. Beside him, Liam shifted uncomfortably.

"The source is what we're trying to kill inside the Wall," Uriah continued. "It caused the war. It controlled both sides. It caused the annihilation of the majority of the human population. Now it imprisons innocent people in order to control their genetic future."

Cole whistled. It came out long and low before he shook his head.

The Wall, yes, yes. He believed that much. Hannah had confirmed it, Lena had confirmed it, Flynn had confirmed it. But this mess about a source, or Artificial Intelligence, taking over the world? *Really fucking hard to swallow right about now.*

It was just too damn convenient, wasn't it? Command Officer Twelve didn't do it. No, it was the big bad non-existent, non-person that lived "out there" behind a wall. Cole wasn't buying it.

"So how do we get to the next step?" Liam pushed

ahead. "How do we get to where the girls can walk around in their own house and you trust us?"

"I could lock you three back up in the jail," Uriah suggested.

"But then we'd just get out," Cole supplied. Not that he knew how they'd do it, but still, the truth is stranger than fiction, or so they say. Plus, Linfield clearly thought Ace and Davey were out there somewhere, waiting.

"Or you could let them out," Liam rushed on. "And you could cuff us to... I don't know... the furniture or something. And if any of your soldier boys touches them, then they get a bullet to the skull."

"That so?" Uriah lifted his eyebrows.

"Just a suggestion," Liam put in. "Although I know you make the final call and your guys respect the hell out of you, so no real worries there."

"Right." Uriah's gaze lifted to appraise the men standing back against the wall.

It was tense for a few moments, no one moved. Cole took the time to scrutinize the adversary across from him. The family resemblance between Uriah and Hannah was undeniable. Same golden hair, same brown eyes and general coloring. She was of course an extremely feminine version, but for sure they were related.

Cole didn't know exactly why he hadn't made the connection before. He'd met with Command Officer Twelve more times than he could count in the two year span of fighting. But then half the time they'd been covered in dirt and dust, with smoke clouds pluming in the decimated land all around them. Command Officers moved around a lot, as buildings were bombed and access to power grew more challenging.

Oh well. Did it really matter? All Cole knew was that he didn't trust Uriah. But at the same time he needed the man in order to get to Hannah. And if Cole had any doubts about Han being here or wanting him, they were gone now. She was a prisoner to her brother. Cole could still hear the sound of his name on her lips, see the look on her face when Jameson had pulled her away. It gutted him.

"Fine," Uriah announced before standing. "The rules are as follows: you three will be cuffed to furniture. If you need a piss break, two of my men will escort you there and back. Try anything? Get a bullet.

If you see Hannah or Lena, you will not call out to them. You do not try to draw them in to you or reach out to them. If you hurt them, so help me, you'll be begging for a bullet, pleading for one, and I promise it won't come quick enough for you."

"What if they come to us?" Liam asked.

"You'll be watched," Uriah conceded. "Don't try anything."

"Okay," Liam agreed, then looked to Cookie and Cole. "We all agree."

"I want to hear them say it," Uriah gestured.

"I agree." Cookie nodded.

Rounding the table, Uriah brought a fresh supply of zip-ties with him. When he got to Cole, he crouched down and peered into his face.

Cole met his stare, unblinking, unafraid. He'd trusted

this man with his life, with the lives of his men, his brothers. He'd never been so betrayed. It stung. Truly it did.

"Do you agree?" Uriah asked quietly.

"I would never…" Cole sucked in a breath, his chest tight all of sudden. "Do anything to hurt Hannah or Lena. Ever. The fact that I even have to swear it makes me sick."

Exhaling through his nose, Uriah tilted his head to one side. They eyed each other for a solid minute, maybe more.

"I'm going to bring someone in," Uriah said finally. "And you're going to listen to what he has to say. I have documents, film reels, blue prints. You *will* know the truth, Tanner. And in the end, you're going to fucking apologize for ever doubting me."

"HE WON'T KILL THEM," JAMESON'S VOICE WAS LOW AS HE stood leaning up against the closed bedroom door, his massive arms folded neatly over his chest.

Hannah just stared at him, she'd run out of words a while ago. Behind her, Lena paced the floor, wearing an obvious track in the plush carpeting of Uriah's bedroom. They were back to square one. Only now they all knew the stakes, and they were high, painfully high.

"How do you know?" Lena asked finally, coming to a stop beside Hannah.

"Because he needs them," Jameson explained. "They have history, apparently. They know each other from the war."

"That's not possible," Hannah cut in, trying hard not to let her voice shake the way her hands were.

"Still." Jameson shrugged. "It's the truth."

The knock at the door was abrupt. It had them all jumping. Through the wood, Uriah's voice could be heard calling for Jameson to let him in. Hannah glanced at Lena who nibbled at her lip before stepping back. Run for it? Now or never, Hannah thought, but then she let her eyes pop over to Jameson who frowned.

"It's not just your boyfriend and his buddies," Jameson spoke quietly, his hand sliding down to the doorknob. "You really don't know them, Hannah Mae. And now there are soldiers in here, too. I can't watch you all the time."

"I know." Hannah backed a step, calculating the distance to the door, hoping her brother would give her an opening.

"Don't run," Jameson warned.

Was she that obvious? Apparently, yes. Hannah let her shoulders slump for a just a moment. But then the door was swinging wide and Uriah was stepping inside. His gaze glanced off of Hannah to settle on Lena. He was worried, distracted. That's when he gave Hannah the opening she needed, the one she'd been waiting for.

But Jameson's warning was still fresh in her mind and Hannah held herself back, she didn't take the opportunity given to her. When had she begun to trust Jameson? When had she decided he was an ally? A friend? She didn't know, but the reality was suddenly here just the same.

"They can come out," Uriah announced. "It's safe but-"

Hannah didn't wait for her brother to finish his sentence. In a split second, her gaze flicked to Jameson who rolled his eyes. That was enough for her. Then she was off down the hall, her hair flying out all behind her, Uriah yelling about rules in the background.

Cole. Cole and Liam. Cole and Liam and Cookie. That's all she could think about, their faces playing over in her mind.

She hadn't heard any gunshots, they weren't dead. They weren't. Then she was at the opening to the kitchen, and flying through it. And there they all were, sitting just as she'd seen them before.

"Cole!" Hannah's voice was strangled as it erupted from her throat. "Oh my God, Cole."

Skidding to a stop, Hannah rounded the corner of the table and launched herself into his lap. The chair rocked back a touch with the force of her weight and Cole's breath came out in a whoosh at her contact, but she didn't care. Didn't care about the murmuring of soldiers, or the shuffling of feet. Wrapping her arms around his neck, Hannah buried her face in Cole's chest and let out a sob.

"Shhhh," Cole's voice was soothing as he shushed her. "You're alive, Han. Thank God you're alive."

Sitting back, Hannah separated her body from his just long enough to look into his face. She ran tentative fingers over his black eye, nibbling subconsciously at her lip in concern. His arms were bound behind his back now, the restraints looped through the back of the wooden chair.

Closing his eyes, Cole tilted his forehead to touch hers, it was the only thing he could give her. But that was the thing about Cole, he would always give her everything he had. Hannah's heart pitched inside her chest. Then she was kissing him, laying her lips against his, feeling that rush he always gave her as he started kissing back.

"What in the-" Uriah's voice boomed out from behind her, causing Hannah to pull away.

Throwing him a look over her shoulder, Hannah absorbed the absolute shock that covered both her brother and Jameson's faces. Beside them, Lena looked wide-eyed, giving her head the slightest shake as if to signal to Hannah.

Rotating back to Cole, Hannah frowned as his face clouded over. He'd bristled at the sound of Uriah's voice. They may have known each other, but it was obviously not a happy acquaintance. Sliding her eyes to the left, Hannah reached a hand to run down Liam's arm, then gave Cookie a teary smile.

"Why are they tied up?" Hannah let the words fall from her lips, but kept her gaze jumping between the men. Cookie was clearing his throat and Liam was shifting around uncomfortably.

"I think the real question is what the hell you're doing, Hannah Mae." Uriah's voice came closer, Hannah could feel his energy collecting in angry bursts at her back.

"These men are my friends…"

"*Friends?*" Uriah cut her off, one heavy hand coming to land on her shoulder. "Have they convinced you to *kiss* all your friends?"

"Don't talk to her like that," Cole snapped.

"Get out," Uriah ordered his soldiers who stood there for a beat too long, mouths gaping open at the spectacle before them. "Jameson?"

"On it," the big man answered, fetching a ring of keys from his pocket.

As the soldiers filed out, Uriah pulled Hannah off Cole's lap and spun her around to face him. Looking up at her brother, Hannah blushed a deep pink as she realized what he must think of her. After all, she wasn't quite sure what she thought of herself anymore.

It was just, seeing Cole after so long, she couldn't stop herself from going to him. She loved him. Such a guilty complicated sort of love, yes, but that's what it was just the same.

"You don't have to do this anymore," Uriah was saying. "You're safe with me. You don't have to kiss them or... or... do *anything* with them. What've they made you do? What've they convinced you to do?"

"Nothing," Hannah protested, trying to back from his grasp, but Uriah wouldn't let go. "I just..."

"You just... what?" Uriah's hands squeezed tighter around her upper arms.

"Well, I..." Hannah wriggled in his grip, her eyes flicking to Lena who began tugging on Uriah's elbow. "I love..."

"Don't say it," Uriah cut her off. "You don't know what you're saying. They've brain washed you."

"No, I-"

"How many?" Uriah again, his face dark, his eyes glinting. "How many of them did you have to be *friends* with?"

"You're hurting her," Liam growled. "Stop."

Hannah could hear all three of their chairs tipping and scraping along the floor now. Glancing over her shoulder, she watched them. Uriah loosened his grip just a fraction, his focus darting over Hannah's shoulder to the men.

"I should kill you," Uriah spat, lifting one hand to point at Liam. "You convinced me you're her boyfriend, that you protected her. Did you just pass her around amongst you?"

271

"No," Cole barked, his chest rising and falling rapidly as he struggled against his restraints. "You're making it into something it's not."

"It?" Uriah's eyebrows raised, his stare falling back to Hannah. "Her head was all screwed up from that chip. First Andy took her and then you assholes. I don't think I can ever forgive myself. Hannah Mae, I should never have left you."

"Uri." Hannah reached up, placed one palm on the side of her brother's face. "My mind was messed up, but by the time I got to Cole and Liam, I knew enough to make my own choices. They didn't force me to do anything, not once, okay?"

"I don't understand."

"I fell for Cole first." Hannah sucked in a breath, squeezed her eyes shut.

How do you explain to your brother what took you so long to admit to yourself? Was she a slut? By the rules of their former world, yes... yes, she was. But this world? This situation? She'd done what was necessary to survive. Then she'd kept doing it because of her heart.

So after a long pause, she tried to explain it to him as best she could, "The thing with Liam just sort of happened. We didn't plan for this... this thing, okay? I've tried to stop, but I can't."

"*I* can make it stop," Uriah countered.

"But I don't want it to." Opening her eyes, Hannah absorbed her brother's expression and her tears began to flow. "I'm sorry I've shamed you."

Dropping his hand, Uriah stepped back. His eyes darted

over her face before landing on both Cole and Liam in turn. What he saw there had his jaw tightening, his fists clenching at his side. Lena rushed forward again, tugging at his elbow, drawing him away.

With a quick shake of his head, Uriah turned on his heel and stalked from the room. Throwing her an apologetic look, Lena scurried out to follow him. Whatever conversation they were about to have, Hannah could be glad Lena was there to take the brunt of it.

Her brother would have harsh things to say; things Hannah could never forget if he said them to her face. Their father had been the same way. The thought of her parents, and what they'd think of her now, had her shoulders trembling. Isn't this what she'd tried so hard to avoid?

"Good to see you, Little Miss," Cookie's voice broke in as she wiped the tears from her face. "The circumstances ain't so good though, are they?"

"No." Hannah kept her back to the men, trying to gain some composure. "They aren't, Cookie."

"Don't suppose you'd be willing to grab a knife from the kitchen and cut an old man free, would ya?" Cookie's tone was playful, but the request was a real one.

"Of course." Hannah sucked in a breath, squared her shoulders and fetched a knife from the block.

When she turned to face them, she kept her eyes averted from both Liam and Cole. She wasn't sure what sort of looks she'd get from them, and she just didn't want to see. Not now.

Starting with Cookie, Hannah sawed through the plastic zip-ties that connected his wrists and then crouched down. Each ankle was fastened to the chair leg and again at the knee position. Working quickly, she freed each of the men before standing.

"Hey." Cole drew her into his chest, wrapping his arms around her body. "It's okay."

"He hates me," Hannah mumbled, fighting a fresh flood of emotion.

"You're an adult," Cole reasoned, placing soft kisses to both her cheeks before resting his chin on the top of her head. "We're all adults and no one's sneaking around. No one's lying. You love me, you love Liam, we both love you. We're not hurting anyone."

"I'm a slut."

"Stop," Cole commanded. "You didn't start out that way and you aren't one now. This world is just... it's different. We ended up in this situation, and we can just try to make the best of it. Right, Lee?"

"Yeah," Liam agreed. Reaching out, he rubbed at Hannah's back.

Cole released her then and Liam gathered her up. Placing a kiss on her forehead, he rocked her a bit before easing her down to sit in one of the chairs. When he landed in one just beside her Liam took her hand in his own and ran his thumb along her palm.

"Food?" He asked.

"Hell, yes," Cole responded.

Together, both Cole and Cookie scouted through the kitchen. Cupboards popped open, then the refrigerator door. The men were busy exclaiming at what they found when Jameson cruised back in. Hannah caught his initial shock before he zeroed in on her.

His brow furrowed, but he didn't move for his gun. After a beat, he simply strode past Cole and Cookie and plopped down in the chair across from Liam at the table.

"You alright?" He asked.

"I've been better," Hannah admitted with a sniff. "Uriah…"

"Let me guess," Jameson offered. "He's pissed?"

"Yeah." Hannah huffed an ironic laugh. "His little sister…"

"Controls one of the most important units in the new war?" Jameson lifted his eyebrows.

"What?"

"These men belong to you?" Jameson asked, gesturing over his shoulder at the bustle in the kitchen.

"I guess so." Hannah shot Liam a look. "I mean, yeah, they do."

"Can you keep them from killing us?"

"Well, yeah…" Hannah frowned.

"Can you get them to fight for us?"

"I guess…"

"Then looks like we're square," Jameson cut in. Turning slightly in his chair he lifted his voice and called, "I'll take a sandwich, too, fellas… and *don't* spit in it." Looking back at Hannah, Jameson gave up a sigh, his shoulders easing noticeably. "Your brother will come around. He always does."

Beside her, Liam just kept stroking her hand, all steady

silence. She'd almost forgotten what a quiet comfort he was.

In the kitchen, Cookie complained loudly about Cole's "overuse" of the mayonnaise. Shooting her a look, Cole made a face before giving Hannah a quick wink. Was this real? Was any of this actually real? After a beat, Hannah nibbled on her lip and exhaled.

COMMAND OFFICER TWELVE DID NOT COME OUT OF HIS room for the rest of the day. Despite that happy fact, all through lunch and on into dinner, Uriah Linfield continued to occupy Cole's thoughts. For Hannah's sake, Cole made sure to play it off. He smiled at her, talked easily to Cookie, and nodded through Jameson's limited tour of the house.

All the while though, his mind churned. The truth was, Cole was utterly divided. A part of him desperately wanted to murder Hannah's brother with his bare hands. He couldn't forget how Uriah had betrayed him, betrayed his entire unit, cost him years of guilt and untimely death.

But the other part of Cole knew he just couldn't allow himself to do that. Because even though the guy was a first class asshole, in the end, he was right. Liam had warned Cole of the fact, but damn it, he just hadn't wanted to believe it. Uriah Linfield could keep Hannah one hundred percent completely safe. Cole could not. That truth burned all the way down.

And what would Cole accomplish by killing Uriah? Aside from immense justice and self-satisfaction, he would lose Hannah forever. Not only that, but then he'd have to kill Jameson and that would put him, Liam and Cookie in the middle of a sea of Linfield soldiers.

There would be no way of getting the women to safety then. None. So... divided Cole kept an easy expression on his face and did his best to work through his own tension.

Alone now, in one of the showers, Cole watched his time limit of water tick slowly down on the electronic monitor. The red numbers counted backwards, using real live electricity that only old world money and technology could manufacture. The largess. It was enviable and also maddening.

Holding his hand under the dispenser Cole watched a perfectly rationed amount of soap squeeze itself out onto his palm. With it, he scrubbed every single inch of his filthy body. He did not go easy. Looking down, he saw the dirt and caked on blood swirl around the drain along with copious bubbles that collected on the tile. His wrists ached from where first the metal cuffs, then the plastic binds had cut into him.

The pain was nothing, though. Nothing compared to the mix of emotions that filtered through him. But the water was hot, so hot that it made his skin pink, and he forced his head under once more. It felt good, he had to admit, the shower felt good.

When he was done, Cole stepped out of the glass enclosure and grabbed a fluffy blue towel. Fluffy. The word hadn't applied to anything Cole had experienced in so incredibly long. With a shake of his head, he wiped the image of his family home from his mind. He didn't want to go back there, not right now. Hannah was waiting for him just on the other side of the door. She would be his tonight.

It was nothing that he and Liam had explicitly discussed but then again they didn't really need to. Liam had simply offered to sleep in the bunk room in the back of the house with Cookie, and Cole had nodded, his blood heating at the implication.

So here Cole was, cleaning himself in the ensuite bath of Hannah's very own bedroom. Jameson had locked them in together after first securing Cookie and Liam in their bunks. The guys may have some leeway for the moment, but nothing would be certain until Uriah took back control. And he would take it back soon, after he digested the new information about his sister.

Cole grimaced at the thought. He wouldn't let Hannah's brother hurt her again. He wouldn't let him make her feel ashamed. She didn't deserve it. If he wanted to punish someone he should start with Cole, for not being able to keep her safe without help; or Liam, for falling in love with her. But not Han. *His* Han.

Wrapping the damp towel low on his waist, Cole brushed a hand through his shaggy hair. He'd needed a trim months ago, he couldn't imagine what he looked like now. Walking to the mirror, Cole swiped a hand through the mist of condensation and frowned at the mountain man staring back at him. Between his beard and his hair he wasn't looking too appealing.

Bending to search through the drawers, Cole found a bottle of women's shaving cream and a pink razor. Another cursory search resulted in a pair of scissors. They'd have to do, he thought as he twisted on the tap of the sink and began his work.

A few minutes later, Hannah rapped lightly on the closed door. Clearing his throat, Cole tapped the razor on the side of the sink and straightened.

"Hey," Hannah's soft voice drifted in. "You okay in there?"

"Yeah." Cole ran a hand over his now smooth chin. "You can come in."

When the door pushed open Cole was rewarded with one of Hannah's little gasps. He couldn't help but smile as she crossed the space to him, running her hands up through his hair and over his face. Wearing nothing but a tiny sleep shirt, she was beautiful, as always, with that golden hair drifting to tangle over her shoulders.

"What do you think?" Cole asked, but he already knew the answer.

"I've never seen you clean shaven." Hannah smiled, her fingers still playing along his skin. "I didn't think you could get any more handsome."

"Is that right?" Cole's voice dropped low.

Reaching up, Hannah's brow furrowed as she messed with his hair. It wasn't so easy to cut it yourself with a pair of scissors. Back at the compound, Ace had always done it.

Suddenly, Cole's thoughts traveled back there, to his home. He wondered how Davey was holding up, and if the guys were staying warm and safe. He hoped like hell they were. When would he be able to go back? He needed to check on them, to check on the livestock and help bury their dead.

"Can I cut it?" Hannah was asking, drawing Cole's attention back to the present and to the warm woman standing so close to him... with her hands all over him.

"Yeah," Cole's voice was husky, his eyes clouding just a bit. He'd forgotten what it was like to be alone with her. "You can cut hair?"

"Um, I used to before," Hannah supplied, coaxing him down to sit on the closed lid of the toilet.

"You're remembering more things?" Cole asked, closing his eyes as snippets of hair began dropping down past his face.

"I am now, yeah."

"Everything?"

"Everything," Hannah confirmed. Cole listened to the slide of another drawer, felt the tines of a comb work against his scalp.

"No more headaches?"

"None."

"That's great, Han." Cole reached forward, found her waist.

Circling his hands around her body, he gripped the thin material of her nightie. Were there panties underneath? His eyes popped open and he studied her briefly. Nope, well... maybe. Wouldn't take much to find out. Cole's fingers pulsed along her waist slightly but then Hannah was stepping away from him.

He let his hands drop back to his lap as his stomach sank. Maybe he was rushing things. She hadn't seen him in months and then there was all that stuff her brother had said. Maybe she was having second thoughts.

"Close your eyes," Hannah said and Cole obeyed, his gut churning around uncertainly.

There was the slide of another drawer, and he felt the faint shift of air as Hannah moved around him. When the hair dryer clicked on, his whole body stiffened with shock. He'd almost forgotten there was such a device. But then the hot air was blowing over his body, warming his bare chest, shoulders and face.

Hannah's hand followed along, brushing the fresh cut hair from his skin. Cole shifted restlessly under her touch. It just wasn't fair. He felt every tickle of her fingertips, every shift of her body so close to him. His hands fisted in his lap as he tried hard to fight the demands of his body. He wanted to do the touching. He wanted her naked, against him, under him.

Gritting his teeth, Cole kept his eyes shut and held his breath. When the blow dryer shut off, he opened his eyes to see Hannah's soft smile. It eased him. Everything about her eased him.

"Do you want to see?" She asked, indicating the mirror on the wall behind him.

"You like it?" Cole countered.

"Yeah." Hannah nibbled at her lip, ran her fingers through his hair once more. "It looks good."

"Then I don't need to see it," he responded. "Now come here."

Reaching out he tugged gently at Hannah's wrist. To his satisfaction, she let herself be pulled down onto his lap. The towel was the only thing separating them now, Cole realized as his hands traced up her thighs. Smooth. He wasn't the only one who'd benefited from the use of a razor.

Tilting his head to once side, Cole eyed her a moment longer. A part of him still couldn't believe she was here, with him. He flashed to the first time he'd ever had her on his lap. Back on his gray horse, with the dirt road to the compound stretching out on either side of them. He'd felt like the luckiest bastard alive in that moment.

Was it possible to feel even luckier now? Maybe so, because then her eyelids were fluttering and she was leaning in close to him. When her lips touched his, Cole's chest expanded. His blood pumped hard in his body, shooting warmth to every extremity. He'd needed this, he'd missed her. Hannah. *His Hannah.*

"You own me, you know that?" Cole murmured against her lips. And it was the truth, the most complete truth he'd ever uttered.

Hannah panted in response as his hands crept up the inside of her shirt, lifting it easily over her head. Then her bare skin was pressing against his and she was shifting her hips down on him. With a groan, Cole buried his hands in her hair, held her mouth closer to his. He wanted more. Deeper. He wanted to own her as much as she owned him.

"I'm in love with you," Cole breathed between kisses,

letting his mouth consume her neck, travel to her collar bone, lower.

"I'm in love with you, too," Hannah gasped, pressing first one breast into his mouth, then the other.

"I thought you were dead." Cole stopped, looked up into her face. That feeling. That terror would never leave him.

"I'm sorry," Hannah whispered, her face falling. "I'm so sorry."

Nodding, Cole frowned before easing back upright. With a sigh, he ran his fingers down the side of her face, brushed his thumb over her lips. When she parted them for him, he pulled her whole body in tight against his. He didn't want to let her out of his sight. Not ever again.

Standing suddenly, Cole picked Hannah up and walked out into the bedroom. She clung to him, her legs wrapping around his waist as the towel drifted to the floor. When they got to her bed, he eased her down onto it before settling himself over her. She would be his now. He'd make her remember.

Gasping at his press of weight, Hannah's warm body wriggled beneath him. Cole pinned her hip with one hand, letting her feel him rest just between her thighs. She was arching and murmuring even before he took her mouth with his own. She seemed ready but he wanted her crazy.

Devouring her mouth, he reached up to stroke her breasts, then down to feel her soft belly. He let his hand graze over her thighs, then around to squeeze her butt. She whimpered and protested. He was dancing around the area she really wanted him to stroke, teasing her with the path of his fingers, sucking a nipple in his mouth one minute, then nipping under her chin the next.

He felt triumphant, like he was in complete control. But then she lined herself up with him, gripped his hips in both hands and that was it. Before he knew what was happening, she'd turned the tables on him. He was inside of her. His mind left him.

All around him, he could feel her, arching to him, drawing back. He couldn't help but follow her lead, pushing into her, pulling out. Again. He had to do it again. His heart was hammering, his breath catching in his throat.

Her little cries panted out against his neck, then her nails were scratching down his back and he came. Shit. She did this to him. He'd forgotten just what she did to him. He managed to keep rhythm for a few seconds more but then he was gasping, groaning into her hair. At that moment she cried out, moaning and pulsing all around him.

He stilled. His breathing hard, matching hers. And in the end he wasn't sure who owned who really. But maybe that's what made it so right. They fit together and nothing else mattered.

CHAPTER THIRTY_
LIAM

"IS THIS REALLY NECESSARY?" LIAM ASKED, INDICATING THE zip-ties that continued to bind Cole's wrists. They'd been living together in relative peace for the past ten days and Liam himself hadn't been tied up in over a week. Even Cookie walked around unhindered, serving up breakfast, lunch and dinner.

"Absolutely," Uriah countered, his eyes darting over to where Hannah sat with Lena on the other side of the room. "Helps him keep his hands to himself."

"Give it a rest, Linfield," Liam countered, as Cole grunted beside him. "We all know that's just an excuse."

"Pardon?" Uriah's gaze flicked back over to Liam and settled.

"She cuts him loose every night." Liam leaned in. "And you do nothing to stop it."

"And neither do you," Uriah countered, his eyebrows raising. "Quite a fucked up little relationship you three've got going."

"Leave her out of it," Liam cut in, lifting a hand to silence Cole who undoubtedly had a few choice words to spew in Uriah's direction. "If we don't deal with the real reason you keep him like this all day, then we'll never get anywhere. It's a waste of time."

"Alright," Uriah leaned back against the couch in the library. "Enlighten me."

"You want something from him," Liam supplied.

"I do," Uriah agreed.

"What is it?"

"Loyalty."

"I've had enough of your fucking loyalty to last a life-time," Cole interrupted.

"And there you go." Uriah smiled. "He doesn't believe me. If I turn my back for more than a second, he'll put a knife in it."

"Not true," Cole countered. "I've had opportunities."

"Bull. Shit." Uriah huffed a breath. "You're locked in the bunk room or Hannah's room, God help me, at night and I'm locked in mine. I get up every morning and open the door with the barrel of a gun ready to blow your head off. No such luck."

"You know what?" Cole began, but then Uriah opened his mouth to speak and neither of them could be heard clearly over the other one.

Standing up, Liam paced a few steps away from the men as they went at it for the millionth time. No matter what he did to try to facilitate a truce, either one or the other of them screwed it up. It was like they were deter-mined to hate each other.

And okay, so they had good reasons. Really good reasons. Death and attempted murder on both sides being at the top of the list.

Across the room, Hannah shot him a worried look as Lena excused herself and walked out. The stress of the situation was wearing on the women. Liam knew it when he got his turn to hold Hannah at night, and he knew it by the drop in Lena's appetite.

All of a sudden, she seemed more pale and fragile to him. More than once he'd heard Lena throw up in the bathroom when she thought no one was around. It concerned him. Lena was probably having flashbacks again but Hannah refused to say. All he knew was he had to put a stop to the tense environment, and fast.

Whirling back around, Liam took a good long look as Cole and Uriah battled back and forth. They didn't touch each other, not with Cole's wrists bound and Hannah always lingering so close. But the animosity vibrated with each word, each angry gesture, every string of curses.

"Enough," Liam announced, then sat down between them once more. "You're upsetting the girls so knock it the fuck off."

Cole glanced over to where Hannah was sitting before swearing and looking down. Uriah's gaze flitted quickly about the room. When he realized Lena was no longer there, he huffed a breath.

"Cole." Liam turned to him like a petulant child. "You want to kill Uriah because he ordered your assassination along with the suicide mission that cost us four brothers."

"That's right," Cole spoke through gritted teeth.

"Uriah." Liam shifted to the other side. "You deny issuing said kill order and suicide mission and instead claim it was an order handed down by the source, or AI."

"I didn't issue the orders," Uriah confirmed.

"So prove it," Liam pushed. "Bring in Dr. Bartholomew. Get out the tapes and blue prints and everything you've got. Let's see it."

"If I show you everything," Uriah warned. "Then I won't be able to release you until after we've taken down the Wall."

"Would you have released us anyway?" Cole asked, a look of disdain painting his face.

"No," Uriah admitted, then shrugged. "I guess it couldn't hurt then."

"Great." Liam sighed. "When can we get started?"

"Today's as good a day as any," Cole put in, daring Uriah to disagree.

"Yeah." Uriah called his bluff. "Today it is."

FOUR HOURS LATER AND THEY WERE ALL SITUATED AROUND that same old mahogany dining table. Papers, maps, blue prints, and documents of all sorts lay scattered across the flat surface.

Lifting his head, Liam surveyed the line of soldiers leaned up against one wall. They were men he'd come to know while working on Uriah's security team. Despite the distraction of having Hannah and Lena present, they all seemed tuned in, absorbed in the hunched figure sitting in the middle of it all.

Dr. Gene Bartholomew. The real one.

That had been the first order of business when Jameson and his team had shuffled the frail man inside. Hannah had taken one look at him and frowned. He wasn't the Dr. B she had known from inside the Wall. Similar. They looked just alike, but it wasn't him. Even now, she still seemed shaken by the revelation.

Shifting his eyes to the left, Liam reached out and took her hand. Hannah's eyes darted up to his a moment before she leaned her head against his arm. On her other side, Cole's brow remained furrowed. His hands, still bound in front of him, were folded neatly together in his lap.

Liam knew his old friend remained skeptical. Hell, he'd been unwilling to believe it himself when he'd first questioned the man. And by questioned, Liam meant just that. He hadn't had to cut him, beat him or even threaten him to get the story pouring out of the old guy's lips.

Sometimes all a man needed was a kind word, the promise of freedom. Plus, it wasn't like Bartholomew was a soldier. No, far from it. He was a civilian, through and through. Not much fight there. Physical or otherwise.

"If you weren't the one running things inside the Wall..." Uriah gestured to a piece of paper. "Then who was it?"

"My- my brother," Dr. Bartholomew said. Lifting his eyes up, he glanced around quickly before settling on Hannah. "Dell was his name. You say he's dead?"

"Yes," Hannah whispered, clutching tighter to Liam's hand. "I saw him."

"I see." The doctor nodded his head as his voice wavered.

"When my father and I invested in your research, you never mentioned your brother," Uriah supplied. All of this information was old news to him. Liam had already reported it, but Uriah was asking the questions for the benefit of everyone else, especially Cole. "What was his involvement?"

"Dell was a computer genius." Dr. Bartholomew's eyes flitted about once more before dropping to the table. He thumbed through a few diagrams before clearing his throat. "I worked on the science side of the project and he developed the means of implementation."

"Implementation," Uriah repeated. "Elaborate."

"Well, he created a sort of super intelligence. Any theories I had were run through it, looking for flaws, or areas of concern, then sometimes it returned suggestions."

"You input all of your research data into this *intelligence?*"

"We did." Dr. Bartholomew lifted his hand, it shook slightly as he ran it back through his thinning array of gray hair. "And together, we had an enormous breakthrough. Together we were able to develop the cure."

"The cure?" Uriah prompted. "That's the vaccine you sold to us. The one you promised to the UN?"

"It is." Dr. Bartholomew swallowed audibly before reaching out and clutching a glass of water.

Liam watched him drink. He watched as the liquid in

the glass trembled along with the man himself. Lifting his gaze he noted the intensity with which each soldier listened. They were as curious as anyone. They wanted to know why their lives had been blown apart. They wanted to know what exactly had robbed them of their families, of their future.

And it was sort of hard to digest, really. In the end it was this little man seated before them that had done them all in. This weak sort of person who, given enough power and money, was able to change the world. Not that he intended for the particular outcome that had come to them, but still, he was the catalyst.

"And it does work," Dr. Bartholomew said suddenly. "The implant prevents all manner of outside disease from developing."

"But not the type of sickness that comes from within, right?" Uriah again, his jaw clenching. "Not the multiple sclerosis, the Parkinson's, the hereditary stuff."

"We were making headway on that," the doctor qualified. "The program had great insight, wonderful developmental suggestions."

"By the program you mean the computer?" Cole cut in, speaking for the first time in hours. "The super intelligence your brother created."

"Yes," Dr. Bartholomew acknowledged.

"Did you realize where those wonderful suggestions would lead?" Uriah's eyes flicked to Cole. "Before you unleashed that thing on the world? Did you know what its long term plans were?"

"We knew there would be genetic screenings," the

doctor rushed in his words. "We knew there would be a culling of sorts."

"Culling," Cole spat, glancing over at Liam with anger in his eyes. "That sounds like a fancy word for mass extermination."

"No, it was never supposed to be like that." Dr. Bartholomew grew more frantic, like he was searching the air for something that wasn't there. "Dell wrote parameters into the code. The program wasn't supposed to be able to defy them. It was supposed to hold human life above all else. Can't you see? That's what this was about in the first place, preserving the sanctity of human life."

"So how do you explain what happened?" Liam asked, they needed to stay on track. As much as they might want to string this idiot up for the war, they couldn't. He had too much information stored up in him, too much that they needed.

"I don't know." The doctor sighed, drumming his fingers over the surface of the table. "Dell was in charge of the computer end of it while I took care of the science aspect. I can only surmise that the code he entered gave too much room for interpretation where human life was defined. Perhaps the program ranked disease-free life above all other forms of life. That's the only thing that would explain the purge."

"And you expect me to believe a computer program that your brother created got away from him?" Cole questioned. "How did he make it inside the Wall and not you? Why was he using your name? Doesn't it make more sense that he was behind this entire thing? That a person is running this, controlling this... maybe even you?"

"Cole," Liam warned. This wasn't exactly the way to get truthful answers to these types of questions. It took patience to get someone to admit they were at fault. It took manipulation to ease a person into confessing their brother was a mass murderer, that maybe they were, too.

"No, it's a valid question," the doctor cut in, surprising them all. "No one really knew about Dell's involvement, let alone the program we were using. I was scheduled to take residence at the refugee center in North America, but the transport I was using was rerouted without my knowledge. It deposited me in the middle of Nevada at the entrance to an underground bunker. Once I entered, I stayed for the duration of the war."

"And your brother took your place inside the Wall?"

"Apparently," Dr. Bartholomew agreed. "After the war ended, I lost all communications ability with the outside world. I didn't know it at the time, but there wasn't any world left to send signals to. That's when I left the bunker."

"And Uriah found you? How convenient," Cole sneered.

"No." The doctor shook his head. "No, not Mr. Linfield. I traveled on my own for awhile until I heard about the city here. There was talk of food rations and clean water, so I came with a group of other men."

"I recognized him when he was brought in for his interview," Uriah supplied. "It was just before Liam arrived."

Pursing his lips, Cole leaned back in his chair. Liam watched his friend's jaw clench and loosen as he processed the information before him. It was a lot to take in.

Hannah crept closer and whispered in Liam's ear. She wanted to know the same thing everyone else did, and she wondered if now was the time.

With a short nod, Liam rolled his shoulders and surveyed the space. They'd watched a few film reels from the United Nations concerning the building of refugee centers throughout the world. There were identical "walls" on each and every continent, save for Antarctica. The span of this thing was quite amazing. But then again, if there really was a super intelligence, then why wouldn't it be able to spread itself wide?

"How do we stop it?" Liam asked finally, not taking his eyes from the doctor's face. Whatever sort of lie detector lived inside Liam, he had to trust it now. This was the information Uriah had originally enlisted him to retrieve. And Uriah had been right, it was of the utmost importance that they get the truth.

"Well, my brother installed a backdoor," Dr. Bartholomew answered. Frowning, the man began shuffling through the papers until he found a lone blue print. He tapped a finger over one area before sliding it over to Uriah. "The program's code prevents it from recognizing this place. Dell told me it was sort of like a blind spot. No cameras register it, all human inferences to the spot are automatically overwritten, ignored."

"It's a physical place?" Liam asked.

"Yes, maybe that's why Dell went to the Wall and I got sent away," the doctor reasoned. "Perhaps he'd already lost control, or saw the way things were going. He would've been next to the input server the entire time."

"So he could have killed it?" Uriah cut in.

"If you knew Dell, he wouldn't have wanted to," Dr. Bartholomew explained. "He loved his creation, it was like a child to him. I think he would have tried everything to fix the problem before ending it."

"Well, it ended him." Hannah cleared her throat, sat up straighter. "He shot himself in the head."

"Where did you find him?" Dr. Bartholomew asked.

"In his office."

"That's where the input server is located," the doctor explained, again pointing to the blue print. "It should be in a cabinet full of food. The program wouldn't think twice about it."

"I've seen that cupboard," Hannah exhaled, staring at Uriah. "I've opened it."

"Well, behind the cans of food, there's a small device, it would look like an old car radio attached to the wall. You just type in the password and it unleashes a kill virus into the program. All instances of it would be wiped out. Each refugee center would go dark."

"My God, could it be that easy?" Hannah breathed the words.

"Easy?" Uriah scoffed. "The only person that was ever allowed in that office aside from fake Dr. Bartholomew was you. We'd have to get inside the Wall, then get into that room, *and* have the kill code ready."

"Well..." Hannah glanced around. "I could do it."

Liam's gut dropped as a wave of nausea took him. Gripping her hand tight in his own, he turned her to face him. No way. He was not letting that happen. At the same time Cole was shaking his head and Uriah was standing up.

"Absolutely not." Uriah leaned forward over the table. "There's no way you're going back there, Hannah Mae."

"Can it be uploaded remotely?" Cole cut in, a look of desperation etched into his face. Liam wasn't the only one breaking out in a sweat.

"My brother was the computer genius," Dr. Bartholomew reminded them. "I wouldn't know how to do it."

"But what if I have a computer guy?" Uriah asked. "What if we could tap into the thing remotely and upload the kill code. Do you have it?"

"Have what?"

"The code. The password," Uriah bit out. "What is it?"

"Oh." The doctor glanced around before nodding. "Yes, it's GeneandDell2."

"You've got to be kidding me," Cole gaped. "That's it? My laptop password was more difficult than that."

"Like I said," Dr. Bartholomew repeated. "I wasn't the computer person. My brother wanted it to be something easy that I could remember."

"Well, shit damn." Jameson whistled, his eyes dancing around to the rest of the men. "When do we get started?"

CHAPTER THIRTY-ONE_
COLE

INHALING, COLE SUCKED IN HIS FIRST BREATH OF FRESH AIR in weeks. All around him the high rises in downtown sparkled in the noonday sun. Spring was coming. It was still a ways off, yes, but it was coming for them just the same. The scent of newness, of warming.

Glancing down, Cole offered his bound wrists to Uriah asshole Linfield. The guy blinked once before his brown eyes cruised up to stare blankly into Cole's face.

"Can't be of much help like this," Cole reasoned as Liam came to a stop at his side. At least his best friend still had the privilege of holding a rifle. Better than nothing, Cole figured, with Cookie staying behind to watch the girls.

"You still haven't apologized." Uriah smiled, flashing those perfectly straight rich kid teeth.

"Now why the hell would I do something like that?" Cole's jaw clenched. *The nerve of this guy.*

"For doubting me," Uriah supplied. "I didn't issue the death order."

"Cut him loose, Linfield," Liam demanded. "It's a long walk to the top."

Tilting his head back, Cole followed Liam's line of sight. They were heading to the top of the tallest building in the city and without electricity the only way to get there was to take the stairs. A lot of stairs. Grumbling under his breath, Uriah turned away from them and signaled to Jameson. The massive guy strode over and ran his knife through the zip-tie, quick as you please.

"Thanks," Cole muttered as he rubbed at his bruised wrists.

"Don't thank me," Jameson quipped. "You're first in line now. And I'll be watching."

"Not a problem," Cole responded, but the other man was already shifting away.

For a moment Cole watched him go, then Liam was striding after him with Dr. Bartholomew following close behind. Today was the day. The day they'd kill that thing inside the Wall, if there truly was such a being. Artificial Intelligence. The source. The program. It had many names and Cole still wasn't quite convinced.

With a look over his shoulder, he studied the two remaining soldiers walking along behind him. One was called Malik and the other Jones. They were the tech guys Uriah had scrounged up and ridden relentlessly for the past seventeen days. They were the ones who'd tackled the impossible, a wireless upload of the kill code into the Wall.

Only problem was, they hadn't tested it yet. In theory, it should work, but it wasn't like they could try it out. If the source did exist, then the second their little device came online and attempted to infiltrate its system, the jig would be up.

Quickening his steps, Cole hurried through the maze of paved streets before ducking into a side alley. Liam was just ahead of him now, holding his weapon at the ready. Not that it was needed. The city itself was on lockdown. Uriah had sent every man he could underground and the ones that wouldn't fit had been moved out of the city limits.

There was a risk to what they were doing. When the device came online, if it connected properly, then the source would be able to trace them back. If the kill code failed, then it left the entire city vulnerable. The source would know where they were, and that it was under attack.

"You're in front, Tanner," Jameson called.

The big guy had stopped at the entrance to an old office building. It was beautiful, with blue shimmering glass that stretched up over twenty stories high. How had this one escaped the bombs and flames? Cole wasn't sure, but from the outside it appeared pristine.

"How many floors?" Cole asked, as the others all crowded around.

"Twenty-six," Uriah supplied. "You first."

With a nod, Cole pushed through the glass double doors of the front entrance and walked into the past. The floors were marble with a creamy-white swirl design and a front desk made of modern wood. No one sat behind it anymore, as they once had. It was empty.

The sound of their team's boots stomping through the space caused echoes to bounce around the abandoned lobby. This was once a great place, a place of humanity and commerce. Now it was a wasteland.

Not surprisingly, when Cole breached the heavy metal door to the stairwell, the signs of apocalypse greeted them. There were chairs and tables shoved into doorways, sometimes down the stairs themselves. Landing after landing contained piles of paper, file folders and office equipment. Each time he approached a door, his instinct had him peeking inside.

There were dead bodies. Old, dried and skeletal now, the scent of their decay having long since dissipated. Who were these people, taking refuge from the war only to starve or freeze to death? Jaw clenching, Cole left them behind.

The ascent itself was brutal and he tried to be quick. Much to Cole's dismay even he was laboring. Uriah hadn't allowed him much space to exercise over the past few weeks, but regardless of how he felt, Cole kept up the brisk pace. To their credit, the others stomped steadily along behind him. Occasionally, Liam's bark of impatience would sound out, most likely aimed at his charge, the good doctor. Bartholomew was lagging.

When they reached the roof, Cole breached the door easily and pushed into the sunshine. Uriah's team had already scouted this location, the lock on the door was punched out.

A steady wind greeted him, whipping around his neck,

brushing over his cheeks, reminding him just where he was. On the tip top of a man-made tower, exposed to the overpowering blueness of the sky.

"This high enough?" Uriah asked. His shoulders were heaving, but his words were even and controlled. Damn, Cole was hoping he'd be more winded than that.

"It'll have to do." Malik ducked his head while Jones slipped off his backpack. Inside was the key to everything.

"Where's the good doc?" Uriah again.

"Three stories down," Jameson answered. "Liam might have to carry him."

"Oh for shit's sake," Uriah spat before ducking back through the door.

With a smirk, Cole paced away. The roof looked like any other that he'd ever been on. All flat gray nothingness surrounded by a low wall and dotted with vents and metal boxes protecting all manner of electrical equipment. None of it worked anymore. None of it was necessary.

The view though, it was pretty spectacular. Stretched out all around them were the unmoving remains of a once thriving city. Office buildings, hotels, businesses, apartments, restaurants. Beyond that were the warehouses, and further still the suburbs. It was like a photograph. A freeze frame from a life before, where you could pause the television, go make yourself a sandwich and come back to it.

Only, there were no cars that zoomed. No people walking along the sidewalks. No busses, no dogs barking or cats mewing. Those poor domesticated animals had been the first to get eaten. Cole grimaced at the thought, although he'd managed to avoid that particular source of food.

At the sound of Uriah's return, Cole stalked back over and folded his arms across his chest.

"We should be able to use this old antenna," Malik was saying. He'd climbed up onto one of the metal boxes fixed to the roof. "And boost the signal even more."

"Will it reach?" Uriah asked.

"Only one way to find out," Malik countered, reaching down for the small laptop Uriah'd had stored in his bunker.

Straightening, Jones handed the thing up along with a few cords and other pieces of equipment Cole didn't rightly understand. Just then, Liam breached the door with Dr. Bartholomew heaving and swaying at his side.

"I don't," the doctor puffed. "Understand... why I... have to... be here."

Liam's eyes flicked over to Cole but his face remained impassive. Maybe the good doc didn't quite get it, but the rest of them did. He was here to make sure he had skin in the game. If the mission went south, it left the seven of them the most vulnerable during an attack. If Dr. Bartholomew wanted to live, then he needed to give them the correct code. Anything less spelled out death.

"Are we set?" Uriah asked.

All eyes shifted to Malik who tapped quietly on the laptop above them. After another moment of silence, the soldier nodded his head. "We're a go."

"Okay Gene, buddy." Uriah crouched next to where the doctor had slumped on the ground. "If you give us the wrong code, then that thing is going to bomb the fuck out of us. Get it?"

"But-" the doctor sputtered. "How do you know?"

"I lived there," Uriah reminded him. "I've seen the defense stores it has. So, this is your last chance. You could barely make it up here, there's no way you'll make it down in time."

"What if it doesn't work?" The doctor whined, fidgeting around as his lungs continued to heave. "I'm giving you the only code my brother gave me. I'm telling you the truth!"

"We'll see." Uriah straightened. "Alright, what is it again?"

"GeneandDell2."

"Is that all one word?" Malik asked.

"Yes, capital G and D," the doctor qualified.

"Is *and* spelled out or is it the symbol?"

"Spelled out, but the two is a number."

"Okay gents." Malik's fingers flew over the keys. "Here goes nothing."

For the next thirty seconds, the only sound among them was the tap of computer keys and the soft whistle of the wind. Cole held his breath. How long would this shit take? How would they know if they'd succeeded? Failed?

"Done," Malik announced, then rocked back on his heels, eyes fixed on the screen before him.

"What's that mean?" Uriah demanded.

"It's in." Malik frowned. "I got access, I put in the password."

"And?" Uriah was impatient, tense.

Cole's shoulders hunched instinctively and his fingers

itched to grip a weapon, any weapon. It was time to bail. They should be getting the hell out of here. They were too exposed, lingering too long.

"I don't know," Malik rubbed at his chin. "Nothing's happening."

"We need to ghost," Cole announced, drawing Uriah's attention. "Now."

"Maybe that means it's dead," Malik offered, tapping again at the keys. "There's no response, just the blinking cursor."

"Out," Uriah gave the order, his eyes still locked on Cole. "It's baiting us."

"But it could be dead," Malik protested as he ripped electronics from their cords and began tossing them down to Jones.

"It was too easy," Uriah spoke, but again his eyes stayed on Cole, like just the two of them were talking. "If my guy at MIT couldn't hack it, I don't know why I ever thought we could. Let's get the fuck out of here."

"Roger," Jameson called.

The word was like a shot of adrenaline among them.

Suddenly, they were a burst of energy. All of them transformed into running legs, skidding boots, hurried breath. The stairwell filled with the sounds of their descent.

Liam was cursing, yanking the doctor along with him as the man tripped and stumbled down the steps.

Jameson was silent, flying downward as Malik and Jones passed them all at a fast clip. Their black backpacks thudded against their bodies, filled with the very equipment that may have just gotten them all killed.

Cole was last along with Uriah, the two leaders hanging back. If anyone was going to die from this mission, it would be them. How ironic, Cole thought, but then his brain turned that side of him off. He was all focus, all drive.

One after the other, they jogged, counting the landings, listening for the distant chug of a plane, or the whistle of a dropping bomb. As if they could hear it over the thud of their hearts, or the deafening sound of their running.

But somehow, Cole knew. It was coming. Death was coming. The only question was, how accurate would the fucking thing be? How fast and how accurate. Because now Cole knew beyond a shadow of a doubt that the source inside the Wall was not a person.

A person would have taunted them. A person would have typed back, *Nice try*, or maybe fought with them a bit, spit code back or tried to crash their computer or something. A person wouldn't have played dead, hoping to delay them on top of that building. A person would've been too curious, too full of ego for that perfection of calculation. AI. Shit. It was real.

Nearing the bottom now, Cole and Uriah were forced to slow down. Just in front of them, Liam had the doctor hoisted over one shoulder. The older man was weighing Liam down considerably and thereby delaying both Cole and Uriah, who refused to go around.

"Leave him," Uriah ordered. "Drop him Byrne, that's an order."

"Can't do it," Liam called, and kept moving.

Uriah growled from his position just ahead of Cole.

Then the first bomb hit.

The stairwell was dim anyway, with no lights from before, but even so, the space seemed to shrink on impact. Instinctively, they all crouched low, bracing themselves on the blue metal railing as the building shook and shivered.

Then for a moment, everything was utterly and completely quiet. Cole blinked. Slowly. Then the ringing in his ears started and turned up. Louder, louder.

Uriah turned to yell at him. He moved his mouth, but no words came out. *Go! Go!* Cole could read his lips simple enough. And then they were going.

Another bomb hit.

The building groaned and swayed. Smoke began to plume in the constricted space, or was it dust? Cole ran. He ran for his fucking life with his heart racing in his chest.

All he could see before him were the vague outlines of Liam and then Uriah. They were flying down, dodging chairs and debris. The doctor was gone now, no longer on Liam's shoulder. Cole didn't have time to think beyond that.

When they reached the bottom, Cole's breath expelled in a rush, his knees almost collapsing as the building began to fold. Another bomb, or no... maybe it was just the building itself. It was giving up finally... falling down on them.

Hands slapping across the marble flooring in the lobby, Cole pushed himself up and kept running. He couldn't see anymore. It was all dust and smoke. All around him chunks of ceiling were falling. Then the groan of metal and the deep rumble of destruction. There was a flash of light. The outline of a glass doorway.

Cole leapt for it.

Fell.

Then nothing.

Then nothing.

Then nothing.

CHAPTER THIRTY-TWO_
LIAM

THERE ARE SOME MOMENTS IN LIFE YOU NEVER FORGET. They're seared into your brain, burned into your eyes so that even when you close them, the full color memory floods you.

Liam had his share of those moments. The way his mom's eyes had grown a little wider just before his father pulled that trigger. The way his acceptance letter to Tulane had been folded into three parts, so crisp and clean. The way Hannah's eyelashes fluttered when she gave him that first kiss.

And now, the look of Cole's body, covered in a layer of dust and blood, buried beneath the rubble of a twenty-six story building. His best good friend. Liam would never be able to escape it.

"You scared the shit out of me," Liam whispered, running a hand down the side of Cole's bed.

He was all tucked in now, plastered in bandages and

ointment. The raspy sound of his breathing was still the most comforting thing Liam thought he'd ever heard.

After they'd dug him out, Cole had been unconscious. First in, last out. The fucker.

And part of it was Liam's fault. He'd slowed them down trying to drag dead weight along with them, trying to save the doctor.

"You," Cole exhaled the word in a puff. "Worry. Too much."

"Shhh," Hannah's brow furrowed as she leaned over Cole. "No talking."

"No talking," Liam echoed, but he choked on the words. Thank God Cole was talking. Thank God.

Behind them, the door to Hannah's bedroom swung open and Uriah made an appearance. Liam glanced over his shoulder quickly before stepping back from the bed. Since their failed mission three days ago, Liam had been unable to leave his friend's side. Leaning his body against the nearby dresser, he settled in to watch.

"He up?" Uriah asked. His face was scratched down one side with bruises blooming over his skin. Of course, Liam didn't look any better. In fact, they were all a bit worse for the wear.

"Yeah." Hannah gave up a small smile, then folded her legs beneath her on the bed.

She sat cross-legged, careful not to disturb the tray beside her. It contained a bowl of broth and a glass of water that Cole barely touched. He had to start eating, Liam knew.

"Good." Uriah cleared his throat and stepped closer, his

eyes dancing from Hannah, to Liam and then down to Cole. "Smelt tells me you're having trouble eating."

"I-"

"Don't talk," Uriah interrupted as Hannah bit her lip and Liam's jaw clenched. "Just listen. You've got to drink this water and have the bowl of broth. It's an order."

Cole's face turned sour before he made a tired attempt at rolling his eyes. When the medical doctor had first examined him, he'd found a broken arm, broken leg and likely rib fractures all down Cole's right side. Partially collapsed lung? Not sure.

Without the use of an X-ray machine or MRI, the extent of his internal injuries was unknown. So far, Cole didn't have a fever, which was a good sign, but the lack of appetite wasn't.

"I-" Cole began again, causing Hannah to reach for his hand.

"Shhhh," Hannah soothed, her fingers gripping onto Cole's gently.

But then Cole grunted and sucked his hand away. The abrupt movement caused him to moan and Liam to swear. *The fuck was Cole thinking?* Shoving up from the dresser, Liam took two steps towards the bed. Cole nailed him with a fierce look and slammed his good hand down against the mattress.

"I. Will talk," Cole heaved through gritted teeth before his face scrunched up and he sucked in a long breath.

Freezing in his tracks, Liam ran his hands up through his hair and caught Hannah's look. She was frightened, her eyes glistening suddenly before she ducked her head. Uriah merely nodded and the room grew silent.

They all waited. They all listened while Cole worked to catch his breath and pant through the wave of pain he'd caused himself.

"I. Owe you." Cole's eyes locked onto Uriah. "An apology."

"What?" Uriah looked shocked then took a step forward. "No, listen-"

"Yes," Cole interrupted. "AI. Real."

"Alright, buddy, alright." Uriah held up his hands. "We're square, okay? You believe I didn't order your assassination?"

Cole nodded, swallowed.

"Guess this means I can't tie you up anymore," Uriah added. "To keep your hands off my sister."

Cole smiled, then. A crooked half sort of grin that made Hannah huff a sad laugh and Liam exhale. Shit. Was he the only one that suddenly needed some air?

"So you got a chance to talk," Uriah said. "Now let's see you eat."

With a nod, Cole tilted his head to look at Hannah. Liam's jaw clenched, his eyes following Hannah's movements. Pulling the tray close to her, she picked up the bowl and cradled it in one hand. With the other, she dipped a spoon and slowly held it against Cole's lips.

When his friend sipped, swallowed and didn't choke, Liam felt light headed. Okay, so this was progress, right? After several spoonfuls, Cole's eyelids grew heavy and he started to sag. Hannah hurried to get him some water, of which he drank a little before passing out.

"The soup was laced with meds right?" Uriah asked quietly.

Hannah nodded, before easing off the bed.

"Any idea why he refuses to take them?" Uriah again.

"No." Hannah wrung her hands. "And he's in so much pain. Liam?"

"No idea." Liam rolled his shoulders, working hard not to get too pissed at his friend. The swing of his own emotions was damn near intolerable at this point.

"Well, he's not thinking straight," Uriah qualified. "Hopefully this will help."

"Yeah," Liam managed, grabbing at the back of his neck. "Any news from up top? What hit us? You think more is coming?"

"Best I can judge is the source used two of its long range missiles." Uriah slid a glance to Hannah before he shifted to go. "Why don't you walk with me?"

"You got him?" Liam asked Hannah, needing all of a sudden to leave.

"Wait." Hannah made a grab for his arm just as her brother slipped out the door. "We have to talk."

"About?" Liam's voice dropped as his eyes flicked back over to Cole's sleeping form.

"I want to help," Hannah whispered. "I lived inside the Wall... *longer* than Uriah. I worked with Dr. B, or Dell, or whatever his name was. I worked directly for the source."

"Hey," Liam shushed her before running a hand down

her arm. "You *will* help okay? When Cole's better, you will help."

"I could go back inside the Wall," Hannah rushed on. "I could get closer to it than any of you."

"Stop." Liam gripped her tighter, a sick sort of panic spreading through him. "The best way for you to help is to give us intel, but stay safe right here."

"But, I-"

"No, Hannah." Liam pressed his forehead down to touch hers. "That's the one thing we all agree on. You stay. Let us bring this thing down."

"But... look what happened to Cole." Hannah let loose a sob, began to cry.

"Shhhh, it's okay." Liam pulled her in closer to him, held her against his chest. "He's okay. We're all going to be just fine."

They were lies.

Liam knew it the same as Hannah knew it. But the words were meant to comfort, to pacify and soothe. And they were pretty, although really and truly false.

He couldn't guarantee they wouldn't all die. Trying to breach the Wall, infiltrate the source, input the code, pray it was the right one. The likelihood of survival was less than slim. In fact, it hovered at just about none. But the truth was, they had to try.

After a few moments, Hannah quieted. Stepping back, she released Liam. He stood there a while, watching her brush tears from her pretty flushed cheeks before she returned to Cole's side. Maybe it would turn out okay, he thought. Somehow, the three of them would all make it through this together, they'd wind up on the other side. But for now, Liam was suffocating and he had to escape it.

Turning on his heel, Liam pushed through the bedroom door and out into the hallway. It was quiet. The come and go of former soldiers was gone. Uriah was too busy with the happenings above ground to monitor the girls like he had before so only Cookie and Jameson were allowed down here now.

"You ready to be done with the nurse routine?" Uriah was waiting for him by the entrance to the kitchen. One black boot was crossed casually at the ankle while his broad shoulders tipped against the white wall.

"Just need something to do." Liam came to a stop, brushed at his wrinkled t-shirt and pair of sweats. Well, really they belonged to Uriah. The guy had stocked clothing in the bunker to last a lifetime. The pants were a tad short, but beggars can't be choosey and all that crap.

"Well, you can't go up top in that." Uriah smirked. "And Jameson could use a rest. I'm thinking you and he will be on opposite rotations. Him down here when you're up there and vice versa."

"What about Cookie?"

"Smelt? He's in love with my kitchen, he won't leave it. And why the hell do you guys call him that anyway? He's never once baked cookies."

"Isn't it obvious?"

Uriah shrugged before shoving off the wall and backtracking to the storage room. Once inside, the two of them sorted through black fatigues, various new boots, socks, jackets, and weapons. Liam's fingers itched and curled around a nice clean new rifle. The one he'd been carrying last had gone the way of the good doctor. Crushed in the rubble.

Liam shed his clothes in silence. By the time he'd suited up, he felt like a new man. The past three days he'd been consumed with thoughts of Cole, of Hannah, of life and death. It was a marvel how close to the line they always walked.

This time it'd actually meant something for one of them to tip too far over. Liam struggled with the feelings. He hated feelings. But then again, it was the cost of having Hannah wasn't it? She brought them out in him, and so he'd pay the price, because he'd tried to walk away before and the separation from her only made his weakness worse.

"Here." Uriah opened one of his many safes and started dishing out ammunition. "Once we're up top, we're going to move quick and quiet. Keep under cover as much as possible."

"We under threat?" Liam raised his eyebrows.

"Far as I can tell, the source fired two long range missiles that hit the office building where we attempted to upload the kill code," Uriah spoke steadily as he shut and locked the safe. "It doesn't have very many of those types of missiles and definitely doesn't have the capability to generate more, at least not at this point."

"So, the threat?" Liam prompted as he followed Uriah back out the door and down the hall.

"If I was the source..." Uriah glanced over his shoulder quickly before continuing to move towards the front door.

"I'd be doing some serious reconnaissance. We're talking unmanned drones, so high up you'd never notice them. Constant monitoring, but with an eye to fuel conservation."

"Do you think it knows?" Liam asked, following Uriah through the front door.

"That it was me?" Uriah frowned. Turning to lock the door behind them, he sighed. "No, the laptop couldn't be traced to me. I'd never used it before and paid cash for it a long time ago."

"So the drones…"

"Are trying to figure out if the missile strike was successful," Uriah continued, their footsteps echoed off the concrete walls as they left the underground and strode for the surface. "The source will want to know how many men are here, who they are, what types of weapons we have. It needs to know if we're worth another strike."

"And we've got to convince it we aren't." Liam ducked his head, shifting his rifle further up on his shoulder.

"Kind of hard with this many men, though," Uriah admitted. "Spring is coming, but it's not here yet. Distributing food rations, water and wood is hard enough without keeping everyone in hiding."

"So what's your solution?" Liam asked.

In silence, Uriah pushed through the final door and out into the parking garage. The light that seeped in from the opening to the street was beautiful, bright and blinding. Liam shaded his eyes but kept walking, following Uriah's figure until he came to an abrupt stop near the edge.

"We're building covers from building to building, but

mostly at night using very small crews. Within a week any number of men should be able to walk around a few blocks without revealing themselves to the sky. I'm connecting the food pantry, the water distribution center, bowling alley and trying to get to where we store wood."

"Alright." Liam cleared his throat, not able to keep himself from looking towards that particular high rise building, the one that had crushed Cole. It was gone of course, leaving a blank spot in the sky where it had stood tall and glistening only days before. "What can I do? You want me to work with a crew?"

"No." Uriah shook his head. "I want you to train soldiers."

"What?"

"Thousands of men that used to walk the streets freely, burning energy and doing whatever the fuck they wanted, are now on lockdown," Uriah explained. "They need something physical to do. They need discipline, a goal, a purpose."

"I'm not a leader." Liam ran a hand over the back of his neck. "That's Cole's gig."

"We're going to run an assault on the Wall," Uriah reminded him. "There are trained soldiers living inside there that will fight to protect it. If we're going to stand a chance of shutting the entire thing down, then we need trained men, too. Time to step up, Liam. We need you."

Sucking in a breath, Liam surveyed the empty street before him. Maybe if he threw himself into this training thing, then the constant replay of what had happened to Cole would leave him. If he was too tired, too focused, too busy, then maybe he could forget the look on Hannah's face when they'd brought Cole back to her.

Then maybe he'd be able to stop the sick twist of his stomach, the drop of his heart, every time the guy groaned or refused to eat. Was this Liam running again? Shit. Maybe. Okay, yeah, in a way, he was running. But it was the only thing that made sense to him, the only thing he could think to do.

"Alright," Liam responded finally. "I'll do whatever you want."

THE IVORY KEYS WERE WARM BENEATH HER TOUCH. THAT'S what happens when you play for hours. As Hannah's hands hovered over the piano, she closed her eyes. The sounds, the music. It floated up around her, consuming her, coming out of her. Inside of it, she found just a tiny slice of peace.

Opening her eyes now, Hannah glanced to Cole first. The past month had gone by so agonizingly slowly. His progress was creeping along, but it was painful. All the time, he was in pain.

Tipped back against the couch, Cole's crystal green eyes were shut. It was something they had in common. They both liked to disappear inside the melody. Whenever she played, his breathing seemed relaxed and calm. Not even sleep had him resting like her music did. That was the only fact that made her smile anymore. Because when Hannah wasn't playing, she was worrying.

Beside Cole, Lena rubbed absently at her belly with one

hand and patted Cole's knee with the other. Her pregnancy was still a secret, at least no one spoke openly about it. And to be honest, Hannah felt probably only Cookie suspected. The others were too busy, too consumed by their own lives to notice the subtle swelling. Uriah was hardly ever down here anymore and Liam only returned to sleep.

Frowning, Hannah reminded herself to focus but the last notes of the sonata faltered. With a slight shake of her head, she pressed on deliberately to end the piece.

When it was done, Jameson stared at her with narrowed eyes. Of all people, he was the only one who knew what she was planning. For now, he was still fighting her about it. They argued almost constantly, in hushed whispers in empty rooms. Despite his many reservations, she knew he would give in. Soon, Jameson would give her exactly what she asked of him.

Meeting his stare with one of her own, Hannah pushed back from the piano and crossed to Cole. His eyes fluttered open and immediately his body tensed. Crouching before him, she reached out to squeeze his hand. He forced a smile.

"I liked that one," Cole said before trying to sit up. "What was it?"

"Chopin," Hannah answered as both she and Lena braced his body.

"I can do it," he protested, using his good hand to swat at Lena. "I can sit up."

With a worried glance, Lena nodded her head and retracted her hand. Nibbling on her lip, Hannah did the same. It was torture, really.

Watching as Cole grunted and exhaled and inhaled and rocked forward, it was torture. But he insisted, and in the end he was able to sit up straight with a thin line of sweat glistening on his brow as a result.

It was the multiple rib fractures most of all that limited him. More so than his leg immobilized in a brace and his arm held fast in a sling. Every little movement he made cost him dearly. Filling his lungs was an effort, laying down was an effort, everything was a painful effort.

"Where to next?" Cole asked. The confinement was getting to him. Even with the game room, the library and the big screen television in the living room, he was bored. Bored and restless.

"Well, I think it's time for your meds and a nap," Hannah ventured.

"I'm not tired," Cole snapped, then began inching himself toward the edge of the couch. "And I can stand up by myself."

Hannah shot Jameson a look but the big man was already striding over. Cole was edgy these days, easily upset and more stubborn than she remembered him being.

"Easy there bud." Jameson gripped Cole's good arm and worked to hoist him to his feet. "I know all these chicks are crowding you, but there's a few thousand guys outside who'd love to trade places."

This earned a grunt and small smile from Cole who teetered a bit on one leg. Hannah and Lena both rose as well, but he quickly motioned them away.

"If you never give me a chance to get better," Cole reasoned. "Then I never will. Just hand me that sorry excuse for a crutch and I'll limp my happy ass to bed, alright?"

"Good plan," Jameson commented as Hannah retrieved the homemade crutch from where it was braced against the couch.

Like a funeral procession, the three of them all followed Cole's progress out of the library and down the hall. As he passed the entrance to the kitchen, Cookie hooted some encouragement before returning to the complex dinner he was making. The delicious smell of fresh baked bread was permeating the entire house.

When they finally made it back to Hannah's bedroom, Lena paused by the door. Taking Hannah by the arm, she pulled her in close. In silence, they watched Jameson help ease Cole back to sitting and then rotate him around before laying him down flat.

"Take a break," Lena murmured, her eyes searching Hannah's face. "I'll get him his meds. I'll stay with him for awhile."

"You sure?" Hannah ran a hand through her hair. She loved Cole. She wanted to take care of him, see him through his recovery. But the reality was, if she was going to move forward with her plan, she'd have to let someone else take care of him soon.

"Of course," Lena answered, before a knowing smile spread across her face. In a whisper she added, "I'll be taking care of a new little someone night and day soon enough. Better get some practice, right?"

"Lena." Hannah shook the other woman's shoulder. "When are you going to tell him?"

"I don't know." Lena frowned. "I hardly see him."

With that the little dark-haired woman traded places with Jameson. Stepping to one side, Hannah let her brother's most trusted soldier exit the bedroom and cruise unhindered down the hall. That didn't mean she didn't follow him, of course. And despite her whisper quiet bare feet, Jameson shot her a scowl over his shoulder.

"Go away," he said before heading straight to the kitchen.

"I'm doing it," Hannah hissed quickly, she didn't want Cookie to overhear. "With or without you."

"That so?" Jameson lifted an eyebrow at her as he strode over to the refrigerator and pulled the door open.

"What so?" Cookie asked. He was chopping some collection of vegetables while a large pot of water bubbled on the stove.

"Hannah's got big plans," Jameson taunted. Popping open the top of a beer, he quirked a smile at her before striding away towards the living room. He wouldn't dare tell, Hannah thought, nibbling furiously at her lip.

"Yeah," Hannah agreed, as Cookie's eyes kept flitting to her. *Reach, reach, make up something.* "I want to remodel."

"Re-what?" Cookie continued to chop, only half listening.

"You know," Hannah pushed on. "This place has been the same since I got here and it's driving me crazy. If we switched a few of the rooms around, changed the position of the furniture, switched out some paintings, it might make it feel different."

"Oh," Cookie huffed. "My ex-wife was always doing that crap."

"Thanks for the vote of confidence Cookie." Hannah rolled her eyes before making a bee line for the living room.

"That's what I'm here for!" Cookie called. "To boost your damn confidence! Not like I spend all day slaving over everyone's meals or anything."

The grumbling continued even after Hannah was out of ear shot. Jameson had come this way, she'd watched him go, but when she rounded the corner, he wasn't in front of the big screen like she'd imagined. Turning on her heel, Hannah huffed a frustrated breath before pushing through the door to the game room.

"Why did you do that?" Hannah demanded, as Jameson came into view. He was working a pinball machine, having emptied the beer already.

"Because it's what I *should* do." Jameson didn't bother to look at her as he punched and jammed at the game. "I should've gone to your brother weeks ago."

"But you haven't," Hannah prompted, her heart pounding suddenly at the very idea.

"No." Jameson cursed then drew back as the ball dropped helplessly through the paddles. "I haven't."

"Why?"

"I don't know."

"Because you agree with me," Hannah supplied, watching him look at everything in the room aside from her. "You know it's the best shot we have. My way will risk the least amount of lives."

"Except we're talking about *your* life," Jameson corrected, his eyes finally shooting to her face. "The life of Uriah's sister. Not to mention how Liam and Cole would feel about it."

"Since when do you make tactical decisions based on emotion?" Hannah countered, taking a step closer, sensing a new sort of weakness in him.

"I never have," he admitted. "But some choices you can't take back. There are some things I would do totally different, if I had the chance."

"Wait." Hannah's brow furrowed. "What are you saying? That you should've made a decision based on emotion?"

"Forget it." Jameson threw up his arms and went to walk away.

"You lost someone," Hannah guessed, saw she hit the mark as his shoulder's hunched. "A woman?"

"I said forget it."

"Could she be up there?" Hannah's pulse picked up the pace, a new sort of leverage appearing to her. "Behind the Wall? Who is she? A sister, a cousin or lover?"

"Stop." Jameson ran a hand over his face, sucked in a breath.

"A lover then." Hannah bobbed her head, reached out to brush down his arm. "She might be alive."

"I can't." Jameson's eyes jumped to hers, so filled with conflict. "I can't trade you for her. I don't know if she's there or if she's dead or anything."

"But it's possible," Hannah countered. "If she was in the right age bracket, no children, reported to a police station. Was she loaded onto a train? A bus?"

"I fucking loaded her myself," Jameson's voice hitched. "I thought… I don't know what I thought."

"It's okay," Hannah soothed. "She's probably there right now."

"Some trains never made it," Jameson offered. "So many of them died locked inside those cattle cars for God's sake."

"But some did make it." Hannah's mind worked quickly, offering him hope, a reason to do what she so desperately needed him to. "What's her name? I could find her."

"What's the point?" Jameson cut in, his voice harsh and low. "Once you're inside, you'll never come back out and neither will she."

"Unless I can enter the kill code."

"What makes you think you can? What makes you think the source would let you anywhere near the input server? Why would it even take you back anyway? You ran away."

"I was taken," Hannah corrected. "It records everything. Even though the cameras inside the Wall were off, it would know Andy led me there. It would have footage of him dragging me out to the woods."

"It could kill you Hannah Mae." Jameson was tortured now. "Then we'd have nothing."

"It won't kill me," Hannah argued, she was so certain of that. "I'm useful to it. Necessary. I'm genetically pure and I worked with Dell. I've been in the same room with that input server hundreds of times. I've opened the doors to that cabinet."

"You're asking me to sneak you out of here." Jameson stepped closer, looked down on her. "Violate your brother's trust, your boyfriend's trust. You want me to steal a car for you and deliver you to the Wall all by yourself. It's a suicide mission."

"We'll need a dirt bike or a motorcycle, too. For when the Jeep runs out of gas, or can't make it any further."

"If I do this..." Jameson paused, pinched the bridge of his nose. "I'll never be able to return to Uriah. They'll kill me for it."

"So you lay low until I enter the code," Hannah supplied. "It might take me a little time, but I'll do it. I know it'll work."

"Hannah Mae." He sucked in a breath, placed a massive palm on her shoulder. "I care about you, too, okay? I can't do this."

"What's her name?"

"What?"

"*Her* name," Hannah insisted. "So I'll know how to find her. I'll let her know you're fighting to get her back. That you've never stopped fighting for her."

As Jameson's hand fell limply to his side, Hannah knew she'd won. He was so defeated all of sudden and then he gave her his answer.

"Cass," he said simply. "Her name is Cassandra Roe. But I always just called her Cass."

THE DAY DAWNED THE SAME WAY IT ALWAYS DID. COLE reached out his left hand and smoothed his palm against the covers. They were cool beneath his touch, so he opened his eyes. Hannah wasn't there. She'd woken already, maybe jumped in the shower or gone to get breakfast.

With a groan, Cole tested his body in the same methodical way he had for the past two months. He wiggled his toes. They sent a shooting pain up his leg, but he bit back a gasp and continued on. The medical doctor had said it could take three to six months before he was healed up all the way. A fractured tibia *and* fibula is a giant pain in the ass, apparently.

Then came his knee, Cole bent it slowly and not very far. The movement stole the oxygen from his lungs. Sweat broke out on his upper lip and he squeezed his eyes shut. Damn that hurt.

Panting now, he eased his leg straight and worked to lift his arm. For the first time since the building collapse, Cole was able to move it with minimal pain. That was a good sign. He'd take it.

Easing his arm back down, he curled his fingers into a fist. Fuck. That still hurt.

Next came the best part, but he'd have to work up to it.

Laying motionless on his back, Cole let the waves of nausea and throbbing pain leave his body. As his head began to clear, he purposefully brushed the negative thoughts from his mind. Was his leg healing right? What about his arm? He was right handed, would he be able to shoot again? Walk without a limp? Make love to Hannah? What good was he? What purpose could he serve?

"Enough," Cole spoke to himself through gritted teeth. He couldn't let his mind overwhelm his body. He would fight this shit, same as he fought everything else.

Sucking in a breath, Cole clenched his stomach muscles and slowly but surely sat up. *Yeah, that's right. You feel that? No fucking pain.* His ribs had completely healed. He could breathe. He could laugh. That was something, and he'd cling to it.

Glancing around, Cole braced himself with his good hand and frowned. The shower wasn't running, and come to think of it Hannah had used her water ration the day before. That meant she was in the kitchen probably. He'd check there first.

Scooting his bad leg off the bed, Cole grunted before shifting to his good leg and standing up. He hop, hop, hopped to the wall where he braced himself against it and caught his breath. Who knew you had to use both arms in order to hop? Shit that ached.

When his head stopped spinning, Cole grabbed for his crutch, tucked it under the armpit of his bad arm and with a bitter slowness, limped his lame ass to the bedroom door. Out in the hallway, everything was quiet.

Looking to the right, Cole eyed the far door to the bunk room. Liam was on day shift now, with Jameson having requested nights. It was possible Hannah was spending some time with him before he left for work, and if so, Cole wasn't going to come a knocking. No, better to start his day alone and she'd show up eventually.

Grumbling under his breath, Cole made his way down the hall to the kitchen. Where else would she go anyway? Although at this rate, if the woman wanted to avoid him it wouldn't be all that hard. With the time it took Cole to change rooms, Hannah would be able to duck through any number of doors and come out on a completely different side.

Not that she would. She was a damn saint actually. Her and Lena both, putting up with him and his grumpy attitude the past eight weeks.

"You're awake." Cookie eyed him when Cole came to lean against the opening to the kitchen.

"Sorry to disappoint," Cole countered, and was rewarded with Cookie's robust laugh.

"Sure, sure." Cookie motioned him in. "Settle at the table and I'll serve up some bacon."

"Bacon?" Cole salivated. "I don't think I'll ever get used to it."

"And..." Cookie smiled before returning to the skillet before him. "Blueberry pancakes."

"Worth their weight in gold, I imagine."

"Frozen blueberries," Cookie admitted. "But still. Fruit."

"Fruit," Cole agreed, and inch by precious inch he got himself to the dining room table without falling over in a faint.

True to form Cookie began a one-sided conversation that blessedly didn't require much interaction from Cole. All the while the older man talked, he prepared food, opened cupboards, mixed batter, took down plates. By the time the finished product was placed in a steamy heap before him, Cole was more than ready to eat it.

After forking the first few mouthfuls down, Liam appeared. The next one to show was Uriah with Lena on his heels. Lifting his eyes, Cole greeted each of them in turn, noting how healthy and glowing Lena looked. She'd finally managed to put on a bit of weight which was a relief to probably everyone. Cole didn't like to remember how she'd looked when he first saw her, standing in that metal cage.

"Hannah still sleeping?" Cole asked, his eyes flicking over to Liam.

"Um." Liam frowned, his large hand wrapping around a mug of coffee. "I was going to ask you the same thing."

"Oh." Cole sat up straighter, glanced to Cookie. "She eaten yet?"

"Huh?" Cookie swept down to the table with his own plate and sat. "No, haven't seen her."

"Have you?" Cole nodded at Lena who looked surprised before glancing into Uriah's face.

"I haven't," Lena said. "But she's probably in the library."

"Yeah," Uriah added, still focused on his food. "She's been reading a lot lately."

"Okay." Cole's brow furrowed but then he gave his head a little shake. It wasn't like her to miss breakfast, but then again, she deserved some time to herself. He'd limp down to the library later, see if he could convince her to play for him.

The rest of the meal moved forward in silence. Forks scraped against plates, cups tapped against the table, chairs shifted with the weight of their owners. Cole used the time to plan his extremely limited, extremely monotonous day.

First he'd find Hannah. Then listen to her play, maybe. Then hobble to the weight room and see if he couldn't manage one of the machines. Surely he could work out just one leg and one arm... *something* for shit's sake. Then lunch. Then... repeat? They could watch another movie, or play Mortal Combat in the game room. At least he still kicked ass at that.

"Well, I'm off," Liam announced, shoving back from the table.

Dipping his head at everyone, he strode out, dropping his dirty plate in the sink before disappearing. Must be nice, Cole thought as he watched Uriah lean in and give Lena a quick kiss. These two bastards got to go up and out every single day. *To work. In the sun.* It made Cole want to scream.

"You'll get there," Cookie murmured quietly from beside him. "Patience, Boy-o. Patience."

Swallowing, Cole worked to unclench his jaw and carefully rise from his seat. It was more difficult than most people realized, getting up from a chair at a table. You had to stand, but scoot the chair out of the way, but not hit the table. It took all sorts of muscles you didn't even think about.

"She's not there," Liam's voice filled the room suddenly and had everyone turning. "Hannah's not reading."

"Oh, well." Lena frowned. "Maybe she's working out?"

Ducking his head, Liam faded from the entrance to the kitchen. He wanted to say goodbye to her before he left, Cole knew. They had a sort of routine now, and with Liam working long hours he didn't spend a lot of time at home.

Bracing himself against the table, Cole gritted his teeth and hopped his whole body backwards before shoving his chair back in place. Cookie clucked his tongue disapprovingly and plucked up Cole's dirty plate before he could reach it.

"If you overdo then you may never heal right," Cookie admonished. "You could re-injure yourself."

"I'm not an invalid, Cook," Cole countered.

"Actually, Boy-o…" Cookie's eyes glinted at him. "That's just what you are. Temporarily, but still."

"She's not there either," Liam's voice boomed out as he slid to a stop back at the entrance to the kitchen. "When did you see her last?"

"She's probably in the game room," Lena reasoned. "Or in the tanning bed?"

"I checked the tanning thing," Liam's voice was strained, his eyes shooting to Cole.

"I'll check the game room," Uriah volunteered, and strode away.

"When did you see her last?" Liam repeated.

"Last night." Cole frowned. "When we went to bed."

"Well, she's got to be here somewhere, fellas," Cookie reasoned. "Just calm down. Maybe she's sleeping in another room or something."

"I'll check." Liam dashed off.

"Nope!" Uriah called as he jogged into the dining room. Fishing for his radio, he picked it up and depressed the call button. "Jameson... Jameson, do you copy?"

Static. Silence.

"Jameson," Uriah again, his face flushing. "Do you copy? Jameson!"

Static. Silence.

No answer. Jameson always answered.

Liam slid back to the entrance of the kitchen. All eyes lifted to him, filled with the same question. He shook his head. Uriah swore.

"Jameson!" He shouted once more into the radio before taking off at a run. "Come back, damn it. Hannah's missing!"

Cole's heart thump, thump, thumped. Time grew still.

Uriah and Liam were gone in a flash, their voices echoing down the corridor. Cole knew they were grabbing keys and weapons. He could hear them shouting to each other, arguing about Hannah, about Jameson. Then they were gone, shoving through the front door and out into the world.

Lena sat heavily in a chair, her hand covering her mouth, her eyes darting between Cookie and Cole. Then

Cookie was dropping the plates he was holding, tossing them at the tabletop as he too took off.

Cole lurched forward, he had to go, he had to move. And he hardly felt the protest of his body, the slam of adrenaline at Han's absence all but erased the flood of sickening pain from his mind. But your brain can only do so much.

He made it halfway across the kitchen on that half-healed, partially destroyed leg before the damn thing gave up on him.

Then all Cole saw was the floor rushing up to meet his face. Then he was breathing against it, with Lena crouching beside him, pressing her hands to his back to keep him down. And even though he gasped and wriggled, turned and twisted, he was no match for the tiny woman.

The shock of it all wore off too quickly, and when the pain messages began to overwhelm his system, Cole was helpless against his own biology. A blinding white screen filled his eyes. He blinked, but it wouldn't go away. He felt like he was falling. Falling through the floor. Then the blackness consumed him and he passed out.

CHAPTER THIRTY-FIVE_
HANNAH

HER HANDS WERE COLD. NO, BEYOND COLD, THEY WERE numb. Maybe it was spring finally, but this far north, it was still bone chillingly cold. Thankfully, dawn had come, and with it, a creeping sort of sunlight and even a hint of warmth.

They'd been hiking for over an hour now and they were close, so unbelievably close. The Jeep had brought them through the night, speeding along until it ran out of gas. Then the motorcycle had gotten them quite a bit further before the terrain became too much. After stashing the bike, she and Jameson had continued on foot.

The woods that shot up all around them now were growing increasingly familiar. The Wall was coming. At any time, Hannah expected to see its flash in the distance.

Coming to a halt in front of her, Jameson took a quick swig from his canteen before handing it back. As she drank, Hannah watched him pull a paper map from his pocket and check their location for the hundredth time.

After that, he consulted a compass and looked up at the sky.

"We're close," Hannah prompted, earning a sharp look from the big man.

"We should be," he acknowledged. "But I've never been here before."

"I have."

In silence, he studied her for a few seconds before carefully folding the map and shoving everything back into his jacket pockets. Adjusting the rifle on his shoulder, Jameson cleared his throat and accepted his canteen back from her. He had reservations. Hannah was well aware. The entire drive up here, he'd tried to talk her out of it. But in the end, his foot kept pushing down on the gas pedal.

"I can do this," Hannah reassured him, reaching out to squeeze his arm. "This is going to work."

"I'm a dead man." Jameson gave his head a shake before turning away from her to resume their hike.

NOT THIRTY MINUTES LATER, JAMESON GOT HIS FIRST LOOK at the Wall. He whistled lowly, stopping in his tracks to shade his eyes. Even through the thick of trees, its height and shiny silver surface was overbearing.

Hannah's gut churned unexpectedly. Glancing down to the scar on her hand, she swallowed. *This would work. She could do this.*

Great, now she was convincing herself.

"Let's turn back," Jameson whispered. "We need a full assault team. Hell, we need an entire fucking army."

"No." Hannah went to brush past him, but he grabbed her arm.

"Hannah Mae," he hissed. "I can't let you do this."

"Then who's going to?" Hannah gripped his hand with her own. "You? Liam? Uriah? The source will pick you off one by one, none of you will ever make it inside."

"What if it picks you the fuck off? Huh?" Jameson's eyes darted over her face. "Have you ever thought of that?"

"It needs me," Hannah insisted. "If anything, it will drug and breed me, okay? That's the worst. It won't kill me and I'm pretty sure it won't even drug me. All the source knows is that I was taken by Andy. I'm innocent. I'm the same woman it had control of on the inside."

"You're Uriah's sister."

"And it doesn't know that I found him," Hannah reasoned. "I've thought this through a dozen times, maybe more than that. All the source knows is that Uriah is gone, not what he's been doing. And it knows I was taken against my will, but not by my brother. This will work. Think of Cass. This is the only way she'll ever be free."

"Hannah Mae," Jameson's voice was whisper quiet but his grip gentled and eventually he let go.

Stepping away from him, Hannah held up her hands to stop him from following. No sense in Jameson getting too close. There could be monitoring systems in the forest now. She didn't need him tripping them, getting her in trouble or himself killed.

"You stay," she said. "I've got it from here."

"But-"

"Thank you." Hannah smiled then. Stepping in close,

she raised up on her toes and gave him a soft kiss on the cheek. "GeneandDell2, right?"

"Capital G and D, the number two." Jameson nodded. "*And* is spelled out."

"Good." Hannah walked a few steps away, then spun around one last time. "Pray this works?"

"It's all I can do," Jameson countered. His face had drained of color, but he stayed still where she left him.

———

THE REST OF THE WAY WAS EASY. SHE WOVE THROUGH THE thick trees, noted the new growth of green shoots on the forest floor and the absence of snow in the shadows. Above her, birds were calling to one another. Nature was blossoming, emerging from a winter of confinement. For some reason, the feeling that consumed her was one of peace.

That all changed though. It didn't take long for Hannah to arrive at the edge of the tree line. Across the clearing, the Wall loomed large. It wasn't more than one hundred yards away. In her mind, Hannah remembered running the distance with Andy. He'd been screaming at her, she'd been bleeding.

Holding up her hand, Hannah noted the way it trembled. She felt the old raw fear growing deep inside her chest. Sucking in a breath, she shoved the feeling down and stepped into the open. The sunlight hit her full force and she lifted her eyes to watch the Wall.

There were no windows in it and no guard towers on top. Every so often, a tiny circle of glass signaled the use of a video camera. Though Hannah couldn't see the guards, she knew they could see her and so could the source. They watched her approach, she was sure of it.

If the source wanted to kill her, Hannah figured this would be the time. After all, the thing had already scanned her face using the cameras so it knew who she was. If it wanted her dead, this would be the easiest way to do it. They'd shoot her in the clearing and not have to deal with bringing her inside, disposing of her body or anything like that.

So with each step closer, Hannah's confidence grew. No shot came. Her lungs continued to draw breath.

At the bottom of the Wall, there was a single door inset into its smooth surface. She aimed for it. When she was about five feet away, the door swung open. In the dark threshold, a soldier stood in silhouette, his gun held off to one side. Hannah hesitated, but then he was motioning for her to come in. So she did.

It wasn't until the door locked behind her that Hannah felt the true gravity of what she'd just done. As her eyes adjusted to the sudden dim lighting, Hannah's heart pumped chaotically and she thought of Liam and Cole. She'd left them. She'd abandoned them and her brother and Lena.

Now the only way to get back to them would be to succeed. Closing her eyes, Hannah inhaled a deep breath and slowly let it go. Game time. If she was going to win, she'd have to eliminate those people from her mind. She'd have to compartmentalize them and shove them away. Her life depended on it; her life and so many others as well.

"Hannah," the soldier spoke, his voice was incredulous. "My God, what the hell happened to you? How did you get out there?"

"Dmitry." Hannah opened her eyes. She recognized this man, he'd worked with Andy. "I was taken. I was only just able to find my way back."

"Holy shit." Dmitry reached out with both hands and steadied her arms, peered into her face. "We didn't know what happened, all of a sudden you were just gone. No one could find you anywhere. First your brother and then Andy and..."

A buzz sounded from Dmitry's side and they both glanced down at his pager. He cringed instinctively, but then reached for the device and read its message.

"You need to be reprocessed," he said automatically, then reached for her right hand, felt along her scar. "Are you sick?"

"No." Hannah shook her head. "I'm fine, I haven't been ill."

"Good." Dmitry exhaled in a rush, his eyes darting up to hers worriedly. "The source will need to run tests, of course."

"Of course." Hannah nodded, then let him lead her on.

RAGE. BLINDING, DEBILITATING, FEROCIOUS RAGE. IT'S A feeling that Liam and Uriah handled very differently. For instance, Uriah hadn't stopped cursing since both Malik and Jones had confirmed Jameson didn't show up to his post the night before. Whereas, upon hearing the news, Liam remained utterly silent.

Even now, stuffed into an old Toyota 4Runner with six other guys, Uriah's mouth hadn't stopped running. He'd used every curse word, every threat, every sound imaginable to vent his underlying emotion... which was fear.

Rage is a result of mind-numbing, soul-crushing fear. Liam knew because he could barely fucking breathe. Every time he tried to suck in oxygen, he was only able to get about half a breath before his lungs pinched in on him. It took work, real honest to goodness work, to exhale that choked on, shaky, worthless air.

"He's a dead man," Uriah said it again. His hands

gripped the steering wheel so tight that his knuckles had turned white long ago.

"You sure he's going this way boss?" Jones leaned up from the rear seat. "Maybe he just wanted to take her... you know, for himself?"

Liam's head snapped around on his neck. He stared hard at Jones, into Jones, through Jones, who managed to look properly contrite before easing back. Of course all these guys would think that. Because that's what they'd of done if they got their hands on Hannah. They'd of driven her a little ways into the woods and... well.

Liam returned his attention back to the road. He *knew* Jameson. He wouldn't have done that. Would he? Fuck.

Glancing down at his hands, Liam noted his fingers were tingling. He tried to inhale again and his nostrils burned.

"He took the Jeep and a motorcycle." Uriah gestured in front of them to the dirt road. "I know the tracks, and no one has come this way since the last rain. It's obvious he came through here so shut the *fuck* up."

"Yes, Sir," Jones intoned and the group dropped into awkward silence.

This was his fault. Liam blinked his eyes, tried to clear the wavy sensation that clouded his vision. This was all his damn fault. If Jameson took Hannah where Liam thought he had, then it was on Liam. She'd warned him. For God's sake, she'd practically yelled her plan right in his face time and again.

Instead of listening to her, reasoning with her, keeping a closer eye on her, Liam had abandoned her. He'd run away. He'd let her deal with the stress of Cole's recovery and the awful confinement below ground.

Beside him, Uriah swerved suddenly around a pothole. The 4Runner rocked to one side and then back. A few of the guys murmured in surprise and all hands reached for something to brace themselves with. Uriah was driving like a bat out of hell. Jameson and Hannah had a head start after all, with an entire night of driving behind them.

The only thing Liam could hope for was that the Jeep broke down, and/or the motorcycle. If they were on foot, then Liam and Uriah could catch them. Otherwise, with the sun up high in the sky… it was probably too late.

"Someone else should drive," Liam announced. His stomach was turning. He just might throw up.

"No time," Uriah spat, then chanced a glance at him. "Puke out the window, piss out the window, do whatever you have to do. We aren't stopping. Not for anyone or anything."

"Roger," a few of the boys in the back called.

Liam ducked his head, then. Oh… the things he would do to Jameson when they found the bastard. And yes, they absolutely would find him. Between Uriah and Liam, there was no doubt in his mind.

Subconsciously, Liam's hand drifted to stroke at his knife. He hadn't used it in so long, hadn't felt the impulse to do so. Slowly, the old demand flooded his system. The bloodlust; it was upon him.

"I get him first," Liam spoke quietly, causing Uriah to spare him a quick look.

"Like hell you do."

"I'll save some of him for you," Liam persisted. "I promise."

"Not a chance, Byrne."

"Don't call me that."

"Whatever Liam," Uriah scoffed. "She's *my* sister."

"She's my-"

"What?" Uriah's eyes flashed as he spared Liam another glance. "She's your what?"

"Lena," Liam said softly. "She's my Lena."

Uriah returned his eyes to the road and bit down hard on his lip. Then he was slamming one palm against the steering wheel over and over and shouting, "Fuck!"

Again and again, Uriah screamed it, until he was out of breath.

Liam closed his eyes, absorbing the shimmer of agony that blasted at him from the driver seat. When Uriah calmed down, the rest of the drive continued in silence.

THEY FOUND JAMESON LATE IN THE DAY ALONG WITH THE Jeep. He was kneeling in some new grass, facing away from them with the sun setting in the sky. Above his head, the oranges, pinks and yellows lit up a fluffy layer of clouds. The motorcycle was laying on its side on the ground a few feet away.

Uriah jammed the 4Runner in park as Liam's heart leapt into his throat. Every soldier in the car was tense, their eyes scanning everything, looking for Hannah. But she wasn't there. The moment Liam saw the scene, he knew she was long gone.

Slamming open the doors, they all poured out at once, boots hitting the soft ground, rifles swinging up. Uriah got to him first and held his handgun pressed neatly up to Jameson's temple. When Liam came to a stop in front of him, Jameson's eyes said it all. He'd given up. He was ready.

"Where is she?" Uriah demanded. "Where's my sister?"

"Inside the Wall." Jameson's eyes tracked to Liam and held. So sad. He was so fucking sad.

"Why?!" Uriah's voice pitched in agony. He pressed the barrel of the gun harder into Jameson's head, making the other man sway. "Why would you do that? Why?"

"Guess I've been taking orders from a Linfield for so long," Jameson offered. "Didn't really matter which one anymore."

"Damn you!" Uriah cried, sucking the gun back a moment, he ran his hands through his hair. "Damn you, Jameson. Fuck!"

"I'm sorry," Jameson said finally, his eyes still fixed on Liam. "She convinced me."

"He's yours Liam," Uriah's words were shaky, his eyes darting amongst his men. "Fuck, I guess he's yours. How could you? Damn it, Jameson. You should've come to me."

"I know it," Jameson qualified. "So let's just get this over with."

Stepping close to Jameson, Liam squatted down and looked him straight in the eye. The guy didn't even flinch.

"What'd she say to you?" Liam whispered it before drawing out his knife. The blade felt heavy in his hand,

351

though. It wasn't like before, when the heft of the thing was all balance and perfection and light. This felt different. For the first time, this felt different.

"You want to hear that she loved you?" Jameson huffed a useless laugh. "A final goodbye?"

With a shake of his head, Liam frowned. Glancing down at his blade, he ran his thumb carefully over the edge. No, that's not what he wanted to hear.

"Because she didn't mention it on the ride here," Jameson's voice grew stronger, his gaze steady. "Course she didn't have to, God knows she showed it enough over the past two months."

Liam's eyes shot up to Jameson and the guy tilted his head to one side before he smiled... actually smiled at him. It was a crazy sort of *I'm about to die* kinda grin, but still.

"That's right." Jameson bobbed his head. "She started in on me right after Cole's injury. Hunted me down every chance she could, berating me. She wanted to help. She could help. We were all going to kill ourselves. She had the best chance."

"You should've come to me!" Uriah shouted it from over Liam's shoulder, causing him to raise a hand and signal for silence.

"What did she say?" Liam asked again. "In the end, something convinced you. What was it?"

"She said the source would never kill her." Jameson sucked in a breath. "I believed her. If worse came to worse, she'd be kept inside there until we could breach. If she did get the code in the server, then it'd save thousands of lives. Your life, my life, Uriah's life. Everyone."

For several seconds the men eyed one another. Liam's breathing was even and slow. Every muscle in his body was taut and controlled. *Jameson believed in her.* The words kept dinging around inside his head as the man himself sweated before him. He had believed Hannah, had listened to her, had done what she wanted, had seen her safely to the Wall.

Was it what Liam would've done? Hell fucking no. But it was something Hannah wanted, something she had pursued, and in the end, it's what she got.

What if... just what if she was right? How would she feel about Liam and Uriah when Jameson lay wasted at their feet? The massive guy was now *her* soldier. Jameson belonged to Hannah and not only that, he was her friend.

Mercy. The word throbbed like a headache inside Liam's skull. Hannah would demand mercy for Jameson. She wouldn't want him touched. And who was Liam to deny her? Especially when this was all his fault. If he'd only spent more time with her, talked through her ideas, kept her safe in that bunker.

Exhaling a slow breath through his nostrils, Liam sheathed his knife and stood up. With a glance over his shoulder, he eyed Uriah. The guy was still pacing, looking so conflicted and torn up. Jameson was more than his second in command, he'd become Uriah's best friend.

"Is there a chance she's still alive?" Liam asked finally, then returned his gaze to Jameson.

"What?" Uriah paused, growled. "Yes, it wouldn't kill her."

"Why not?" Liam tilted his head to one side, considering. "She ran away. She's your sister."

"The source would drug and breed her before it would kill her," Uriah bit out. "Happy? Huh? If it traces her back to us and what we've been doing, then she's going to be made into a vegetable in there."

"A living vegetable?" Liam qualified, his gut churning.

"Yeah," Uriah spat. "A living pregnant vegetable."

"Then seems like we need him." Liam motioned to Jameson who dipped his head low. "Plus, as long as Hannah's living, then he's under her protection and thereby, under mine, too."

Behind him, Uriah began once more to pace and rage. He shouted, threw curse words at Jameson, then at Liam and finally at himself. The soldiers who were gathered all around still held their weapons, but they breathed quieter. Everything was tipping towards a stand down, they could feel it.

"Fine." Uriah came to a stop finally. "She's got three months to kill that thing herself, if it doesn't die by that time, then we're burning the fucker down."

"Roger," Liam echoed.

But his attention wasn't on Uriah. No. Liam's eyes tracked the silent tears falling from Jameson's face as one by one, they hit the ground.

CHAPTER THIRTY-SEVEN_
HANNAH

SHE'D FORGOTTEN. ALTHOUGH THAT PARTICULAR WORD WAS sort of a sensitive one for her, it was still the truth. Hannah had forgotten just how beautiful civilization was. When Dmitry pushed open that final metal door to reveal the inside of the Wall, Hannah's breath caught in her throat.

Manicured green lawns, carefully maintained paths, an array of evergreen trees dotting the expanse. People. Women. Bundled up in coats, riding bicycles, walking, laughing, calling to one another. And children. The first crop of a new generation, born in safety, in peace, toddling across blankets spread out for them.

Hannah stilled, her hand shooting instinctively up to her mouth. Dmitry came to a stop beside her after securing the door shut.

"Are you alright?" He murmured, his dark eyes questing but kind. "I can't imagine what you've been through out there."

"Yes," Hannah managed to gasp out the word and replace her arm neatly at her side. "Thank you."

"Of course," Dmitry replied. Again, his pager buzzed at his side and doggedly he retrieved it. After checking the display, he gestured for them to keep walking. "You'll be reprocessed through medical first. The routine hasn't changed from when you and Flynn handled it."

Ducking her head, Hannah nodded her agreement and fought the swell of sadness that overtook her. Flynn would never make it back here, or anywhere else for that matter. The fiery redhead with all her smarts and vigor had met a truly awful end, and worse, it was one Hannah couldn't even talk about.

The source was always listening, always watching and monitoring. There was no way she could confess anything out loud. Any slip could cost Hannah everything.

"After you clear through medical," Dmitry went on, aiming for one of the many polished new buildings stacked up before them. "Then you'll be able to move back into your old apartment. No one has needed it since you disappeared. The new family units still aren't full."

"Alright." Hannah couldn't think of anything else to say.

Nibbling on her lip she twisted her fingers in the fabric of her canvas jacket before purposefully making herself stop. Nervous habits, ticks and tells were monitored as well. Though it would make sense if she showed some signs of stress at being back here, after all, she'd been gone for what... almost a year?

When they reached the pristine office building, Hannah paused at the foot of the wide concrete steps. On either end were planters containing a few flowering bushes just starting to spit out buds. She knew the grounds crew would pull them in at night, or cover them to keep the frost at bay.

"Ready?" Dmitry had climbed the steps and was holding open the front door.

"Yes," Hannah replied, ducking her head and closing the distance between them.

This place was so familiar. She'd walked the hall countless times before, but it was always for work. This time she was the patient. Stopping at the door marked *Female Medical*, Dmitry held it open but did not join her in crossing the threshold. Inside, genders did not mix.

Reaching out, Dmitry gave her forearm a quick squeeze before departing. Words were few here. You learned to interpret gestures, eye contact or lack thereof, instead. Of course, the source was probably doing that, too. Tracking, learning, growing, adapting. Dmitry had questions for her and by his quick touch, he wanted to see her again, but he didn't voice any of it.

Rotating around, Hannah absorbed the quiet peace of a doctor's waiting room. As the door clicked closed behind her, a few other women glanced up before returning to their tablets. There was a collection of padded chairs lining the walls, a water cooler in the corner with little metal cups and a coffee table in the center of the room.

Crossing to the receptionist window, Hannah placed her palm flat against the tablet on the counter until it beeped once. A small woman in pale green hospital scrubs sat behind the desk and smiled gently at her before gesturing to an open seat.

"The nurse will see you shortly," she said, her hazel eyes blinking.

Hannah didn't recognize her from before. As she took a seat, she wondered what became of Trudy, the receptionist that had worked for Flynn. Maybe it was her day off, or maybe she'd been reassigned.

After an hour of waiting, Hannah's name was called and she rose from her seat. She was greeted by a nurse's assistant at the door and led to an open area where her height, weight, blood pressure and temperature were taken. This was the job Hannah herself used to do.

Peering at the woman's name tag, she read *Belinda*, in small black letters. She was another new face. Hannah held back a frown.

After providing a urine sample, she was led to a closed examination room where she was given a cloth gown to change into. It was also pale green, like the scrubs, and hung open in the back. For several more minutes, Hannah sat awkwardly on a padded table that crunched and crinkled with a thin sheet of disposable paper. So this is it, she thought, my first test to pass.

When a knock on the door sounded, Hannah's pulse jumped reflexively, but immediately she coached herself to stay calm. In walked two women pushing a tray full of instruments between them. The same nurse's assistant busied herself arranging the various tools while the nurse, a tall woman with wavy black hair and wide brown eyes, did all the talking.

"Good morning, my name is Zoe." The woman clasped her hands together and smiled. "From the scan of your palm I take it your name is Hannah and you've been here before. Am I right?"

"That's right," Hannah acknowledged, the woman had an endearing way about her. "I used to work here with Flynn."

"Yes." Zoe bobbed her head before grabbing for a small black electronic box. "I was on rotation with her for only a month before she disappeared, but you'd been transferred by then. May I scan your back?"

"Of course." Hannah sucked in a breath and shifted around. After a second, the scanner beeped and Zoe stepped away.

Turning back around, Hannah nibbled on her lower lip while the nurse switched from the scanner to her tablet. She click, swipe, clicked for a minute before her brow furrowed and she began to read. At one point, her eyebrows raised, but only slightly. When she was done, she sucked in a breath and returned her focus to Hannah.

"The source informs me that about a year ago you were forcibly abducted by a male associate and taken outside the Wall."

"Yes," Hannah whispered it.

"And now you've managed to return... alone."

"I have." Hannah swallowed, her throat was suddenly dry.

"Is that what happened to Flynn? There others who've disappeared, but we never knew how or why. Have you seen them? What's it like out there? Is it dangerous?"

Zoe's questions tumbled from her mouth, one right after the other, until the pager at her side began to buzz.

The source was calling. Right here, right now, just like with Dmitry.

It was following every step of her progress. Hannah gripped her hospital gown in her fingers while the nurse's assistant stood wide-eyed. Zoe stopped mid-sentence, her hand shooting to her side as she retrieved the pager. After reading it, she heaved a quick breath before arranging her face in a complacent smile.

"Forgive me," Zoe intoned. "My questions overstep my role."

Hannah held her breath as the nurse continued on, her eyes disagreeing entirely with the words coming out of her mouth. Reaching behind her, she pulled a new tablet from the instrument tray and handed it to Hannah along with a new pager.

"You will find great resources for dealing with sexual assault and trauma included in your tablet contents. I will also refer you to our staff psychologist for a series of interviews concerning your time on the outside."

"Thank you," Hannah managed before accepting the tablet and pager in both hands.

"Now I must draw blood, continue with a physical examination and insert a new microchip into your hand," Zoe informed her. "I can see your old one was removed."

"Yes," Hannah agreed, before glancing down at her scar.

It was time to get the source placed back inside her. She only hoped the thing hadn't learned to read minds. As the slap of latex gloves and click of plastic cases sounded,

Hannah watched the nurse's assistant ready her blood draw equipment. When Zoe approached, tourniquet and anti-bacterial swab in hand, Hannah looked away.

"Did you become pregnant while you were gone?" Zoe asked, cleaning the small spot on Hannah's arm.

"No."

"Was your IUD removed?" Zoe again as she inserted the needle. "Small pinch."

"No."

"I'll have to check and then remove it today."

"Why?" Hannah's eyes popped back over to search Zoe's face.

"Your breeding phase is past due," Zoe explained. "It's time for you to choose a mate."

"But I've been gone…" Hannah began to protest but the look of warning on Zoe's face cut her off.

"You will have ninety days to select your own mate. If you cannot find someone, then you can opt for a pre-selected male chosen by the source." Zoe handed a bright red tube of Hannah's blood off to the assistant who switched her for an empty vial. "If you choose not to conceive, then your eggs will be extracted and implanted into donor women."

"Donor women?" Hannah's eyebrows raised.

"Yes, all sterilized women are now considered maternal donors." Zoe stared straight into Hannah's eyes. "Their genetic material has been removed and so now can be replaced by yours, which is considered pure."

"How…" Hannah pushed the words out. "How many of my eggs would you take?"

"As many as possible." Zoe tilted her head to one side, handing off another full vial of blood. "You'd have to undergo fertilely treatments first, of course."

Hannah's mouth dropped, this was a new procedure. At the time she'd left, the source hadn't implemented it yet. Removing the needle, Zoe pressed a small piece of gauze to Hannah's arm and proceeded to tape it down.

"The best course is to choose your own mate," Zoe instructed. "You can always switch after two births if it doesn't work out."

"I-"

"Alright," Zoe interrupted. "Ready for the microchip?"

"Um, yeah," Hannah mumbled. "Yes, of course."

LEANING HER SHOULDER AGAINST THE THRESHOLD OF THE door, Hannah looked into Flynn's old bedroom and tried hard not to cry. The space was exactly as she'd left it. Everything was in order, from the neatly made twin sized bed to the small white ceramic lamp on the dresser. Up in the corner of the room, the little red light below the camera glowed.

Folding her arms over her chest, Hannah cleared her throat. She couldn't set foot inside this room. She couldn't set foot inside Lena's either. If she did, if she let herself collapse against their clothes hanging in the narrow closets, then the source would wonder why.

Hannah couldn't let on that she cared. At least not beyond a normal sense of loneliness. The women had been taken by Andy before her, but she didn't know if the source knew that. He hadn't had to force them the way he had with Hannah, maybe their escape was more clean.

Retreating back into the hall, Hannah moved to her

own bedroom. The silver doorknob beneath her hand was cool to the touch. The temperature controlled apartment was hovering at sixty-eight degrees. With a twist, Hannah pushed inside. This time, she let a few tears escape down her cheeks.

Walking to her own closet, she pulled out her collection of modest clothing, running her hands over worn denim jeans and soft shirts. On the floor were a variety of shoes. There was a department store of sorts inside the Wall along with a fitness center, library, movie theatre and so on. The source was trying to keep things as close to before the war as possible.

If you worked, which everyone was assigned a job of some sort, then you earned stipend. The amount you got was tallied up in a virtual bank that each store automatically kept track of. All you had to do was place your palm on a scanner and it would register whether or not you could afford the merchandise you wanted.

Flopping on the bed, Hannah threw an arm over her eyes and sniffed. Absently, she wondered if the source would allow her access to her former unspent stipend. She supposed it didn't really matter. After all, she wasn't planning on being here for long. Although, she would need it in order to get food in the cafeteria or at the restaurants.

Speaking of which, her stomach was rumbling unhappily. Since breaching the Wall this morning, Hannah hadn't stopped to eat. After her medical check, she was released to walk freely out the door and her feet had taken her here... taken her home.

With a sigh, Hannah rolled off the bed and got up.

Shrugging out of her jacket and travel worn clothes, she padded naked to the single bathroom and got in the shower. The water was hot almost instantly and fresh and not restricted. Between the shampoo, conditioner and body wash, Hannah lingered under the never-ending spray. It was the longest, hottest shower she'd had in a year.

When she was done, she retrieved an old towel that'd been hanging in the lonely bathroom for forever. Bringing it to her nose, Hannah inhaled the staleness of time. After drying off, she returned to her room and changed into a pair of simple jeans and warm sweater.

On the surface of her small desk, her tablet glowed. With a frown, Hannah stepped to it and swiped across the screen. A welcome message displayed with a reminder about meal times at the cafeteria as well as the balance of her former stipend account. Swallowing the lump that had formed in her throat, Hannah stared down at her right hand. The microchip lay just under her skin but she couldn't feel it, at least not yet.

Could the damn thing read her mind? Track her thoughts? Or was the source simply running algorithms that so accurately predicted human behavior that it would know she must be hungry? Hannah preferred to believe the latter. She preferred it because if not, then she was really and truly screwed.

On her way out the door, Hannah's pager buzzed. Glancing down at her desk her brow furrowed, she'd forgotten to place it on her hip where all pagers were required to be. After retrieving it, she checked the display.

The source had an appointment for her to keep, and dinner would be provided.

Closing her eyes briefly, Hannah reminded herself to remain calm. She checked her breathing, slowed it down, cleared her mind and proceeded to go exactly where the source indicated. Back to the medical office building, with its clean white facade and glistening windows.

On the second floor, Room 201 was the first door on the right after cresting the staircase. Hannah placed her trembling hand on the doorknob, sucked in a deep breath and pushed into the Office of Psychotherapy.

Again, a pleasant receptionist welcomed her inside with a scan of her palm print. The waiting area was devoid of other people however, so Hannah took a lone seat and swiped absently through her tablet. There were informative articles about life inside the Wall, photos of people enjoying a live band at the outdoor amphitheater, and participating in a bicycle race.

Hannah was so absorbed in the colorful display that she didn't notice a woman approaching her. When the woman cleared her throat, Hannah jumped, letting the tablet tumble to the thin carpeted floor.

"Oh my," the woman spoke in a quiet voice. "I didn't mean to startle you."

"I'm sorry," Hannah fumbled, before reaching to retrieve her tablet. "I wasn't paying attention."

"It's alright." The woman blinked soft brown eyes and brushed a hand at her careful sweep of short dark hair. "My name is Miriam Tomey and I'll be your facilitator today."

"Facilitator?"

"I can't claim the title of Doctor," Miriam admitted with a smile. "But I've been trained specifically to speak with those who've endured trauma."

"I see."

"Won't you come with me? The source has sent us a meal to enjoy while we talk."

Hannah ducked her head before rising to stand. Trailing after Miriam, she entered an intimate office space. It looked like any psychologist's office Hannah ever remembered seeing. There was a wide window with a wooden desk situated beneath it. In the center of the room was a coffee table flanked by a soft couch and a pair of overstuffed seats.

Miriam gestured for Hannah to take a seat on the couch, surprise surprise, while she herself chose one of the seats. A tray of food was arranged on the low coffee table. It included two perfectly measured and portion controlled plates filled with roast chicken, a vegetable medley and lightly seasoned white rice. Healthy. All the food served by the source was healthy.

"Are you hungry?" Miriam asked, while handing Hannah a plate.

"Yes," Hannah admitted, her mouth had begun to water the second she'd laid eyes on the food.

"You've been on the outside a long time," Miriam again, this time retrieving her own plate and settling it on her lap. "What was your diet like out there?"

"Not like this," Hannah offered. Stay as close to the truth as you can, she thought. It was easier to remember a lie if it had truth woven into it. "When Andy first took me, he hunted a lot. We ate small animals mostly, rabbit, even squirrel."

"Were you often hungry?"

"Yes." Hannah proceeded to shovel cooked carrots and corn into her mouth. "One time we even ate wolf."

"That's interesting," Miriam commented, her fork pausing on her plate. "Because you look quite healthy now. Your weight is within the acceptable parameters for your height."

Dropping her eyes to her plate, Hannah broke into a cold sweat. Yes, that's true. She looked too healthy. She was going to have to come up with an explanation, and fast. One good enough to fool Miriam as well as the source.

"I understand discussing trauma can be very challenging," Miriam continued on. "But I promise you this is a safe place. What you say here is very important to your future recovery. Giving voice to what happened to you is healing."

"Yes." Hannah nodded, feeling instantly guilty as a solution came to her mind.

What she was about to do felt like a betrayal of the highest order. Lena had confided her own story to Hannah, sometimes in excruciating detail. It had helped her friend, in the end, and Hannah was glad of it. But now... now she was going to use it to her own advantage. The thought made her slightly sick.

"The source wishes for you to be cleared back to work," Miriam spoke into the silence. "You could return to your job as a nurse's assistant. But first, we need to work through your time out there."

"Alright," Hannah conceded.

Dropping her eyes to her right hand, she felt a quick pulse from the microchip, then an instant flood of nerve-swamping peace released to flow through her blood stream. When she opened her mouth to speak, Lena's story just flooded right out. "Andy sold me to a group of men. They're the ones that fed me."

"Ah." Miriam gave an encouraging nod before reaching for her tablet. She swiped and clicked and then settled her gaze back on Hannah. "Tell me more."

CHAPTER THIRTY-NINE_
COLE

COLE GRIPPED THE LONG METAL BAR IN BOTH HANDS. IT WAS warm beneath his touch, and slightly slick. Sucking in a breath, he pushed it up into the air, away from his chest. With a grunt, he held it still above him before slowly lowering it back down. Again, he thought, his back pressing against the padded workout bench.

He didn't care if his right forearm hummed in pain. He wanted to feel it. Physical pain was the only thing he wanted to feel.

"Fifty," Cookie counted, as he hovered over Cole. "I think that's enough, Boy-o."

"No." Cole pushed the barbell up once more, then lowered it back down. "More."

"Five more then," Cookie conceded, his brow furrowing. "I shouldn't have put the extra weight on."

Ignoring him, Cole pumped through another set of ten. By the time Cookie stepped in to forcibly retrieve the barbell, Cole's muscles were jumping and his lungs burned.

Sitting up, he wiped the sweat off his brow with the back of his hand.

Injury or no injury, the past eight weeks since Hannah'd left had been pure and utter torture. Cole used the time the only way he knew how, to get stronger, better, bigger, faster, than he'd ever been before.

It was slow work, especially at first, but now that his bones were healed, Cole was able to push himself even harder. Though it wasn't without cost. Cookie's harping being the number one annoyance.

Getting up from the bench, Cole limped his way over to the door and pulled it open. That damn right leg just hadn't healed right. Everyday he kept waiting for the lameness to smooth out, but it didn't. He was starting to realize the inevitable. He was starting to realize that this was his new normal, that he'd never be quite the same.

"Where are they?" Cole threw the question over his shoulder, knowing Cookie would be close on his heels.

"Up top," Cookie answered. "I think Liam's showing Mr. Big Stuff his progress with the specialty units."

Ducking his head, Cole aimed for the bunk room. He would have loved to shower, but today wasn't his day and all his clean clothes were stacked up beneath his bunk. Neither he nor Liam had the stomach to stay in Hannah's room after she'd gone. Even now, her name in his head caused a sort of pinching sensation to bloom in his chest.

As usual Cookie dogged his steps, peppering him with needless conversation. Cole grunted and shrugged and generally ignored ninety-nine percent of the remarks.

After changing into pants and a long sleeve shirt, he laced up his boots, grabbed his rifle and was on his way.

"Where do you think you're going?" Cookie questioned as they cruised back down the hall.

"Out," Cole's answer was gruff, they were just passing the closed door to Hannah's bedroom.

"Well, who's going to stay with Lena?"

"You." Cole smiled to himself as the older man launched into a series of lamentations.

Cookie didn't like being left behind any better than Cole did, but that was rule number one around here now. Lena wasn't ever left alone. And it wasn't because any of them thought she'd bolt. It was because she was freaking pregnant. Yeah, shock and awe.

When Uriah'd found out, he'd practically brought the house down. As if the guy needed anything more to stress out about. First there was running the city, then the assault on the Wall, then his sister fucking ghosts them and now his girl was carrying his baby. His first and only baby.

Needless to say, the place had been on lockdown ever since, though Lena didn't seem to be bothered by it or anything else. She was all peace and zen, all the time.

Remarkable really, under the circumstances. In a few months she'd be giving birth, without a hospital, or medication, or anyone with an ounce of experience. Even the resident medical doctor admitted to only ever assisting in one birth and that was decades previous while he was still training.

Coming to a stop at the open door to the library, Cole

peeked his head in and spied Lena. She was curled up on one comfy couch, stroking that small protruding belly with one hand and flipping the pages of a book with the other. Sensing him, she looked up and offered a relaxed smile. She was beautiful. Cole'd never thought there was much truth to that whole pregnant woman glow thing, but apparently there was.

"I'm heading out," he announced, and in response the little dark-haired pixie rolled her eyes.

"Tell him I need some sun." Lena held up the book she'd been reading and waived it side to side. "I can't use the tanning bed and it's important."

"So says the book?" Cole asked, eyebrows raised.

"So says the book," Lena confirmed. "And tell Cookie he can go up top, too. I'm perfectly safe down here by myself."

"Yeah right," Cookie chirped from behind Cole's shoulder. "I'm not going up there so Mr. Big Stuff can deliver his boot unto my backside."

"Oh guys." Lena shook her head. "He's not that bad."

Cole and Cookie shared a glance before both of them retreated back into the hallway. Lena's voice followed them.

"He's not!" She called, but Cole was already at the front door with Cookie grumbling in the background.

Fishing for his set of keys, Cole unlocked the heavy metal door and shoved it open. As he turned to close and lock it, he caught Cookie's gaze. The older man was leaning up against the wall inside the hall, his mouth shut for once. It made Cole pause.

"Someone's gonna have to stay behind with Lena," Cookie whispered, and he didn't mean today. No, Cole knew what he meant. Someone was going to be left behind on babysitting duty during the assault on the Wall.

"I know." Cole dipped his head, his pulse jumping. There were only four men that Uriah Linfield trusted to be alone with his woman. Only four.

"You know it ain't gonna be me," Cookie supplied. "And it's got nothin' to do with your leg."

"Fuck. You." Cole growled before slamming the door.

For a few moments, Cole's shoulders shook. Each breath he took was ragged as he sucked it into his lungs. He'd spent months working, healing, improving. He knew he could fight just as well as he had before, maybe better.

Sure, he limped a little when he walked, and even more so when he ran. But he could still shoot. His hand to hand was on point. Hell, he could whip the shit out of the vast majority of Liam's trainees.

This leg would not keep him from going to war. This Godforsaken leg would not prevent him from taking part in the assault. He would participate. He would be there when they got to Hannah.

So what... he couldn't outshoot Cookie. The truth was, no one here could. But Cole had other things to offer and when it came down to it, Uriah would choose him. He would make Cookie stay home and look after Lena while the rest of them did their duty. Cole was sure of it. Wasn't he?

With a quick shake of his head, Cole twisted his key in the lock and turned to go. The sound of his boots traveled down the concrete halls, past the bustling bowling alley and out into the world. He took a series of covered walkways between office buildings until he arrived at a tower two blocks over.

Once inside, Cole pushed through the empty lobby and headed for the stairwell. At the door to it, he paused. With his hand clasped around the handle, Cole worked to control his breathing. His heart jumped, his body tensed and a line of sweat burst on his upper lip.

It's okay, he coached himself, just open the door and walk up the steps. Blinking, he released the handle and took one step back. Stairs. They fucking spooked him now. Sure, he'd almost died in a place just like this, not that long ago, but even still, the weakness made Cole crazy. He hated it.

Hopping in place on both feet, Cole blew out a slow breath and then grabbed the handle. Yanking the door open, he charged up the stairs. As he climbed, the steps swayed and a slow roar built itself from deep underground. The sound grew and grew in intensity until Cole swore they were having an earthquake. Only, he knew they weren't. This had happened to him before. It was all in his head.

Trying not to trip, Cole kept his vision focused on each step as he sprinted up the four flights of stairs. During flight number two, his throat closed up on him, making it so he couldn't hardly breathe. He pushed through anyway.

When he got to the fourth floor, Cole dove for the door to the hall and wrenched it open. Stumbling into the empty corridor, he braced himself against one wall and tried not to black out. He'd made it, just like he'd made it before and just like he'd make it again.

This bullshit mental hallucination he endured would not go on forever. Cole simply refused to let it. And if Uriah knew, then for sure he'd choose Cookie to go and force Cole to stay. That was not going to happen.

After a solid minute, Cole was able to collect himself. The humming in his brain subsided and was replaced by the far off shouts of men. Behind every door on this floor were groups of soldiers training. Their planned assault wasn't too far off now, another month at the most.

Shoving upright, Cole walked along the corridor listening and looking until he found the right door.

"Hey," Liam called when he spotted him lingering in the doorway. "Come look at this."

With a nod, Cole entered the room as smoothly as he possibly could. He did his best to hide his limp, but even so, he was unable to make it disappear completely.

At a long table positioned against a far wall stood Uriah and Liam along with three other soldiers and Cole's least favorite person... Jameson, the giant asshole. Cole still couldn't believe how easily that guy had gotten off. He'd delivered Hannah to the fucking Wall and there wasn't a scratch on him.

If it'd been up to Cole, the other man wouldn't be breathing. Unfortunately, Cole had been passed out in the bunker during that particular time and Liam, with all his talk of mercy, had won out. Who the fuck would've seen that shit coming? Not, Cole.

But alas, Jameson's just deserts would be served eventually. If Han was hurt in any way, that guy was first on Cole's hit list.

"As you can see there aren't many weaknesses," Uriah was saying, as he pointed to a blue print of the Wall. "The power plant is situated within the perimeter wall so we can't just cut a line."

"Can we overwhelm it in some way?" Jameson asked. Cole glared, he couldn't help himself.

"The power grid?"

"Yeah."

"Not that I can figure," Uriah went on. "That would be the easiest solution but it would take a crew getting inside the perimeter and then another breach of the power station building, which is heavily guarded."

"What about water lines? Sewer?" Liam this time, looking down, frowning. Cole followed his gaze.

"All self-contained, if you can believe it," Uriah countered, then pointed. "That's why this location was chosen in the first place, it sits on a giant underground aquifer. All waste water is processed through a plant and used on site. It's how they water lawns, farm, launder clothes, the list goes on."

"What about the perimeter wall itself?" One of the soldiers asked. "Can we use ladders or climb it? Launch over it?"

"I suppose it's possible," Uriah acknowledged. "But keep in mind there are thousands of soldiers on the inside that will sit there and pick us off with rifle fire. I don't think it's a wise choice, too many casualties."

"There were trains." Liam brushed his fingers against the paper in several locations. "Lena told me the tracks led right up to the Wall and then stopped."

"That's true." Uriah's brow furrowed. "All large material was inside the Wall before they completed the build. Now the biggest opening in the perimeter wall itself is the same size as the door to this room."

"What type of incendiary do you have?" Cole asked, drawing Uriah's gaze up and over to him.

"The perimeter wall is made of steel and filled with concrete. It's up to fifteen feet thick in some places with narrow walkways traveling here and there. I don't have quite the firepower necessary to drop the thing."

"What if it was from inside one of the walkways?" Cole's eyes fell to the paper once more. "What if you blew it up from inside one of these doors?"

"Well..." Uriah sucked in a breath and considered. "There are four doors positioned all along the perimeter equal distance apart. They are not opened often."

"But they are opened," Cole ventured, his eyes zeroing in on Jameson. "Like for Hannah."

"Yeah." Jameson swallowed. "I hid in the tree line and watched them take her in."

"How thick do you think the door was?" Cole pressed.

"I don't know."

"It's four inches of solid steel," Uriah supplied.

"Could we breach using explosives?" Cole asked. "I mean, do we have enough of the right kind of stuff?"

"Look, what you're suggesting is suicide," Uriah cut in. "It would take a team of men minutes to get the entire thing rigged up. They'd be exposed from the moment they stepped into the clearing until the moment they left it... *if* they had time to leave before the damn thing blew up on them."

"But it *is* possible." Cole's eyes darted all around as Liam ran a hand down his face and groaned.

"Yeah." Uriah sighed. "I guess it is possible."

CHAPTER FORTY_
HANNAH

HANNAH'S LIFE WAS A SERIES OF REPETITIONS NOW. IN THE morning, she woke up in her empty apartment, took a shower and got dressed for work. On her way to the medical building, Hannah stopped by the cafeteria and spent some of her stipend on breakfast. A two egg white omelet with red bell peppers and a sprinkle of cheese in particular.

With coffee in hand, she'd then take a seat at the same table each day next to a few friends she'd had from before. After about ten minutes, Dmitry would arrive and sit across from her. Everyone would smile and nod and talk of absolutely nothing that mattered.

They spoke of spring, of planting new crops, and whether Hannah would come to the recreation center and play the piano again. Those were the words their mouths spoke, but they weren't the ones their eyes communicated. The truth was, everyone really wanted to hear the story of Hannah's life beyond the Wall.

She knew it. They knew it. Maybe the source even knew it. But unfortunately, it was something Hannah was never going to give them. It'd taken her four weeks of therapy with Miriam to earn a release back to work, and Hannah wasn't about to blow that up.

So with a smile on her face and a glance to the ever-present cameras, Hannah would rise from the table and depart for a day spent working on the medical needs of women. She did paperwork, took vital signs, and assisted Zoe in all manner of patient treatments. When something happened that made Hannah uncomfortable, she'd swallow her words and inevitably her microchip would release its customary flood of relaxation. Her mind would numb out a bit and Hannah would find herself floating through her tasks for the next several minutes.

After the impulse wore off, Hannah was left with a sick sort of dread. She'd forgotten the extent of the microchip's influence over her mind. By now it was clear that the source couldn't actually read your thoughts, but the damn thing was able to make pretty accurate guesses based on your heart rate, body language and who knew what else.

The extent of the microchip's control was definitely a major concern, but not the most pressing in Hannah's life. Somehow, someway she had to make it back into Dr. B's old control room. The source had transitioned her from the nurse assistant position to Dr. B's assistant before and so with continued good behavior, Hannah could only hope it would repeat the pattern.

She knew from prior experience that the location of the

room was under guard and locked by a palm scanner. There was no way she would be able to sneak in or break in. This sort of heist would take time, patience, and a lot of it.

Glancing down at the tablet in her hand, Hannah swiped across its screen, searching for the next patient on her list. On the other side of the door, the waiting room was teeming with women. It was almost midday and though Hannah's stomach grumbled, she knew they wouldn't break for lunch for another hour or so.

When her eyes found the name, they widened a fraction. Hannah's mouth dropped slightly and her heart gave an involuntary thump before settling. Blinking, she worked to remain calm, slow her own vital signs and not provide any sort of tell to the source. With a relaxed sort of smile painted carefully on her face, Hannah laid her palm against the waiting room door and pushed it open.

"Cassandra Roe," she called, her eyes darting around the room. "Cass?"

The woman who rose from her seat had stylish clothes that complimented a curvy figure. Curly ringlets of soft chestnut hair flowed over her shoulders to frame a lovely face accented by mossy green eyes. When she drew close to Hannah, her forehead pinched slightly as she murmured beneath her breath.

"It's Sandra here," the woman said. "I haven't heard anyone call me Cass in a very long time."

"Alright." Hannah stepped aside before directing her further into the office. "Sandra it is then."

"No." Cass shook her head before her eyes caught Hannah's. "I like it. I mean… it reminds me of someone."

"Who?" Hannah asked.

She had to hold back from supplying the name herself. The source was here, all around them. Hannah couldn't say the word Jameson, even though it was streaming on an endless loop inside her head. Stopping at the vitals center, she bade Cass sit down and fixed her arm with a blood pressure cuff.

"A man," Cass offered, but then her words dropped away and she glanced down.

In silence, the two of them went through the typical routine. Blood pressure, pulse, weight, height, urine sample. Then Hannah directed her into a waiting room and withdrew. As she busied herself collecting a tray of sterile instruments, Hannah's stomach twisted and turned on her.

Jameson. The man's name throbbed like a knife inside her, demanding to be let out. Was he still alive? Was he hiding nearby, or had he turned himself over to Uriah? If so, his chances of continuing to draw breath were much less. That made Hannah feel both responsible and worried.

After all, she'd convinced him to help her by using Cassandra's memory. Now that she was faced with the pretty woman, Hannah couldn't even fulfill her end of the deal. In order to maintain her cover, she couldn't even say Jameson's name. She couldn't tell Cass he remembered her or was coming for her or anything. It bit deep into her, this sort of lie she was living.

"Who do we have next?" Zoe stopped beside Hannah

and pulled out her tablet. While she scrolled quickly through it, she frowned and sighed. "Ugh, I know this one. Alright, Hannah Banana, you ready?"

"Yes," Hannah responded easily to the pet name. Ducking her head, she pushed the rolling tray behind Zoe as they entered the room.

"Good morning Sandy," Zoe intoned, fixing a reassuring smile on her face. "How are we feeling today?"

"Fine," Cass answered, her fingers twisting and twining in her cloth hospital gown.

"So it looks like we have more bad news," Zoe again, lifting her tablet. "Your pregnancy test came back negative again."

"Oh." Cass heaved a sigh and glanced away. This news didn't seem surprising to her. Hannah worked to keep her own expression plain.

"You've had twelve months of unsuccessful attempts with your source selected mate," Zoe offered. "And with both of you testing within the normal fertility limits, there is no real explanation I can offer as to why you haven't become pregnant."

"I see," Cass again, not maintaining eye contact.

"Unless you two aren't trying," Zoe continued. "In the physical sense."

Cass's eyes popped over to Zoe once before sliding away. Hannah's stomach dropped out completely. This would be her own life soon enough. Hannah's ninety days were almost up and she hadn't selected anyone yet. She couldn't bring herself to.

"You have two options going forward." Zoe brightened,

but forcibly so. Her voice did this pitchy thing that Hannah had grown to recognize. "We can start the process of artificial insemination using your partner's genetic material and your own, or we can start the process of egg extraction."

"But..." Cass's voice trembled as her eyes lifted to the camera in the room. "What if I'm just not ready? Can't I wait? What if I don't want a baby yet?"

Simultaneously, both Zoe and Cass's pagers began to buzz. The sound itself triggered a sort of adrenaline rush for Hannah. Despite her best intentions, her pulse jumped and sweat broke out on her palms. Glancing down at her microchip, Hannah felt the inevitable pinch followed but a slow seeping release of chemical-like ease.

As her vision slowed, Hannah inhaled a lazy breath and watched the goings on as if at a distance. Zoe explained how that choice was not one any living woman got to make. The health and longevity of the human race depended on them and they couldn't let their fellow man down. Cass clutched at her right hand where her own microchip lay before releasing a long sigh.

Rotating slightly, Zoe held out her hand and asked Hannah for the first set of fertility injections. Hannah tilted her head to one side, her eyes tracking along the tray before her. Reaching down, she selected the correct syringe and calmly handed it over.

Then, quiet as you please all three woman participated in the drugging. Cass sat still. Zoe injected her. Hannah did nothing to stop it.

Somewhere in the back of Hannah's suddenly thick

brain, thoughts swirled and competed for attention. This is wrong. This isn't how life is supposed to be. You should stop this.

Then... this is going to be you. You're next. You have a sacrifice to make and this is part of it.

CHAPTER FORTY-ONE_
LIAM

"Alright, boys," Uriah whispered. "Remember, we want as few casualties as possible on both sides. Our objective isn't to kill everyone in there, our objective is to get to Building Ten and shut the whole thing down."

"Roger," a few soldiers whispered back. Liam nodded his head, his gut turning.

"He shouldn't be on that crew," Liam hissed at Uriah.

In the light of the half moon, Uriah's glare morphed almost instantly into an eye roll that could be seen easily. It only served to piss Liam off all the more.

"Not your call," Uriah reminded him before returning his attention to the shit show unraveling before them.

Cole and a crew of three other volunteers were all geared up and ready to go. The armored Jeep they'd jury rigged themselves was tucked neatly in the thick of the tree line, along with several thousand men. Across the clearing, lay the massive shining metal wall. Liam swallowed. It was taller than he'd imagined.

"He can't hardly run," Liam spat. "It should be me."

"Don't fucking question me the minute before battle, asshole." Reaching up, Uriah gripped the back of Liam's neck and squeezed. "He needs this, now go fucking prep your guys before I lose more of my precious shit with you. I need every ounce of it I can get."

Shoving away from him, Liam held back a growl and stalked off. He hated this. He hated that Cole was putting himself out there, heading up a breach crew. He had no business doing it but yet there he was, driving the damn thing.

As Liam wove through the trees in the dark, his eyes tracked the thousands of soldiers they had hiding. It had taken weeks to get up here, making night marches, no fires, minimal noise using scattered groups. They could only hope like hell the source wasn't flying night drones. They could only pray the damn thing wasn't wasting precious fuel monitoring their city so many months after that initial hit.

So far... so good. Too good, maybe.

A foreboding sense of dread filled him. It shouldn't be this easy to get so many soldiers this close to the Wall. Glancing up, Liam squinted high into the darkened forest. Jameson said when he tracked Hannah he'd been searching for cameras. He never found any, but that didn't mean some weren't around here somewhere. Why wouldn't there be?

A few things came to mind. Battery life. Someone would have to charge the damn things, which meant regular exits by multiple people from inside the Wall.

Hubris... *if* an AI could claim such an emotion. The idea that its defenses were so superior to anything left in the rest of the world that exterior monitoring wasn't needed. Possible... but likely?

Fuck. Liam shook his head and came to a stop beside his second in command. Crouching down, he silently took the night specs from Malik's hands and held them up to his own eyes. And what's behind door number four? Liam thought ruefully.

To his right, his own volunteer incendiary crew was locked and loaded inside yet another armored SUV. Sucking in a breath, Liam removed the handheld radio from his side and held it up to his ear.

Click. Static. Silence.

That was the all ready call by Uriah.

Standing up, Liam slinked to the door of the SUV and patted the helmet of the sorry fucker sitting driver. The man offered him a thumbs up before crossing himself and gripping the wheel. Yeah, Liam thought, say your prayers brother.

Click. Click. Static. Silence.

That was position number two's all clear. Liam adjusted his own helmet. It felt so strange not being the first in. Slanting his eyes sideways, he reviewed the faces of each man in the vehicle. That spot used to be reserved for him.

Snorting softly to himself, Liam suppressed a smile. Was it possible he actually envied the fuckers? Yes. Yes, it was.

Click. Click. Click. Static. Silence.

That was position number three's all clear, Cookie's

crew. Now it was Liam's turn. Sucking in a last breath, Liam glanced around one last time then depressed his thumb on the call button.

Click. Click. Zip.

The shot came out of nowhere, knocking Liam clean off his feet.

With a whoosh of expelled breath, he barely managed to keep hold of the radio as his back impacted the ground. Pain bloomed on the left side of his chest. He gasped and rolled to one side. Then all around him bullets were whizzing through the trees. They were under attack. He'd been hit.

"Go! Go! Go!" Liam screamed into the radio as the men all around him scrambled for cover.

A few feet in front of him, the engine of the SUV roared to life. As hell continued to rain down all around them, Liam's breach crew floored it into the open. Suddenly the car was drawing most of the enemy fire.

A pair of soldier's hands grasped at Liam's shoulders then and he was being dragged back. He twisted and clung to his radio, listening and shouting in turn. Uriah's section was being peppered too, as was Cookie's. No one was getting feedback from sector two.

"I'm fine!" Liam screamed into the face of his medic.

The guy ignored him and instead proceeded to rip open his jacket and shirt. When the soldier pressed his fingers to the depression in Liam's bullet proof vest, Liam let loose an involuntary cry. Tears flooded his eyes and he swore.

"You're one lucky fucker, Sir," the medic whispered as

he retrieved the smashed up bullet remnant. "The vest worked."

"Get the fuck off me," Liam growled before holding the radio up to his mouth once more.

He wanted to ask about Cole. He wanted to verify the idiot was still alive. But then the first explosion let loose and the blast filled the night sky.

Tilting his head up from his position on the ground, Liam watched his own crew in the distance. One guy was laying dead on the ground while the others huddled up against the small steel door. They were still working. His soldiers in the trees were continuing to lay down suppression fire like no other. All around him, war raged.

That fact calmed him. Focused him. The violence spoke to him.

Then Liam was rolling up and grabbing his own rifle. He shouted into his radio once more before taking aim. They were going to breach this piece of shit. *Damn it...* they would take this thing down, even if they all went down with it.

CHAPTER FORTY-TWO_
HANNAH

HER SLEEP, AS IT HAD BEEN FOR THE PAST THREE MONTHS, was deep and dreamless. Tucked into her twin sized bed, Hannah's breathing was even and calm. Beneath her, the sheets were warm from her body. Stretching one hand up under her pillow she sought a cool spot and exhaled.

Then her eyes were fluttering and her brain began to circle. It was still dark. Outside her single small window, Hannah could just see the dim light reflected from a half moon. She was awake. Frowning, it took her several seconds longer to repeat the realization in her mind and then of course she began to wonder. Why? Why was she awake?

Boom. The massive percussion caused the building beneath her to shake and the glass pane to rattle in its frame. Sitting up, Hannah's heart beat out a furious pace. An explosion. She knew that sound. During the war, it had been the most familiar of all nighttime music.

Boom.

Throwing the covers off, Hannah stumbled across the floor as the lights inside her apartment automatically flickered on. Just as she braced her palms along her small wooden desk, her pager began its incessant buzzing. Snatching at it, Hannah read the display.

Report to Building Ten, Floor Six, Office of Manual Resources.

The source office. Hannah blinked once before squinting to read the display again. Boom. Another explosion lit off and then her microchip discharged.

"Ow." Hannah sucked in a breath at the rush of angry tingles that flooded her system. Her pager vibrated in her hand once more.

Your knowledge of manual code monitoring is required immediately. Please report.

"Of course," Hannah spoke the words out loud before dashing to her closet.

As she stripped off her pajamas and hurriedly got dressed, Hannah's mind flipped through her time working with Dr. B, or Dell, or whoever the man had truly been. He'd used her on several occasions to input manual stipulations and make certain protocol changes. It had been when he was too busy managing something else and needed to alter some background phases.

Slipping into her running shoes, Hannah pushed out into the hallway and blanched. Everyone was in the hallway. Bodies stumbled and shuffled and mumbled their way towards the stairs. The building was being evacuated even as the sound of far off gunfire let loose in rapid bursts.

Attack, they were under attack.

Hannah's pulse kicked and she glanced worriedly at her chip. Thankfully, no flood of impulse doping came. The source needed her primed for this work and apparently attributed her boost in adrenaline to the shock of what she saw before her.

Shoving her way through the collection of people, Hannah breached the doorway to the stairwell and began a measured descent. The area was crowded. As more and more bodies pressed into the space, the air began to sing with voices. People were waking up, becoming suddenly more aware. This was no drill.

Even as she reached the bottom and squeezed out into the night air, the sound of gunfire filled the space. Then people were calling to one another, yelling and shouting. Panic simmered all around her. Why wasn't the source doping them? The question came to her absently before she found herself rushing off into the night.

Hannah's feet took her across gently rolling lawns, still damp with evening moisture. When she inhaled, she could smell burning. Lifting her eyes to the far perimeter wall, she saw a few plumes of smoke lit by a burst of dancing flames. They'd come for her, she thought, but then quickly banished the idea. No ideas. No thoughts. No names.

Purposefully, Hannah cleared her mind and filled it instead with directions. Building Ten. Veer left past the cafeteria, then make a hard right. Cross one more lawn, two bike paths and a raised garden bed. There it was.

Checking her speed, Hannah reached a hand out for the door just as a collection of soldiers ran by. They didn't bother her, didn't notice her even. The sound of buzzing pagers, shouting and rumbling continued to dominate the air.

Once inside the lobby, Hannah headed for yet another stairwell and jogged up. This building was blessedly empty. No one lived here. It was pure office space.

By the time she reached the sixth floor landing, Hannah was completely out of breath. Her lungs burned and she braced both of her hands on her knees, working hard to suck in oxygen.

But the source had no time for this. Beneath her skin, the microchip pinched once and again a series of angry tingles rushed through her system.

Biting down hard on her lip, Hannah slapped her palm against the electronic reader next to the hall door. It beeped before the lock clicked. Stepping back, she watched the door swing slowly outward. When it was wide enough for her to fit through, she wedged herself in and jogged down the dimly lit corridor.

At the end, two guards holding rifles eyed her. She could feel their tension as she approached and made sure to keep both hands up, palms facing them.

"What business..." one of them began but then his pager buzzed and he gave it his full attention.

Without further commentary, he motioned for the other soldier to step back and he nodded to Hannah. At the same time, they each placed a palm against the dual electronic reader next to Door Zero. It beeped and just like that Hannah was admitted once more.

When she crossed the threshold, her heart did a funny sort of dance. It was pitch black inside, just like before. No windows. No lights.

Glancing over her shoulder, she watched the guard turn away from her as the door rotated slowly closed. The lock clicked. The light automatically flickered on. Hand slapping over her mouth, Hannah stumbled back at the sight before her.

Dr. B's body was still lying there, just as she'd left it. His dried out corpse was slumped over, fully clothed, the handgun having tumbled from his hand when he'd shot himself. Dried blood spotted his now blinking computer monitor. Her pager buzzed and her microchip dosed her with another shock... but this time she barely felt it.

He'd just been left there... to rot. Bile rose up in Hannah's throat but then her pager vibrated again. This time she grabbed it off her hip before reading the words.

Move his body aside. Sit at the monitor and follow the prompts.

No, she thought, but she didn't say it out loud. Turning quickly, Hannah stepped to the corner where the tall metal cabinet stood. She should be in the blind spot now. She should be completely off the feed, but that in itself would be a trigger for the source. She had to work fast.

Tearing open the cabinet doors, Hannah began

clutching cans of corn and green beans and chucking them on the floor behind her. It had to be here. Oh, for God's sake please let it be here. Behind her, she could hear the buzz of her pager. A continual stab of pain released from her microchip and overtook her system.

"Ow," Hannah gasped the word as her muscles tensed and cramped.

Boom.

Another explosion lit off somewhere nearby and the building shook. Outside the door, she could hear the guards begin to call to her. They were yelling and then the electronic reader from the hall was beeping.

Come on, come on, come on.

Sweat poured down Hannah's back as she continued to empty shelf after shelf. As the door behind her swung open, her eyes lit on her prize. A tiny black box that looked like an old car radio. It was fixed to the wall on the very bottom shelf, right hand side.

Dropping to the ground, Hannah lay on her belly and began punching at the key pad.

G-e-n-e-a-n-d-

"What the hell?" A male voice called from behind her as the two guards entered the space.

"Stop!"

Hannah struck at the keys as her body was hit with another flood of pain.

D-e-l-l-2

A pair of hands wrapped around her ankles. She was being hauled back, her belly dragging along the thin carpeted floor. Writhing around, Hannah kicked out, causing the hands to drop away. With a final leap, she stretched for the cabinet and hit the final key.

Enter.

IT'S AMAZING WHAT YOUR MIND CAN ABSORB IN ONLY A second's worth of time.

In front of her, Hannah's field of vision filled with a blinding bright flash of light. It was white and sudden and all encompassing.

Behind her, both the guards dropped to the ground. She heard them. Their heavy bodies were a twin thump, thump as they made contact with the floor.

Then it was Hannah's own body that was releasing. Every muscle betrayed her at once. Her eyes rolled back in her head and her neck gave out. She could do nothing to stop her own face from smacking down against the bottom of the cabinet.

Inhale. A final semi-conscious breath.

Release....

and she was gone.

Groaning, she scrunched her already closed eyes tighter and licked at her lips. Her face... it *hurt*. Gathering both hands beneath her body, she pushed up. The back of her head impacted something hard and metal. The clanging sound was loud and forced her to drop back down.

"Ow," she moaned the word slowly, her eyes fluttering open.

She was in the dark, no semi-dark. Occasionally, a single distant light would flash and she could see for a second or two after. It was like an emergency power failure or something. Every few seconds the light would turn on and a beep would sound before it went dark once more.

Scooting back carefully, she extracted her head from inside the bottom shelf of a metal cabinet. All around her, cans of food were strewn on the floor. Easing up to her knees, she stretched her head to one side and then arched her back. Why did she hurt so much? Everything just hurt, like an aching soreness, like she'd run a dozen miles.

Another flash and beep had her glancing over her shoulder. Two men were stirring just behind her. They were groaning too and going slow. Something had happened to all of them... but what?

Earthquake? The word came to her mind in a shimmering sort of softness but nothing more accompanied it. If she'd been asked at the time, she would've been unable to explain what an earthquake actually was. Strange. Something's wrong with me, she thought, but then she sucked in a breath and tried to stand up.

"What happened?" One of the men on the floor asked.

"I don't know," she answered, swaying slightly on her feet. "Do you?"

"No," the man said. "I don't remember anything."

Frowning, she stumbled in the brief flashes of light to the wall and leaned a hand against it. She didn't remember anything either. Then all of a sudden, all the lights in the room came on and the beeping stopped. The men on the ground were also staggering to their feet. They were wearing military clothing and had guns strapped to their bodies. *Soldiers.* The word echoed a moment inside of her before dropping away.

"You okay?" One of them asked her.

"I hurt everywhere," she confessed.

"Are you bleeding?" He ran a hand over the back of his neck before trying to crack it.

"I don't think so," she answered.

From somewhere far away, a door popped open. All

three of them looked to the metal door of the room they were standing in. It was still closed. Feet pounded closer and closer, lots of footsteps. Hannah took a step back and glanced to her right.

Clapping a hand over her mouth, she muffled a scream. The soldiers gaze popped between her and what she was looking at as she scrambled away. Her back bumped into the metal cabinet and the two soldiers drew their guns. A dead body. There was a dead body in the room with them. Had they killed him? Had she?

Looking down at her shaking hands, she began to hyperventilate. She didn't know. She couldn't remember, but there was no blood. Her eyes traveled the length of her body, looking for signs, but there were none.

Then their own door was slamming open and more men were flooding inside. More soldiers. Guns were being pointed and orders yelled.

"Stand down fellas!" One man shouted, he seemed to be in control. "We're all on the same side here!"

"What?" One of the men with her asked. "What's happening?"

"Look, see?" The soldier with the golden hair and broad shoulders lifted his gun, fixed it back by his side. "I'm your commander, Uriah Linfield. You've just gotten a little shook up, that's all."

"Oh."

Both men that had woken in the room with her lowered their weapons and relaxed. That's when all eyes became fixed on her.

"Holy shit," the commander who called himself Uriah

exhaled the words and stepped closer. "Hannah Mae, thank God. It was you, right? You input the code?"

"Who?" Holding up both her hands, she managed to stop the man before he touched her. "Who are you? I don't understand. I don't…"

The man's face fell and he glanced quickly over his shoulder. Behind him, a soldier with impossibly green eyes limped forward before stumbling down to his knees.

"Han," he let loose the word on a whisper, his eyes searching her face. "It wiped you again. It wiped all of you."

"WHERE IS SHE?" LIAM DEMANDED, HIS HAND FELL HEAVILY on Uriah's shoulder but the guy refused to stop.

"Cole has her," he supplied before barking more orders and dispatching more men. "I want no violence of any kind. Do you hear me? No instances of abuse. Absolutely none!"

"Yes, Sir." Malik and Jones bobbed their heads before scurrying away.

They took about thirty soldiers along with them, but that didn't seem to hardly dent the flow. As Uriah and Liam pushed through the open area between buildings, men continued to swirl and descend on them.

It was post-battle, enemy mixing, bizarre surrender, chaos. After all four doors had been breached, with soldier teams rushing inside and commencing an assault... every single person inside the Wall simply passed the fuck out. If Liam hadn't been there to see it, he wouldn't have believed it himself.

One second, they were taking enemy fire, pursuing soldiers and laying suppression. Then the next, it completely stopped. Eyes rolled back in heads, guns fell from hands, and bodies dropped like stones to the ground.

"What do you mean, he has her?" Liam pressed, his long legs working hard to keep up with Uriah's punishing pace. "Is she okay? Is she like them? Is she-"

"She doesn't remember a damn thing okay?" Uriah snapped the words at him before rounding on a second group of soldiers. "Bojoroquez, Chu, Parks, Ramierz."

"Sir," the men echoed at once.

"Take your respective teams to Buildings Three, Eight, Six, and Fourteen. Clear them of civilians and Wall soldiers. You will treat them all as your own. None of these people has any memory whatsoever, okay? They don't know their own fucking names."

"Sir," a few whispered, glancing at each other.

"I want beds set up in the recreation center, the cafeteria and the indoor theatre. All women will be separated from all men at this time. I mother fucking swear if there is one instance of abuse I will have your asses made into a new pair of boots for me. Is that clear?"

"Yes, Sir." With a final salute, the men turned to gather their soldiers and discharge their duties.

Liam halted in his tracks a moment and watched Uriah press on. He was barking out orders, reining things in, organizing a plan. It was necessary. The focus, the precision. They had just introduced thousands of men that hadn't seen a living woman in years to a facility containing tens of thousands of women who had no fucking clue what was going on. And Hannah was one of them.

"How long did it last?" Uriah called over his shoulder, causing Liam to jog up to him.

"How long did what last?"

"Hannah's memory thing," Uriah's voice was strained, dropping low. "How long until she could at least tell good from bad?"

"I don't know," Liam exhaled, felt the color drain from his face. "Months. Andy had her for months and even after he died she believed everything anyone told her until she saw Flynn."

"Fuck." Uriah rolled his shoulders before finding and berating another set of his men.

When he was done, Liam dogged him to the next section. His mind was whirling, collecting every bit of information it could before he couldn't take it anymore.

"Where is she?" Liam demanded again, this time yanking Uriah around to face him. "Where is Cole? *Where* is Hannah?"

With a growl, Uriah ripped Liam's hands off him and shoved him once, hard. The men around them backed a few steps, but kept watch.

"Do you trust him?" Uriah stepped forward, raising his eyebrows. "Huh? Isn't that what your whole fucked up sharing deal was about? You and him and her? Do you *trust* him?"

"I do," Liam gritted the words out between clenched teeth. "I just have to see her."

"I need you here," Uriah countered, before gesturing

around. "Go get your team, secure the perimeter. Send out scouts, make certain the teams I've assigned aren't taking advantage. For fuck's sake Liam, do your damn duty!"

Uriah turned away, his shoulders heaving. Liam was about to open his mouth, when the man himself whirled back and closed the distance between them. Leaning up into Liam's face, his eyes were glistening as the next set of words dropped from his lips.

"You'll have plenty of time to stare at Hannah while nothing that recognizes you stares back, okay? My sister doesn't know me. She won't let me touch her; won't let Cole near her. She's scared and fucking alone, trapped in her own mind. You don't want to see it right now, Lee. *Trust me...* you do not want to see it."

With that, Uriah gave his back to Liam and strode off into the crowd. Soldiers parted for him, making room as he transitioned from man to man. He spit orders, rattled off commands and sent groups of bodies scurrying in all directions.

Liam stood still there, the blood drained from his body, and watched him go. Casualties of war. Hannah was just another casualty of war now. What if she didn't come back this time? What if she never remembered any of them? Could a brain withstand being wiped twice?

"Sir." A soldier crept up beside him, paused, then repeated his request. "Sir?"

"What?" Liam's eyes came back into focus as his attention snapped to the man.

"What are our orders, Sir?"

"Orders," Liam repeated the word, his gaze narrowing.

Yeah, that's right. He was the one giving the damn orders around here. Because... what the hell else was he going to do? Shit. The thought of Hannah had him wanting to break. To run and scream and beat the shit out of someone or something.

But fuck. Fucking. That.

Liam sucked in a breath. He never, ever broke and he swore that he'd never run again.

Straightening his shoulders, Liam surveyed the crew surrounding him and got the fuck to work.

CHAPTER FORTY-FIVE_
HANNAH

BENEATH HER FINGERTIPS, THE IVORY KEYS DIPPED EASILY. With her eyes closed, Hannah let her head move in time with the music. This wasn't hard for some reason. When she played, it took no effort from her mind. There were no headaches, no throbbing pain, no stutters or halting bursts of almost remembering.

When she sat at the piano, the songs simply came to her... from memory or something like it. She didn't read the music, though sometimes the man who called himself her brother would set a particular piece before her and request that she play it, which she would.

Uriah Linfield. That was his name and her name was Hannah Mae Linfield. In particular, he had a habit of using both her first and last name together. The sound of it didn't upset her, but it didn't create a memory either.

Inhaling a deep breath, Hannah continued to shift her hands over the piano. It was beautiful, the music was, and as it lifted into the air, it helped other people, too. If she opened her eyes right now, she would see an auditorium filled with people. Men and women both, sitting in silence, listening to her play.

They liked to hear her. At least, that's what Uriah always said. And sometimes, she was approached later by a certain man or woman who told her she'd helped them. That they'd gotten some breakthrough out of it. And that was good. Hannah was glad for them. It just wasn't her.

Each morning that she woke in her little apartment, her brother was there to greet her. He was usually sitting quietly on the short gray couch in her living room, waiting. He'd strum his fingers on his knee before standing up to give her a hug. She let him, of course, but then she'd pull back, look into his eyes and not recognize him beyond the past three months.

His instant disappointment never failed to shimmer back at her. She didn't know him. Not really. And that fact hurt him every single day.

As the sonata circled to an end, Hannah kept her head bowed a moment longer. The remaining thrum of the final chords faded into the air and for a split second it was entirely silent. It was these moments that Hannah enjoyed the most. The absolute quiet when she was finally done.

But then the people were clapping and rising to their feet. She could hear the shuffling and murmuring. Opening her eyes, Hannah raised her head and stood up. A warm blush crept up her cheeks and she couldn't help but duck her head. The attention made her uncomfortable. All those eyes resting on her at once. It made her nervous.

And of course, there were a few sets of eyes in particular that contributed to that. Glancing over to the rear of the room, she spied the both of them. Liam and Cole. They were positioned just beside each other. Liam, the tall dark and extremely hot one was leaning against the wall, arms folded across his chest. Cole, with his crystal green eyes and classic good looks was standing in the aisle, clapping along with the rest of them.

Ugh, they made her feel so twisted up and silly. Ducking her head, she fought the rush of butterflies that built in her belly. Did they know how impossibly attractive they both were? Of course, whenever they came around with her brother she clammed up. She couldn't hardly make eye contact, let alone participate in a normal conversation.

Why did they both stir such a reaction? She didn't know, and she wished it would stop. It wasn't right. She shouldn't feel this way about two men she didn't know and it was the strength of her feelings that confused and upset her the most. She just needed a moment to breathe. She just needed a moment to feel normal.

Stepping down from the raised platform, Hannah made way for the next series of players. It was a band complete with guitar, bass and drums. Though everyone living here suffered from some sort of cognitive problem, the musicians were still able somehow to play. Uriah said they'd all been hit with an electrical sort of EMP that affected large areas of their brains. It originated from a microchip that had been implanted inside them, which was why everyone had theirs systematically removed.

Hannah recalled that procedure and pretty much everything since then with perfect clarity. She'd sat in a medical office while Uriah and Cole watched. Liam took hold of her hand, produced a knife and slit her skin open. It hurt, but not as much as she'd expected. He then extracted the tiny tube-like plastic thing and threw it away.

Hannah knew from talking to some of the others that normally Cole would proceed to read a series of marks located on the skin of the person's back. He'd tell the person their name and estimate their age. But he didn't do that with Hannah. They all seemed to know her name already.

Frowning now at the implication, Hannah shoved out the side door of the auditorium and into the warm summer air. There were people everywhere, walking, riding bicycles and talking. To her right, there was an expansive green lawn where a few children ran by screaming. With a smile, Hannah watched them. They didn't have a care in the world. None of the babies had had a microchip, though all of their mothers did.

Hannah recalled Uriah really stressing about that at first. He'd come in at night to her apartment and sit in the dark on her couch with his head in his hands. He'd murmur about pairing the right child with the right mother. But now a lot of people here were fully recovered, including most of the moms, which was great. And others were gaining more traction all the time. Not Hannah though, she still had no memories and she knew that upset her brother more than he let on.

"Hannah Mae," Uriah called to her.

Glancing over her shoulder, Hannah saw him crossing

the bike path from the auditorium and held back a cringe. Oh, how she wanted to roll her eyes. Instead, she gave him a placating smile. He rarely left her alone and it was getting pretty... okay no... *really* old.

If it wasn't Uriah following her around, then it was Cole or Liam. They usually kept their distance, but still. The three of them were like the ultimate shadow babysitting team. And with them constantly hovering it was hard for her to just have a moment alone to think. Cole and Liam made her in turns giddy and nervous while her brother annoyed the crap out of her.

"Uriah," Hannah said his name as he came to a stop beside her. At the sound of the word, his face fell just a fraction, but then he caught himself and plastered on a fake smile instead. Hannah sighed before asking, "What's wrong with what I just said?"

"What?" Uriah's eyes slid quickly across her face.

"I said your name and you did this thing with your face," Hannah crossed her arms. "Like it wasn't right."

"Don't worry about it."

"Just tell me," she demanded. "Why don't you just give me the answers, Uriah? It might help me to remember."

"But I want you to remember on your own," Uriah's voice took on a pleading quality. "I don't want to prompt it. I want it to be genuine."

"What if I never do?" Hannah countered, then looked past his shoulder as his eyes squeezed shut. "What if I never recover like the others?"

"Don't say that," he whispered. "You will, I know you will."

For several tense moments they stood there in silence facing one another. Hannah stared out past his shoulder and listened to the muted sounds of the band start their first set.

"Uri," her brother conceded finally. "You mostly called me Uri, not Uriah. It was a nickname or whatever."

"Uri," she repeated, hoping that something would spark in her mind. When nothing did, she bobbed her head and cleared her throat. "Thank you."

"Listen, there's someone I'd like you to meet," Uriah pressed on, forcing her to look up into his face. "Someone new, she just got here today."

"She?" Hannah's brow furrowed and her curiosity piqued.

"Yes."

In the past three months, she'd never seen her brother with a woman, or at least not with anyone in particular. He did his job, which seemed to be to run the entire place, and he dogged Hannah. Other than that, he was an island unto himself, so to speak.

"Are you going to tell me her name?" Hannah's foot began to tap impatiently.

Uriah had this annoying way of bating her. He was constantly dancing around saying certain things in order to get her to remember. *It. Was. Really. Old.* She had no doubt in her mind he truly was her brother, no one else pissed her off quite to this extent.

"I'd rather-"

"You know what?" Hannah threw up her hands and stomped away. "Just have one of your henchmen come get me when you're ready. I'm so freaking tired of you, I can't hardly stand it."

"Henchmen?" Uriah's voice called after her.

"Yeah." Hannah whirled and pointed back to the auditorium. "Cole and Liam. You know, your little buddies."

"*My* little buddies?" Uriah's eyebrows hit his hairline and his mouth dropped. Then almost as quickly, he snapped it shut and bit back the words he was about to unleash.

"Oh great. Is that not right, too?!" Hannah ran her fingers up into her hair and held back a scream before turning away from him once more. Why couldn't she remember? Why?

"Where are you going?!" Uriah called.

"To my apartment!" Hannah shouted back, refusing to turn around this time. "Just bring the mystery woman to my place, whenever."

<hr />

THE KNOCK ON HER FRONT DOOR SOUNDED ABOUT AN HOUR later. By that time Hannah had showered and changed into a light cotton sundress from her closet. Padding across the bluish carpet with her bare feet, Hannah rose up on her tiptoes and looked through the peephole.

Immediately her gut dropped out on her. Her brother was standing out there, and he'd brought the whole damn brigade with him. Nibbling on her lip, Hannah stepped back and paced a few steps away, placing a trembling hand on her chest. He'd brought some dark-haired pretty woman with him alright, but Liam and Cole were out there, too.

Ugh. Couldn't she have just a little time to adjust without the audience?

"Hannah Mae?" Uriah's voice called and the knock came again.

Sucking in a steadying breath, Hannah straightened her shoulders and approached the door once more. This was going to be okay. This was no big deal. She would just smile and keep a friendly look on her face when she saw them. It didn't matter that Liam burned her with his gaze and Cole stopped her heart with that crooked smile of his. She would maintain eye contact. She would act like a normal human being.

Placing her hand on the silver handle, Hannah twisted the knob and pulled it open. Four sets of eyes hit hers and as usual it caused her to frown. Stepping back, she dropped her head to stare at the floor as they all filed in.

Great. That's it Hannah, instead of looking pretty and friendly, make sure to fix your face with an ugly grimace. Yeah, that's perfect, you're so desirable and approachable.

With the last of their boots passing her line of sight, Hannah let the door swing shut of its own accord. Forcing herself to raise her head, she avoided the two men she most wanted to look at and instead settled her eyes on the far couch.

"Please," she intoned. "Won't you sit?"

"Thank you," the woman answered before waddling slowly over to the sofa.

Waddling, that was definitely the word to describe it.

Hannah's eyes popped wide. The mystery woman was pregnant. Like very, very, almost ready to pop pregnant. As Hannah watched, her brother braced the woman's arms and helped ease her down to sitting.

With a groan, the woman patted her belly and smiled beautifully up at Uriah. His whole body relaxed beneath her gaze and Hannah blinked. Interesting. There was something between those two.

"Um…" Hannah let her eyes dance quickly to Cole and then over to Liam before she cleared her throat and side-stepped them. "I have nothing here to offer you. If you're hungry or thirsty, I could maybe make a trip to the cafeteria and bring something back."

"Oh, no." The dark-haired woman smiled easily and exhaled. "I'm fine at the moment."

"Good," Hannah agreed, before pulling a wooden chair from beneath the living room table and sitting down in it. "My brother wanted me to meet you, but I'm afraid he wouldn't tell me your name."

"Ah." The woman's eyes glanced to Uriah's face quickly then settled back on Hannah. "My name is Lena. It's nice to meet you."

"I'm Hannah," Hannah said, then paused. What else was there to say? "So, you're pregnant."

"Yes." Lena gave an indulgent chuckle. "How could you tell?"

"Well, you're only showing a little bit." Hannah felt herself relax into the friendly joking. This woman was nice at least. She wasn't full of heated stares and uncomfortable silence like the men in the room. Even now they were all just standing around, watching. "Do you know if it's a boy or a girl? When are you due?"

"I'm hoping to evict this particular tenant any day now." Lena shifted in her seat. "And I'm not sure of the sex, I haven't had access to an ultrasound machine or anything."

"I do," Hannah offered, then tilted her head to one side. Why had she said that? Well... because it was true. It felt true anyway, though she couldn't bring any particular experience to mind.

The room around her tensed and Hannah squirmed immediately under its collective pressure. She'd said something again. Something wrong.

"That's wonderful," Lena leapt in to save her. "Do you know how to use it?"

"Yes." Hannah bobbed her head with the immediate response before nibbling on her lip. At least, she felt like she did. "Would you like to find out now?"

"I would." Lena glanced up to Uriah who was staring hard at Hannah.

"Do you know the way?" He asked carefully.

"Well..." Hannah trailed off, thinking. "I believe I can show you."

"By all means." Uriah glanced quickly to Liam who was shoving off the wall and grabbing Cole's arm. He'd been moving towards her with this look on his face. Hannah stepped back and crossed her arms.

"Please," Lena interrupted, drawing Hannah's eyes back to her. "I'd love to go with you."

"Um, okay." Hannah cleared her throat and made for the front door. "Just follow me, then."

She led the woman and trail of men out into the hallway and down several flights of stairs. It was slow going, with Lena being so pregnant and her brother hovering like... well, like a concerned partner.

Behind them, Cole did his best to hide his ever-present limp and Liam outright scowled. He didn't like her maybe, Hannah thought, or there was something about this whole situation he didn't like.

When they hit the bottom, Hannah pushed out into the late afternoon sun. It was so lovely outside, with the heat of the day waning and a small breeze picking lazily at the leaves of the trees. Hannah didn't think about where her feet were taking her, nor did a particular series of steps enter her mind. She just proceeded across the grass, down a bike path, took a left around the cafeteria and then headed straight for a two story office building.

Once inside, Hannah led their party straight to a door marked *Female Medical*. When she glanced over her shoulder, Hannah's brow furrowed and she eyed the men.

"I'm not sure you're allowed in here," she said.

"Trust me." Uriah gave her a quick nod. "We're allowed everywhere... and Hannah?"

"Yes?"

"Do you remember coming here before?" Uriah asked the question even as Lena tugged at his elbow and Liam grumbled under his breath.

"No," Hannah admitted, her shoulders slumping slightly. "Should I? I mean, obviously I should because I led us here, right? I... I um..."

Pressing her fingers to her forehead, Hannah stepped

back from the door. She should remember. She should. Right? Her heart rate picked up and a strange sort of panic released inside her body. Her right hand began to pulse where that old ugly scar was and a cold sweat bloomed down her back.

"Hey, Han," Cole was speaking, his voice coming out soothing as he reached for her shoulder. "It's alright. Don't worry about it okay?"

"Please." Hannah shivered beneath his touch and moved away. This was too much. All she felt was pressure and failure and confusion.

Immediately the small hallway burst with tension. Liam was hissing in Uriah's ear and her brother was growling right back at him. Cole looked so hurt. He was shoving his hands in his pockets and staring purposefully at his toes.

This was a bad choice. She shouldn't have volunteered to do this. But then Lena was piping up and drawing Hannah's attention back to her and her big round belly.

"Let's find out," the pixie woman said. "I'm excited to know."

"Oh." Hannah felt a tug of curiosity. "Yeah, I want to know, too. Plus, we can check if you're dilated at all. I mean, someone can. Someone in here."

"Great." Lena waddled up to the door and shoved it right open. Behind her, the men dropped into silence.

The waiting room was mostly quiet as they all filed in. Several women sat in chairs, sipping water from tiny metal cups or chatting with one another. More than a few were pregnant, but some were not. Hannah moved with Lena over to the receptionist who beamed at them both before gesturing for them to sit.

As they did, the entire room dropped into silence. Uriah, Cole and Liam remained standing. No one said a word. Hannah frowned, and glanced around at the other women. They were all looking at the men.

"Are you sure you're supposed to be in here?" Hannah zeroed in on Uriah as the women in the room began to giggle at her question.

"We're the exception to the rule," Uriah assured her then lifted his eyes to address the room. "Good afternoon ladies, some of you may remember Lena... she's my... she's my..."

"I'm his baby mama," Lena supplied and everyone erupted with excited commentary.

Uriah grumbled something about needing a ring and finding the right time, but his protests went unnoticed. As some of the women got up to give Lena hugs and pat at her belly, Hannah blanched.

Some of you may remember Lena, that's what Uriah had said. That meant Hannah should know Lena as well. Duh... why else would Uriah spring this whole introduction thing on her in the first place?

Ugh, her crazy blank empty mind, it just wasn't fair. She felt so stupid and out of sorts all the time. It was so hard when her body and emotions didn't match what was inside her brain. There was hardly a moment where Hannah could feel equal to anyone around her. They all knew more about her than she did, so much more.

And... wait... that's *Uriah's* baby? That meant...

"I'm an aunt?" Hannah exclaimed suddenly, turning to Lena. "That's my niece or nephew in there?"

"Yes." Lena smiled, so lovely, with a glitter of tears building in her eyes. "It is."

"Oh, have you picked a name yet?" Hannah jumped in, forgetting herself. "I always thought Flynn for a girl or Ian for a boy. Aren't they the most wonderful names?"

"Ah…" Lena's eyes lit with a spark, before they tracked up to the men standing against the far wall. "Those are. Yes, I love both of those names."

Following Lena's gaze, Hannah looked over her shoulder. Cole was pressing his fingers over his eyes. Liam was walking out the door.

CHAPTER FORTY-SIX_
LIAM

IT FUCKING HURT. SEEING HANNAH BUT NOT HAVING HER see him, it really, really fucking hurt. And it didn't help that Uriah was always getting their hopes up only to have them smashed into the ground over and over. The Lena experiment had been the worst one yet.

Hannah didn't *know* Lena. She didn't even remotely recognize her. Sure, she'd been able to show them to her old job, but she hadn't remembered any of the women she used to work with. And yeah, she'd spit out the names Flynn and Ian. But she didn't understand why they were special. She didn't remember Chan or the fiery redhead she'd lived with from before.

Hannah did not fucking remember. Not anything. Hell, she couldn't even stand to look at him, or Cole either. It was torture.

But Liam guessed in the end he was a glutton for punishment. Because here he was, participating in yet another one of Uriah's fucking experiments. Strumming nervous fingers on the white tablecloth, Liam took a survey of the bustling restaurant around them. It hadn't been very long after the original takeover that Uriah got this place up and running.

He'd restored power, destroyed all tablets and pagers and had Malik and Jones eliminate as much computer tech involved as possible. Most everything here was run manually by people turning things on, or shutting things off. That sort of thing. It was like the world had been before computers were invented and most people were assimilating just fine.

In fact, thousands of men and women who'd suffered a memory wipe were completely normal again. Just not the one person Liam cared about.

No, Hannah's mind was still blank. Liam was no longer in there and neither was Cole. The two of them handled this happy fact differently, of course. Just beside him, Cole ran his fingers through his hair for the millionth time, then smoothed at his button down shirt.

"Your hair isn't going to make a difference," Liam whispered to him. Some people like to face reality head on, others like to live in a big fat river in Egypt. Cole was the latter.

"Don't listen to him," Lena interrupted, waging a finger at Liam from across the table. "He's just afraid."

"I'm not afraid of shit," Liam corrected, leaning in. "I'm just not into lying to myself."

"How long has he been like this?" Jameson lifted his chin at Liam but spoke to Cole.

"Since he removed the chip and she didn't fall into his

arms," Cole answered, bracing both elbows on the table before shifting them down to his lap.

"For God's sake, stop squirming," Liam spat, then grabbed his beer and swallowed half of it down.

Jameson had been the one left behind to watch Lena during the attack and they'd both just made it up here two days ago. Liam had forgotten how damn irritating the man could be. Immediately he'd sided with Cole and the rest of them. It was like Liam was the only one seeing the real world.

Well, Cookie had agreed with him, but then high-tailed it back to the compound months ago. He just couldn't deal with the whole Godforsaken business, as he put it. Liam's throat closed up on him and he slammed the beer back down on the table. *Wake the fuck up!* He wanted to scream it, but then there she was.

Hannah walked into the room and it was like time stood still. Liam couldn't hear Jameson's response or Lena's hiss of disapproval. They were all just background buzz. Beside him, Cole stiffened instantly. The two of them together made quite a pathetic pair these days.

As she approached, Uriah walked beside her, keeping a hand at her back. He was always the one guiding her now, maneuvering her, placing her here and there. Liam didn't like it, but what could he do?

Uriah was Hannah's brother and this was normal for them. Before the war, Uriah had controlled every aspect of Hannah's life and now he did again... and she let him. Because unlike Liam and Cole, his touch didn't cause her to jump away.

"Oh," Hannah exclaimed the word as she and Uriah came to a stop at their table.

Her pretty face instantly flushed and she looked down. She doesn't want to be here, Liam thought, watching as she sucked her bottom lip into her mouth and nibbled on it. Fuck. That did things to him.

Grabbing for his beer once more, Liam downed the rest of it before sliding a glance at Cole. The guy was gesturing to Lena who was motioning for him to stay seated.

"Hey Hannah," Lena spoke cheerfully. "We were all just going to catch some dinner. Won't you join us?"

"Um..." Hannah's eyes swept the table once more before she frowned. "Yeah, sure."

Uriah pulled out her chair and as Hannah sat, she brushed some of that golden hair back over one shoulder. Lena handed her a menu and immediately started gabbing. What's good here? What have you tried? Oh, I have all sorts of cravings. Basically anything spicy.

Liam supposed the rush of female nonsense was a good thing. As the beer flowed through his blood stream, he watched Hannah visibly relax.

Around him Uriah, Jameson and Cole talked shop. Liam refused to participate. He could care less about the groups of people leaving. It made sense after all. When they finally remembered everything about the Wall, they no longer wanted to live on the wrong side of it.

A waiter stopped by and took their order. Liam requested more beer. Hannah shot him a quick look that had his gut dropping. Tilting back in his chair, Liam grabbed the guy's sleeve before he could scurry off and requested a steak, too. Rare, damn it. Rare.

About halfway through their meal, things began to even out. Hannah was relaxing, actually looking around and talking for once. Cole engaged her a few times and her responses were in turns teasing and funny. Liam felt the perpetual tightness in his chest ease.

Good. So this was more like it. Liam couldn't trust himself not to fuck it up, so he kept quiet. Cole, on the other hand, was good at this sort of stuff. Liam had forgotten just how good. Maybe, Cole could charm his way back into Hannah's good graces, and by a small miracle, manage to bring Liam's bumbling ass along with him.

The thought gave Liam hope and it was that dangerous emotion that ruined him in the end.

Because just when things were feeling normal, Cole had to push it. A soft song was playing over the speakers and Hannah made some comment about it. Standing up, Cole reached a hand across the table to her.

"Would you like to dance?" He asked.

Hannah's eyes fell to his open palm. The table tensed. Uriah's gaze popped up to Cole with this questioning sort of... *are you out of your damn mind...* look and Lena was holding her breath.

It was all Liam could do not to outright groan. Baby steps. How many times had Uriah coached them. Take this easy, don't overwhelm her all at once. She gets confused and it really upsets her.

"Okay," Hannah answered finally and Liam's eyes

popped wide. Okay? Holy shit he almost didn't want to know how this was going to play out.

Pushing back from the table, Hannah waited for Cole to come around to her. When he again offered his hand, she took it. Liam's eyes tracked them as they moved a few feet away to the corner of the room where a small space was cleared for such things. No one else was dancing at the moment of course, but why would that stop Cole?

"Oh God," Liam murmured under his breath. Involuntarily, he reached for his third beer.

"Just... let's see how this goes," Lena coached. "And everyone try not to stare, okay?"

"Fuck that," Liam hissed.

He couldn't tear his eyes away if he tried. A part of him desperately wanted to be Cole in this moment, and the other part was scared shitless. Yeah, he could say it inside his own head. Scared. Like a teenage boy who's voice was about to crack as he asked the hottest chick in school to the prom. Gonna be shot down... writing is on the wall buddy.

"You know what?" Jameson turned his back on the spectacle. "I don't know if I can do this."

"You?" Liam was incredulous, glancing to Jameson. "*You* don't have to, you lucky bastard."

"Yeah." Jameson's eyes flitted to Lena who looked suddenly sad. "Right."

"Uh oh," Uriah groaned.

Liam's gaze locked back on Hannah just in time to see Cole loop his hand around the back of her neck. Wait. Liam's heart stopped. Too soon. Damn fucking it Cole, too soon. But the guy just couldn't help himself. He was lowering his head and brushing his lips against Hannah's and she was curling her fingers in his shirt.

Liam counted it. One. Two. Three. The seconds ticked by in perfect rhythm with the slow thump, thump, thumping of his tortured heart.

She was kissing him back. She seemed okay... but then... no. Hannah shoved away and gasped.

Cole was apologizing, reaching for her, then sucking his hands back to run them through his own hair. Hannah had this look on her face. Shit. Then her eyes were darting to Liam with a sort of flash and then she was running. Like *running*.

Before he knew what he was doing Liam was up and after her. He brushed past Cole who was fixed in place and barreled out the back door of the restaurant. Hannah was ahead of him, her running having slowed to a brisk walk. The swing of her hair reflected in the moonlight and when she tossed him a look over her shoulder, Liam was gone. He lost all coherent thought.

"Wait," Liam called to her and to his amazement she stopped.

Coming to face her, Liam couldn't help but take her elbow in his hand. His eyes searched hers, noted the wretched look on her face and he felt so awful. Everything was so awful.

"Are you okay?" He managed.

"I..." Hannah blinked hard, then sucked in a breath. "I think I've slept with him before."

Liam's eyebrows raised but words escaped him. Well... she had. Did that mean she remembered or...?

"It's this feeling I get," Hannah supplied before her eyes fell to where Liam was touching her. "And I know something is wrong about it."

"Wrong?" Liam's eyes narrowed. "What do you mean?"

"Because..." Hannah bit hard at her lip, her eyes traveling slowly up his body before she met his gaze. "I get this feeling like I was with you, too."

"Uh..."

"Have I?" Hannah demanded suddenly. "Have I been with him?"

"Well..." Liam was at a complete loss.

"Kiss me," she interrupted. "I feel like we have before. Have we?"

Liam's breath released in a rush as he pulled her up against him, his body ached from the closeness. They hadn't touched like this in so long. Bending low, his mouth found hers and she parted her lips for him.

He kissed her, just like she asked, but really it was just like he wanted. Did that make him a greedy bastard? Yeah, probably it did and suddenly it was the best feeling in the entire world, the only feeling he ever wanted.

But then she was breaking away from him and even though his body screamed at him not to, he let her go. She stumbled back, her hands pressing to her cheeks as they turned an irresistible shade of pink.

"Have I slept with both of you?" Hannah's eyes were pained, and it made Liam so guilty, so sad.

"Hannah," he sighed.

"What kind of person am I?" She asked. "Why are the two of you always together? Why are you both here?"

Stepping back, her eyes darted all around. She was searching for memories, for answers, and they weren't coming to her. Liam ran a hand down his face before looking to the heavens. Was there no solution to this anywhere?

When he looked back down, all he saw was her silhouette running away from him in the night.

Drawing her legs up to her chest, Hannah laid her forehead down against her knees. She was sitting on her couch, in her apartment, alone in the dark. When she'd run from them, and all these feelings she was getting, she could think of no place else to go.

Because that was the crux of the issue right? Nowhere was familiar. Nothing was recognizable.

Rocking slightly, Hannah mumbled to herself. Everything had been going fine. Dinner was lovely. After a little while, her nerves had calmed and she'd been able to smile and talk. Maybe not with Liam, with all his intent energy, but Cole had made things easy.

And she'd really enjoyed it. The rush of butterflies in her tummy had subsided a bit and when he'd shot her that crooked smile of his, the feeling was pleasant. For once she hadn't clammed up and made a complete awkward fool of herself.

But then he'd asked her to dance and she'd said yes. She'd

wanted to, of course and was flattered by the invitation. The song had been slow, one she enjoyed playing on the piano herself. With Cole's hand on her waist and another gripping her palm, her body flooded with heat. Then there was that kiss. Cole's mouth on hers was a sparking sort of demand and then the feelings began consuming her.

They weren't memories exactly, she saw nothing in her mind, had no visions. But where her mind was empty, her body was full. It remembered things. And it was scary.

"Why?" Hannah whispered the word out loud, though no one was around to hear it.

She just wanted to know her story. Everyone around her seemed to know it, but she didn't have a clue. What type of person was she to want these two men? To maybe have *been* with these two men? Oh God, she thought suddenly, were there any others?

No. The answer came from within and had a surety about it. She didn't have this problem around anyone else. It was just Liam and Cole.

The knock at her door was so soft, she almost didn't hear it. Raising her head, Hannah swiped at the tear streaks that marked her cheeks and sniffed.

"Hannah Mae?" Lena's voice was barely louder than the knock. "Are you in there?"

"Yes," Hannah called.

Getting up, she crossed to the door and pulled it open. Lena stood there by herself, which was a complete and utter relief. Retreating into her apartment, Hannah returned to her position on the couch and sat down. Lena waddled in after her and shut the door. In her hand, she clutched a large purse.

"Are you having memories?" Lena began. Setting her bag on the table, she lumbered to the sofa and lowered herself with a groan beside Hannah.

"Not exactly," Hannah admitted. "My mind sees nothing, but it's like the rest of me can or does."

"Wow." Lena tilted her head to one side. "That sounds scary."

"It is." Hannah glanced away. "I hate it."

"Can I ask you a personal question?" Lena ventured, causing Hannah to huff a laugh.

"Sure, I probably don't know the answer," she countered, her eyes darting all around the room.

"How do you feel about Liam and Cole?"

Pressing her lips together, Hannah felt her cheeks go pink with embarrassment. How did she feel? Talk about a loaded question. When she gave no immediate answer, Lena's hand left her belly to rest on Hannah's arm.

"Are you afraid of them?" Lena asked, her voice quiet. "Do they make you uncomfortable or...?"

"No." Hannah shook her head as a flood of nerves cruised through her system.

Should she just say it? It's not like she had any girlfriends, or anyone else she could confess her problems to. After a beat of reluctance, she turned to face Lena.

"Did we know each other well?" Hannah asked. "I mean, did we tell each other things?"

"Yes." Lena let an easy smile crease her lips. "We were

best friends. I've trusted you with my most precious secrets."

"Really?" Hannah's brow furrowed before she reached up to place her hand over Lena's.

"Really," Lena replied simply.

"Alright, well then here goes nothing." Sucking in a ragged breath Hannah just spit it out. "I think I'm in love with both of them."

"Oh... well-"

"I mean, that's crazy right?" Hannah rushed on, the words tumbling one on top of the other. "I don't even know them. They're my brother's friends or soldiers or whatever, but everytime they come around I can't hardly think straight. My stomach does this flipping thing and the only thing I can do to keep the dumb smile off my face is to frown or look away."

"Hannah-"

"Then when Cole kissed me, I just freaked out on him and... oh I'm sooooo embarrassed." Hannah buried her face in both hands and sighed. "Then I did the same thing to Liam when he came after me. I was saying all this crazy stuff about how maybe we'd kissed before or even... oh God. Or even how I'd *slept* with him?"

"Well, listen..."

"I just want to know the truth, Lena. I'm not playing with a full deck of cards here and it seems like they are. I just want to know my story."

"Okay." Lena reached out to clutch Hannah's wrists and gently tug them from her face. "Your brother has all sorts of theories about how to handle your memory loss," Lena confided. "Not everyone who cares about you agrees, but Uriah tends to get his way."

"Is that how it's always been?" Hannah asked. "Uri runs the show?"

"Yes." Lena gave an indulgent smile. "And he means well. When it comes down to it, I think the thing he's most afraid of is that someone will influence you. He's afraid it won't really be you making your decisions."

"But then it's just him making my decisions," Hannah countered. "I want to know things. I deserve a chance to take back control of my life."

"I know and I agree." Lena gestured to the bag on the table. "Will you grab what's inside there? I just can't bring myself to get up."

With a nod, Hannah rose to her feet and reached for the purse. It was heavy. Peering inside, Hannah tilted her head as she pulled out a series of leather bound journals.

"So that's our story," Lena spoke quietly. "I've had a lot of time to myself the past few months and keeping a diary helped me to deal with some things in my past."

"Things?" Hannah glanced over her shoulder before thumbing through some of the pages. "These are hand-written."

"Yes," Lena acknowledged. "It started as sort of a tribute to a few special friends we had that didn't survive all this. There's no one around to keep track of events or how things come about anymore. At some point my writing changed. I went back and started from when I arrived here the first time, when I was originally placed inside the Wall."

"You were here before?"

"I was." Lena cleared her throat. "I lived in this apartment with you and a woman named Flynn."

Flynn. That's the name Hannah had liked for a baby girl. Too bad Lena and Uriah were having a boy. Ian Ryder Linfield. That's what they'd agreed to call him. Maybe next time, Hannah thought, they'd have a girl. But wait... she'd known a woman with that same name? She and Lena had lived with her?

"If you start there," Lena ventured. "It follows my experiences chronologically, but when I met up with you again, I did include a few things about your life that you told me."

"My life?" Hannah let her hand stroke down the ivory colored pages.

"Yes. Why don't you take some time to read them and you can ask me any questions you have. If you let me, I could move into my old room here."

Closing the journal in her hand, Hannah replaced it on the table and thumbed through the volumes. There were four. When her finger paused on the first one, Lena spoke once more.

"Cole and Liam are both in there," she said, then wiggled her eyebrows as Hannah gave her a quick look. "No time like the present, right?"

"Yeah..." Hannah picked up the book. "Especially when all you remember is the present."

CHAPTER FORTY-EIGHT_
COLE

Staring down at his scrambled eggs and bacon, Cole pushed his fork uselessly around his white ceramic plate. All around him, the noise from the cafeteria filled the space. People were busy today, grabbing their breakfasts, talking and laughing. Most of the men and women here would be off to work in one capacity or another.

Some were grounds crew, some were soldiers, some were cooks and some were farmers. Cole envied them. He envied the easy direction of their lives. After what he'd done to Hannah at the restaurant last night, he could hardly eat. What the hell had he been thinking?

Well... that one was pretty simple to answer actually. He hadn't been thinking. Hannah did that to him. He should've remembered what it was like to have her in his arms.

"Uriah thinks we need to split for awhile," Cole finally gave up the words he'd been battling since last night. "He thinks it would be better for Han if she didn't see us."

"What?" Liam shot him one of his classic scowls. "That's bull. There's no way we're leaving. I've done enough leaving."

"Well, it wouldn't be forever," Cole qualified, remembering Uriah's insistence after the kissing fiasco. "We could take a trip to the compound for a few months, check in on how Cookie and that group he took back with him are doing... see Ace and Davey."

"Yeah, that's a no." Liam shifted on the bench seat beside him.

"For real?" Cole gave up, dropping his fork down on the table before turning to eye his oldest friend. "Walking away is like your MO."

"It was," Liam corrected. "And I finally learned my lesson. I'm not leaving her. Not again."

"Even if she doesn't want anything to do with you?" Cole's eyebrows raised.

"All I'm saying is that if old Hannah ever makes her way back, then she's going to discover I'm right fucking here." Liam tapped a finger on the rim of his coffee mug before lifting his head to stare at Jameson. "Isn't that right, big man?"

"Huh?" Jameson shifted in his seat, ripping his eyes away from the group sitting two picnic tables over.

"You going to ask that curly-haired brunette out, or what?" Liam pushed. Both he and Cole were rewarded when Jameson actually began to squirm.

"I don't know who you're talking about," Jameson countered, then focused entirely too hard on his own plate.

"That chick." Liam jabbed a knife in the woman's direction. "The one you keep staring at. What's her name Cole?"

"Um…" Cole rocked forward and eyed the pretty thing. "Starts with a C. Casey? Or no… maybe it's Cali?"

"Cass," Jameson spat the word at the table before he shoved up to standing. "Her name's Cass, now go fuck yourselves."

As the big bastard stomped away, food tray in hand, Cole's mouth hung open. Apparently they'd touched a nerve. Leave it to Liam, Cole thought, as always the definition of tact and grace. Cole was just about to lecture his friend when Hannah strode over to their table and plopped down in Jameson's spot.

Now Liam's jaw dropped along with Cole's and they both sat there side by side looking like frozen idiots. In her hands, Hannah held what looked like a brown notebook or journal of some kind. She clutched it to her chest and eyed the both of them for a moment before setting it gently down on the table between them.

"So how did it work exactly?" She asked, her eyes darting from Liam to Cole and back.

"How did what work?" Cole ventured.

"Us." Hannah tapped a finger on the cover of the book, causing Cole to glance at it quickly before looking back at her face. "We were a thing right?"

"You remember?" Cole's heart leapt in his chest one moment only to plummet to his toes the next.

"No." Hannah gave her head a shake, but her gaze on him remained steady. "Not exactly."

"Wait," Liam interjected. "What's not exactly?"

"I can't see it." Hannah's focus shifted between them, as if she was trying to make sure to talk to them both at once. "My mind has no memories, but I feel things. I have strong *feelings* about... well, about both of you."

Cole could hear Liam's quick release of breath, but he didn't look over. This was the most Han had spoken to either of them in months. It was enough to make Cole measure every single word he said. He didn't want a repeat of last night. He didn't want to send her running again. Somehow, someway, he had to make her stay.

"So how did it work?" Hannah repeated her earlier question and waited. When neither of the men jumped into the pause, she continued on. "Did we all... like... *together*... or?"

"What? No." Liam's face twisted slightly before Cole spoke up.

"No, it wasn't like that," he said.

"Then what was it like?" Hannah pressed.

"Well, there were rules." Cole shot a sideways glance at Liam who lifted his eyebrows and held up both palms.

"What sort of rules?" Hannah again, suddenly undaunted. "The book says we were all dating and that I slept with both of you. Were we serious or was it like kind of casual?"

"Okay, okay," Liam interrupted. "It was *not* casual. What the hell book is that?"

"Lena wrote it," Hannah said and slid it over. "She knew some things but not how it actually was between us. I want to know how it really was."

Reaching for the book, Liam began immediately to scan

through the pages. Cole, on the other hand, just stared at Han's face. *His* Han. Was this her way of trying to get back to them? The past months had been agony for him and Liam, but maybe it hadn't been any easier on her. After all, she hadn't had anyone to talk to. At least they'd still had each other.

Suddenly, Cole felt he'd failed her again. All the times he'd been tasked with watching over her, he'd kept a respectful distance. She'd seemed so vulnerable and wary of him. Maybe that'd been the wrong move. Maybe he'd owed her an explanation right away.

"The first time I saw you," Cole began. "You were all alone and starving. You didn't remember anything that had happened to you beyond about six months. I think I fell in love with you from that very first moment, but I couldn't really say for sure."

"You..." Hannah stuttered a moment, her eyes fixing on his. "You were in love with me?"

"Oh yeah, Han." Cole gave her a small smile. "I still am."

"But..." Hannah frowned, her gaze shifting to take in Liam.

"Your turn," Cole prompted his oldest friend who swallowed visibly before setting the book aside.

"I tried really hard not to like you," Liam admitted. "You were with my best friend, and I wasn't good enough for you. I'm still not."

"You two are childhood friends," Hannah repeated, pointing at the closed book.

"Yeah," Liam acknowledged. "And circumstances being what they were... well, I got fucking lucky is all. You agreed to be with me and I knew I had to do everything I could to make it easy for you to stay. I'd already fallen so hard Hannah."

"So..." Hannah trailed off.

"So the three of us agreed to share," Cole filled in the blank spaces. "And it was hard at first."

"We went through some shit," Liam put in, looking suddenly worried. "I left for awhile, but it was the wrong move. I'll never do it again, Hannah. I'm in love with you, and I won't leave again."

"Is any of this..." Cole chose his next words carefully. "Getting through to you?"

"I don't remember it," Hannah admitted. "But I do feel things. I know it sounds crazy, but I feel like I'm in love with you guys too... with both of you. Was there ever like a time limit? Was I supposed to choose between you at some point? Do you want me to choose now?"

"No," Liam and Cole spoke at the same time before eyeing one another.

"We're good moving forward," Cole continued. "However you feel most comfortable."

"Okay." Hannah leaned back a moment, contemplating. Cole held his breath. "I want you to take me home."

"What?" Liam's customary scowl returned.

"To the compound." Hannah nodded her head. "That's where we started, right? I want to go back there, to our home. I don't want to live here anymore."

"Do you think you'll remember something?" Cole asked.

"I don't know," Hannah admitted. "But I know that's

where I want to go and I'd like to go with both of you. Will you guys take me?"

"Of course," Cole responded, it wasn't even a question.

"Yeah." Liam glanced to Cole before continuing, "Han... we'll take you wherever you want to go."

6 Months Later

KNEELING ON THE ICY GROUND, HANNAH REMOVED HER gloves and reached out to brush some snow off the wooden cross. Beside her, Cole continued to shovel. They'd had a break in the weather so of course, this is the first place he'd insisted on coming.

Glancing over her shoulder, Hannah spied Liam watching her. He didn't share in Cole's compulsion, but he always came to witness it.

With a sigh, Hannah uncovered the name that had been so carefully carved into the grave marker.

Ian Xiu Chan

That was all it said. When Ace and Davey had buried

their dead, they hadn't known the year. Well, technically there wasn't a year count anymore, no government to record things, no certificates to file. Letting her eyes drift down, Hannah thought about the man buried in the frozen ground below her.

Cole hated to have the graves covered in snow. He was working on uncovering Flynn's now, then the next one he would get to was Ryder's, then would come Trey.

"I think I want to build a shelter," Cole huffed between shovelfuls. "Something to cover them, you know? Something to keep the snow off."

"Yeah." Hannah cleared her throat before getting to her feet. "I'm sure everyone would help with that."

Stepping back, Hannah turned to eye Liam who nodded in agreement. He would make sure the shelter got built. Between him and Davey, new buildings were popping up all over the compound. Of course, the winter season had ground most outside progress to a halt, but with twenty people living here now, there was always something being done.

Sliding her hands back into her gloves, Hannah watched quietly as Cole continued to work. A stiff breeze picked up, tossing the tops of the pines all around them. They were near the horse pasture here, in a clearing that during the summer was filled with lovely tall grass. It was a pretty spot.

"Hey," Liam murmured against her ear as he wrapped his arms around her. He'd crept up on her, he was good at that.

"Hey," Hannah echoed his word.

Covering Liam's hands with her own, Hannah rubbed a thumb over the ring encircling the finger of his left hand. He'd made it himself, along with a ring for her and one for Cole. They didn't have a big ceremony or anything. After all, there were no churches around, no priests or government officials to sanction things.

One night the three of them had just sat around the table in their new little living room and made promises. Liam put a beautiful bracelet around her wrist and Cole slid the ring on her finger. Then she gave them each a ring of their own. It was silly maybe, but for them it felt right... it felt permanent and okay.

Hannah still had no memories from before, but in the past six months, she'd made plenty of new ones. While Liam and Cole worked to build more rooms onto their cabin, Hannah helped Cookie prepare meals or gave sewing classes to a few of the new women. While she'd grown to love her new neighbors and friends, Hannah continued to miss the ones she'd left behind.

She'd stayed long enough inside the Wall to witness the birth of Lena and Uriah's first child. A perfectly healthy baby boy. Although Lena had wanted to come back with them, her place was with Uriah and his was to keep things running at the Wall.

Leaving her brother and his new little family was hard, but Hannah knew it was the right thing for her. Besides, both Cole and Liam had agreed to visit first thing this coming spring. There were no radios that reached that far and no one dared to use electronics, so instead, Hannah wrote letters.

When she saw the little dark-haired pixie again, she'd be able to hand them all over. After all, like Lena had said, someone had to record their story.

Someone had to list the names of the people that mattered, the people that sacrificed so that they could be free. Someone had to write down the truth of what it was like surviving the Wall. Because they had survived.

And now... well, now it was time for them to really live.

CLICK HERE TO START BOOK 4 IN THE SERIES: BREAKING BEFORE

A word from the author:

Don't stop now! Get the 4th book in the Outlasting Series
BREAKING BEFORE... this is Jameson and Cass's story
and it will not disappoint ;)
PS. No cliffhanger this time!!!

Book hangover much?
Might I suggest my other completed series...
THE CAPTIVE BORN
It'll be right up your alley... wink, wink.

Join my email list...
LK MAGILL NEWSLETTER

Join my ARC Team!
ARC TEAM - LK MAGILL

Reviews, pretty please...
Each and every positive review makes a huge difference.
Be it Amazon, Kobo, iBooks, Barnes and Noble; no matter
the retailer, I read and appreciate them all.
Thank you and I hope to see you in the future.

Websites:
www.lkmagill.com

Like me on Facebook:
https://fb.me/LKMagill1
Follow me on Instagram:
https://www.instagram.com/lk.magill.author
Check out my Amazon page:
http://amazon.com/author/lkmagill

ALSO BY LK MAGILL_

Standalone novels:

VANISH ME

The Captive Series:

THE CAPTIVE BORN - Book One

THE CAPTIVE MISSING - Book Two

THE CAPTIVE RISING - Book Three

Outlasting Series:

OUTLASTING AFTER - Book One

CHASING TRUTH - Book Two

SURVIVING THE WALL - Book Three

BREAKING BEFORE - Book Four

TAKING TOMORROW - Book Five

FINDING FOREVER - Book Six